CAUGHT
stealing

LEIGHTON U BOOK TWO

CE RICCI

Epigraph poetry: _hydrus
Editing: Angie Hazen of Lunar Rose Editing
Proofreading: Amanda Mili of Amandanomaly
Cover Design: Emily Wittig Designs

To Dork:

For keeping me focused, motivated, and sunburn-free

during our time in T&C.

And to the anxiety that almost had me throwing in the towel on this one:

I would have preferred to do this without you.

Go kick rocks.

"YOU ARE WORTH EVERY KISS MY LIPS CAN STEAL."

_HYDRUS

Theme Song

bad decisions — Bad Omens

Playlist

Criminal — State Champs
Sugar We're Goin Down — Fall Out Boy
Last Night — Drew Jacobs, No Resolve
Degenerates — A Day To Remember
Saints of the Sinners — The Faim
Fake Fiction — Picturesque
Wish I Never Met You — Loote
Bad for Me — FNKHOUSER Bad Nature — Nerv
sugar honey ice & tea — Bring Me The Horizon
True Friends — Bring Me The Horizon
Bad Habits — Ed Sheeran, Bring Me The Horizon
Monsters — All Time Low, blackbear
Dirty Little Secret — The All-American Rejects
Smile In Your Sleep — Silverstein
F*CK YOU, GOODBYE — The Kid LARIO, Machine Gun Kelly
Stuck In Your Head — I Prevail
Holding Me Down — Picturesque
Enough, Enough Now — Bad Omens
You & I — VRSTY
MIDDLE OF THE NIGHT — Loveless
Someone Else — Loveless, Kellin Quinn
1 Last Cigarette — The Band CAMINO
Can't Take This Away — AVOID
Haunting Me — Loveless
Hey Baby, Here's That Song You Wanted — blessthefall
forget me too — Machine Gun Kelly, Halsey
heartLESS — You Me At Six
Some Kind of Disaster — All Time Low
Intoxicated — ALESTI, Until I Wake
my ex's best friend — Machine Gun Kelly, blackbear
LosT — Bring Me The Horizon
maybe — Machine Gun Kelly, Bring Me The Horizon
With Me — Sum 41
Granite — Sleep Token

Listen to the playlist on Spotify.

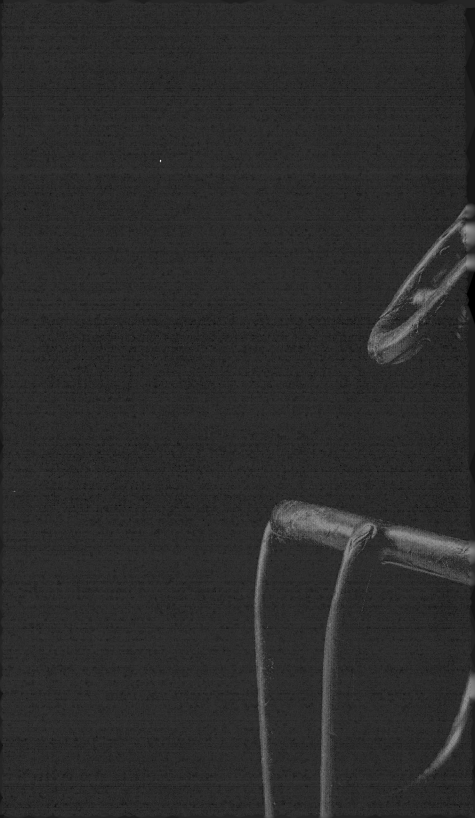

Disclaimer

As a dedicated sports enthusiast, I've done my best to portray all aspects of the NCAA, NFL, and MLB seasonal schedule, rules, and regulations as accurately as possible. However, sometimes rules, when applied in a fictional setting, need to be bent to fit within the narrative, so some creative freedoms and liberties were taken for the plot purposes of this book.

Leighton University, along with any other university within this work and series, is completely made up, fabricated so as not to misrepresent the policies and values, curriculum, or facilities of real institutions. The views in this book in no way reflect the views and principles of the NCAA, NFL, or MLB, as it is a work of fiction.

Author's Note

Caught Stealing is the second book in the Leighton U series, and while this is a series of standalones—where each book is a different couple—there are crossing timelines between some of the stories. So while it is not a necessity, it's highly recommended to read the series in publishing order. For example, *Caught Stealing* follows a very similar timeline to *Iced Out* (Leighton U Book One). Some overlapping scenes are to be expected because of this, but from another character's point of view and more context to drive this specific story.

I'd also like to note, this book is not going to be for everyone. In technicality, this book is neither a cheating trope or a love triangle, as it does not fit the required criteria to be classified that way. **However,** these characters make some choices that fall into a very gray area surrounding those topics, and not everyone will agree with their decisions.

PROLOGUE

Holden

May—College, Sophomore Year

"**U**nless you're looking to be plastered before nightfall, you might want to slow down."

I glance up from the keg and over to where Oakley's leaning against the deck railing, watching me with those Judgy McJudgerson eyes of his. He's the only person at this stupid Kappa Sig party who'd try being the voice of reason at the last kegger of the semester, a task no sane person would ask for.

I raise my solo cup toward him in cheers, because little does my best friend know, his tip is already lost on me.

He's right about one thing, though—there's easily still another couple hours of daylight left. Maybe it is a little too early to be as far gone as I am, but in my defense, I've been here since two o'clock. And it's the last day of finals week, so why wouldn't we start partying the second we hand in our exams to the proctor?

"Too little…" I start before drinking the overflow from my cup. "Too late."

"C'mon, Hold," Oakley says, crossing the grass and making a grab for my drink. "Give me the beer, and let me get you back to the house."

"I'm fine," I slur, pulling away from his grip and trying my damndest not to stumble on the uneven ground. "And last time I checked, you're my roommate, not my fucking babysitter."

"It seems like you need one right now," he rebuts, his brows crashing together as his brown eyes harden. "You can be one sloppy drunk, you know that?"

"No one said you had to stay and watch," I mutter, and honestly, all of me wishes he wouldn't. It's probably better for our friendship if he goes home now before I get really bad. Any other day of the year, fine. He can take care of my drunk ass all he wants. He's done it plenty of times in the past couple of years since we've become friends.

But not today.

Certainly not like this.

Oakley rolls his eyes before holding his hands up in surrender and backing away. "Fine, just don't come bitching to me in the morning when you're hungover on your flight back home to Cali."

Home.

My mind snags on the word, and in my intoxication, I fixate.

On the word, on the *meaning* of it.

On what is missing from *my* home, which is the entire reason I'm this fucked up to begin with.

Because today marks the anniversary of when I lost them.

As if reading my mind, Oakley's gaze softens. "Your parents wouldn't want you doing this shit," he says, barely loud enough for me to hear over the thumping bass. "You know they'd want you to move on and keep living."

"Living is exactly what I'm doing," I say, a small hiccup leaving me on the last word. "Which is a lot more than I can say for them."

He winces, as most people do when I choose to make a morbid dead-parent joke. But hey, what doesn't kill you just gives you seriously fucked-up coping mechanisms and one massive self-destruct button.

"Can you just text me so I know you make it on the plane tomorrow?" His brow hitches up before he tacks on, "Please?"

"Yes, sir." I toss a mock salute his way, completely done with this whole conversation. Which is why I'm glad to see him roll his eyes again and head toward the gate leading to the alleyway where he parked.

"Now that my babysitter's gone," I mutter under my breath.

I move inside, where more people are laughing and dancing to whatever shit is blasting through the speakers, because the K-Sigs are known to have the worst taste in music.

Taking another sip of beer, I head up the stairs, doing my best to brush aside the empty feeling Oakley's words have brought to the forefront of my mind. Still, the thoughts have infiltrated the drunken state my mind's been occupying most of the day, forcing me to, once again, think about things I'd rather forget. Or at least ignore, if only for a little while.

That's when I spot a dark-haired guy with even darker eyes staring at me from his spot in the hall, even while he's in the midst of a conversation with someone else. His eyes heat my skin, and when his gaze lifts to collide with mine, I know exactly how I plan to escape every thought plaguing me.

It's improbable, but not impossible, that I'm mistaking his attention for interest, but from the way his eyes track me as I close the space between us, I'd bet my throwing arm I'm in the clear with this one.

My lips part, and I'm about to interject his conversation when a familiar voice drags me away from the dark-haired hottie I'm two seconds away from propositioning.

"I thought Oakley was taking you home ten minutes ago."

Theo.

My gaze shifts to another one of my roommates, and I glare daggers at him. "Wasn't in the mood to be bossed around by Dad tonight," I reply, my tone clipped. "So if you're looking to take over the role, do us all a favor and walk away now."

Theo's dark brows hitch over two light green eyes, but there's more amusement than irritation written in his expression. "Someone's testy tonight."

"You would be too if your roommates were trying to babysit you all evening," I remind him, my own brow arching before allowing my attention to drift back to the guy I came over here for. "Now, you could stop being rude and introduce me to your friend here."

Understanding about what I'm attempting to do crosses Theo's features before he lets out a sharp laugh. "Not a fucking chance, Hold." He glances from me to the sex on a stick beside him before clapping him on the shoulder. "I'm heading out, but you played one helluva game, Merce. Don't think too hard on it."

Merce.

Even drunk, I'm able to deduce the nickname must mean he's one of Theo's teammates. Meaning Theo could get me an in with *Merce*—if he was a real friend and roommate.

"Thanks, man," Merce says, and *shit*, he has a nice voice. Not too deep, but a little rasp that's sure to sound phenomenal saying my name while we—

Theo takes a second to clap me on the shoulder too, before leaning in to whisper in my ear. "You're in the clear. Good luck."

All right, so maybe Theo is a pretty good roomie for confirming that

I wasn't barking up the wrong tree with his teammate. Something all my roommates have saved me from in the past when it comes to hooking up with the male population of Leighton, especially when I'm too drunk for my gaydar to work.

Merce watches Theo head down the stairs before he drags his attention to me, only to find I've been watching him the entire time. His eyes really are dark—almost black in the dim light of the hallway—and they bore into mine with a heated intensity capable of searing me to my bones.

God, he's fucking beautiful.

And tonight, he's gonna be mine.

A semblance of a smile curls his lips as he leans his shoulder against the wall. "Well, that's one way to get a guy's attention."

"It worked, didn't it?" I muse, stepping closer to him.

"Apparently so." His brow lifts, attention flicking between my eyes and my lips. "I'm Phoe—"

"I don't care," I mutter, and before I can think, I crush my mouth to his.

No preamble, no names, no more mincing words.

Nothing.

If I was even an ounce more sober, I probably should have exchanged names before straight-up mauling him in the middle of a frat house, but desperate times call for desperate measures.

Though I was right about one thing: this is exactly what I needed. Just the feel of his mouth on mine—tongue slipping between my lips on impact—calms the chaos inside my mind. Takes the edge off. Every glide it takes against my own, twisting and tangling in an erotic dance, makes my already drunken brain a little more intoxicated.

Not to mention the way it goes straight to my cock.

He might've been surprised initially, but he recovers quickly, only to turn things up a notch. His hands grip either side of my face as he spins us, backing me into a door and turning this kiss into a full-body experience. I feel every hard inch of him when he rolls his hips into mine. Not just of his cock, either. Every toned line and muscle of his body presses against me, crushing me against the wall in a way I've never been handled before.

If I wasn't already intoxicated from the alcohol swimming through my veins, this kiss would easily do the trick.

"Let's get out of here," I murmur when he breaks the kiss to bite down the column of my throat.

He nods, hands gripping my hips. "Where?"

I don't have it in me to wait for an Uber or to walk back to the townhouse, so those are out. "Your place close?"

"Not close enough," he mutters, the sexy rasp in his voice telling me he's just as desperate for this as I am.

I can work with that.

A smile tilts the corner of my lips as I fumble blindly behind me for the doorknob that was just digging into my spine. I give it a twist once I find it, praying to whatever God exists for some sort of horizontal surface behind the wood.

Merce and I stumble backward into the dark space, his arm swinging out to close the door, and we only stop when the back of my knees collide with a mattress.

Bingo.

I drag him down onto the bed with me, need and desire the only driving forces for my actions. They're the only things that matter now.

The pitch-black room does nothing to subdue the fuzziness creeping further into my vision, and it only seems to get worse as he continues kissing me like I'm the oxygen he needs to survive.

His hands slip beneath my shirt, and the first true brush of his skin against mine sends my pulse into hyperdrive. Every inch his fingers skitter up my abs only serves to build the need inside me to an insurmountable level, until I'm overcome with lust.

And that's before his hand moves to cup the underside of my jaw, tilting it when he breaks the kiss and opting to explore my neck instead. Every bite and nip down my throat sends an electric shock straight to my dick, the appendage throbbing behind my zipper.

"Fuck me," I whisper, gripping his shirt at the hem and ripping it over his head.

He does the same, peeling mine off before his entire body weight pins me to the mattress. Yet there's a small amount of hesitation in his touch now as he continues exploring me in the darkness.

"I…I'm not this guy. The one-night-stand kind."

Oh, how the irony of his statement isn't lost on me, knowing full-well my reputation around campus.

"Seems to me like you're doing a great job of it," I tell him, my hands gripping his smooth, muscled biceps. "But if you're planning to implode afterward, at least let me sneak out so I don't have to watch."

He groans, his hands tightening at my throat for a brief second before his mouth collides with mine again, no doubt in an effort to shut me up. I don't mind though, because his tongue works magic as it fucks into my mouth, drawing a moan from my chest before he swallows it whole.

It could be the alcohol or the heat from our kiss, but the need for oxygen comes far too soon, and I'm forced to break away for air. But even as I pant against his lips, I make my request known once more.

"Fuck me."

His head drops into the crook of my neck, a breathy chuckle floating over my skin. "I'm going to regret this, aren't I?"

"Sounds like a problem for tomorrow."

There's a moment of silence where I wait for him to decide, but lust must win out over common sense in the long run, because his mouth is on mine again. More aggressive this time. More desperate for me to meet every press of his lips and roll of his hips.

The darkness and the intoxication I'm feeling take over as every nerve ending in my body becomes overwhelmed by his touch. His taste and scent.

My brain seems to be drowning in equal parts alcohol and him until it's fully submerged in pure black.

One I'm lost in, only to wake up the next morning with no idea whose bed I'm in, how I got there...or a single recollection of the events from the night before.

ONE

Phoenix

Six Months Later—November, Junior Year

"So…why are we here again?"

My attention shifts to Kason, who seems to be scanning the crowded living room of the Kappa Sigma house like he's looking for someone. He must not hear me over Breathe Carolina blasting through the speakers, since his attention is still locked on the plethora of groping, grinding bodies on the make-shift dance floor.

The weather's been cooling off—what with it being autumn in Chicago—but the room has gotta be nearing ninety degrees, thanks to everyone packed in such a tight space. Add in the stench of body odor and beer, and it's a wonder why everyone loves college parties.

"We're just having a good time," my best friend says, giving me an off-handed shrug as he continues looking around the space. "Aren't you having fun?"

Not one fucking bit.

I like parties just fine, though not when the only person in the room I even know is Kase. Those types of parties end up with me glued to his side while he socializes, and it's just weird. Not to mention awkward as shit.

This is one of those situations.

Which is why I'm about to tell him I'm bored out of my mind, even more out of my element, and have been ready to get out of here the moment we walked through the door thirty minutes ago. Too bad for me, I don't get the chance, because a tiny blonde tries to squeeze between me and the random guy to my left…and she completely drenches the side of my thigh with beer in the process.

"Oops! Sorry," she says, righting her solo cup with a sloppy smile and continuing on her merry way.

Wonderful.

"Yeah," I shout over to Kason, who doesn't even notice what happened. "I'm having a great fucking time."

Not.

Honestly, it's moments like this when I really hate college.

The days I wish I never came to Leighton have become much more frequent lately. Though it's got nothing to do with the school or party life or drunken sorority girls spilling beer on me, and everything to do with having too deep of a loyalty to my best friend. To the point where I let him drag me out on a Thursday night when I should be studying.

Or maybe the time I gave up my first choice in school so we could room together here.

But I guess the first step is acknowledging there's a problem. I just have no idea how to *stop* putting him first.

"See? Just let loose and have a little fun."

I roll my eyes, irritation setting deeper in my bones with every passing second we spend here.

"Who are you looking for?" I ask as best I can over the music.

He doesn't hear me, so I give him a slight elbow jab to the bicep.

"Ow," he mutters, rubbing the spot and finally looking at me. "What was that for?"

"In case you weren't aware, you go deaf when your eyes are working overtime."

All I get for a response is a distracted, *oh, yeah,* before he goes back to searching for what or whomever he's waiting for, still entirely oblivious to my annoyance.

I wipe my beer-dampened hand on the dry part of my pants, wishing now more than ever I would've stayed back at our apartment. But, unfortunately for me, Kason has noticed the dramatic shift of my demeanor into anti-party mode and is looking to change it.

"There's beer pong in the backyard," Kason tells me, still scanning the crowd. "Go call the next game and start having some fun."

"Kind of need a partner for beer pong," I mutter under my breath, knowing damn well he won't hear me. Then again, I could probably shout it in his ear and he'd still be too distracted to know what I said.

Shoving down my frustration, I head out toward the keg and grab a beer. Beer pong and flip cup tournaments are in full swing on the patio, and I watch for a while before deciding to take Kason at his word and mark us down for the next game.

I haven't been to a party since the finals week rager last May, and I'll admit—despite being ignored by my best friend—it's not as bad as I remember. Granted, I'm not drunk or pissed off about losing a game or lonely as fuck after being dumped.

A night spent drunk and desperate to escape reality is a toxic combination: a fact proven in this very house last year when I made the single greatest mistake of my life.

Sleeping with Holden Sykes.

I try pushing the thoughts away, yet being back here makes it nearly impossible. The memories this place holds only amplify the self-loathing and regret as each one comes flooding back, making me sick to my stomach. Even months later, I can't understand how I thought getting obliterated after a shitty week—just to screw the biggest player on campus—was a good idea.

I am the definition of a cliché.

A cliché only made worse by his refusal to acknowledge my existence when I see him *everywhere* now. In class, around campus. At every one of Kason's games, thanks to them being teammates.

He's impossible to escape. Like fucking herpes.

So why wouldn't he be standing next to Kason, chatting away, when I walk back into the house? And looking way too good, to be fair, I might add. Even for a super-douche.

"You're lookin' good, Kase," I hear Holden say when I reach them, and the way his whiskey brown eyes take their time drifting up and down Kason's entire body makes my stomach roll. Not to mention the way his hands keep touching him—a little too friendly for my comfort.

After all, there was a moment in time he looked at me that way. Touched me like that too.

But now, as his eyes meet mine, there's not a hint of recognition crossing his face. And it only serves to piss me off even more than his presence.

"Uh, thanks," Kason says awkwardly before his attention shifts to me. "This is Phoenix. Mercer. I, uh, don't think you've officially met."

We *definitely* have, but if Holden wants to play it off like we haven't, then two can play his game. Which he does, keeping his poker face intact as he gives me one of those stupid bro nods that causes his honey-blond hair to flop over his forehead.

"Hey, I'm Holden."

Anger bubbles up inside me, and I bite out a forced, "I know who you are."

Once again, not a single ounce of awareness crosses his face before his focus moves back to Kason like I'm not even here.

Fine, so maybe I'm not okay with playing this game of his, because every moment he spends acting like we've never met—like that night never happened—simply pisses me off more. How he can just stand here and act like he has no clue who I am is beyond me. But then again, he hasn't said anything to me in the history class we share, where he sits a couple rows in front of me. There have been moments where our paths have crossed on campus too, yet he's never given so much as an inkling about what happened in this very house being a blip on his radar.

I'm just another notch on his bedpost—utterly unworthy of a second thought.

The annoyance I felt earlier only intensifies as I stand here awkwardly while the two of them talk—Holden shamelessly touching and flirting with Kason the entire time. It makes the discomfort I was already feeling all the worse, making no signs of getting better when it continues for a solid fifteen minutes. The only reason it ends at all is because I finally speak up after the third-wheeling reaches the point of unbearable.

"Aren't we waiting for someone?" I finally ask Kason, cutting off whatever Holden's about to say.

Kason's brows furrow as he shakes his head. "Not anymore."

What?

"You were standing here searching the crowd for fuckin' half an hour before I went out back," I remind him.

Kason's green eyes flare a bit before his head gives the slightest nod toward Holden.

"Not anymore," he says again, this time through gritted teeth.

What is happening right now?

Holden's inquisitive gaze shifts between us before a little smirk forms on his lips. "You were looking for me?"

"Uh, I mean…" Kason stutters and stumbles over his words for a second before he finally strings together enough words for a sentence. "I said I'd meet you here."

I'm so lost; I might as well have been dropped in the middle of nowhere without a road map. Because there's no reason in the world for Kason to be waiting for *Holden* at a party. I mean, sure, they're teammates. Maybe even more friends than acquaintances, since they spend so much time together.

Besides that though, they don't run in the same circles. So why—

"You ready to head out soon?" Holden asks, slicing through my thoughts.

The question is clearly aimed at Kason, seeing as Holden still hasn't offered a hint of recognition toward me. Which creates far more confusion on my end. It's only when my eyes catch the way Holden licks his lips—an action brimming with pure, predatorial sex—that the puzzle pieces start coming together, smacking me in the forehead like a fucking V8.

Kason was waiting for Holden. And now Holden wants them to leave *together*.

Emotions course through me in rapid succession, circling round and round like a carousel. Anger. Betrayal. Sadness. Hurt. Regret.

Maybe even a bit of jealousy, though I'm not quite ready to unpack that at the moment. But, regardless, it sticks, now causing me to lash out at my best friend in ways I'd never dreamed of in the past. Not until this moment.

My brows crash together, and I feel my nose wrinkle up in some mixture of disbelief and disgust before uttering a single question.

"You're *fucking* him, Kase? Seriously?"

Kason's mouth drops slightly, evidently shocked by my crass outburst. He recovers quickly, though, and goes to explain himself.

"Phoe—"

"Save it," I scoff, taking a step backward. "I don't wanna hear it."

Kason takes a step toward me and grabs my forearm, guilt and pleading written all over his face.

"We're not...Just let me explain," he says, glancing at the people around us to make sure no one is paying attention. They aren't, of course, but even if they were, I doubt I'd so much as blink an eye. Not when I'm still reeling from this bombshell.

Holden Sykes.

Out of everyone else attending Leighton—hell, in the entire world—it had to be Holden fucking Sykes.

The same jackass who is watching this exchange with a blend of amusement and disbelief...and still not one ounce of recognition on his face when his eyes land on me.

Un-fucking-believable.

"I'm outta here," I mutter before pulling my arm from Kason's grip.

I shove my way through the crowd to get away from them both, my emotions still swirling as much as my thoughts. The back door is the nearest exit, and I make a beeline for it.

I need to get out here. *Now.* So I don't have to watch Kason go home with the campus man-whore. There's no way I can ever be okay with it. Not after having gone there myself, only to regret it with every fiber of my being.

Fingers wrap around my bicep before I reach the back door, and I glance over my shoulder to find Kason attached to the hand, keeping me from escaping all over again.

"Phoe, hold on," he says, drawing me away.

"We're best friends," I tell him, not holding on one iota.

His brows clash together. "I know we are."

"Right, so I was under the impression we'd tell each other everything."

And as those words leave my mouth, I feel the full weight of their hypocrisy. Especially since I've neglected to tell him about the night *I* spent with Holden last year.

Confusion and irritation mix in Kason's expression before he bites out, "We're not a couple of teenage girls. I don't need to clear my sex life with you."

I cannot believe he just said that.

A sharp bark of disbelieving laughter leaves me. "Then, by all means, go get your dick wet. Holden's a pro by now, so I'm sure it'll be good. But don't come crying to me with your morning-after regrets."

I go to walk away again, but Kason tightens his hold on my arm.

"Can you just hold on for a second?"

"No, Kase," I snap. "You wanna act like a cool jackass to get laid? Go for it. But don't sit here and treat me like shit when I'm just looking out for you."

Kason's hands raise in clear surrender. "I'm hearing you, but you don't have all the facts."

"And whose fault is that?"

"Mine, but it's about to be yours if you don't shut up and let me fucking talk," he snaps, a hint of irritation in his voice.

My teeth clamp down on my tongue. "Fine. Then talk."

"We aren't sleeping together," he starts, gauging my reaction. The disbelief must be written clear as day on my face, because he amends. "Okay, we *haven't* slept together."

"Meaning you're planning to," I say, a statement rather than a question. He remains silent, neither confirming nor denying. But his silence speaks louder than words, and I scoff. "Do what you want, Kase. Just don't say I didn't warn you when he shows his true colors after getting exactly what he wants from you."

We lock eyes in a stare-down of wills, waiting for the other to back down. But I know what I'm talking about in this situation, so I won't be the one to concede first.

"Fine. You've made your point," he mutters with a sigh before glancing longingly over his shoulder at Holden. "Just let me go say goodbye at least, and then we can head home."

I nod and watch as he heads back over to Holden, the same unsettled, nauseous feeling still rolling around in my gut. Yet I don't quite understand it. After all, I'm getting what I wanted—though it seems kind of ridiculous to put it that way.

But the feeling is there regardless.

Like a bad omen.

A premonition that this is only the beginning.

TWO

Holden

After he finishes his little chat, Kason doesn't even have to speak for me to know precisely what he's planning to say. It's written all over his stupid, handsome face.

I'm going home *alone* tonight.

Still, I'm not about to let it deter me from being the charming, easy-going guy he's known for the past few years. Which is why I plaster on a smile as he closes the remaining distance between us.

"Trouble in paradise?"

Some mixture of a wry smirk and pained grimace crosses his face, before he shakes his head. "We're gonna have to take a raincheck."

Called it.

"Yeah…" I say, trailing off for a second. "I kinda picked up on the vibe when your bestie pissed all over your leg like a territorial dog the second he walked over here."

This time, he definitely winces. "I'm sorry about Phoenix. He's just a little protective. Best friends, you know?"

My attention flicks over his shoulder to where Phoenix is standing, only to find him glaring daggers at me. An action reading less *best friend* and more *jealous boyfriend*.

I'm not about to point it out, though.

Kason's been on my radar since he let his interest in guys slip at the beginning of the season. But as much as my interest in him has piqued, I'm not about to fight for his attention—especially if someone like a best friend is involved. I might like getting laid as much as the next guy, but I'm far from fucking desperate.

"Look, Kase," I start, shifting my gaze back to him, "If you've already got something else going on with him, then—"

"With Phoenix?" he interrupts, shock evident in his tone. "Absolutely not. Like I said, we're just friends, and he's protective of me. Plus, I think most of the issue is that he's new to the idea of me dating."

My brow arches. "We're dating now? I'm glad to have been included in that discussion."

A sharp snicker leaves Kason as he rubs the back of his neck, noticeably uncomfortable. "You know what I mean. Seeing people, hanging out with people who aren't him."

"The only way he's gonna get used to it is for it to keep happening," I point out.

"You're probably right. Though I don't think it'll happen anytime soon."

"Regardless of your bestie's approval, I don't think it should stop you from heading back to my place."

Instantly, the smile turns into a grimace when he glances back at

Phoenix. "It's not that I don't want to, because I do. It's just…not tonight."

Irritation creeps in, though I play it off. "The offer still stands."

"Good to know," he says, blowing out a breath.

I can feel the nervous tension radiating off him—how he's torn between what he wants to do and worried about pissing off Phoenix. It's not something new, yet I'm surprised by the dynamic in this circumstance. Kason's never given off the vibe of relenting to anyone.

Then again, ever since we started talking in a more than friendly way, he's changed a bit. Becoming less self-assured and more of a bumbling fool. A trait I might find endearing if it wasn't about to end my night without getting laid.

"I swear it," I tell him, doing my best to counteract his nerves. "Even if it means you sneak out of the apartment later, and I pick you up off the street like a prostitute."

He cracks a grin, easing some of the tension. "I've been called many things, but that's never been one of them."

"There's a first time for everything." My brow arches before I motion to him with my cup. "And, hey, they used to sell virgins into prostitution for some serious cash."

Kason chokes out a laugh. "You saying you're willing to pay?"

A smile curves my lips as I step closer to him and lean forward to whisper in his ear. "Guess you'll have to wait and find out."

My gaze collides with Phoenix's over Kason's shoulder before I have the chance to back away, noting the drop of his lips and lines etched into his forehead. The stiff, rigid way he's standing, arms crossed and pissy.

The pure rage written in his body language is unmistakable.

And it only gets worse when my hand lands on Kason's arm, my fingers skating up and down the length of it.

"Until then, you better go," I tell Kason, stare still fixated on Phoenix. Once I pull back, I break eye contact in favor of looking at my teammate. "Your chastity belt is waiting."

Another strangled laugh comes from Kason's mouth, and he peers over at Phoenix...whose stare doesn't leave me.

"You're probably right. He looks ready to rip your throat out."

"Just being a good little guard dog."

Kason's head shakes as he steps out of my reach and toward his gatekeeper, somehow finding amusement in this shit situation. "I'll see you later."

I fake yet another smile and nod. "Yeah, sure."

And as quickly as I found him, he disappears into the crowd without another word.

I'll be the first to admit I'm disappointed. Still, if he'd rather go back to his apartment with his pissy-as-fuck best friend, the more power to him. I'm more than happy to head toward the keg and attempt to salvage the rest of my night rather than dwell on Kason's missed opportunity.

I'm in the middle of yet another heated Bronco versus Wrangler debate with Theo, my abysmal attempt to entertain myself after Kason left the party with Phoenix. Which clearly isn't going well, seeing as I'm barely paying attention to Theo while we talk, opting to people-watch while I wait for Oakley to reappear.

"I think you just need to drive it," Theo says, taking a swig from his solo cup.

I try picturing myself in his ostentatious mustard-yellow Bronco, rolling through town with the top off, and I just shake my head. "No way, man. If I'm driving the thing anywhere, it's off the nearest fifty-foot cliff."

All Theo does is laugh. "You say that now, but I promise you'll convert once you do."

I'm about to rebut yet again when I catch sight of Oakley making his way down the stairs.

Finally.

His cheeks are flushed, like he just ran a marathon or something, and he glances around the crowd like he's in search of someone. It's more flustered and disoriented than I've ever seen him. Then I realize the *someone* he could be looking for is probably me, and it's time to head out.

"We can continue this later," I tell him, nodding toward Oakley.

"You do realize *I* could take you back to the house, and we could finish this now?" Theo shouts as I start to walk away, me waving him off as I go.

There's no way he's converting me anyway, no matter how hard he tries.

Oakley's at the bottom of the stairs, still searching the crowd, when I reach him. Yet, he doesn't see me until I lean in to shout over the music. "You good?"

Two brown eyes flash to my face, and he briefly nods.

Thank God.

"Then let's get outta here."

We weave our way through the mass of people between us and the front door, more than a couple of girls grabbing at my arm to stop me. Something I wouldn't normally mind, but rejection and boredom have long since set it, and I'm ready to call it for the night.

It's nearly twenty degrees cooler outside the Kappa Sig house, and I follow Oakley over to where his car is parked on the side street.

"Thought you were going to get laid?" he says as we reach the car.

So did I.

I give him a shrug before sliding into the passenger seat, not necessarily wanting to get into the details. "Plans change."

Oakley's brow quirks as he hops in beside me. "And from how you're trying to vaguely play it off, I'm assuming it wasn't your idea."

I open my mouth, ready to lie through my damn teeth, seeing as I'm not one to get bothered by striking out. But something about the way tonight went rubs me the wrong way. Enough to have me spilling the most minute details.

"There's nothing like being cock-blocked by an overprotective bestie to ruin the night."

He lets out a bark of laughter. "Why do I feel like this isn't the first time that's happened?"

"Because it's not," I say with a sigh, my eyes locking with Oakley's in the darkened car. "And if we're being honest, it probably won't be the last either."

Oakley laughs again before steering his car onto the streets, heading toward our empty townhouse. At least, I'm assuming it's empty, seeing as I saw two of our other roommates at the party. Camden was the only one I didn't catch sight of, but if there's a party on campus—especially on Greek Row—he's usually not far.

"Quit laughing at me."

"Why? It's funny."

"Yeah, it's hilarious," I deadpan. "I wouldn't be laughing at you if the roles were reversed."

His brow arches, but he doesn't look away from the road. "That's a lie, and we both know it. You'd laugh, announce it at the party with a megaphone, and then keep laughing louder."

Yeah, definitely sounds like something I'd do...

"Fair enough," I mutter.

"You know better than anyone, it's the life of a playboy to strike out once in a while." He glances my way again. "Or is your ego too large to handle it?"

He's not wrong about one thing: it's undoubtedly par for the course to strike out every once in a while, though I wouldn't classify myself as a playboy. Just a lover of many with a set of simple rules when it comes to hooking up that has yet to fail me thus far.

No cuddling or overnights. No strings with repeat hookups. And most importantly: no involving anyone's fucking heart. Especially mine. And seeing as I don't stick to one person long enough to get attached in the first place, this last one is pretty much a given.

Of course, that's not to say attachment doesn't happen on the *other* end of things, but I always make sure the score is known. If whoever it is can't hang— which isn't very often—then feelings get hurt and shit ends badly. Like getting bitch-slapped at parties or drinks thrown at me. Or decked by boyfriends. Although those moments, specifically, are ones I'd rather not recollect.

So best friends looking out for each other isn't uncommon, but it's still a blow to the balls—

"Holden?" Oakley says, cutting through my thoughts.

I blink over at him. "What?"

He laughs and just shakes his head. "Your ego really must not be able to deal if you go all *Twilight Zone* on me after getting shot down."

"I was thinking," I say, an iciness to my tone that's more playful than irritated.

"Something you're not used to, obviously."

"Oh, fuck off," I laugh, my mood lightening despite his jabs. What's a best friend without a little lighthearted roasting, anyway?

Or judgmental cock-blocking, it seems.

"Enough about me, where the hell did you disappear off to?" I ask, flipping the conversation back to him—anything to get my mind off Kason and the looks Phoenix was giving me.

Like I was the dirt beneath his shoe. Or the scourge of the Earth. Both make me feel like there's some other dynamic I'm missing between me and Phoenix, despite having never met the guy before tonight.

Except, for some reason, I feel like I know him. More than knowing he's on the baseball team or having vaguely recognized him from studying at the townhouse with Theo, seeing as they're teammates.

"I was upstairs," Oakley says, eyes focused on the road.

"With the stoners?" I let out a low whistle. "Damn, Oakie. I've always said you needed to let off steam, but I didn't mean like that."

"I wasn't getting high," he snaps, shooting me a glare. "Especially after all the shit de Haas went through earlier this season."

Yeah, getting pegged for drug use isn't really Oakley's style.

"Were you hooking up with someone, then?"

His eyes shift to me. "Yeah, Hold. I took a page straight from your playbook and let someone get on their knees for me in the upstairs bathroom with a bunch of other people right outside. Best blowjob of my life; the scent of weed and stale beer truly was the best kind of aphrodisiac. I get why you enjoy it now. Ten outta ten, highly recommend."

I snort out a laugh and shake my head at the snarky bullshit that just left his mouth, knowing it's for sure that—a bunch of bullshit.

"Well, I'll be damned," I muse. "I fuckin' called it."

THREE

Holden

onday morning comes far too quickly, and with it, another week of boring, monotonous classes we're required to attend. Honestly, I wouldn't have even bothered with college at all if it weren't for football—which is about the only thing I actually give a shit about. And it shows when my grandmother harps on me about every chance she gets about dedicating more time to school than football—even all the way from California.

My phone vibrates in my palm as I cross the quad toward my history class, and when I check the display, I can't help but laugh at the name of the person texting.

Gran: Don't forget you need to pass your history exam this week to keep your playing eligibility this weekend.

A smile lifts the side of my mouth, and I shake my head. I swear, it's like her ears start to ring whenever I think of her, let alone talk about her.

Me: Shouldn't you be watching The Price Is Right instead of texting me?

Honestly, I'm not upset about her checking in on me. As my guardian after my parents passed, I'm sure it's difficult for her to loosen the reins. Especially when I'm halfway across the country.

Gran: Don't treat me like I'm some ancient, decrepit sack of bones. I can multitask.

Me: I wouldn't want to take away your time with Drew.

Gran: And I wouldn't want you to take too much time away from your studies.

I chuckle softly at her smooth redirection of the subject. She's always been sly like that.

Me: I really shouldn't have sent you the syllabus for all my classes.

Gran: Hindsight, my dear. Always 20/20.

Me: I've got it, I promise.

Gran: Good to hear it. I'd hate having to disown you for failing out of college.

I snort, knowing Hell would have to freeze over for either of those things to happen, and pocket my phone as I enter the auditorium. I'm only a few rows down the steps, ready to take my seat in yet another dreadfully boring lecture about the French Revolution, when I catch a familiar face in my periphery. One that, not more than seventy-two hours ago, could have buried me six feet deep with loathing alone.

It's enough to have me sneaking a quick glimpse to confirm it's him, and when I do, I find his dark eyes already staring at me.

How long has he been in this class?

He holds my gaze for a moment before breaking eye contact, opting to look back at his phone rather than give me another second of his attention. It's a quick, meaningless interaction by any standard. Yet, after the major cock-blocking performance he did this weekend, it has a way of getting under my skin.

Which is why I do something ballsy. Even for me.

Rather than heading to my usual spot next to one of LU's cheerleaders a few rows down, I make my way toward Phoenix and drop into the seat right beside him.

My sudden presence must startle him, making him yank his headphones from his ears at the same time those dark eyes lift again. Of course, the second he registers it's me, they only fill with annoyance and disdain.

"Hey there, Nix. This spot taken?" I pluck the headphone from his fingers and go to put it in my ear. "Whatcha listening to?"

"Don't call me that," he says, grabbing the headphone back before shooting another glare my way. "And what's the point of asking if it's taken when you're already sitting in it?"

"It's called being polite."

A dark brow arches. "Really? I'd call it being a douchebag."

I let out a sharp laugh; he's quick witted. "You really don't like me, do you?"

He scoffs, the sound brimming with disinterest. "Thank you for the astute observation, Captain Obvious, but if that's all, you can go now."

The grin spreading over my face can't be helped. Ruffling his feathers is fun. "Why would I go when I'm having such a great time pissing you off with my presence alone?"

"Because, unlike you, I actually plan to *learn* something in this class," he snaps before jutting his chin toward where I normally sit. "So why don't you go back to flirting and fucking your way through college and leave me alone?"

This time, it's my brows that hitch up. "I'm just trying to have a conversation. No need to get so...prickly."

"Before this weekend, you've been perfectly content with acting like I don't exist." His lip curls back in some mixture of anger and disgust. "Which was perfectly fine with me, so why have you suddenly flipped the status quo?"

"I figured we needed to have a little discussion after the party."

"I said all I needed to say. And seeing as we have absolutely nothing in common to chat about, I think it's safe for you to go now."

"See, but that's where you're wrong, Nix."

The muscle in his jaw ticks as he stares me down. "I told you not to call me that."

I ignore his comment, opting to prove my point instead. "You see, I think we do have *one* thing in common. Kason."

His eyes are hard, giving nothing away as his stare bores into mine. Yet, the more impenetrable he tries to look, the more he ends up giving away.

"What do you want with him?"

"Whoa, now. Put away the shotgun, *Dad*."

Phoenix's eyes roll so hard, I'm surprised they don't get stuck. "Funny, jackass, but excuse me for being protective. The last thing he needs after coming out is the likes of you using him for a night, only to drop him when you realize you're ready to find the next notch in your bedpost."

Spoken like someone who knows from experience, though I doubt Mr. Monogamous here has ever had a one-night stand in his life. Yet the tone of his voice and the fury in those dark eyes make me think maybe he's had a night or two of regrets.

"First of all, you should know better than to project your own issues on Kason and me," I chide, brow arched. "And B, what makes you think I'm only after sex with your bestie? Have you ever considered I might be interested in getting to know him for more than what lies behind his zipper?"

"Oh, please," he snarls under his breath. "Don't act like you're unaware of the reputation you've built over the past few years. You're the stereotypical playboy jock who screws anything that moves and refuses to commit to anyone for longer than a night. Of course, I don't want you anywhere near my best friend. Any sane person would feel the same way."

Well, damn.

My hand comes over my heart, feigning hurt. "You wound me, Nix. Even if I'm as big of a fuckboy as you make me out to be, I've gotta have some redeeming qualities to make me worthy of your blessing."

Those deep brown eyes finally meet mine, and there's not an ounce of amusement in them. "Not any that I can see."

This is proving to be far more difficult than I realized. Normally I'd cut my losses and just deal with his distaste—after all, I've never felt the need to be everyone's cup of tea. Only, this interest in Kason will never be satiated if Phoenix continues cock-blocking me at every turn.

It's that thought which sparks an idea of sorts, and I twist toward him.

"What if I proved to you I'm not after sex with him? If I truly date him, court him, whatever they called it in the 1950s. Would you approve, then?"

"You mean date him without getting in his pants?" When I nod, he lets out a low scoff and shakes his head. "There's as much likelihood of that happening as turtles sprouting wings and learning to fly."

"I think the saying involved pigs, actually."

"Does it really matter?" he grits, fingers running through his hair. "Either way, we both know it's not gonna happen. You dating my best friend *or* managing to stay out of his pants. Not if I have any say in it."

My own irritation starts flaring as I lean back in my seat, letting out some mixture of a scoff and a laugh. "If I didn't know any better, I'd swear you're jealous or something."

He gives nothing away, his eyes hard and nostrils flared as he stares me down in contempt.

The comment was a one-off, meant as a joke. I mean...it has to be it. It's the only thing that makes sense for this kind of adverse reaction to my interest in Kason. After all, this is only the second time we've ever spoken—and he made his contempt for me evident the very first time we met only a few days ago.

There was no time for him to form any opinion on me, even if my reputation precedes me. And there's no way it makes that much of an impact without him having some kind of stake in the game.

Jealousy is the only logical option at this point.

"That has to be it," I say slowly, more to myself than him. "You don't want me with Kason because you want him for yourself."

Again, his expression gives nothing away. If anything, there's a hint of confusion that adds to his response. "What the hell are you talking about?"

For a brief second, I'm wondering if I'm wrong, and maybe he really does just dislike me this strongly on principle alone.

"Look, you've got some unresolved feelings for your bestie. But let me give you a little piece of advice." I lean in and whisper in his ear, "If he thought of you that way, getting with me would hold no interest to him."

"You're disgusting."

He shoves me away and fixes his eyes at the front of the class, a clear sign he's done with this conversation. Too bad for him, I'm not.

"Thou doth protest too much, Nixy."

"And childish, apparently," he mutters under his breath before adding, "I don't have feelings for Kason. Even if I did, it was years ago, and that ship has long since sailed."

Or you've been harboring the feelings for years without acting on them, only to see your time is running out.

"If you say so."

"I do." He chances a quick glance at me before whispering, "Now shut up and pay attention or go find a new fucking seat."

And just because I know it'll piss him off more, I mime zipping my lips and settle in beside him for the next ninety minutes, scrolling mindlessly through social media the entire time.

FOUR

Phoenix

I'm still reeling with irritation and anger the same afternoon when I get back to the apartment, deciding to skip our optional lifting session because I need to catch Kason before he heads off to practice.

It's a good thing I do too, because he's in his room grabbing a change of clothes when I stop in his doorway.

"What's really going on with you and Holden Sykes?"

He glances up from his duffle, brows crashing together at the center. "Apart from the major cock-blocking you did at the Kappa Sig party?"

I shake my head, tongue pressed into my cheek.

"Cock-blocking. Funny. The guy must be rubbing off on you," I reply with a little more snark than necessary. It only takes a second to realize my unintentional innuendo, and from the grin curling his lips, Kason catches it too. But I'm not in the mood for jokes. "Don't you fucking dare touch that."

He raises his hands in surrender. "Wouldn't touch it with a dream or a ten-foot pole."

Rolling my eyes, I cross the room and plop down on the end of his bed, not planning to let either of us leave this room until the full picture has been painted for me.

"So?"

Kason drops his bag and straightens to his full height, clearly unamused. "So, *what*, Phoe? We're friends, we're teammates. He's hot, and we're both kind of interested in each other."

"Only kinda?"

"Jesus," he mutters under his breath, his cheeks tinting a little red. "What's with all the questions? You've never been interested in my sex life before, so why are you now?"

I blink, not sure where the defensiveness is coming from on his end.

"Because there wasn't a sex life before now," I say slowly. "And the last thing I want you to do is regret screwing around with the wrong guy."

Something I've learned the hard way. And with Holden himself, no less.

Except, where I see my so-called *cock-blocking* as being a concerned friend, Kason must be seeing something else entirely. It's the only explanation for the frown still etched in his features.

"You ever think maybe I need to make mistakes on my own instead of just taking your word for it? Besides, it's not like you're some kind of expert on sex when you've only done it with one person yourself."

"Still more than never."

His huff of indignation grates on my nerves, though not nearly as much as his response. "Well, if you'd stop playing guard dog, then maybe I'd be able to change that."

"So you want me to just let you go fuck whoever, knowing you might regret it later?"

"Yeah, Phoe, maybe I do!" Exasperation is evident in his tone as he throws his arms out to his sides. "I didn't say shit to you when you started seeing Nico, who I thought was a grade-A asshole the moment I met him, by the way. I kept my mouth shut the whole time, even when I could tell he would only end up hurting you. Which is what a supportive best friend does."

"If you'd have told me how you felt about him, I'd have taken it into account. I'd have—"

"That's a bold-faced lie, and we both know it," he cuts in, crossing his arms. "You were head over heels for the guy before he ended things. Besides baseball, *he* was the thing that took up most of your free time. No amount of complaining about him or trying to make you see him for what he was would have swayed you into not sleeping with him, let alone not dating him."

My teeth gnaw at my bottom lip as his words sink in.

The thing no one mentions about having a best friend for as long as we've had each other is the fact that they can see where the weak spots are. The deep, dark shit no other soul will ever learn, they know. The shameful mistakes. The forever regrets. They have access to it all.

And because of that, they have the power to use all of it as a weapon, should they choose.

I just never thought Kason would use mine against me.

"There's a difference between my relationship with Nico and this thing between you and Holden," I say quietly, my ex's name tasting bitter on my tongue.

His brow arches as he calls me on my shit. "If that's true, why are you being like this about Holden?"

Truthfully, Kason isn't entirely off base with these accusations.

Because, yeah, Holden does remind me a lot of Nico. Not so much in looks, but rather in persona with his charming and charismatic nature. The same smooth lines with a silver tongue to match. He's good-looking, knows it, and uses it to his advantage at every opportunity. I'll be damned if a single person has ever told him no for anything because of it.

And he'll throw you out on your ass without the blink of an eye…all exactly like Nico.

But it's only because of what happened with Holden, how he's been acting since we slept together, that I know he's just like my ex. I'd be insane if I *weren't* wary of Kason seeing him.

"I think you can do better than him, Kase. Especially for someone to lose—"

"It's. My. Choice," Kason says slowly, words coming out in staccato.

"I know it is."

"Then act like it is. Because right now, it's feeling a lot more like you're trying to get a do-over through me."

Maybe I am projecting some of my shit with Nico onto Kason right now. After all, it was the shitty ending of our relationship—paired with a tough loss going into the conference tournament—that led me straight into bed with Holden.

Nevertheless, it doesn't change the place I'm coming from here. Which is a place of concern and friendship more than anything else.

Blowing out a sigh, I lean back against the wall and look up at him. "I hope you realize I'm only telling you this because I care about you. I don't want to see you get hurt by yet another person."

His green eyes soften around the edges before he runs his fingers through his hair. "I know. But at some point, you have to loosen the reins and just let me do my thing."

"Kinda hard to do when it goes directly against the way we looked out for each other as kids."

For as long as I can remember, it's always been us against the world. He became a brother to me the moment we met, and our bond only grew with time. After all, we understood each other on a level no one else did.

Both athletes. Both gay. Both closeted.

Both far too afraid to ever change that—though his reasonings were far more dire than mine.

I'd do fucking anything for him. Look out for him and keep him safe, the way family does for one another—the way his real family never has. After all, there were times he needed to be protected *from* them.

As if peering straight into my thoughts and reading them like a road-map, Kason gives me an understanding smile. "I know you mean well. But we aren't fourteen anymore, Phoe."

I sigh in resignation.

No, we really aren't fourteen anymore—and thank God for that. Because idiotic, virgin, eighth-grade Phoenix had just figured out he was gay and became whacked upside the head with attraction for Kason. Or, at least, that's the way my pubescent, hormone-filled brain translated the emotions I was feeling.

My mind rewinds back to Holden earlier today and his ridiculous accusation. *You don't want me with Kason because you want him for yourself.*

I know he's wrong—feelings for Kason haven't entered the equation in years. Truthfully, I don't think it was anything other than my wires getting crossed to begin with.

The love I have for Kason—love coming from a place of friendship—turned into this misguided idea of wanting more with him, and heading off to college fixed that too. It shifted those strange, warring emotions back to the typical kind of love best friends feel toward each other, and nothing more.

Kason's knuckles rap on my skull. "Phoenix?"

I blink up at him. "Yeah?"

"Just making sure you're still in there." His head cocks to the side. "Did you not hear anything I said?"

A sheepish grin takes over my face. "No, sorry."

He rolls his eyes, even though I can tell from the tilt of his lips he's not all that upset.

"I asked if you could just…" He pauses for a second, choosing his words carefully. "You don't have to like him, and you don't have to be his friend. But if you could trust me to know what I'm getting into, I'd be grateful."

Sighing, I relent as much as I dare. "I just wish you'd pick anyone else except him."

He shakes his head again and lets out an exasperated laugh. "Is there something specific you have against Holden? Or is this just one of those *no one will ever be good enough for my best friend* things?"

It's definitely Holden. Ten thousand percent, it's Holden.

He's the guy no one should ever want their daughter dating—or son, for that matter. And here he is, fixating on the most important person in the world to me.

"A little of both," I hedge, not wanting to sound like a straight-up asshole. Only, from the arch of Kason's brow, he can tell I'm holding something back, so I quickly add, "But leaning more toward just Holden."

"Then what is it? I believe you when you say it has nothing to do with Nico…but there must be something else. You're not the type to just hate on someone like this without reason."

Part of me wants to tell him.

Tell him *everything,* and let the chips fall where they may.

Fuck, I *should* tell him. After all, he's supposed to be my best friend. If anything, letting him know about the colossal mistake I made could prevent him from repeating it. But I can't bring myself to open my mouth and admit to my drunken one-night stand with his teammate.

Because it's embarrassing to be so easily tossed to the side and forgotten immediately after it happened. Because I'm ashamed of falling under Holden's seductive spell so quickly and easily, all to simply get out of my head for a few moments. Because if I was going to tell Kason, it should have been when it happened. Six months ago. Not now.

And—maybe most importantly—because even if we are best friends, Holden is still Kason's teammate. With football being Kason's life right now, the last thing I'd ever want is to severely mess with the juju between them mid-season. Even if he's willing to do it himself by jumping into bed with Holden.

So rather than let this secret spill from my lips, I lock it down and lose the key.

"I just think you can do better than him, Kase," I tell him, repeating the sentiment from earlier. "He's…"

"A fuckboy?" Kason supplies, a smirk on his face when he says it.

Understatement of the year.

"I think you're putting it mildly." I pause, hedging a little further. "And if you already know that about him, I don't understand why you'd even entertain the idea of getting with him."

"He's a good guy, Phoe. And it's nothing serious, we're just testing the waters." His shoulders lift in a shrug. "Who knows, he might not even be into me like that after we've been teammates this long. Sharing a locker room kinda leaves little to the imagination."

"Which would make total sense when he was trying to take you home last week," I deadpan.

Kason smirks. "Okay, smartass."

"Just saying," I say, raising my hands.

"You have to admit, fuckboy or not, he's really hot." His lips quirk up from a smirk to a full-blown grin. "Anyone with eyes and two brain cells to rub together can see that."

I laugh under my breath. "If you say so."

"Don't act like you haven't noticed."

I just roll my eyes and shake my head, not daring to touch his comment. Because, unfortunately, yes. I have noticed just how good-looking Holden is.

Up close and very, *very* personally.

FIVE

Holden

The week passes quickly, and before I know it, I'm suited up and running through the tunnel for yet another Saturday on the field. We're getting late in the season—this week's match-up against the Crown Point Hawks—and we're all aware this will be the biggest test of our abilities, as the Maine-based school still remains undefeated. A fact which has nerves swirling through my body, causing me to bounce up and down like a deranged idiot as special teams lines up for kick-off.

The ball sails through the air toward the Hawks until it lands safely in the arms of a returner who calls for a fair catch around their thirty-yard line. Special teams leaves the field, and I watch as the offensive line and Chase King, QB for the Hawks, takes position behind his center to start their first drive of the day.

He's good, I'll give it to him. I've been following his career as much as any other quarterback in our conference. Except there's no way he's gonna be leading Crown Point to victory today. Not if the boys and I have anything to say about it.

"You ready for this?"

Kason's voice from behind me is startling, and I twist to look at him. Completely ignoring his question, I ask one of my own.

"Am I blind, or were you in stealth mode while standing here this entire time?"

"Nah." He says with a smile before nodding his head back toward the stands. "Grabbed something from Phoenix quick before coming over here."

My brows crash together. I'm not sure what response I was expecting, though it certainly wasn't that. "He's here?"

"He comes to all our games."

I'm not sure why it surprises me, seeing as these two are about as codependent as two people can be—and both are entirely oblivious about it. But somehow, it still does.

For reasons I can't quite place, I'm itching to look over and find him in the stands. Maybe even catch his attention and rile him up a bit. Still, through sheer willpower or stubbornness, I manage to keep my focus locked on Kason instead.

"I didn't realize he liked football."

Kason laughs and shakes his head. "Oh, he doesn't."

I frown some more, mostly not understanding how someone doesn't like football. But also… "Then why does he come?"

"Show support. Being a good friend."

I'd like to think of myself as a great friend to my inner circle, but Hell would have to freeze over before I'd be caught dead watching Oakley play hockey. I freeze my ass off enough just living through Chicago winters—

there's no way I want to do it for sport too.

"I see," I murmur, watching our guys stop King from completing a quarterback sneak up the middle. "And what did he bring you?"

"Blue Gatorade," he says, holding up the sports drink. "He brings me one before every game, and I'll bring him a bag of dill pickle sunflower seeds during baseball season. Kinda been a ritual of ours since high school."

The sentimentality of this little exchange makes me want to vomit nearly as much as the thought of eating sunflower seeds by choice. Then again, I'll never understand the allure of playing baseball, let alone their mid-game snack selections.

"Adorable."

Kason must hear the tiniest hint of sarcasm in my tone, because he knocks his shoulder pad against mine. "You're telling me you don't do anything nice for Oakley? Or the other way around?"

I doubt I could tell Kason his favorite color, to be honest. Then again, our friendship is more of the trolling, jabbing kind. The lighthearted fun rather than the heartfelt shit, even if he is one of the few people who knows the whole story about my parents.

"That would require him to stop thinking about hockey every waking moment."

A lilt of laughter leaves him. "How did the two of you even become friends? You're not from the same place, and you don't play the same sport, so…" He trails off, but I'm easily able to follow his line of thinking, even if it is a bit unexpected.

"I answered an ad he'd posted about looking for a roommate near the end of my senior year, and I moved in the summer before starting at Leighton."

"Seriously?"

"Yeah," I say with a nod. "He was living alone in the townhouse at that time of year, seeing as he's the only one from Chicago. All our other roommates at the time weren't due until closer to school starting."

"So it was just the two of you."

"Yeah, and it was awful," I say with a laugh. "We butt heads constantly the first week, and I swear, I was this close to murdering him when he left one of his weird socks with red chili peppers printed on them in the washer. By the time I'd realized it, all my white clothes were fucking pink."

He lets out a laugh. "Not a great way to kick things off."

"Seriously. And he blamed it on me for washing my clothes in warm water." I shake my head, recalling more of the fuck-ups we shared that summer before any of the other guys showed up. Like the time I flooded the kitchen by putting dish soap in the dishwasher instead of the little pod thing, or the time we set all the smoke detectors off when we accidentally put a frozen pizza in the oven still on the cardboard.

"We spent a lot of time together, just the two of us. Made us bond, I guess, even if we don't have a whole lot in common."

The Hawks manage to get a first down on our guys thanks to King throwing one helluva pass to his tight end. He runs it a good twenty yards before one of our corners, Colson, takes him to the ground.

Standing on the sidelines watching our defense always makes me antsy to get out on the field to help the team. But I can't do that if they don't stop the damn ball.

Which is why I glance over at Kason, needing a distraction.

"What about you and Phoenix?" I ask, and I realize I'm intrigued as to how they ever became friends.

"We've been friends for as long as I can remember. I moved to his school around…sixth grade, maybe? Got thrown together on some class project, and it just kinda stuck."

I blink at him, waiting for more of an answer, only for none to come tumbling from his mouth. "That's it? That's your great, grand story?"

"I take it you were expecting some great, epic saga?"

Yeah, kinda.

"Considering you talk about him like he hung the moon or something…" I point out, letting him fill in the details. Then a wicked smile curves my lips, and I add, "Besides, I gotta know what my competition is here."

His focus leaves the game and flicks to me, his brows furrowing in noticeable confusion. "Competition?"

"For your love and affection, obviously." I aim another winning smile his way. "Seems from what happened last week, he's got one up on me."

A smile cracks his composure before he lets out a soft laugh. "You're never gonna let me live that down, are you?"

"Highly unlikely."

He laughs some more, though it's quickly drowned out by the cheers and screams of the Crown Point fans as King drives them further down the field with yet another first down—this time with a twenty-yard pass to their star receiver.

"Well, shit," Kason mutters, and when I glance away from the field, I find him frowning. "Guess we have our work cut out for us on this one."

I'll say.

"But to answer your original question…" he says, rerouting our conversation, "I dunno how or why Phoe and I became friends in the beginning. We just clicked, even with us being so different. And over time, he became more like family. A brother. My person."

My brows collide and I turn to look at him, cocking my head to the side. "Your person?"

"You know, *Grey's Anatomy?*"

I bark out a laugh and shake my head. "Nah, Kase. Can't say I do know."

"Well, for one, you're missing out because of McSteamy alone." He offers me a sheepish grin when I look at him like he's lost all his marbles. "But essentially, it means Phoenix is the person I'd do anything for. Cross oceans, bury bodies, you name it. He calls me for anything, and I'm there."

Yeah, that's a little much to do for a best friend. For anyone, really. And if those are the general requirements, then…shit, I feel sorry for Oak. Guess he's gonna be rotting in jail or stuck in Europe, because I don't think there's anyone I'd do those things for.

"And vice versa, I'm assuming?"

"He's more like family to me than my own, so I'd like to think so," he says with a laugh. "And he did come here with me for college, so I think it's safe to say he'd do anything for me too."

My mind catches on his words, and I frown. "What do you mean *came here with you?* He's on the baseball team, so he's gotta be here on an athletic scholarship just like we are?"

"Oh, he is." Kason's green eyes flash from the game back to me. "But he also got one to Foltyn College over in Oregon, which was originally his first choice."

As it should have been. Besides Vanderbilt and LSU, Foltyn's baseball program has been on the rise for the past few years. At least, according to Theo, it is.

"But he willingly came here instead?"

He nods. "Yeah, though it took a little convincing."

Interesting.

Phoenix choosing to follow Kason here over heading to one of the top baseball programs in the country only adds to my assumption that there's a little more than friendship on his mind. Something he's been adamant about not being the case, yet all signs point otherwise.

Very interesting, indeed.

Our focus is again brought back to the game when Crown Point's kicker takes the field. They're fourth and long now but are in easy field goal range at this point. Not ideal, but I'll take them scoring three points over six or seven. Our guys line up for the kick, and a rush of adrenaline spikes through me the way it does every time I'm about to take the field.

But my focus wavers momentarily along with my resolve, and my eyes slide back to where Kason said Phoenix was sitting. He's easy to spot, seeing as no one would be texting away on their phone from the first row at the fifty-yard line.

Or wearing Kason's away jersey.

For whatever reason, the sight fills me with annoyance and jealousy. The latter is misplaced, I'll admit, but the feeling is there regardless.

As if feeling his eyes on me, Phoenix's gaze lifts from his screen to collide with mine.

There's a niggling feeling in the back of my mind as we lock eyes, and it's got nothing to do with the pure hatred radiating from him all the way to where I'm standing on the sideline. It's something else entirely, but I can't put my finger on what, and it's driving me mad.

Almost like there's a piece of the puzzle I'm missing. Some memory I've lost or interaction I've locked away in the recesses of my mind, yet I can't quite figure out why I'm getting that feeling in the first place.

All I know is there's gotta be some reason for the animosity he holds for me. A reason not at all related to Kason—who was no help in figuring out what it might be. But when the whistle blows, signaling the change of possession, I realize right now is certainly not the time to dwell on it.

Our offensive line begins rushing out to the field, and a mixture of anticipation and adrenaline churns in my gut.

"Show time," Kason says, and I catch him bouncing out of my peripheral, clearly trying to hype himself up to take the field.

Phoenix's gaze still bores into me, even after I break away to give Kason my full attention. I'm not one for words of encouragement—giving or receiving them—so I just give him a grin. "Damn straight, man. Let's do this shit."

And then, because I can still feel Phoenix's attention burning me like a blow torch, I give him a nice little smack on the ass. For extra luck.

Kason doesn't even notice as he takes the field, but when I glance back over to his bestie in the stands, I know he saw. At least, if the steam billowing from his ears like in those cartoons is any indication.

A smirk curls the corner of my mouth before I blow Phoenix a kiss, knowing it's all that's needed to get under his skin before I head out on the field for our first drive of the day.

SIX

Phoenix

"There you are," I grumble as I drop my tray on the table where Kason is all but devouring his lunch in the middle of the crowded dining hall. "I've been looking for you everywhere."

A mild exaggeration. Then again, the dining hall reserved for any of the college's athletes is packed at noon, so we normally eat later. Not sure what made him decide to change things up, but since lunch is pretty much the only time I see him until the end of the day, I'm not gonna complain.

"Yeah," he says back absently, eyes glued to his phone screen while he stuffs another fork full of vegetables into his mouth. "Not used to this many people here."

I slide into place across from him and start digging into my food. The time change means I only have thirty minutes to eat and book it over to the main lecture hall for history—the wonderful class I share with Holden.

God, I'm annoyed just thinking about having to see him.

I do my best to brush away the thoughts, opting for any sort of distraction.

"Am I still helping you study for your poli sci exam tonight?" I ask Kason between bites of chicken. "I think I've still got the flashcards I made last semester."

He chose the elective class thinking it'd be easy, but the course is quickly proving to be more than he can handle—at least without a little help. I'm happy to provide it, seeing as I already passed the class; the only issue is finding nights we're both home at a decent hour. They've become less and less frequent—thank you, football season—so the time we have to go over the material is dwindling before his next test.

Two green eyes flick up to meet mine from across the table, and I can tell from the lines etched between his brow that something's wrong.

"Shit," he curses, dropping his fork to his plate with a loud *clink*.

It's all the answer I need.

"You forgot." It's not a question, since we've been friends for a decade. And while I love him, he's one of the most absent-minded people I've ever met. To the point where both my parents would poke fun at him, saying he'd forget his head if it wasn't already attached to his shoulders.

There's a plea of forgiveness in his eyes as he continues to stare at me. One that gets my forgiveness every fucking time he's bailed in the past—albeit on accident—and I'm certain this time is no different.

Kason might be forgetful, but Mom always did say I'm loyal to a fault.

"I'm sorry, Phoe," he says, his tone matching his expression. "Holden asked if I wanted to grab dinner and catch a movie tonight. I must've spaced on our study session when I said yes."

The mention of Holden causes ice to trickle down my spine, and I bristle. A raincheck of any other kind, I can handle. But to do it so he can go on a date with *Holden?*

"You're the one who asked me to help you with this shit, Kase," I grind out through clenched teeth. "Something I can't do if you cancel on me to get laid."

"Don't be like that."

Pettiness isn't in my nature—I'm normally a lot more easygoing than this. I should be happy that Kason is branching out, meeting new people. Dating a guy, or at least finally exploring his sexuality after being closeted for so long. He was for me when I first started seeing Nico last year, though he's since admitted he wasn't a fan of the guy.

It should be easy for me to put my own feelings aside here and support him.

But I just can't. Not when—

"Hey, guys," an annoyingly familiar voice comes from behind me.

This motherfucker.

I stare straight at Kason while Holden slides in beside me, praying to God I have the willpower to not strangle my best friend on the spot.

And now I know why we're eating at a different time today.

"What'd I miss?" Holden asks as he takes a swig of water.

Kason watches me silently, the expression on his face begging me to play nice, at least for the next fifteen minutes. Which very well might take every ounce of strength in my body and still not be enough.

I shift in my seat to face Holden. "Kason was just telling me that he won't have time to study tonight because the two of you are going out on a *date.*"

There's a gleam of amusement in Holden's eyes at the apparent venom dripping from my voice. "Yeah, I'm excited for tonight."

"Of course you are," I mutter under my breath. Not quiet enough, though, because Holden's brows quirk up.

"Is there a problem?"

"Yeah, I think there is."

He studies me for a moment, eyes cataloging my face with scrutiny before he responds. "Well, the only problem I can see is your parents never teaching you how to share."

My nostrils flare, annoyance growing as I stare him down. "Sharing is easy if the other person is deserving of it."

"You two about done here, or do we need to whip them out and measure to end this?" Kason snaps. For a second, I completely forgot he was at the table with us; all my attention barely veering off Holden and all his irritating glory whenever he's in the same room as me. I can't help it, though. I'm sick of his smooth, silver tongue and cocky attitude. It radiates from him like a toxin.

"Not necessary," Holden says, a smirk sitting on his lips. "We both know who'd win."

"Fitting, seeing as you're the biggest dick."

"Jesus take the wheel," Kason mutters, eyes shifting to the ceiling before landing on me in a death glare.

I raise my hands in surrender. "Just saying, irony works in many ways."

Kason's thoughts are written all over his face, so I'm not surprised in the slightest by what comes out of his mouth next.

"Can you not be an asshole for five minutes?"

"Happily," I say, plastering a fake, innocent smile on my face when I glance over at Holden. "So glad you could join us for lunch."

There's a slight lift of his brow, amusement and challenge in the action.

"Really? Then maybe we should make it a regular occurrence."

I'm one smart-ass comment away from losing my shit on him—maybe even causing a scene in the middle of the dining hall. Something that would not only embarrass all three of us, but also piss Kason off to no end—the latter being something I'm trying *really* hard not to do.

Which is why I bite my tongue and shove back from the table before grabbing my half-eaten tray of food.

"I better get going," I tell Kason, even though I still have ten minutes. But leaving now is the best thing I can do for everyone involved, considering I have the massive urge to wipe Holden's smirk clean off his stupid face.

"Already?"

I nod. "Yeah. I'll see you later."

The heat of Holden's gaze on my cheek as I attempt to ignore him is searing, and I make the mistake of looking over at him while grabbing my bag from the ground.

"Save me a seat," he says with a taunting lilt.

"Only in Hell," I whisper, just for his ears, before rising to my full height.

Not giving him a chance to make another comment, I drop the remnants of my lunch in the trash and push through the exit, needing the fresh air and space from Holden and Kason and this entirely fucked situation I've found myself in.

The cool Chicago wind hits me the second I step outside, yet it does nothing to temper the anger bubbling inside me.

"Fucking asshole," I curse under my breath as I storm off toward the lecture hall.

More than anything, I wish I could just ignore him. Pretend he doesn't get under my skin or irritate me to the levels he does. Life would surely be a lot simpler if that were the case.

But I can't.

I can't ignore him and pretend he's not the most irritating person I've ever met. So at this point, the only thing I *can* do is try limiting the amount of time I'm around him.

Like that's possible if he and Kason are seeing each other.

Just thinking about the two of them getting closer and Holden spending more time infiltrating the dynamic between Kason and me only serves to frustrate me even more.

I shove open the door to the lecture hall with far more force than necessary, wracking my brain for some sort of solution. A circumstance where Kason would finally see what's in front of him—and that he can do far, *far* better than the one-and-done king on campus. But the more I think on it, the more I realize the only way it would happen is if Holden starts severely screwing shit up. Something he's made very clear is not happening if he can help it.

Unless I make it so he can't *help it.*

Ideas swirl in my brain as I slide into my seat, and I start silently working out the details and logic behind them. And as 'Operation Cock Block' takes form, I figure the likelihood of pulling it off and also having the desired effect are highly, *highly* probable.

Movement out of my periphery causes my gaze to slide over to the aisle, and I watch as more people file in for the lecture—Holden being one of them. He catches me staring at him within seconds of entering the room, his eyes staying locked with mine as he closes the space between us.

He's barely dropped into the seat on my right when I turn to him and ask, "What time are you supposed to be picking up Kason?"

A crease crinkles his forehead. "Seven-thirty."

Not long after practice ends, giving him maybe…forty minutes to shower, change, and make it to our apartment.

Perfect.

"Okay," is all I give him for a response, but it's not enough for Holden.

His imploring eyes analyze my face before they narrow on me. "Why are you asking?"

I offer him a sardonic smirk before lacing my tone with the perfect amount of malice. "Just making sure I'm not there to watch."

A soft snort leaves him as he pulls out a notebook and pen from his bag, though I've witnessed firsthand that he has no intention of using either. "Remember that thing I said about jealousy?"

"Remember that thing I said about not giving a fuck?" I counter, brow hitching up. My quick reply and sharp attitude must surprise him, though, because he doesn't respond.

Good.

"That's what I thought," I mutter before pulling my phone out and feigning disinterest.

He drops it, though I can still feel the weight of his stare on the side of my face—much like back at lunch. Only this time, I don't let it bother me. Instead, it acts as fuel as all the pieces of my plan start coming together.

I have no idea how to pull this off without being caught—by Holden or anyone else.

But shit, it's worth a shot.

SEVEN

Phoenix

"**W**ould you just sit down?" I mutter from my spot on the couch where I'm attempting to study, all by my lonesome, thanks to Kason's last-minute cancellation. "Your pacing is making it hard to focus."

There's a long sigh, and I lift my gaze to find Kason linking his hands behind his head, clearly trying not to let nerves and panic get the better of him.

"Where is he?" Kason mutters, more to himself than to me. "He should be here by now."

I glance from him over to the microwave in our kitchen to check the time. *Seven-fifty-three.*

A victorious smirk lifts the corners of my lips as I focus back on the textbook in front of me. There were plenty of times I thought my entire plan would backfire or go awry, yet seeing as Holden is almost a half-hour late to pick up Kason, I'd say it was successful.

"Maybe something came up. Did you try texting him?"

"Ten minutes ago, but no answer."

I let out a sigh and shrug. "I have no idea, then."

Except, I do have an idea as to why Holden isn't here and why he hasn't texted. Because when I decided to sneak into the football locker room and steal all Holden's clothes from out of his stall, I made sure to take his phone, wallet, and car keys too.

If I'm getting my hands dirty with sabotage, I'm damn well gonna be thorough.

Leaning back against the couch cushion, I bask in the glory of a hard-earned victory when a knock on the door has my blood freezing in my veins. My attention snaps to the door, where Kason has already spun on a heel and bolted to it.

There's no way—

Yet, as Kason yanks open the door, I discover there *is* a way when I've underestimated the guile and determination of my enemy.

Tenacious fucking bastard.

Because there on the other side of the threshold is Holden Sykes, naked as the day he was born, save for the baseball glove he's using to cover his junk and pair of sneakers on his feet.

"What're you…Uh, Holden…You're not…" Kason stumbles over his words as he gawks at Holden, blinking rapidly in the way he does when he's nervous. Hilarious, considering they already spend so much time barely dressed in a locker room together. "Clothes…"

"Yeah, I know," he says, a bright and shiny smile on his face as he steps into the apartment. His eyes trace over the kitchen and living room, only stopping when they land on me. "And here I thought you said you wouldn't be here when I came to pick Kason up for our date."

"Couldn't resist seeing you off," I tell him, my tone flat and unyielding of any information. "Now, I can see it was a good choice."

"Glad to be of entertainment to you, Nixy," he says, and from the slight bite to his tone—probably imperceptible to Kason—I realize he knows I was behind this little prank.

Then again, with it done, I don't necessarily care if he knows I did it; I just care if it prevents this date from happening. But from his presence here, sans clothing, I have a feeling the only thing I've managed to do is poke the bear.

But as the saying goes: in for a penny, in for a pound.

"You know, *The Naked Mile* is just a movie, right? Unless…did you join a nudist colony since the last time I saw you? I think they have those back in California." I sit up, tossing my textbook on the couch. "Or wait, are you trying to start a new streaking club on campus? Because I doubt the administrators or the NCAA would be okay with it."

There's an inferno in Holden's eyes as he stares at me, wreaking of defiance and revenge.

"Someone stole my clothes," he says, masking his irritation with a shrug of indifference. "My whole bag, actually. Phone, wallet, keys and all."

"What?" Kason says, finally gathering himself enough to speak.

"Yeah. Some kind of prank, probably," Holden replies, eyes locked with mine. "Though it wasn't all that funny walking across campus like this, seeing as I couldn't drive. Or call you to come grab me."

"What the shit," Kason mutters, and when I tear my gaze away from the naked jackass in my apartment long enough to look at Kason, I see he's red as a tomato. "I can't believe someone would pull that crap."

"Yeah, me neither. But no harm, no foul." Holden continues, and once my focus shifts back to him, he adds, "I wasn't about to let it ruin our *date*."

This dickhead.

The only person utterly oblivious to what is happening here is Kason—though I have no clue how he's blind to the sheer amount of hostility between Holden and me. But I'm grateful for his obliviousness; he'd no doubt skin me alive if he knew I was the reason Holden showed up naked and thirty minutes late for their first date.

Crossing my arms, I lean back on the couch. "Pretty sure they don't let you into the movies wearing only a glove there, Sykes."

Another bright smile is aimed at me before he looks over at Kason. "Oh, it's okay. I don't mind ordering in and watching something here instead, as long as that sounds okay to you?"

Absolutely the fuck not.

I cock my head, eyes darting between the two of them. "Doesn't sound like much of a date to me."

"No, it doesn't," Kason says, cutting into the conversation. His eyes stay locked on Holden's face as his own finally returns to a normal pigment. "I don't want to ruin the plans you made. Plus, you already got the movie tickets, right?"

God, this is ridiculous. I can't explain how much I wish he'd see through Holden's shit right now and end whatever this weird dynamic is between them.

But of course, he goes playing right into his hand instead.

"Nah, it's fine. I honestly don't mind." Holden's attention shifts to me. "Phoenix can join us even. The more, the merrier, as the saying goes."

A smile sits on his lips, and I can hear the unspoken words swirling in his eyes.

So you can witness the entire thing.

Well played, Sykes. Well fucking played.

"He needs to study, and I don't want you to be out cash by us not going." Kason glances over at me, then to Holden, before finally ending on me. "Phoe, you're about the same size. Holden can just borrow—"

"Oh, fuck no," I say at the same time as Holden says, "Works for me."

I shoot him a death glare, but he just smiles—bright, shiny, and unbothered. It's infuriating.

"C'mon, man," Kason says, a plea in his eyes. "I know you're pissed about me canceling on you, but will you just do me this solid?"

At this point, what else can I do? Being petty out of spite only turns this around on me, once again making me the asshole best friend who can't be supportive. A role playing right into Holden's favor.

So I reluctantly nod toward my bedroom before speaking through gritted teeth.

"The door on the left."

"Thanks, Nix," Holden says, going as far as patting me on the shoulder when he passes by. "You're really a lifesaver."

"I'm about to be a life-ender if you touch me again," I mutter low enough for only his ears.

The threat misses the mark, though, and Holden just keeps on smiling. "I'll be out in a bit."

I shove my irritability under lock and key while Kason babbles on about hazing and stupid pranks, not paying attention enough to give away my involvement. Kason figuring out I was the one who did it is sure to only backfire on this entire plan more than it already has.

True to his word, Holden emerges from my room five minutes later.

Wearing...*his clothes.*

The clothes I had kept in his duffle, stashing the whole raid so far back in my closet, he had to dig and root around to find it.

Blood pools on my tongue, the coppery taste filling my mouth as I bite the inside of my cheek to keep from screaming. Because...fuck! I've never met another human being who can fall into a pile of shit and still come out smelling like a damn rose garden.

Kason comes up beside me, and I glance over to find a smile on his face as he looks at Holden.

"Knew you two would be a similar size." His eyes shift from Holden to me. "Though, I've never seen you wear that before. Is it new?"

"Yeah," I say through gritted teeth. "I was saving it for something special."

A seemingly innocent grin appears on Holden's face. "Well, I think a first date is a pretty special occasion."

"I guess so."

Keeping calm and composed is nearly impossible as the two of them chat amongst themselves about switching their dinner reservation to after the movie because of the delay. And though it was my intention to keep this date from even happening, I'm ready for the two of them to get the fuck out so I no longer have to be in Holden's aggravating presence.

Thankfully, it only takes them a few minutes to head for the door, Kason calling goodnight behind him and saying he'd be quiet coming back tonight.

Well, at least he's planning on coming back. That's gotta count for something.

I wave him off, not bothering to respond, while I wait in silence for the telltale *click* of the door to alert me that I'm finally alone again. Only... the sound doesn't come.

Instead, I hear the one sound that grates on my nerves more than all others.

"Oh, hey, Nixy?"

My lips roll into a firm, flat line as I slowly turn to look at where

Holden lingers in the doorway. An arched brow is all I give him, not trusting myself not to pop off at the fucker.

"I left you something on your bed. You know, as a thank you for the clothes."

A jolt of dread hits me in the stomach as my mind races through the hundreds of possibilities, each one taking a far worse turn than the last.

"Not necessary," I tell him, swallowing down the bile in my throat.

"Regardless." A smirk lifts the corner of his mouth before he adds, "And if you could put my bag back in the locker room before we're back, it'd be greatly appreciated."

And with that, he's out the door and following Kason down to the car.

I'm quick to work up the courage and face the disaster sure to be left in Holden's wake. Clothes strewn across the floor and every available surface, books ripped to shreds, the whole nine yards as retaliation for stealing his clothes.

Yet, to my surprise, my room is just as pristine as I left it. Not a single thing is out of place except Holden's *gift* sitting at the end of my bed.

It's the glove he used to cover his junk while he trotted across campus. But it's only when I get closer and grab it off the comforter that I realize…

It's *my* glove.

The one that's supposed to be in my stall in the baseball team's locker room instead of on my fucking bed, having just been used…

Ugh.

A Sharpie falls out of it as I go to flip it over, and my blood is set to a boil as my eyes trace over the words written in black ink on the back side.

Holden's cock cover. Est. 2023.

I throw the damn thing across the room, where it hits the wall with a *thwack,* and drop to my bed, frustration coursing through my bloodstream like a tidal wave.

Not only did I fail to ruin this date, but now I also have to break in a brand-new glove before the season starts.

That motherfucker.

I should've known from that day in class, we'd be evenly matched in this battle. It's my fault for underestimating him, but never in my life did I think I'd be this severely outplayed.

Still, the score speaks for itself.

Holden: 1, Phoenix: 0.

EIGHT
Holden

The house is in complete chaos when I get home from practice over Thanksgiving break, and for once in my life, I'm not the reason for it.

There are at least fifteen people jam-packed on the first floor of our three-story townhouse, and I can tell there are more spilling out onto the deck in the backyard for beer pong—even if it is late November in Chicago. Add in the music thumping through the floor, my guess is there's a good amount of people in the rec room we have downstairs too.

What the hell?

It takes me a few minutes to find someone who actually lives here, and I'm not surprised when my eyes finally land on Braxton manning the beer pong table out back.

"What's happening here?" I ask slowly while he aims for a cup.

"We've finally started winning," he says with a shrug, as if it's enough to answer all my questions. "I only invited a few guys from the team over for a few beers to celebrate, so if you're pissed, don't look at me. It's not my fault it turned into this."

This being one step below a full-blown kegger in the middle of our townhouse.

"Of course not," I mutter as I continue taking in the scene before me.

Most of the people I vaguely recognize from other frat or sorority parties I've attended the past few years, and true to his word, there are a bunch of Braxton's teammates back inside the house. But when I glance through the window, I don't see the two other hockey players I live with. And while that's not *not* normal, I'm a bit surprised by it.

"Where's Oak?" I ask, still looking around for my best friend.

Braxton shrugs for what might be the eighth time since I walked into the backyard. "Beats me. But with our game tomorrow, I'd assume he'll be home soon."

And he's gonna be thrilled when he sees the state the house is in. Ever the golden boy.

"And Cam?"

"Fuckin'..." is all Braxton says before catching the pong ball his opponent throws a little long.

"Theo?"

"Downstairs with some of the baseball guys." His attention shifts to me after he throws again, and this time the ball bounces off the rim of one cup before bouncing into the one beside it. "And you're right here, annoying the shit out of me with all your goddamn questions."

Well, all right then.

I've never been much of a Braxton fan, but he's Oak and Cam's teammate, so I shut my mouth and deal. Except moments like this make it really fucking hard.

"Just wanting to make sure you cleared it with the other people living here before throwing a house party."

Braxton doesn't so much as bat an eye when he replies, "Not like you don't do the same thing."

I'll be the first to admit I'm the usual perpetrator when it comes to parties at the house. The main difference is, I tend to let the rest of the people who live here know when a party is being thrown, rather than everyone being greeted by a sight like this when they get home.

So if *I* know better, there's no reason Braxton shouldn't either.

"As long as everyone knows," I say dryly, which is as close to biting my tongue as I can get.

"And now you do." His attention shifts back to the game at hand. "So, if you don't mind, you're kind of ruining my vibe."

He just pulled two cups on the last throw while I've been standing here, though I'm not about to point it out. I've got no reason to keep talking to the asshole as it is.

Ducking back inside, I grab a beer from the fridge and pull out my phone, two ideas battling in my head as to what to do. In the end though, I decide what's done is done, and there's no use trying to end this prematurely—especially when my roommates don't say shit when I have people over. Besides, the last thing I want is Braxton retaliating when I decide to bring in a keg and my fifty closest friends.

So I do the only logical thing at this point.

I open the football team's group text and extend the invite—making sure to text Kason again separately.

I haven't had much time outside of practice with him since our date last week. A date that was downright abysmal, filled with far too much awkwardness—mostly on his end—to consider a success. Especially when the most fun I had all night was seeing the look on Phoenix's face the moment I showed up at the door with his glove covering my dick to pick Kason up in the first place.

We could've ended it right there, and I'd have been just fine. But I'm still hoping it was a fluke incident; first date jitters or whatever, and maybe another time hanging out in a group setting will make him a bit more comfortable around me.

Which is why I'm happy as a clam to see he texts back seconds later, opting to head over here and join the party.

Kason: Where are you? This house is packed.

The corner of my mouth curls up in a grin as I read the text twenty minutes later.

Me: Downstairs. Rec room.

Kason: Meet me somewhere a little more private?

Me: How private are we talking?

Kason: Private enough that we won't risk someone walking in and finding us in a precarious situation.

A smirk spreads across my lips into a full grin at the same time my brain thinks a single victorious word.

Finally.

Kason has been adamant about letting things progress naturally, taking it slow and whatnot. And while my agreement has given me a killer case of blue balls—they honestly might be purple now—it's also enabled me to prove a point to Phoenix. Though, if I've learned anything from the past few weeks, it's that it was the dumbest agreement I could have ever made.

Me: Meet you in my room?

His reply is almost immediate.

Kason: Five minutes. Lights off. We don't want anyone walking in.

Me: And why's that?

Kason: Because I want you naked when I get there.

Excitement shoots through me as I reread the second text enough times I think I'm hallucinating the words altogether. Because if this conversation is leading where I think it is, I'm about to fold like a house of cards; agreement with Phoenix be damned.

Then again, if we don't have *sex,* maybe I haven't broken this unspoken deal at all?

Hell, if I know. And it's not like I'm gonna track down Phoenix to find out.

Yet even throughout all the excitement, there's a weird, nagging feeling in the back of my mind as I reread the text. As if this is too good to be true. Especially when the house has an additional thirty people milling about.

Fucking—or even messing around—with a house full of people doesn't seem his style.

It's still not enough to keep me from texting back.

Me: I better not be the only one naked for long.

Kason: ;)

I glance up from where I've been sitting on the couch with Theo and a few of his teammates, ready to head off to my room and wait for him. Except I don't make it into the hallway before a familiar figure comes walking down the stairs.

Phoenix.

He sees me. I know he has to, but he makes it a point to ignore me as he moves to brush by me. That just won't do. Not after the little stunt he pulled last week when he found out I was taking Kason out for a proper date.

I reach out my arm in front of him, pressing my palm to the wall to prevent him from going any further.

"Seriously?" His dark, penetrating stare lands on me, entirely unamused. "Move."

"I don't think so."

Phoenix lets out an indignant huff before going to duck under my arm. Little does he know, he's not getting away that easily.

With a quick maneuver, I cage him with his back to the wall, my arms on either side of his head.

"Fuck off, Holden. I'm not doing this with you right now."

"Didn't realize they were inviting just anyone to this little gathering," I say, ignoring his commentary.

"Not even you get to control the guest list."

"I definitely should have some sort of veto power, especially after the stunt you pulled last week." I lean forward, my lips brushing the shell of his ear when I speak. "Tell me, are you planning to steal my entire wardrobe this time, Nix? Because if that's the case, I think I need to go lock up my room."

"Feel free to lock yourself *in* it so I don't have to look at you the rest of the night."

I pull back to stare at him, our noses close enough to touch. "Maybe I will. But feel free to send your buddy Kason my way once he arrives."

I'm expecting irritation or anger from him, so when a grin appears on Phoenix's lips, I'm taken by surprise. Although not nearly as much as by the response leaving his mouth.

"I'll be sure to pass along the message."

I'm left gaping at him, completely shocked that he's not making some sort of snide remark. I don't even try fighting him when he ducks under my arm again and heads toward his teammates, because my brain has just been whipped, scrambled, and tossed in a blender.

What…?

I watch after Phoenix far longer than I should—waiting for my equilibrium to return—only to find him smiling and laughing with his teammates the second he joins them. Like he's a normal guy for once, instead of the anti-social, cock-blocking demon who has been making my life hell these past few weeks.

It's then I realize this is the first time I've seen Phoenix out without Kason, and my confusion only grows.

There's no way he doesn't know Kason's coming; they're roommates, after all. They had to have come here together. So why isn't Phoenix acting like the guard dog he usually is?

All these questions run through my head at warp speed as I stare at him, not sure what to think while also knowing I don't really have the time to worry about it.

Shaking my thoughts free, I push through the door to my room and let it fall closed behind me.

I keep the lights off as I strip, surprised to find that the more articles of clothing I remove from my body, the more anxious I get. And not in the fun, sexy, exciting way I get when I'm ready to tear someone else's clothes off. It's the same unsettled feeling from earlier, telling me something isn't right.

I can't shake it, even as I drop onto my mattress and wait for Kason to show.

There's a good chance this feeling can be chalked up to Phoenix right outside the room, who will surely know exactly what happened the second Kason and I emerge looking sex-touseled and satiated. Or worse, catch Kason on his way into my room and stop him from coming in here altogether.

Oh, shit.

I swear, if Kason is finally ready to take things a bit further and Phoenix pulls one of his stunts, I swear, I'm gonna wring his damn neck—

The door to my bedroom cracks open, simultaneously pulling me from my thoughts and putting them at ease. But we're not in the clear until we're locked in complete privacy.

"Get in here and lock the door," I murmur, my eyes locked on the silhouette in the doorway.

Kason doesn't say anything as the door falls shut behind him.

Anxiety turns into anticipation as the soft footfalls get closer and closer to me, only to have my heart rate kick up a notch when I feel the bed dip beneath his added weight.

"Those five minutes felt like an eternity." My hand slides under his shirt, tracing up his back as he settles over me. "I thought I was gonna have to take matters into my own hands."

He doesn't say anything, just gives a raspy chuckle that goes straight to my cock as the heat of his breath coasts over my neck. And it only gets worse when his lips skim the column of my throat in a teasing caress.

"Fuck," I mutter, my fingers digging into his muscular obliques.

I beg my libido to stay in check—to let him explore and tease to his liking so we don't move too quickly. But every minuscule brush of his skin sets my nerve endings on fire, lighting me ablaze with a need too deep to ignore.

So I turn my head and capture his lips with mine.

I expect him to pause or pull back at the sudden contact, but he surprises me by sliding his tongue against the seam of my lips, seeking entrance I'm more than happy to give.

My cock thickens as his tongue slides against mine, twisting and tangling until a moan rumbles deep within my chest.

Something about this kiss feels different from the few we've shared. Yet somehow, it's eerily familiar at the same time.

Maybe because it's finally missing all the awkwardness and quirky fumbling. Instead, every press of his lips is filled with passion and… aggression. An almost fury that pours into me, filling me to the brim with a ferocity of my own.

My teeth sink into his lower lip and I tug, loving the brutality he's showing me. He answers in kind when I release him, his tongue now flicking and teasing against mine in a torturous game of cat and mouse. Give and take.

Catch and release.

Another moan fills the otherwise silent room when his hips finally drop against mine, and I couldn't say which of us it came from. All I know is the friction of his jeans against my bare cock is both heaven and hell.

"You're making it really hard to behave," I murmur, my fist balling in his shirt at the small of his back before dragging it up and over his head. "So you better tell me if you wanna stop."

I feel his smile against my lips right before he captures them again, and I take it as a sign to no longer hold back.

My hips roll up into his while our tongues tangle some more, loving the slight bite of pain from the denim that accompanies the pleasure. He's hard behind his jeans too, and I snake my hand between us to free him— wanting to finally feel him skin to skin.

I've barely worked open the button when his hand wraps around my wrist, halting my movements. I let him pull my arm away, assuming we've reached his limits. But he surprises me once again when he grabs the other wrist and drags them both up over my head, my knuckles brushing against the metal headboard.

It's a move I'd usually hate, preferring my hands to be tracing, touching, and groping naked skin. Yet, when he uses a single hand to pin them to the bed above me, it only increases the fire already raging like an inferno inside me.

It's a sexy, downright sinful move; one only made better when his free hand trails a single finger down my throat to my sternum. He makes no sign of stopping there, and it continues down a path over my abs until it finally traces me from root to tip.

I feel every single atom of his body as it presses against mine, but it's the skin-on-skin contact that's electric.

Intoxicating.

Fucking euphoric.

The need for more overwhelms me until I'm ready to beg him for pity or sympathy, anything to get him to really, *truly* touch me. If he doesn't, I might die on the spot from an explosion of need and testosterone. But there must be a masochistic side to him, because instead of having mercy on me and wrapping his hand around my length, his touch disappears entirely.

"More," I pant, my head thrown back against the mattress in frustration. "I need more."

Another dark, sinful laugh comes from him as he changes his torment by scraping his teeth over my throat instead.

His laugh, his silent command, his touch; all of it together creates the hottest, sexiest encounter I've ever had—with a guy or girl. Nothing compares to the way I'm being truly manhandled, explored, and teased.

That is, until the clicking of…metal registers.

Dread fills me instantly when the cool bite of the handcuff fastens around my wrists, and I go to pull away, only to find I'm already restrained.

"The fuck," I hiss, bucking his body off mine as I start tugging against the cuffs to the point of pain. It's no use, though—the only movement I get is the scrape of metal on metal as the links slide over the rails of the headboard.

The lights illuminate the room without warning, and I slam my eyes closed to prevent going momentarily blind.

But nothing could prepare me to meet the gaze of the shirtless man standing beside my door.

The one who has quickly become the bane of my fucking existence.

Phoenix.

NINE

Holden

As much as I'd like to pretend it wasn't Phoenix's body and mouth on mine, there's no way around it. Not when I'm staring at his half-naked form across the room, complete with flushed cheeks and kiss-swollen lips that make my cock take even more notice.

What I find more puzzling than anything is that I'm not even pissed about him tricking me or besting me in this messed up little game we've begun. As far as I'm concerned, it's all par for the course.

The reason I'm so fucking irate is because of how turned on he made me. How sexy, fun, and *familiar* his touch and kiss were. It's disarming and more than a little maddening.

"What the hell, Nix," I growl, bucking up from the bed against my restraints despite knowing it's pointless. I'm cuffed in place until he decides otherwise; naked and at his mercy.

"I knew you couldn't stop yourself from trying to get in his pants," he says, chest rising and falling with quickened breathing, his dark eyes searching my face.

And just like that, everything clicks into place.

The dread and anxious feeling while I waited for *Kason,* the way Phoenix didn't even react to me egging him on out in the hallway, the way he so boldly touched and kissed me. All the way down to the very un-Kason-like texts.

Because it was never Kason to begin with.

"Did you steal his fucking phone?"

A smirk forms on his lips as he pulls Kason's phone from his back pocket. "The great thing about being best friends with Kason? He trusts me. Implicitly. So when your text popped through on his phone while he went to the bathroom, it was pretty easy to use the passcode I've known since I was thirteen to text you back."

I can practically see the whole scenario play out in my head as he grabs his discarded shirt from the ground, and even by my own scheming standards, it's brilliant.

"Well played, Nix. You win this round," I grind out. "Now uncuff me."

His response is immediate. "Call it off with Kason, and I will."

My brow arches, not at all surprised by his terms. What I find astonishing is his thinking I'd give up so easily just to save myself a little embarrassment.

"And if I don't?" I ask slowly. "What happens then? You'll leave me chained here? Or will you come back over and finish what you started?"

As he pulls his shirt over his head, Phoenix's dark eyes flare with heat and rage. "You're never gonna win this war with me, Sykes. I told you, there's no way I'd allow it."

"You think so? Because I'd be willing to bet my life that Kason won't forgive you when he discovers what we just did." I keep my voice low and as menacing as it can be when I'm naked and subdued. "Because when I tell him, there's only one of us who isn't complicit in what just happened. And it sure as hell isn't the one holding the key to these cuffs."

"Except, who do you think he'll believe?" Phoenix leans against the wall and twirls the handcuff keys on his finger. "The best friend he's known for half his life who tells him you drunkenly made a pass at me… or the cocky playboy with a reputation for meaningless one-night stands."

My teeth sink into my cheek until I taste blood, having now found myself caught between a rock and a hard place. Or, in this case, a best friend and a set of handcuffs.

"That's what I thought," he murmurs. "So you can admit defeat and be released…"

I shake my head, ready to call his bluff. "You won't leave me here like this. There's no way."

"If you say so," he says, before dropping the keys to my freedom on the desk near the door.

"Nix," I growl as he takes a step toward the door, a small amount of panic setting in.

He stops with his hand on the knob and arches a brow at me, waiting for me to wave the white flag.

I should. It would be the smart move here. Although something inside me—some sick, masochistic part that enjoys this back and forth with him—won't let it happen.

So I remain silent and accept my fate, whatever it might be.

"All right," His eyes are dark and hooded as he watches me. "Consider the scores even now."

"We're not even close to even, Nixy. But mark my words, we will be."

A crooked smirk curls at his mouth, accepting the challenge. And then, without another word, he opens the door...and walks out.

I'm not sure how much time passes while I lie there, cuffed to the bed and debating my poor life choices, but it's far longer than I'd like it to be. But it's the only option I've left myself with, considering there's no way anyone will hear me shouting over the music blaring through the speakers just outside my room.

And believe me, I tried.

Thankfully there's a large enough break in the music for me to hope my cries will be heard. I shout the only name I can think of, the only one who might be within hearing distance, hoping I don't get some rando answering the call instead.

"Theo!"

I wait for an answer, hearing nothing but the music increasing in volume as the new song starts building. God only knows when my next chance will be, so I shout again.

"Theo!"

Still no answer.

My head slumps back, the realization that I could very well be here until the party is over sinking in—and by my estimation, it'll be hours from now.

I really fucked this one up.

Irritation—with myself, with Phoenix, with this entire situation—fills me, fueling me with fire for one final attempt at freedom.

"Theodore!"

His name leaves my mouth on a long, screeching howl—more animal than man—but it's enough to have the music level drop dramatically. I hear murmurs and talking on the other side of the wall, before the sound of Theo's voice comes from the other side of my door.

Relief floods me the second it opens, my roommate and savior, stepping into the room.

"You bellow—Jesus fuck!" Theo shouts as he slaps his hand over his eyes. "A little warning would be nice, Hold!"

A warning? Seriously?

"I was a bit preoccupied trying to get your attention," I snap as he quickly shuts the door behind him. "Or, in case you hadn't noticed, I'm a little tied up here."

He looks ridiculous when he smirks with his eyes still covered, clearly amused by my word choice. "Well, can you include nudity as a preface when you're in need of rescue next time?"

I scoff and pull at my restraints some more. "Oh, please. You're an athlete. Don't act like you've never seen another dick besides your own."

"Yeah, but not your diseased one," he mutters, shifting his hands to act as blinders while he grabs my discarded shirt and tosses it over my now flaccid cock. "Now, where's the key so I can unlock you?"

"On the table by the door," I tell him, nodding toward it. "And I'm clean as a whistle, thank you very much."

He spots it immediately and grabs it before heading back to my aid.

"With as much action as you get? I doubt it." The handcuffs rattle against the metal headboard while he fiddles with the locking mechanism before he looks down at me. "This might take a second."

"Not like I haven't been waiting here for a while as it is," I mutter. "But I'm offended by your assumptions, ye of little faith."

He snorts out a laugh as he releases the first lock. "You're not offended by anything."

The second lock clicks open, and I shoot up to a sitting position the moment I'm free from the cuffs, rubbing at the raw skin on my wrists. "I'm offended by being left rock-hard and handcuffed to a bed by the most infuriating person I've ever fucking met."

"Yeah…" he says slowly. "Do I even want to know what kind of sex game you were playing to end up like this?"

"Not a sex game."

"Again, don't believe you."

"Then you should probably get out so I can start making my plans of retaliation."

"Figured as much." Theo sighs, shaking his head while he rises to stand. "But you might wanna do it with some clothes on."

I toss the shirt that was providing my only means of decency at him, the fabric hitting him square in the face.

"Dick."

TEN

Phoenix

December

"We need to talk."

My blood instantly turns to ice as Kason's voice registers, and I glance up from where my laptop is strewn over my mattress to find him leaning against the doorway. There's a slight frown to his lips and lines worrying his forehead, both of which set me on edge.

"Hey," I say, my voice a little higher pitched than I'd like. "About what?"

But I'm pretty sure I know *exactly* what Kason wants to discuss.

It's been a week since I tricked Holden and left him handcuffed to his bed, and I've been walking around on eggshells, anxious about this exact moment happening. Where the guillotine drops, severing all the trust Kason and I have because of one stupid decision.

Now with it here, the anxiety rippling through me might cause me to burst at the seams.

Holden must've told him what happened—no doubt making it seem like I was seducing him for my own benefit—only for my best friend to be absolutely pissed.

Except, the expression on Kason's face isn't angry so much as...nervous?

"About our trip to Florida."

Both relief and guilt flood me simultaneously as my brain registers his words. Especially if he still doesn't know anything about my history with Holden. And as much as I hate keeping it from him, I know it's better this way. Easier as well, because it's far too late to suddenly bring up the real reason I consider Holden to be public enemy number one.

"Oh, okay," I say, pushing my books aside for him to sit. He does, and I swear, he looks even more nervous after. "What's going on?"

With the way things have been going lately—specifically him ditching me to spend time with Holden—I'm wondering if he's planning to cancel on me yet again. And when he starts his explanation with, "Try not to be mad at me about this," I'm fully prepared for my line of thinking to be correct.

"Okay."

"I'm serious," he insists. "You have to promise me you won't revoke my friendship for this."

Oh, hell.

"I'll do my best to not be pissed," I say slowly, keeping my temper in check. "Now, just spit it out, Kase."

Reluctance still consumes his features while he looks at me. "Okay, I um..." He clears his throat twice, and then, "I invited Holden."

This is not how I pictured this conversation going when I saw him in my doorway, but this probably is just as shitty of one. To the point where

I might honestly prefer him finding out about my failed attempts to get Holden to run in the other direction, consequences be damned. Anything would be better than having to spend ten days with the two of them in one house—no matter how big it is.

My eyes sink closed, and I let out a long sigh. "And why the fuck would you do that?"

More guilt slides over his face. "He saw it on my calendar the other night when we were hanging out," Kason explains.

"And invited himself?" I surmise, not bothering to keep the disdain from my tone. "Sounds pretty on brand, if you ask me."

"No, didn't you just hear me? I said I invited him."

I take a deep breath through my nose and exhale. "Which brings us back to *why*?"

"You said you wouldn't get pissed."

"I'm trying very hard not to," I say through gritted teeth. "Now explain. In detail."

Kason starts fiddling with the stitching of my comforter, tracing the lines as if they're the key to getting out of this conversation.

"Kase," I say again, my patience practically gone.

Green eyes flash up to meet mine, and I see a plea for mercy in them. "He was asking about it, and I explained how we always take a trip down to your family condo every winter break. But then I told him how your sister had all these new ballet lessons, so it was just the two of us going this year." He goes back to playing with the stitching, no longer willing to hold my gaze. "It got us talking about his winter break plans and how he wasn't planning to go back to California since his Gran was going on an old-folks cruise, and so…" Kason trails off, but it doesn't prevent me from filling in the rest of the story on my own.

He invited Holden because he felt bad. Worried he would be alone for the holidays instead of with friends or family.

This guy really isn't going down without a fight.

In fact, he might be getting even sneakier with his strategies. I'm gonna have to up my game if I have any chance of killing whatever is brewing between the two of them before it ends badly.

I sigh, pinching the bridge of my nose. "And he couldn't have just gone home with Oakley or any of his other teammates?"

"Phoe…"

"Nah, don't do that right now." My eyes analyze his face, noting every little line of stress and worry written there. "I know you're just trying to look out for him and be his friend. I get it. But seriously, Kase? Your bleeding heart will be your greatest downfall."

Just like mine is not being able to tell you no.

Kason only nods, letting the silence linger in the space between us. It feels suffocating—like every single mention of Holden Sykes is poisoning the air and our friendship with toxic fumes we might not survive.

"Who else?" I ask, my voice not more than a whisper.

Kason's brows collide. "I only invited Holden."

Sometimes this man is so fucking dense, I wonder how we're even friends at all.

My fingers curl over my laptop screen as I snap it closed. "Yes. Holden. Who is the biggest party animal around, and we're spending ten days in a condo down at the beach with zero parents or anyone to keep us from acting like idiots. So I'm asking you again, Kason. Who else is coming?"

He shoots me a pleading look. "I know you don't have much faith in him, but he knows it's your house. There's no way he'd just go off and invite a bunch of other people when it's not his invite to extend."

"Right," I say dryly.

I believe what Kason is saying as much as I believe this whole situation was mere happenstance. If I only had a dollar left to my name, I'd still bet it on Holden fabricating the entire conversation until Kason invited him along for the ride.

Kason's phone chimes in his pocket with a text, and I take it as an opportunity to end this conversation and cool back down. But Kason sighs and rubs his temple as his eyes read the screen, and my gut sinks.

"What?" I ask.

He doesn't speak, just hands off his phone after turning the screen to face me.

Sykes: Do you care if I invite a couple of the guys on the team down to the condo too? Nothing nuts, just thinking Noah, Harrison, and Luca. None of them had plans for the break either. Figured it could be fun.

The glare I aim at Kason as I return his phone could melt ice.

"Try not to say I told you so," Kason says with a groan as he flops backward onto my mattress. "I can already hear it inside my head as it is."

"You have too much faith in people." My eyes shift over to him. "And for the record, having all those meatheads joining us doesn't sound like fun at all."

Kason gives me a look of exasperation. "You don't even know them."

"I know Holden enough to know who he hangs out with," I snap. Honestly, I have no idea how Theo can stand being his roommate. "Besides, isn't Noah the teammate you said has been acting super weird around you since you came out?"

Kason adjusts his body weight, rising up on his elbows. "Yeah, but—"

"No. No *but* anything." Irritation starts settling into my bones, and I do my best to shake it off. Again, my best friend might be dense as shit, but he's also a pretty awesome guy. It's one of the things I love most about him.

He just needs to learn to rein in his Mr. Nice Guy routine every once in a while.

"Noah always hangs out with Holden and Oakley," he tries reasoning. "And both of them are open about their sexuality."

Sounds like a crock of shit to me. Like simply being friends with someone in the queer community automatically exempts you from ever being homophobic. It doesn't fucking work that way.

"I just don't want to see you water yourself down to make other people comfortable. You shouldn't have to do that—not for a single person on this planet." My stare is pointed and firm, leaving no room for debate.

"I won't be."

I arch a disbelieving brow. "So you're planning to be all cute and lovey-dovey with Holden right in front of Noah, knowing he's already been acting weird around you? And your other teammates too?"

I've known Kason long enough to know the answer to both those questions is no. He just doesn't want to admit it. To me, or himself.

"Things aren't like that with Holden," he says quietly. "We're not anything serious yet, and while we aren't keeping it on the DL, the guys won't care if they saw a little PDA."

"You say that now, but what happens when they do, and you're left feeling like garbage due to some shitty comment they make to be funny?"

A disgruntled sound leaves him and he runs his fingers through his hair. He must be getting just as frustrated with me as I am with him. Or realizing how right I am, as much as he might wish I wasn't.

"It's your family's place, Phoe. They don't have to come if you don't want them there. Just say the fucking word. Even Holden will understand if I tell him he can't come either. I'm sure you need to run it by your parents as it is."

Mom and Dad already told me I'm more than welcome to invite any friends down—something they've made clear to me since starting college. That's not the issue here. I just wanted to get Kason *away* from all of this shit to talk some sense into him about Holden. Or maybe gaining some distance from him might allow him to remove whatever rose-colored glasses he has on when he looks at the guy.

Having him *and* the rest of those Neanderthals won't help my efforts.

Plus, after what happened with Holden in his bedroom, the last thing I need is to be trapped in a single house with him for a week and a half. Or a vehicle on the way down there, for that matter.

Too bad saying no and disinviting Holden only makes *me* look like an ass.

I pinch the bridge of my nose and let out a long sigh, already regretting my decision before it's even been made. "Fine. They can come. But don't be surprised if I end up inviting Theo and Wyatt and any other people I actually want to hang out with too."

Hurt crosses Kason's features immediately, but I'm too pissed to care. He's the one who didn't care about how bringing the fucker with us on vacation would make *me* feel. This thing with him and Holden is changing us and our friendship into something...I don't even recognize anymore.

"Phoe—"

"I've got work to do," I mutter, lifting my laptop back open. My focus stays fixed on the screen as the bed shifts from Kason rising off the mattress. He must be taking the agonizing silence between us as a sign that this conversation is over.

His footfalls retreat toward the door, but when I chance a glimpse, I find him standing in the doorway, staring back at me.

"Can you at least try to forgive me before we leave next week?" he asks softly.

I swallow back the desire to right this moment, and whisper, "Shut the door on your way out."

ELEVEN

Holden

I'm not exactly sure why I agreed to be the one driving seventeen hours down to Florida for this trip over winter break. The only time I've ever taken a road trip of this magnitude was to move from California to Chicago, and it was a drive I hated every minute of.

My desperation to get laid—and under Phoenix's skin—must be at an all-time high. It's the only explanation for why I'm suffering through the daggers being glared at me through the headrest. Or the hateful stare I'll randomly catch in the rearview mirror whenever I change lanes or talk to Noah, who's beside him in the back seat.

At this rate, I think Phoenix might be getting under *my* skin more than the other way around. It doesn't help that every time our gazes collide, my attention snags on his lips, and I can't help the way my blood heats when I remember the stunt he pulled in my room.

It only takes a second for me to realize he's probably plotting yet another way to ensure my demise while our eyes are locked through the reflection. Then I snap right out of it.

Those moments alone have already made for a less-than-desirable trip, and we still have fourteen more hours to go. But I also know it could also be much, much worse.

Still, the tension is enough for me to crave the pit stops for gas and food every few hours, if only for a slight reprieve from the toxic cloud filling my Jeep.

I glance to where Theo pulled into the pump behind me and is refilling his Bronco. Meanwhile, Phoenix, Kason, and the others head inside to order lunch and hit the restrooms, leaving the two of us here alone.

"How's your drive going?" I call over to Theo as I screw the cap back on my gas tank.

"Long," he replies, leaning against the driver's door. "Yours?"

"It's a disaster, honestly." Blowing out a breath, I shake my head and walk in his direction. "Thank God we're stopping for the night, or I'd be inclined to run us off the road."

"Already sick of driving?"

"If only," I say with a laugh. "Just sick of Phoenix aiming evil eyes at the back of my head for hours on end. I swear he's plotting murder back there. Simply looking for the right opportunity to act."

Theo snorts, amusement evident in his tone when he asks, "I take it things between the two of you didn't end well, then?"

The question catches me off guard, and my brows clash together. "End well?"

"At the Kappa Sig party?" When I don't acknowledge what he says, he lets out a laugh and shakes his head. "Man, you really need to start keeping a log of the people you sleep with if they're starting to run together this badly."

My brain comes screeching to a halt, attempting to recalibrate and make sense of what he's saying. Only, it doesn't. Because Phoenix and I have never slept together. Apart from him making out with me, dry humping me to high heaven, and cuffing me to my bed for Theo to find, nothing has happened between us.

And even then, I haven't told a soul about that night. Theo might have an idea of what happened, but even he doesn't know who it was with.

"What the hell are you talking about?"

It's Theo's turn to look confused, dark brows slashing down over light green eyes. "The final's week party in May. The same night as—"

"Oh, my God," I whisper, piece after piece clicking into place in rapid-fire succession—all the answers I was missing to create a clear picture in my head.

The anniversary of my parents' death. Blacking out, only to wake up naked and alone the next morning with no memories from the night before.

No idea who it was I'd spent the night with.

It was Phoenix?

"There's the lightbulb," Theo jokes, oblivious to the plethora of epiphanies slamming into me like a fifty-car pile-up.

Why Phoenix's hatred for me seems to run so deep for no reason. Why his image of me was tainted from the moment we met. Why he wants me nowhere near Kason. Yet the most significant being…why my body felt familiarity in his touch when he left me chained to my bed.

It was because my body subconsciously remembered it.

Shit.

"Yeah," I choke out, doing my best to recover from the onslaught of emotions rampaging through me. "Takes a second sometimes."

He laughs again before going to say something, but the commotion behind me causes him to glance over my shoulder. Turning to look, I spot Harrison, Noah, and the rest heading back out with ten bags of food and piling back in the cars.

"Ugh, I'm starving," Theo says as Phoenix approaches and hands him his order. "You're the best."

Phoenix gives him a weak smile. "No problem, man."

He must feel me staring at him, because his attention shifts to me. And while so many questions have been answered, there's now a new one pinging around in my brain.

Why hasn't he said anything?

I don't have a chance to even think of a reason, let alone ask him, because he takes me off guard by shoving a greasy bag of food in my chest.

"What—"

"Your food," is all he says before turning back toward the Jeep.

I'm left staring after him, wordless and more confused than ever, when a chuckle comes from beside me.

"Yep," Theo muses with a shake of his head. "Definitely didn't end well."

Apparently. I just wish I had a fucking clue why.

Dread fills my gut as I realize we have another four hours before we reach the Mercer's place in Nashville; our halfway stop for the evening. Meaning four more hours of death glares while my mind attempts to figure out what happened back in May.

But rather than dwelling on it, I do my best to shove down the thousands of questions swirling inside my brain and fake a smile. "Guess we better get back on the road."

"Probably," Theo says with a heavy sigh. "But hey, if you need to escape the tension for a bit, you're more than welcome to drive the Bronco."

"You don't want me to."

He gives a shrug. "I swear, I don't mind."

My eyes shift from him to the mustard-yellow contraption he calls a vehicle. "I meant what I said. The only place I'd be caught driving this thing is off a damn cliff."

He aims a smirk at me before yanking open the driver's door. "From the sounds of it, you're ready to anyway."

Shit. After the bomb he just dropped on me? Me turning kamikaze on all their asses is less of a possibility and more of a guarantee.

"More than you know, man. More than you fucking know."

Thankfully, the time spent in the car after lunch is much more mellow—though I'd like to merit it to Phoenix falling asleep about thirty minutes after lunch. It's a little hard to give death glares when you're in a food coma, I guess.

Yet the peace wasn't all that peaceful, seeing as I couldn't stop sneaking glimpses at his sleeping form in the rearview mirror, begging the recesses of my mind to remember something.

Anything.

But as another few hours pass and we close in on Nashville, I'm starting to see the light at the end of the tunnel. Maybe even having a bit of fun—with Noah, at least.

"Okay, this has been bothering me since we got in the car, so I have to ask," he starts just after we cross the state line into Tennessee. "Why do you have a duck named Jerry on your dash?"

I can't help the smile curling across my lips as I glance at the rubber duck he's speaking of perched via a piece of tape on the top of my dashboard. There's a little *Hi, my name is* sticker on its chest, and I filled out the blank space with a black Sharpie, dubbing him Jerry.

"It's a Jeep-people thing," Phoenix says before I can reply.

I didn't realize he woke up, and my eyes shift to the rearview to find him already staring at me. "Why do you say it like that?"

"I didn't say it like anything."

"Except you did," I insist before glancing at Kason—who is dead asleep in the passenger seat.

So much for being the mediator like he promised.

"You kinda did," Noah confirms, and hell, at least someone's on my side. "You said it like you just found out he has an STD."

This time, Noah is the recipient of my irritated frown. "Why the fuck does everyone equate me with STDs?"

"I dunno," Phoenix says, tone laced with equal parts sarcasm and venom. "Maybe it's because you've spent the last couple years defining yourself as a man-whore who will screw everything that walks on two legs."

I watch his face silently for a minute, waiting for even the slightest hint of anything. Any clue as to what happened between us. But all I pick up on is a big, fat nothing, so I let my focus shift back to the road.

"It's a label I've been given."

"It's one you've earned."

My attention stays locked on the road, knowing it's either that or risk crashing into oncoming traffic. And I can't get answers out of Phoenix if I'm gorked from a head-on collision.

"Okay, but back to the duck," Noah says, simultaneously diffusing the tension and rerouting us back to the original conversation. "I have to know the story."

"There's not much of a story to tell," I insist. "I wasn't ducked or anything."

"Ducked?"

"Duck, duck, Jeep," Phoenix interjects, before adding, "Again, a Jeep-people thing."

Noah laughs. "You're acting like they're a cult."

"Because it is."

"Am I even needed for this conversation?" I snap from the front, my ability to play things off officially gone. "Because it sure doesn't seem like it."

Phoenix meets my glare in the rearview once again, a little smirk on his lips.

It's then I realize his entire goal was just to rile me up. Fray my edges. Lose my carefree persona he's slowly starting to slice through, one jab at a time. And I fed right into it without a second thought, thanks to my mind being so occupied with Theo's little slip-up.

Points to Nix on this one.

"I'll smother his face with a pillow to shut him up," Noah says, and true to his word, he slams his pillow right into Phoenix's face. And while it's not enough for me to completely compose myself again, I do get a small amount of enjoyment from it.

"Whatever, I'm done with this," I hear Phoenix mutter, and I glance back just in time to see him shove his headphones in his ears—no doubt in an attempt to drown out our conversation.

"Didn't want to tell you anyway," I snark back, aware it might be brushed aside. Which it evidently is, so when he doesn't respond, I fall into storytelling mode.

"I found the duck, actually. Move-in weekend of freshman year. It was the same weekend as the Duck Derby they do in the Chicago River, and my Gran and I were exploring the city before she flew back to California.

We'd caught the end of the race by chance and watched the winner slide into the massive net to catch them all. But this one fell outta the net."

"So you just kept it?"

I nod. "Yep."

"Why?"

"I'd just bought my Jeep a few weeks before and knew of the so-called cult," I say, aiming a barb at Phoenix—even if he can't hear me. "So I gave him a name and taped him to the dash. He's been there ever since."

Noah lets out a low hum. "Never took you for the sentimental type."

"Only with my Gran," I say, thinking of the woman I owe everything to. Without her, God only knows where I'd be. Certainly a lot more fucked up than I am already.

Noah catches me off guard by asking for the first truly personal piece of me in the years we've known each other.

"Did she raise you?"

I hedge for a second as I switch my attention to the mirror. Relief floods me when I find Phoenix staring out the window, still not listening.

Good.

The duck story—whatever. I don't care about him knowing the little, seemingly meaningless things about me. But if what Theo said is true, then his knowing something like this...is just different.

Too personal and intimate.

"She helped, yeah. And she became my guardian after my parents died."

My gaze slices to Noah as I wait for the look of sympathy I'm used to getting whenever someone finds out about my parents' passing. And sure enough, there it is, written all over his damn face.

He's silent for a second before asking the second-most fundamental question. "How long ago?"

I glance at Phoenix—once again grateful to see him tuning us out—before answering. "It'll be six years the first week of May."

"Shit," he whispers. "I'm so sorry, man."

"Thanks, but it's fine." I swallow down the knot encroaching on my vocal cords, but the rest of my response still comes out a little gruff. "It was a while ago."

"Still doesn't mean it's easy."

I nod, knowing that truth all too well. Even if it feels like the time that's passed should have lessened some of the pain. Or I'd have learned to cope better, at the very least. But if I've learned anything, there's no timeline for something like this.

Silence fills the car again, the only sound being the cadence of the engine and the quiet lull of music coming from the radio. I'm grateful for it. For having a moment to think. Except thinking and talking about them steers my mind straight back to the night I can't remember.

To Phoenix, and the memories of him that continue to evade me.

My eyes find the mirror again subconsciously, only to discover him already staring at me. Not in contempt or irritation like normal, though. There's a flash of empathy in those dark depths, an emotion so out of place, I almost miss it entirely before he looks back out the window.

But it was there, making me realize one thing.

He was listening, after all.

TWELVE

Phoenix

Stopping at my parents' for the night was the best idea I've ever had, because if there's anything worse than being forced to share a house with the constant source of my misery for ten whole days, it has to be driving seventeen straight hours with him to get there. My patience was already wearing thin before we stopped for lunch yesterday, so breaking it up into two days was necessary.

And I'll admit, after overhearing Holden had lost his parents, spending the night at home with mine ended up being an added bonus. I hugged them goodbye a little longer than usual this morning because of it too.

"Dude, why didn't you say you're loaded?" Noah says as we pull out of the driveway to officially hit the road.

"My parents are loaded," I correct him, not bothering to look up from where I'm scrolling through my playlist. But nothing sounds good to drown the three of them out for the next ten hours of driving.

"Typical rich person's response," Kason reminds me.

I glance his way, finding him already peering at me over his shoulder from the passenger seat. But he's got a soft smile on his face that I know well enough to realize he's poking fun.

My family's money has never meant anything to Kason, even when we were growing up. In fact, it's one of the many reasons we became so close, despite him coming from a completely different lifestyle.

Doesn't mean he passes on the opportunity to troll me for being a trust fund kid.

"What do they do?" Holden asks, and my attention shifts to meet his eyes in the rearview mirror.

I silently debate how much to tell him before going with the watered-down version. "Dad works for a record label."

Kason snorts, and I catch him shaking his head. "Try *owns* a record label."

"No shit," Noah muses beside me. "Country?"

I let out a short laugh and shake my head, since that's what everyone assumes when they think of the music business in Nashville. "No, actually. More alternative rock and metal stuff."

"Anyone I've heard of?" Holden pipes up.

"Doubtful," I mutter, still focused on my phone.

Kason decides to join the conversation with, "He signed Icarus Ignites last year."

"For real?" This comes from Holden, and I glance up to see him looking at me in the mirror for the eight millionth time in two days.

My eyebrows lift in surprise. "You know them?"

"Of course. They've exploded in the past few months." A little smirk forms on his lips. "Well deserved, since their new album is a masterpiece.

Nash Kaelin has the voice of an angel and the scream of Satan himself."

I couldn't have said it better myself—though I'm a bit taken aback by him having even heard of the band at all.

"He listens to a lot of the same stuff you do, Phoe," Kase says. "Maybe it's enough for you two to call a cease-fire for the rest of the trip?"

"Highly unlikely," I say at the same time Holden says, "Absolutely not," and our gazes lock in the mirror again.

At least we can agree on something.

"What do you mean by *a lot?*" I ask skeptically, my interest piqued.

Rather than listing out his music tastes, Holden unlocks his phone and tosses it at me in the back seat. I quickly scroll through his downloaded music and find out Kason is right. There's a ton of music on here that I already know. A Day To Remember, I Prevail, and Bad Omens roll out his top three artists. Bring Me The Horizon isn't far behind—though I'm chalking it up to his sharing the same last name with the lead singer rather than having actual taste.

But as I keep searching the list, I'm shocked to see some obscure bands it took me *years* to find, Nerv and AVOID being two of them.

"Shit," I whisper before holding the phone out for him. "You're telling me Holden Sykes, campus playboy, and literal golden retriever, is a closet emo?"

Noah snorts out a laugh. "*Holden* retriever."

"That's going a bit far with it," he says as he takes the phone from my hand while ignoring Noah's joke. Yet, from the flash in his eyes, I'm taking it as a yes.

Well, I'll be damned.

"At least you're not a closet Swiftie," Kason says, and I watch him visibly shudder.

His nose wrinkles up in disgust. "Unless it's a metal cover, I refuse to listen to her songs."

Once again, he's stolen the words right outta my mouth, which leaves me in nearly as much shock as his taste in music. Never in my lifetime would I have thought we would have that in common.

Truth be told, I never thought we'd have *anything* in common, yet here we are.

Add it to the growing list of things I'm learning about Holden Sykes.

God only knows how many hours we've been in the car now. It feels like close to an eternity, and after hitting multiple slowdowns through Atlanta and Tampa, I'm getting antsy for us to finally arrive at the condo.

We all are, if Noah's constant tapping on his leg or Holden's inability to pick a single song to listen to are any indications. The only person who seems relaxed is Kason—and that's because he's passed out yet again.

I swear, he could sleep through a fucking hurricane.

However, a buzz of excitement fills the car when we finally pass the sign welcoming us to St. Petersburg, Florida, giving all of us a burst of new life.

"I've never seen such a beautiful sight," Noah says as he stares out the window at the sign.

"You haven't seen the beach yet," I tell him, grinning.

"Hope it's worth it, 'cause that ride was brutal, and I never wanna do it again."

I glance at him, brows raised. "We get to do it all over again in ten days. Unless you forgot, we don't get to stay here forever."

He lets out a long, low groan. "Fuck, don't remind me."

"At least we'll all be tired," Kason pipes up, and I hadn't realized he was awake again.

"That's true." This comes from Holden. "The anticipation is always the worst part, so it always feels a million times longer."

Yet another thing we can agree on, as trivial as it might be. But I'm hoping it means spending these next ten days with him won't be nearly as painful as I initially thought they'd be.

At least, here's to hoping.

"So since we're almost here, what's the rooming situation gonna be like?" Noah asks, glancing between the three of us. "Because as much as I love you guys, I'm not looking to snuggle up with another guy the entire time we're here. Homo or no homo."

I roll my eyes before looking over at him. "There are enough beds for everyone. I get the master, but besides that, you fools can figure it out."

"I already got my roomie," Holden says, causing my attention to lift to the rearview mirror. His eyes are already staring through it, waiting to lock with mine, and he smirks before glancing over at Kason.

I'm not sure why I didn't expect this to be the case. Of course they'd probably want to stay in the same room if they're seeing each other—even with *taking things slow*. But it's yet another unexpected twist to this vacation, and it makes me sick to my stomach.

The last thing I wanna think about is these two fucking while I'm under the same roof.

"Well, then, I hope you're not a light sleeper," I say, trying to act unbothered by the two of them pairing off. "As you've witnessed, Kason snores like a freight train."

"That's a mild exaggeration," Kason says before shooting me a look over his shoulder.

"I can hear you through the wall back at the apartment," I say, my brow arching in challenge. "You really wanna argue with me on this?"

"Considering you're asleep when it happens, I have to take Phoenix's word on this one," Noah chimes in. "Besides, you were snoring like half an hour ago."

I smirk when Holden looks at me again. "Hope you brought earplugs."

"That's okay," Holden says, his eyes flaring with challenge. "I've got other ways of shutting him up."

Kason chokes on his own spit, forcing Holden to smack him on the back several times before laughing out a gruff *fucking God*.

"Might be a little too much information," Noah remarks with a half-hearted laugh.

"Just didn't want Nixy back there worrying about my well-being."

My teeth sink into the fleshy side of my cheek, once again finding myself irritated with Holden still being a step ahead of me in this fucked up little game we've created. But I've got ten whole days to cause as much mayhem and destruction as I can between them—all under the radar, of course.

After telling Kason I'd do my best to be supportive, the last thing I need is for him to find out about Operation Cock Block.

But it's also become painfully obvious that I can't do this alone, so if this scheme of mine is gonna work, I'll need a bit of help. And as I open my texts, I know just who to recruit.

Me: What's your ETA?

Theo: Less than thirty minutes. Why?

My eyes widen as I glance up at the GPS on the dash, noting we still have almost an hour left thanks to traffic.

Me: Holy shit. How fast were you driving?

Theo: It's all Wyatt. I swear, he thinks the speed limit is just a suggestion.

A grin tilts my lips up, and not just because I can hear Wyatt saying that exact thing in my head. Their early arrival will actually work out, should recruiting Theo go according to plan at least.

Me: You'll be there half an hour before us.

Theo: Is that a problem? We can pull off at a gas station and wait for you guys to catch up. Or we can swing by the store and get food and alcohol before you get there.

Me: No, it's fine. I'll text you the door code, and you guys can get settled in. Makes more sense for us to get the food and beer together anyway.

Theo: *thumbs up emoji*

I smile to myself as I type out my next text, feeling downright giddy about my plan seemingly falling into place. A tiny part of me feels a little bit guilty for it, but it's quickly overshadowed by annoyance when I glance up to find Holden staring at me in the rearview mirror.

Lifting my free hand, I flip him the bird...and then I hit send.

Me: Can you also do me a massive favor when you get there?

Theo: What's up?

The same giddy, stomach-fluttering feeling returns as I type out my request.

Me: When you claim your rooms, don't let anyone take the one on the third floor.

Theo: Sure. That your room? I thought you were taking the master?

Me: I am. It's Kason and Holden's.

The three little dots in the corner appear and disappear for a straight minute while Theo types and retypes his response about a hundred times until one finally comes through.

Theo: Why do I feel like you're scheming?

My lips quirk up in a grin.

Me: Don't worry about it. Just tell me you'll do it.

Theo: I can't do that until I know the plan.

Me: It's need to know.

Theo: I feel like all evil masterminds are supposed to share their plans with their sidekicks.

I roll my lips inward to keep myself from laughing.

Me: You're not a sidekick, you're an ally.

Theo: Like there's a difference?

Me: One has plausible deniability. Which you're definitely going to want.

Theo: Fair point. But I'm still not happy about it.

Me: Thank you. So do we have a deal or not?

Theo's response of another thumbs-up emoji sends a spike of serotonin coursing through my bloodstream I hadn't realized I needed. But it's enough to have me leaning back to enjoy the rest of the ride to the condo, knowing all hell will break loose once we arrive.

"Holy shit," Noah whispers as we pull up to the condo that's been in my family for as long as I can remember. "You really are fuckin' loaded."

"Parents," I correct again.

"Same shit, different pile."

I snort out a laugh and shake my head, though I can't help the pride surging through me as both he and Holden gape at the place we'll be staying for the next week and a half.

It's a three-story, single-family unit with six bedrooms in total, but the entire condo could easily sleep fifteen people; it's that large. First floor has all the living spaces, a bedroom, a bathroom, and some storage, and the second floor has three bedrooms and a couple of bathrooms to share between them. Finally, the top floor has a fifth bedroom, a laundry room, and a killer master suite complete with a massive balcony opening to the beach. The whole thing is raised on stilts, leaving space for a carport large enough to fit Theo's Bronco and Holden's Jeep more than comfortably. But my favorite thing about the condo has to be the in-ground infinity pool out back, and past it, a nearly panoramic view of the Gulf and St. Pete's Beach.

It truly is a paradise I've been lucky to have growing up.

The four of us pile out of the car, grabbing all our crap before heading into the condo, and Noah wastes no time exploring the entire thing the moment he walks in. He doesn't even stop to drop his bag, instead carrying it with him as he races though the house like a kid on Christmas morning.

Meanwhile, Kason, Holden, and I join the other four where they're lounging around in the living room that boasts a massive balcony with a stunning view of the gulf.

"Look who finally decided to show up," Luca calls from where he and Harrison are playing some card game I've never seen before.

"Wyatt was driving like he committed a crime," Theo reminds them before shooting an unamused look at our third baseman, who just grins sheepishly.

"You were just as ready to be out of the car as I was," he reminds Theo before shoving off the couch to head for the kitchen. "Besides, there's only so many times I can listen to the Top 40 before I start losing my mind."

"It's called Bluetooth," Kason says, dropping his bag to the floor near the kitchen island. "I'm assuming y'all already claimed rooms since you've been here a while?"

"Yeah, three of us grabbed all the bedrooms on the second floor," Theo mentions from the couch, eyes locked on his phone. "And I think Noah asked Luca to room with him, so they're in the one with the twins down here."

I smirk, realizing my devious little plan is working out perfectly, thanks to my teammate. Because if all the bedrooms on the first two floors are filled, and I get the master, that only leaves—

"Leaving only the room with the bunk beds upstairs," Kason says, brows furrowed. "Unless they got a bigger bed in there since we were down last summer?"

Bingo.

"Still the bunk beds," I confirm, trying not to sound too elated by finally getting one up on Holden. Of course, I can't help sneaking a glance at him, only to find him already watching me with an intensity that I feel down to my marrow.

"Damnit," Kason mutters before he looks at the other guys. "Would any of you mind switching?"

Luca and Harrison glance between themselves before both decline, and Wyatt and Theo quickly follow suit.

"Sorry, man," Theo says with a bout of indifference. "You snooze, you lose kinda thing."

"Because we're five now?" This comes from Holden, who shifts his attention from me to Theo.

Wyatt grins at him while filling a glass of water from the spout in the fridge. "Guess you should've driven faster."

"Hadn't realized getting down here was gonna be like racing in the Daytona 500," he says, though the forced smile on his face doesn't match the gritted tone his words take.

Kason blows out a breath. "It'll be fine. It's just to sleep, right?"

Holden nods in agreement, but from the way his eyes narrow on me after my gaze slides to him, he's seeing right through this wholly inconvenient turn of events. But I just smile at him before heading upstairs to the king-size bed that awaits me.

Good luck getting laid now, asshole.

THIRTEEN

Phoenix

My hopes for things to be smooth sailing after the drive down are quickly snuffed out once Kason and Holden found out they'd be—quite literally—bunking together. I swear, Holden is going out of his way in retaliation for it, and by day two of this messed-up vacation I've found myself on, my frustration is at an all-time high.

I don't even feel at home at my own vacation house, and it's got everything to do with all those damn football players currently taking over the condo.

Well, four of them are fine. It's mostly their quarterback I'm taking issue with.

I glance off the back balcony of my room—the master my parents usually take—and down at the idiots in the pool below.

Luca and Harrison are playing some weird version of chicken against

Kason and Wyatt while Noah and Theo act as referees. Meanwhile, Holden is perched on the giant flamingo float my little sister loves, drink in hand, without a care in the world.

Fuck, I can't stand him.

What's more, I can't stand the way my body wants him. *Craves* him after that stunt I pulled in his bedroom. The feeling's only gotten worse over the past few days, too. One, because I keep catching his gaze or find him watching me when I look his way. And two, because he's always half-naked, making it impossible to ignore him and all his sinful glory.

Like right now.

My eyes trace over his shirtless form sprawled over the inflatable. Even in a pair of fucking light pink trunks with bananas all over them—a level of ridiculous that should make him look idiotic, not sexier—he nearly reaches God-like perfection. Especially the way they hang low on his hips, drawing my eyes down the smooth, lean muscles of his abdomen to focus on a sinful V carved from stone.

And soon enough, my mind starts thinking about him. Recalling memories it has no right to. About *him* and how it felt to be inside him, his skin hot against mine as his ass clenches—

Shit.

The frustration I've already been feeling only grows into self-loathing when I glance down, noting the way my cock is straining against the zipper of my shorts. Of course, the asshole only amps up my irritation when he catches me staring down at the pool and raises a hand to his head, giving me a mock salute.

A growl rumbles from my chest as I storm back inside, letting the screen door slam closed behind me.

I'm so sick of him and his constant presence. Of the reminders of that night in May, which never ceases when he's around. Especially with his body on display.

It's infuriating. *He's* infuriating.

I need to release some of this tension coiled up inside me like a snake. If I don't, who knows what I'll be liable to do. Which is why I find myself stripping out of my board shorts and sprawling over the king-size bed before taking my aching cock in hand.

It's just a fantasy. No one has to know.

The mantra bounces around in my head as I do the very thing I've prevented since finding out Kason was interested in Holden. I open the box in my head where I've locked away those stolen moments with the campus playboy...and I let the memories of our night together in the Kappa Sig house take hold of me.

The heat of his breath against my skin as it skimmed over my pecs and down my stomach. The swirl of his tongue around my cock before he took me deep to the back of his throat. His soft groans and pants as I fucked him—hard and ruthlessly—like he was the only thing grounding me to Earth.

And God, the way his ass clamped around my length as he came, long and hard, with a moan that will remain ingrained in my brain for the rest of my life.

Every one of those moments is a mini highlight reel in my mind, and I mentally shuffle through each clip as my hand moves over my shaft. Reliving them one by one as I bring myself closer to release.

The pressure in my balls has built to a cataclysmic level, and if I don't come soon, spontaneous combustion might be my demise. My movements become quicker and more sporadic as I chase my climax toward the cliff. I'm almost there, ready to hurdle myself over the edge and—

"Well, if this isn't a sight."

My eyes fly open the second his voice registers, but not even hearing his voice could prepare me for Holden standing in the open doorway—half-naked and blond hair still dripping wet from the pool—while I've got my cock in my hand.

"What the hell are you doing?" I snap, pulling myself up into a sitting position against the headboard, and grab the sheet in a sorry attempt to hide the evidence of what I was doing. I don't know why I bother since he already got an eyeful. And God only knows how long he was standing in the doorway, watching me before he even spoke up.

His brow kicks up and he nods toward me. "I could ask you the same thing."

"I meant, what the hell are you doing in my room, uninvited."

"Oh," he says, stepping through the threshold and closing the door behind him. "I just wanted to see where you were off pouting."

"I'm not pouting."

"Clearly not," he says, nodding to where my aching cock is still pitching a tent below the sheets. "Need some help with that?"

My jaw ticks as my temper flares. "Are you being fucking serious right now?"

He shrugs and leans back against the closed door, but I don't miss the heat in his eyes as he stares at me. "Just making an offer."

"The fact that you even offered only serves to prove my point," I snap, grabbing a pillow to cover myself completely. "You're just looking to get laid. It doesn't matter with who."

"Hmm," he hums, arms crossed over his chest. "Too bad. Because if there's one good thing that comes outta being a man-whore, it's knowing how to give."

"Can you just get out of here?"

A wicked smile curves his mouth. "But where's the fun in that, Nix?"

"The fun is me having some peace and quiet away from you."

"You're the one who left the door unlocked," he says, and instead of moving to leave, he takes a step further into the room. "Maybe you were hoping for the guy you're thinking about to join you."

I'm fully aware he thinks I was just jerking it to Kason, but knowing it was him—*us*—only makes his statement all the more horrifying.

"Get out. I'm not asking this time."

"Or maybe you were hoping I'd return the favor from the night back in my room." The smile on his sinful lips turns into an ear-to-ear grin as he pulls the pillow out of my grip to reveal my erection still tenting the sheet.

I'm both slightly impressed at my cock still being harder than granite despite Holden's interruption and mortified about him being the reason it's like this in the first place. But if he wants to believe it's because of Kason, that's fine. It's better than him knowing the reality.

His eyes don't leave mine as he peels the sheet back, letting it pool at my knees, before taking a seat on the edge of the mattress. I can feel his body heat radiating against my bare skin, and the second his eyes finally drop down to where my cock salutes him, I might as well be doused in lighter fluid and set ablaze.

I'm consumed in white-hot desire.

My gaze lifts to his, watching his expression as he takes me in, and it's immediately apparent that he's as affected as I am. I just don't know if it's a good or bad thing.

Regardless, I'll chalk it up to him being sex-starved due to our little wager, and not because he actually wants—

Don't go there.

"What're you doing?" I whisper, and I hate how breathy and turned-on it sounds. But he's so close, mere inches away, and the scent of sunscreen and what must be his body wash wafts over me as the breeze blows through the open window.

Why does he have to smell as good as he looks? It should be a sin against humanity.

"You left me hard, naked, and handcuffed to my bed for my roommates to find," he murmurs. "I think it's about time we were even."

Panic sets in, not entirely sure what he's planning in retaliation here. But beneath the worry, I realize there is a fair amount of anticipation too, which only means I'm as fucked in the head as I am stupid.

"You brought the handcuffs, did you?"

A sharp gasp leaves my lips as he runs his thumb from the base of my shaft up to the head. My cock twitches as he rubs the sensitive underside just below the tip, and the pressure is just enough to have my balls drawing up, ready for release once again.

"Nah," he whispers. "I just want to fuck with your head as much as you've been fucking with mine lately."

My breath hitches as he continues massaging that singular spot, simultaneously building my pleasure and dragging it out of me in soft pants and moans.

It's the strangest juxtaposition I've ever felt.

And if this is what he can do with two fingers, I can only imagine what he can do with—

"Do you want to come?" he whispers, breaking through my thoughts.

I hadn't realized I'd closed my eyes, letting go and simply allowing myself to feel. But when my lids lift, and I catch Holden staring at me, I'm left breathless.

His eyes are locked on my face, watching and gauging my every reaction as he touches me. Two plush lips are slightly parted and glistening, like he's recently wet them, and the idiotic, self-destructive side of me wants nothing more than to lean in and take them as mine.

A part of me almost wins out until he speaks again.

"Are you going to answer me, Nix? Or are you content to just stare at my pretty face?"

"Repeat the question," I utter softly.

The corner of his mouth curls into the tiniest, yet sexiest, smirk I've seen yet. "I asked if you wanted to come."

God, yes.

I want it more than anything. I need this release more than I need food, water, oxygen. There's a possibility I might die without it—or worse, my dick could fall right off from the worst case of blue balls in history.

Yet I can't bring myself to answer him.

Giving into the lust, taking the pleasure he's so willingly giving…it's a slippery slope. One I doubt I'll find my way off of easily.

He must be witnessing the war waging inside my brain, because he cocks his head to the side while those whiskey-brown eyes turn into liquid gold.

"I'll let you come, Nix. But you have to ask me for it."

I let out a frustrated groan as his wicked ministrations continue, creating an urgency inside me I've never felt before. One hell-bent on release, no matter the cost.

Still, I know I can't give in, so I allow my eyes to sink closed again, if only to prevent the look on his face from making me cave. Yet as he keeps stroking and rolling his thumb in that one spot with expertise, I become desperate for more anyway.

More friction, more skin, just fucking more.

My hips finally join in of their own accord, thrusting up into his touch. Giving into the lust and desire coursing through my veins like a drug. But it's no use. I won't get what I want from him. Not unless I—

"Ask for it," he whispers again. I swear I can feel the heat of his breath coasting over my lips when he continues, "Ask, and it's yours."

My fists grip the sheets, and the second his tongue flicks out against my lips, I know I'm a goner. Lost to the abyss that is my lust and desire for the one man on this planet I know I shouldn't want.

"Hold, I—"

A rap on the door cuts the words off before they can form on my lips, and my eyes fly to the door. Another knock comes, and then I hear Kason's voice muffled through the door. "Hey, Phoe?"

My gaze flicks back to Holden, and I hold a finger up to my lips, signaling him to keep silent. To his credit, he manages to keep his mouth shut…while still teasing the tip of my cock with his thumb.

"Stop," I mouth, before trying to smack his hand away. There's no point in continuing, what with the moment of release I was desperate for having been doused by a bucket of ice water in the form of my best friend's voice.

There's another knock, and this time, the doorknob rattles like he's trying to get inside. "Phoe? You in there?"

My eyes widen as I look at Holden, and a devious little smirk sits on his lips when he sees the fear sure to be written all over my face.

"Don't worry," he whispers, giving my tip a gentle squeeze. "Unlike you, I locked it. Now, are you gonna answer him?"

My lips part slightly, and I swear, I'm halfway torn between kissing him for ensuring no one could walk in on this and tossing him into the pool from the goddamn balcony for putting me in this position to begin with.

"I, uh, yeah, Kase. Just kinda" —I suck in a breath as Holden rubs the sensitive spot below the head again— "occupied at the moment."

"Shit, sorry," he calls, undoubtedly a little embarrassed. Probably because he knows what I was up to. Just not *who* with. A fact made only more apparent when he asks, "I was just wondering if you've seen Holden. He said he was getting us drinks but hasn't come back yet."

Holden's eyes flare as he continues tormenting me with merely two fingers and his hypnotic stare. "I did say that, didn't I? Guess I got distracted."

Oh, for the love of fucking God.

"Answer him," Holden commands, this time squeezing the tip to nearly the point of pain.

"I…haven't," I say loud enough for Kason to hear, still keeping my gaze locked with Holden's. "He's probably in the bathroom. Fixing his hair or something."

There's an awkward laugh on the other side of the door. "Okay. I'll leave you to, uh…whatever you're doing and try to find him."

Holden and I both remain silent, waiting for the telltale sound of Kason's footfalls retreating down the stairs.

"You're unbelievable," I mutter, my fingers digging into his forearm.

"Not the first time I've heard that," he whispers back.

"It wasn't a compliment."

"Well, it should be."

On the last word, he presses and rolls that nerve one final time, and my release slams into me like a Mack truck without warning. Cum spurts free from my cock, the warm liquid spilling onto my chest and over Holden's fingers.

"Oh, shit," I curse, my teeth sinking into my bottom lip to prevent myself from making more noise than I already am.

Holden works me through my climax, eyes never leaving me the entire time. He makes no sign of stopping his wicked ministrations either, milking every last drop of pleasure he can from me until I force him to by wrapping my hand around his wrist.

My chest heaves as I come down from the high of my orgasm, and as soon as I do, the shame for what just happened hits. Hard enough, I close my eyes and hope that maybe Holden will be gone by the time my heart rate slows.

But luck has never been on my side when it comes to this guy, so why would that change now?

"I'll be damned," he whispers, his hand slipping from my grip. "Never would've taken you for an exhibitionist."

My eyes open at the sound of his voice to find a mixture of amusement and lust in his gaze. Irritation settles in at the former, but I'm not quite sure how to feel about the latter.

"I'm not."

He shrugs before rising from the bed. "With the way you just came? I'd beg to differ."

I go to rebut, but I'm left silently gaping when his attention shifts to the hand he used to get me off. Two fingers are still coated in my release, evidence of my wrongdoings there for us both to see. Only rather than heading into the bathroom only ten feet away to wash it away, the fucker pops each of them in his mouth and sucks them clean.

And despite having just been wrung dry not two minutes ago, my cock throbs with an aching want at the sight.

What is wrong with me?

"You can come out and join us, you know," he says nonchalantly, as if he didn't just sample my cum like finger food.

I continue to gape at him, a mixture of irritation and disbelief taking over, rendering me incapable of responding.

He must take my silence as a rejection, though, because he shrugs and takes a step toward the door. "Or not."

I watch as he crosses the room, and only when his hand is on the knob do words come barreling from my mouth without permission.

"I never asked for it."

My words give him pause, and I don't need to see his face to know he's smiling. It's clear as day in his voice when he responds.

"Your eyes did the talking your mouth wouldn't." He glances over his shoulder with a wink. "And don't worry, Nixy. The first one's always free."

FOURTEEN

Holden

One of the things I've always struggled with is impulse control, and what happened yesterday afternoon in Phoenix's bedroom is the perfect example.

Theo's insight on the way down to Florida has severely messed with my head; uncontrollably and without end. The newfound knowledge and unanswered questions have festered, creating intrusive thoughts that keep ramming against the front of my skull like an enraged bull until they've become something I just *have* to act on, consequences be damned.

But lemme just say, the consequences of this? Well, no doubt they'll be fucking huge. I'm just not sure *how* huge yet.

"Ready to get going?"

The question breaks through my silent musings, and I glance up from where I'm laying across one of the pool loungers to find Kason looking down at me, shirtless and in board shorts sitting low on his hips.

It's a sight that should make me all kinds of hot and bothered, and yet…nothing.

"I've been ready for an hour," I tell him as I rise from the lounger. "What's taking you guys so long?"

"Theo was arguing on the phone with his mom, and Luca was video chatting with his girlfriend to show her the house and the view of the gulf. Noah got annoyed with them taking so long, so he went to take a nap until we were ready to go," he says, naming off a few of the guys. "I think Phoenix was packing the cooler for the beach. Not sure about the others."

"Better late than never, I guess," I mutter as we head over to the carport, where Phoenix is adding ice to the cooler and avoiding looking at me.

Fantastic.

It takes another ten minutes for the eight of us to gather our shit together—towels, chairs, cooler, the works—and as I stare at the pile we're supposed to take down to the beach, I realize we might be worse than a group of girls packing for a weekend trip. Especially when we're only going a few hundred yards from the house and could easily come back up for anything we need.

Luca and Harrison grab the cooler and head for the beach, leaving the smaller stuff for the other six of us to split. However, it's only when I notice the boogie board tucked under Noah's arm that I realize what I'm missing.

"I'll meet you guys down there. Just gotta grab something." I tell them before circling back to the pool to fish Francesco the Flamingo Floatie out of the water.

I grab the giant inflatable and haul it over my head before starting toward the beach again when I hear a voice call out from behind me.

"You're actually bringing that thing with you?"

I glance over my shoulder to find Phoenix staring at me like I've lost my goddamn mind. Then again, I am holding a giant inflatable flamingo over my head—the float acting like a kite or an umbrella in the gulf breeze.

"Why wouldn't I?" I ask slowly. "The entire point of a floatie is to use it to float."

He opens his mouth to respond, but then closes it and shakes his head instead. But there's no way in hell I'm letting him off the hook. If he wants to pass judgment or be a dick, he can say it to my face.

Lord knows he's already keeping enough secrets.

"Don't even think about just walking away. Not without saying what you gotta say."

"You're just such a…man-child." His teeth are bared as something between a grimace and a sneer lift his lips. "I can't fucking stand you."

A deadly smirk curls the corners of my mouth. "Believe me, Nixy, you've made sure the feeling's mutual."

"Then why come?" He takes a step closer to me, gaze lit on fire with fury. "Why spend ten whole days down here, all the while knowing you'd be under the same roof as me?"

"Because I knew it'd piss you off," I say with a shrug.

A huff leaves his lips as he shakes his head. "Fucking unbelievable."

I can't help the smile curling my lips. "You already know just how unbelievable I am, don't you, Nixy?"

Hatred flares in his eyes, although I don't miss the hint of lust in them too. "It was a mistake."

Do you say the same thing about our night together as well? Or do you not remember, just like me?

The questions are on the tip of my tongue, but I can't bring myself to ask them. Because if there's a chance he doesn't remember it either…

well, shit. That knowledge might only add fuel to the fire between us, and I already don't know how much more I can take.

"Just how many mistakes are we gonna make together?" I take another step toward him. Close enough for my chest to brush his if we inhale at the same time. "I can squeeze you in between rounds with Kason. All you have to do is ask. Or maybe you'd be interested in joining us. The Eiffel Tower happens to be one of my *favorite* positions."

"You're disgusting."

"And you're into it," I counter with a cant of my head.

"Hardly."

I lick my lips—not missing the way his eyes track the movement—before leaning forward to whisper in his ear. "Then why haven't you pushed me away yet?"

As if suddenly realizing just how close we are, Phoenix clears his throat and takes a step away from me. Probably a good thing, because the electricity flickering between us when we're that close…it's too much. Too powerful.

He must be reading my mind, as he puts more and more distance between us, now heading down to where the rest of the guys are setting up near the water's edge. But he does stop and stare back at me to give some parting words.

"If you lose that flamingo and my sister finds out, I won't stop her from killing you."

Turns out, I don't need Francesco after all.

The moment we make it down to the beach, we spot a sand volleyball net set up a little ways down from the condo. It takes some convincing on

Luca and Kason's part, but eventually, everyone agrees to a nice, *friendly* game.

Or, at least, I hope it's friendly.

We break off into two teams on either side of the net; Luca, Noah, Wyatt, and Harrison on one side. Meanwhile, Theo, Kason, and Phoenix are on my side. It's a pretty even match-up regarding height—the only one with a true advantage being Luca since he's nearly six-foot-five—but I have no idea what everyone's skill level is.

The only one I know that has any experience is Theo, seeing as he plays in a league during the summer back home in Missouri, which is exactly why I picked him for my team. Even if it is just a lighthearted game between friends, we're all still athletes. And athletes like to *win*.

My thinking is on point, too, since as soon as the eight of us start getting into the game, it's quickly becoming apparent that we're all in it to win.

It's also becoming quite obvious that sand volleyball is *not* my sport. Though I think the reason is wholly because I can't seem to focus on the ball; I'm far too busy looking at Phoenix.

Hard not to when I've become *painfully* aware of the sex appeal he holds.

I'm not blind or stupid; of course, I've noticed Phoenix is attractive. I thought as much the second he walked up to Kason and me at the Kappa Sig house the first—*second*—time we met.

But fuck, I can't stop myself from noticing now. Can't keep my eyes from snagging on his obliques and abs, or the way they draw down into a sinful V rivaling my own. Entirely helpless to stop watching the sweat droplets as they slowly drip down the path those muscles create before disappearing into the waistband of his trunks.

Lust swirls in my gut as my eyes continue to map over his body greedily, and it's then I realize the only thing keeping me from mauling him right here in public is the tiny threads holding my self-control together.

The same ones that fray a little more with every second I spend staring at him, right until he turns and catches me red-handed.

He walks over to me, ball in hand, before shoving it straight into my chest.

"Stop it," he hisses, and I can feel the heat of his stare behind his sunglasses.

"Stop what?"

His words come out through clenched teeth. "Looking at me like you're thinking about what happened yesterday."

Fuck.

I quickly avert my gaze and give my best attempt at serving, surprising myself when the ball not only makes it over the net, but in bounds. Though I can't say my luck lasts much longer after that, since standing back here gives me a perfect view of Phoenix's back muscles, which are unfairly toned and perfectly chiseled like some sorta Greek god.

"How can you be *this* bad at a sport?" Theo asks after I miss my serve, the ball veering off wide to the right.

"Throwing balls and hitting them are two very different things," I say before taking my place by the net.

If it wasn't for Theo—who is truly in beast mode—and Phoenix, we'd be losing by a landslide. Thanks in no part to me; I'm ashamed to even call myself an athlete at this rate.

But as the game starts closing in on game point, both sides begin upping the ante; diving for loose balls, spiking harder, doing sneaky little dumps on the other side of the net. It's an all-out battle—a war of who wants it more—by the time it's my turn to serve again.

And it's also game point, with our team in the lead.

"Try not to fuck this one up, Sykes!" Noah calls from the other side of the net as he bounces between his feet.

"Shit talk your own teammates," Theo says before looking back at me. "But seriously, Hold. Don't screw the pooch."

"Be nice," Kason chides, kicking sand toward Theo. "We all have weaknesses. Volleyball just happens to be Holden's."

My eyes lock with Phoenix, waiting for him to make some snarky, smart-ass comment next. Except, rather than joining in with Kason and Theo, all he does is give me the hint of a smile and a tiny nod of... encouragement.

Which, at this point, is as welcome as it is unexpected.

Letting out a deep breath, I toss the ball in the air and pray like hell for solid contact. By the grace of God, I get it, but as the ball sails toward the net, I realize it looks a little low. A little *too* low.

Shit.

Defeat takes over my body as the ball smacks against the tape that runs along the top of the net, waiting for it to drop to the ground on our side of the net. Yet, to my surprise, the net bends with the movement of the ball before it flips over to their side and falls to the ground.

"We win? We win!" Theo says, jumping up and down as he flips Noah the bird. "That's for talking shit."

Kason is just as excited, plowing through the sand until he picks me up like we just won the National Championship.

"Fuck yes, Hold!" he shouts, swinging me around like I'm light as a feather...and he plants his lips directly on mine.

Surprise and panic blend together at the sudden affection before instinct takes over, and I kiss him back. But everything about it feels wrong. The taste of his lips, the sweep of his tongue. None of it feels *right* because he's not the person I want to be kissing.

Because he's not his best friend.

I break away, putting some space between us and rub the back of my neck self-consciously. "It was just a stupid game, Kase," I tell him before chuckling awkwardly.

A laugh leaves him. "Sorry, got a little excited."

"Well, you gonna kiss me now?" Theo asks, tossing his arms out to the side. "I was part of the team too."

"Yeah," Kason says slowly. "Not happening."

Kason and Theo start tossing jabs, which leads to Theo tackling Kason to the ground—a feat in itself—all the while making loud, obnoxious kissing noises at him. It's truly a ridiculous sight to behold, which is why I keep my eyes firmly focused on them.

I don't have it in me to meet Phoenix's stare as it burns into me hotter than a thousand suns.

I already know I won't like what I see written on his face if I do.

FIFTEEN

Holden

uilt has been eating at me since the volleyball game a few days ago, and it's making no sign of dissipating, either. It's not an emotion I often feel as it is, seeing as guilt is so often paired with regret—and that is something I've rarely experienced.

But fuck if I don't regret letting Kason kiss me in front of Phoenix.

Which is precisely why I've been sleeping on the couch in the living room ever since, only to sneak as quietly as possible into the bedroom we've been sharing in the early hours of the morning. Reason being, I don't want it to happen again.

It sounds stupid, and I'm not even saying it out loud. Because I'm here with *Kason. He's* the one I'm supposed to be unable to keep my eyes off. The one I should be lusting for and excited to kiss, rather than regretting it or trying to prevent it from happening again.

I do like the guy, don't get me wrong. I'm just finding out I don't like him in *that* way. If I'm being honest, at some point, my interest in Kason became less about him in general and more about riling Phoenix up. Getting Phoenix to pay attention to me. Messing with him and crawling under his skin, just like he digs under mine, now more than ever.

It just became about Phoenix.

It became about him well before I ever found out about our elusive one-night-stand back in May.

So while it might not make any sense, the guilt and regret are there nevertheless.

And what might be even more confusing is now…I actually care about him. About hurting his feelings. About what he's thinking. About where he is right now, because he sure isn't present. He's here physically, sitting across the table from me while we're out at dinner. Mentally, though? He might as well be eating his crab legs on Mars.

Theo must've also noticed, because after we pay our bill and head to the cars, he grabs Phoenix by the shoulder and steers him away from the group.

My nosiness and newfound caring create a desire to follow them, to get some answers even. Yet a part of me knows I'd only make it worse, so instead, I keep my feet firmly planted and lean against the Jeep to watch them from a distance.

"Any idea what's going on over there?" Luca asks from where he's sitting on the hood of my Jeep.

"Ten bucks says Theo is telling him to get his head outta his ass and start having fun," Noah says absently while he texts away on his phone.

Kason's eyes flick to Noah. "You'll have to give him a break. This wasn't exactly the trip he thought we were gonna have."

"So he's gonna sulk about it the whole time?"

"Just leave it alone," I find myself snapping at Noah, who looks to me with surprise. They all do, in fact, and I don't blame them, seeing as I've made it my life's mission since this trip started to be a thorn in Phoenix's side. So I can see why they'd wonder what made me suddenly change my tune.

Shit.

Clearing my throat, I reroute as best I can. "If he's gonna be pissy, let him. We shouldn't let it ruin the time we have left here for the rest of us."

There's a murmuring between the guys before they come to the conclusion that I'm right, though from the look on Kason's face, he's torn and worrying about Phoenix still. A boat I also find myself in, as much as I wish differently.

I'm just grateful Theo is the one over with Phoenix, considering he'd be the asshole to see through my shit…and potentially call me out on it too.

The two of them head back toward us after a few minutes, and if possible, Phoenix looks more irritated than he did before. But he does make eye contact with me as they approach, so I guess that's a plus.

Theo, on the other hand, has a bright smile on his face when he reaches the rest of us at the cars.

"We're going out tonight," Theo says, clapping his hands together. "There's a club called The Wharf down just a little ways. I'm happy to drive so we don't have to Uber, as long as someone else will man the Jeep."

Theo's eyes land right on me, and I return his insinuation with an arched brow and a snicker. "Me? Seriously? You want *me* to DD?"

"It's your car."

"Yeah," Luca says slowly. "But if we ask Holden to DD, we'll be stranded 'til morning."

I give Luca a winning smile and toss the keys in his direction, which he catches on instinct alone.

"What—"

"Thanks for volunteering."

With a roll of his eyes, Luca yanks open the driver's side door as the rest of us pile into the vehicles to head off toward The Wharf.

But a sinking feeling lingers in my gut as we drive the streets of St. Pete's, and the reason is entirely because, when I glance over my shoulder from the shotgun seat, I realize Phoenix got in the other car.

Guess he's back to avoiding me.

A hand anchor's itself on my waist a few hours—and drinks—later, and I glance over my shoulder to see Kason holding another shot for me. I don't even have to ask if it's tequila; it's the same thing he's been feeding me all night. If I didn't know any better, I'd think he was trying to get me drunk to take advantage of me.

A thought that's hilarious, considering it holds absolutely no appeal to me anymore.

I pass the empty glass back and suck on the lime, not missing the way his eyes watch my mouth as I do. He's been going shot for shot with me since we got here, so the alcohol swimming in his veins is loosening him up a lot more than usual. I know he can hold his liquor, just not nearly as well as I can, making me place him firmly in the drunk category. Or at least well, *well* past tipsy.

Still, it's enough for him to reel me toward the group of grinding bodies when the Bring Me the Horizon remix of "Bad Habits" comes blasting through the club's speakers.

Meanwhile, I'm out here with only a slight buzz and wishing my attention would stop sneaking back over to Phoenix.

He's leaning against the bar, still nursing his second beer, and chatting away with Theo. Has been all night without so much as casting me a glance, and it's driving me crazy.

Then again, the little self-destructive part of me thinks maybe it's because I haven't given him anything to look at.

Kason circles around behind me and grabs my hips, pulling me so my back is flush with his front. I take the opportunity to unbutton the red floral print shirt I'm wearing, letting it hang open down the center instead. God knows it's already hot enough in here to merit taking it off altogether.

The alcohol has loosened my inhibitions some, and I throw my arms over our heads, lacing them behind his neck. It was an instinct more than anything, except the move has Kason gripping my hips even harder. Vice-like, even, and there's a good chance I might have bruises there tomorrow.

He keeps our bodies pressed so close together, a piece of paper wouldn't fit between us while we move in time with the music, and it doesn't take long for it to turn him on. The ridge of his erection glides against my ass with every grind and press of my hips; the feel would normally cause my own cock to take notice. Perk up, ready to get in on some action.

It's all heat and sweat and grinding and tension, and I should be into it.

Only, my eyes are locked on Phoenix. Waiting for him to notice the filthy way his best friend and I are dancing together—though I'm not even sure it can be called that.

Yet he's still too occupied with Theo on the other side of the room.

"You're so fucking hot," Kason shouts in my ear over the blasting bass, and I can hear the slur in his voice.

I know I look good tonight. And truthfully, Kason looks hotter than sin himself in shorts that show off his sculpted ass with a short sleeve button-down I'd usually want to rip open with my bare teeth. Those dark auburn locks are styled with perfection and his sinfully green eyes—the color I'm a sucker for—are two shiny emeralds when the light hits them.

He's any gay man's wet dream.

So why does my attention keep getting snagged by Phoenix across the bar?

Ignore him, the little voice in my head chimes in, and I do my best to listen.

But just when I go to reinforce my resolve, Phoenix's eyes slide over to me, and I swear I can feel the heat and fire in them from all the way over here. Maybe even see the tick in his jaw before he glances away and responds to whatever Theo just said.

Doesn't matter though, especially since it's exactly the reaction I was looking for.

The music shifts into some pop/EDM remix, but Kason makes no signs of wanting to stop. In fact, one of his hands leaves my hips, slipping up to where my shirt hangs open down the center. His calloused palm scrapes over my abs before trailing down to the edge of my waistband. A stray finger dips below it, teasing ever closer to my dick, and still, nothing.

Something's fucking wrong with me.

I look up again and am greeted with the sight of one devastatingly infuriated Phoenix, who's positively fuming from where he's leaning against the bar. The heat of his stare is palpable, burning into my skin like a white-hot brand. Painfully searing but still somehow addicting.

He's clearly pissed with the scene before him, and he might just burst into flames right here until he's nothing more than a pile of ash where he once stood; a true embodiment of his namesake.

Bingo.

I shoot him a grin while grinding my hips back into Kason, and it only makes the fury in his eyes more intense. And it's the hatred, paired with the way his heated gaze drifts down my torso where Kason's hands are exploring, that stirs my cock to life.

Apparently, I'm more turned-on by Phoenix's glare from across the bar than I am by Kason's touch. If that isn't messed up, I don't know what is.

The weirdest part about this whole thing with Phoenix is I *always* separate myself from my attraction. I never let it cloud my judgment or make me do stupid shit. Or at least, stupid shit I actually *regret*. Yet something about him isn't letting my old ways stick.

He's crawled under my skin, burrowed beneath the surface and made a home there. And while it was irritating at first, it's gotten to the point where…I like him there. *Want* him there.

My eyes sink closed, finally allowing myself to admit what I've known for a while now.

I want him.

This stick-up-his-ass, frustrating-as-hell guy who, quite frankly, wants nothing to do with me.

And I don't know how to navigate it. Nor do I know how to navigate the pure, jealous rage that slams into me when my lids lift to find some random dude chatting it up with him.

Motherfucker. Where the fuck is Theo?

Fury ignites my own blood as I watch the two of them. The curly-haired surfer jackass is noticeably more into the conversation than Phoenix is. Then again, how can he possibly be interested in the guy when his eyes keep darting back to me every three seconds?

But then the fuck-face puts his hand on Phoenix's arm, and Phoenix *smiles*.

Not at the douchenozzle.

At *me*.

Oh, hell no.

"Gonna get a drink," I tell Kason, freeing myself from his grasp. Not waiting for a response, I storm to where Phoenix is still chatting it up with this dickweed, his eyes locked on me the whole way over.

Once I reach the bar, I slide into the space behind Phoenix and slip my arm around his waist.

"Hey, baby," I say loud enough for numb-nuts to hear me. "You want another drink?"

Cum dumpster's eyes lift to meet mine, the blue orbs widening when he realizes what I just said. It has the desired effect too, because he quickly removes his hand from Phoenix's arm.

"Shit. Sorry, man. I didn't realize."

He doesn't wait for a response, just grabs his beer and walks off toward the other end of the bar.

Gold star for the asswipe.

"What the fuck are you doing?" Phoenix seethes. He turns in my arm before attempting to worm his way from my grip. But even when I'm drinking, there's not a chance in hell of that happening unless I want it to.

"Me? What're *you* doing?"

His nostrils flare as he aims his infamous death glare at me. "I'm letting loose. Having fun. Isn't that what we're supposed to be doing?"

It is, but goddamnit. Not like that. Not when—

"You don't even know that guy."

The words come flying out of my mouth before I can stop them, and I really should stop them. What Phoenix does and who he does it with should be of little to no consequence to me. Yet here I am, all ragey and pissed off when another man was just *talking* with him.

Granted, his hands were on Phoenix, but still.

Something between a smirk and a snarl curls his lip up. "Careful,

Holden. That sounds an awful lot like jealousy."

I'm floored to realize…yeah, I'm jealous. Of some twat-waffle who has nothing to offer Phoenix that I can't give him myself. The epiphany smacks me clear in the face, and it's enough to have me releasing him.

He must see it in my eyes as he nods and steps away from me.

"Thought so," he mutters. "Now, why don't you go back to Kason and dry hump some more on the dance floor?"

I'm still reeling as I watch him cross the space toward the back hallway.

Something snaps me out of it, though, because I'm quick to follow as he disappears around the corner, heading toward the bathroom. Either he's genuinely oblivious to me being behind him or doesn't care, but regardless, he doesn't see it coming when I grab his arm and drag him toward me.

His chest collides with mine, momentarily stunning him as I back his body against the drywall.

"Get off me, Holden," he snaps, his dark eyes appearing pitch-fucking-black in this lighting.

I shake my head, alcohol and confusion swirling together as I stare at his pink lips and dark lashes, truly hating myself for noticing just how… beautiful he is.

My words come out in a harsh whisper; an angry, desperate plea for reprieve.

"What are you doing to me, Nix?"

"You're the one pinning me up against the wall of a club," he growls. "So I'm not the one doing a damn thing."

"Not what I meant," I bite out, inching in closer. "What are you doing to my head?"

"Someone finally getting sick of the mind games?"

"Yeah, I am." My attention shifts, dancing between his eyes and mouth. "And I'm sick of knowing how sweet you taste, when in reality, you're not sweet at all."

He scoffs, and it's filled to the brim with all the hatred and contempt he's been trying to keep under wraps since we made it down here. But it's all there now, pouring over the surface.

"Because people always want to be equated to a Sour Patch Kid, right?"

I can't help but laugh, shaking my head. "See what I mean?" I implore, my hands fisting against the wall. "So. Fucking. Abrasive. It's driving me insane."

"You don't think you're making me feel just as crazy?" He shakes his head, equal parts disdain and desire laced in his tone. "I wish I'd never met you."

His words instantly sober me, a slow smile creeping over my lips.

"You remember that thing I said about your eyes and your mouth not matching?" His Adam's apple bobs as he swallows before he gives me a slow nod in response, and I can't help the smile that curves my lips. "Well, you're doing it again."

Phoenix's eyes flare with resentment. "You're full of shit."

"I'm full of a lot of things. Hormones, lust, alcohol. But I know a lie when I see it, Nix."

He scoffs, but there's not the usual snark to it. And the same goes with his words when he says, "You're sex-starved, drunk, and delusional."

"I've already admitted to the first two, but the only one acting delusional here is you."

I crowd in closer to him, my body nearly enveloping his against the cool drywall. We're chest to chest, every inch of our bodies plastered together, and I know he has to feel my cock pressed into his hip.

I sure as hell can feel his.

"You want me, you're just too loyal and proud to admit that not having me is killing you."

"Like I said. Delusional."

Avoidance has been his forte far longer than should be allowed, and I'm done letting him off that easily. It's why I catch his jaw between two fingers and turn his head to face me again.

"You sure about that?"

He smacks my hand away, irritation once again bubbling to the surface as his demand comes out in a growl. "Touch me again, Holden. I fucking dare you."

"Oh, you've got teeth," I murmur, not at all affected by his venom. "Feel free to use them on me later."

"Never again."

He realizes his mistake the moment after I do, because his eyes flash up to mine. Worry and regret swim at the surface of their dark depths as he stares at me.

"Oh, so we're finally gonna talk about this, huh, Nix?" I snap, pressing in even closer. Close enough for me to feel his breath and taste the hint of beer on his lips.

"Talk about what?"

"Us sleeping together," I say plainly, not bothering to mince words. We're long past the time for that. "Or were you gonna try keeping me in the dark about our little hook-up forever? Or better yet, maybe you were hoping Theo might let it slip so you'd never have to tell me?"

Phoenix's lips part slightly as a look of astonishment takes over his features. His eyes dart back and forth between mine until something inside him just snaps.

"What do you mean by *keeping you in the dark?*" he snarls, teeth bared. "You're the one who has been acting like you have no clue who I am or what happened at the Kappa house back in May."

"Because I *didn't.*" My eyes dart back and forth between his, feeling the anger diffuse. "I didn't know. I thought the first time we met was in November. You know, the night you decided to turn into the world's biggest cock-block? It wasn't until Theo mentioned something on the way down here that I found out it wasn't."

Something on my face must finally convince him—make him understand that this entire conversation is as foreign to me as the idea that he and I have slept together—and he blinks as if he's seeing me for the first time.

"I...I don't understand—"

"Hey, there you are," Kason says, appearing out of nowhere from around the corner. I can tell he's drunk before he even approaches, only to be confirmed when I turn to him to find a massive, drunken grin on his face. "I've been looking everywhere for you."

"Bathroom," I tell him as I step away from Phoenix. "Ran into Phoenix on the way out."

I feel Phoenix's gaze on me as I take another step back, only for it to get worse when Kason wraps his arm around my waist.

"You owe me a dance."

Then he links his fingers with mine and drags me back to the dance floor. And just like the kiss after the volleyball game, I feel Phoenix's eyes on me the entire time.

SIXTEEN

Phoenix

The party rages long after we all return to the condo, and for once, I let loose a little more than normal. I'd like to say it's due to the break we're on and that it's my last chance to let off some steam before baseball season begins. But honestly, I just need the distraction from Holden and the entire conversation from our run-in by the bar bathroom.

It doesn't veer far from my mind, only worsening with Kason being all over him ever since.

And like the trainwreck I am, I can't seem to look away.

Holden was right about one thing when he cornered me: I do want him. Even when I know I shouldn't. It's why I've been watching him the whole time, the same way I've caught him watching me.

It's something that can't be helped. Those seductive whiskey eyes ensnare me, dragging me under wave after lustful wave every time they lock with mine.

Just like right now, as I catch him staring at me from where he's lounged on that fucking flamingo floatie again. Our only saving grace is everyone else has long gone to bed, leaving no one around to—

"You're doing it again," Holden murmurs, barely loud enough for me to hear over the crashing waves against the shore in the distance.

"Doing *what* exactly?"

"Don't play coy with me, Nix," he chides, a slight bite to his tone. "No one's here. You can cut the shit." His head drops back against the neck of the flamingo. "And I'm talking about how you're straight-up fucking me with your eyes right now."

Irritation flares within me as I swish my legs in the pool water, my fingers gripping the edge a little tighter. "I'm not fucking you with my eyes or anything else, for that matter."

"But you have."

My blood runs ice cold, and more than anything, I wish I'd gone upstairs with the rest of the guys—anything to avoid having this conversation with him. But luck never seems to be on my side when it comes to Holden Sykes, which means he can't just drop it.

With no one else around, nothing is going to stop him from digging until he gets all the answers he wants.

"I'm not talking about this with you." It feels like that's all I ever say to this guy. But avoidance is the only weapon I have in my arsenal anymore. The only thing keeping me from fucking things up and giving into whatever is happening between us.

"Like hell, you're not." He sits up in his float, causing ripples in the water to splash against my shins like a mini tsunami. Fitting, since it feels like I'm being drowned by one made of emotions right now.

"Hold—"

"No," he says, cutting me off. "You might hate me, and that's fine. I've never been the kind of person who needs to be liked by everyone. But if Theo wasn't just screwing with me, and we really do have history, then I should damn well know what it is."

Nausea hits me as I war internally, knowing that telling him is the only option. No matter how much I don't want to.

"Theo wasn't lying," I utter.

"Then tell me everything."

"I don't know what you know, all right?"

"Nothing!" he shouts, the water beneath him rippling some more. "I don't know anything except something happened between us that night, only for me to wake up alone. And I've been going crazy since Theo said something, trying to find the missing pieces. But I can't. So, please, I'm fucking begging you to just put me out of my misery and tell me."

Swallowing, I shake my head. "The details aren't important anymore. The fact that it happened at all is bad enough—replaying it now isn't going to change anything."

His eyes darken as he leans back against the flamingo's neck, seemingly dropping the subject per my request. But from the frown etched at the corners of his lips and the way his eyes gaze up at the stars above, he seems lost in thought. Once again, attempting to pull the pieces together without my help.

Silence falls between us, the only sound coming from the crashing waves and the wind rustling the palm trees. It's peaceful enough to lull me to sleep, if I wasn't so attuned to Holden's dissatisfaction with my answer.

Which he makes apparent when he just won't let it go.

"You're not the only one holding onto secrets, you know," he says, his raspy voice slicing through the quiet.

A quick glance at him reveals he's still staring up at the stars, his hand swishing back and forth in the water absently.

"Is that supposed to hold some kind of allure?"

"Maybe. Or you can think of it as an offer." Dark eyes shift to me, and I sense unease in them for what might be the first time ever. "Tit-for-tat. My secret for yours. I'll even go first."

I mull it over for a second, knowing even if I don't agree, there's a huge possibility he'll only keep pressing. Stubborn and tenacious as he is.

Though, sharing secrets—alone and in the darkness—feels awfully... intimate. More so than anything else that has happened between us.

I grab the bottle of tequila I've been nursing since we got back and take a long swig, needing all the liquid courage I can get before I nod in agreement.

Holden's gaze burns the side of my face as he watches me intently, setting me even more on edge. But it's his words that might as well have shoved me off a cliff.

"I knew it was you."

I lick my lips—drowning in tequila and his gaze—before asking, "Knew it was me?"

"The night you left me chained to my bed."

Just the mention of that moment sends a bolt of lust rushing straight to my cock, and the way his voice drips with sex and sin as he slides off the float to swim closer has the appendage pitching a tent behind my trunks altogether.

"Of course you did," I say with a scoff. "I flipped the lights on afterward. We had an entire conversation. Or did I traumatize you into blacking out again?"

A sardonic smirk lifts his lips as he shakes his head. "I meant while it was happening."

Despite the warmth of the breeze and the water, my blood freezes the instant his words register. Because once again, Holden has a way of throwing me for a loop with a single sentence—flipping my world on its axis in the process.

"Bullshit," I whisper through the knot in my throat.

"The only one full of bullshit here is you," he murmurs as he continues closing the distance between us. And he does, not stopping until he's standing directly between my legs. "Because the second your lips landed on mine, I knew damn well it wasn't Kason in my room. Wasn't him kissing me, touching me…" He trails off, his palms land on the edge of the pool on the outside of my thighs—the heat of them scorching me more than the Gulf Coast sun ever could. It's searing, his proximity when he's close enough to touch, yet contact isn't made.

It's driving me mad, but not in anger.

In *want*.

His teeth roll over his bottom lip before he murmurs, "But there's one thing I couldn't figure out."

"What?" I find myself whispering, still held captive by his gaze.

"How I knew." His eyes search my face, taking in every line and curve of my features before adding. "But it all makes sense now. The familiarity was because I'd already tasted you before."

Pure, carnal desire roars through me at his words, ripping and clawing at the mask I'm desperate to hold in place. But the only problem is— thanks to his nearness and the alcohol—it's slowly slipping out of place.

"So you…"

"Blacked out," he finishes, nodding slowly. "I'm not proud of it, but yeah. I was gone."

I clear my throat and mutter, "Clearly, you have zero self-control."

"Oh, believe me, Nix," he whispers, attention now fixed on my mouth. "If that were true, you'd be on your back beneath me right now."

Shit.

The ache inside me intensifies to a level almost impossible to ignore, and it's at this moment I realize something I should've known all along.

This is all a game to him. A dangerous one.

One I certainly know better than to play.

It's why I should push him away—shove him back into the pool, get up, and go to bed. Or better yet, hold his head underwater and drown him the way I've been itching to since we arrived. Anything would be better than going along with this, falling further into the trap that's been set for me.

Even knowing this isn't enough to snap me out of the seductive trance he's pulled me into, though.

If anything, he's dragging me further and further under. Drowning me in want, lust, desire…until all I can do is succumb.

"Why are you doing this?" I whisper.

"Because it's all I can think about anymore." His attention drifts from my eyes back to my lips. "*You're* all I think about. And I can't do anything to stop it."

An electric surge rushes through me, and more than anything, I wish the alcohol swimming in my veins was the reason behind it. Too bad we're long past the point of pretending any differently.

I want him.

And while that fact also makes me want to drown him, it's still true.

I want him more than oxygen; the very thing I need to survive in this fucked-up reality where he's supposedly with my best friend.

Regardless of all the reasons why I shouldn't, despite all logic that defies it…I want him.

It's the only explanation for why my fingers curl around the back of his neck, and I drag his mouth to mine.

Something inside me breaks—splinters apart piece by piece—the second our lips collide, and it only gets more intense when his hands leave the concrete to grip either side of my face. The moment the heat of his skin seeps into mine, I become unglued. Dismantled.

Destroyed at a cataclysmic level, and all that remains is the bone-deep desire for him I've been trying to fight.

A soft groan slips free when the tip of his tongue teases the seam of my lips before spearing between them altogether, no part of him willing to wait for permission. Everything with Holden is at warp speed—all acting first and thinking later. I shouldn't be surprised he kisses the same way.

One hand slides around and anchors in the back of my hair, holding me in place while he feverishly explores my mouth. Tongues roll and tangle together in a frenzy as hands glide over bare skin and toned muscles, a feral kind of desperation taking over us both.

His other hand drops down to my waist, sliding around my lower back, dragging me closer to the edge. To him. Except chest to chest isn't enough for either of us, so he slides his palm down my leg until it reaches my calf in a silent request. One my body listens to instantly, igniting under his touch as I wrap my legs around his waist, and he drags me straight into the pool.

The cool water lapping against my skin does nothing to negate the fire I've been consumed in, especially now with our bodies perfectly aligned. It only gets worse when he shifts until my back collides with the wall of the pool, because now, I can feel the hard ridge of his erection against my own with every press and roll of his hips.

It's possessive, the way he takes control of me. Barbaric and brutal when his teeth scrape over my lips hard enough to draw blood. As if the thread holding together his sense of control has snapped, and he's suddenly taking all the pent-up lust, anger, and frustration out on me. Channeling it into a kiss I could drown in.

It's downright erotic, the way I feel it and him in every single nerve ending.

And I never want it to end.

But even in my oxygen-starved state, I know it has to. Soon, or I'll never break free from this hold he has on me. I'll let myself be consumed to the point where we complicate things further.

I groan into his mouth before jerking away, needing to distance myself from him. Before this goes further, before we make more mistakes than we've already racked up.

Before we do more damage we can't come back from.

I shake my head, my breathing coming out in heaving pants against his lips.

"Hold—"

"Don't you dare," he whispers harshly while tightening his hold on my hip. "You're not ending this now. I'm not fucking done with you."

Then he crashes his mouth back to mine, and I drown all over again.

SEVENTEEN

Holden

Every molecule in my being has been lit on fire by Phoenix, and the only thing I want right now is to keep fanning the flames. Keep kissing and touching him until I'm nothing but a pile of ash and debris on the ground at his feet.

From the way he's kissing me back, full of anger and passion, there's no doubt in my mind he's thinking the same thing. It's also not enough. Nothing will be until he's as wrecked and shattered as I am; as needy and feral.

And I have no intention of stopping this until that happens.

I break our kiss, only to carry him safely up the steps of the pool before capturing his mouth all over again. My every intention is to get him naked and under me, if only to show him everything he's been missing by denying this uncontrollable desire coursing between us.

Except the second I step toward the door leading inside, his hand tightens around my forearms and he shakes his head.

"We can't go inside. Someone will hear us," he mutters in harsh pants against my lips.

"Well, we can't stay out here."

Confusion mars his features as he tries to slip out of my hold, but my fingers tighten on the underside of his thighs to keep his legs locked around my waist. Fuck if he thinks he's getting out of my grasp right now. He'll be lucky if I ever let him out of reach ever again, especially when it took this long to get him here in the first place.

"Why not?"

"Because," I growl as his back collides with one of the columns supporting the carport, "a pool lounger won't be stable enough for all the things I plan to do to you."

I catch his arched brow in the dim glow of the pool deck lights. "What makes you think you're the one who's gonna be doing anything to *me?*"

The smirk forming on my lips can't be helped. Always so damn abrasive, this one.

"If I didn't know any better, I'd take that as a challenge."

My hips press into his for emphasis, and the ridge of his erection grinding against my own is something between Heaven and Nirvana. But the fabric from our trunks preventing us from being skin on skin is pure torture.

I need to touch him again—every bare, hard inch of him.

It feels like I might die if I don't.

An idea takes hold of me, and before he can change his mind and bolt, I walk us the twenty yards toward the outdoor shower, where the edge of the property meets the beach. He either must realize my intention or not care what my plan is, since his lips and teeth start carving a path from my jaw to my collarbone. And thank God it's not any farther, because, by the time I step into the three-sided bamboo enclosure, my cock is hard enough to cut diamonds.

His back collides with the wall of the privacy screen, and I take my turn to devour him right back. My teeth skate over his jaw as I rock my hips into him again, letting him feel just how desperate I am for him.

A raspy chuckle leaves him when his elbow knocks the knob into an on position, causing water to start pouring from the shower head above us. And if I thought he was sexy before, it's got nothing on the way water cascades down his face and body. Catching on his eyelashes and dripping off his lips in a way that…I just have to kiss him all over again.

"You really like slamming me into things, don't you?" he muses when we come up for air.

"Are you telling me you don't like being manhandled?" I rasp against his lips and loosen my hold on his thighs, finally allowing him to stand. "Or would you rather be the one manhandling me?"

The cord lights running along the top trim of the enclosure are the only thing illuminating his face, but it's more than enough for me to watch his teeth scrape over his bottom lip.

God, he's beautiful. Beautiful and finally fucking mine.

"I want both," he finally says slowly, fingers dancing down my bicep. "I want you to drive me to the brink of insanity only to stop and let me return the favor."

A hellish smile curves my lips before I whisper a single word against his mouth.

"Done."

And with that, I drop to my knees and pull his trunks down past his ass; waiting to get my hands on him is no longer an option. His cock pops free from the waistband, hard and ready for me, and I wrap my fist around it and stroke him slowly.

Phoenix sinks his teeth into his plush, kiss-swollen lower lip again as he watches me, a hunger in his eyes that I'm positive mirrors my own.

"Are you planning to suck it or not?"

"Maybe I want to play with you a little first." My lips curl up in a smirk as I roll my thumb over the nerve beneath his swollen head. "I already know how much you like this."

Fire and lust darken his gaze as he continues staring at me through the water raining down on us, and I realize being on my knees for him like this only adds to the potency.

It's enough to spur me into action, and I flick my tongue out over the head, swiping the precum up with a single lick. The salty tang bursts on my taste buds, and I beg my memory to recall something. Anything to fill in the gaps. But all I get is a growing need and desire—both of which quickly become too strong to withstand, and I wrap my lips around the head to take my first long pull of him.

His length slides over my tongue until he reaches the back of my throat, eliciting a throaty, tortured gasp from his lips.

"Oh, fuck, baby," he groans.

His hand grips the back of my head, fingers sinking into my hair, and he rolls his hips forward. The motion sends him even deeper, and I hollow my cheeks as he inches down my throat.

I pull back, running my tongue along the underside of his shaft, before taking him again—this time to the hilt. Tears prick at my eyes as I continue working him over like this, the water cascading from the shower rinsing them down the drain immediately.

Despite wanting to unravel him my own way—despite Phoenix asking for just that—I allow him to take the reins when his hand tightens in my hair. The way he takes control is undoubtedly one of the sexiest things I've experienced. His hips set the pace for us, giving me slow, deep thrusts while he slides over my tongue all the way to the back of my throat.

My hands roam up and down his calves and thighs, mapping and memorizing every inch of his skin. He picks up speed, now fucking my face like it's his dying wish. Hell, it might be mine as well, since I can't seem to get enough of it.

Of him.

God, I want all of him.

I moan around his cock when it twitches between my lips, my own aching behind the confines of my board shorts. But just when I think I've got him there—that I'll finally get to taste him again—he tightens his hand and forces me to release him.

"We have to stop," he gasps after he drags me up to stand in front of him.

I shake my head, water flinging off the ends of my hair. "Not until we're both wrung dry," I murmur the words against his lips before sealing my mouth to his again.

I knew I was drunk that night—at the Kappa Sig house. Knew I blacked out, too, seeing as I woke up the next morning in a stranger's bed with no recollection of the night before. Yet, I had no clue just *what* moments were evading my memories until now.

Now? I wish I could remember everything.

In vivid, explicit detail.

But if I can't? If they're truly gone for good?

Then I'm damn well gonna make some new ones.

"It's your turn to drive me mad," I mutter against his lips before shoving his soaked trunks to the ground. I do the same with mine before tossing them outside the enclosure.

His nearly black eyes darken further as they trace over my naked body.

"Then I need you to turn around," he utters, his voice raw and grated with lust. It sends bolts of desire down my spine, and I shiver.

Doing as he asks, I place my hands flat against the bamboo screen. Anticipation builds inside me as Phoenix's chest collides with my back, every hard inch of him pressed into me. His shaft nestles between my cheeks, and the water pouring over us makes it just slippery enough to slide up and down my crease with ease.

"You're so. Fucking. Hot," he rasps against the back of my neck.

It's the second time I've been told that tonight, but *hell,* if hearing it from him isn't a million times better than it was falling from Kason's lips. Hearing that Phoenix is just as affected and attracted…it's exhilarating.

Not as exhilarating as his palm wrapping around my cock, though. That just about makes me come on the spot.

Every pull and stroke he makes over my length has my balls drawing up in pleasure, and God, if I don't welcome it. His hands on me are the things my fantasies have been made of lately, as much as I hate admitting it. But even as he continues jacking me while exploring my skin with his mouth, I can tell it's not enough. It's not even close.

"More," I pant as his teeth scrape against my shoulder. "Need more."

It's a plea, not a request. At this point, I'll beg for him. Whatever is needed to take anything he's willing to give.

"How much more?"

"Inside me," I say between ragged breaths. "Right now, Nix. I want you inside me."

His forehead rests between my shoulder blades, and I hear him utter a soft curse. "I don't have a condom."

Shit.

I don't either, and there's no way we're ending this just to take a trip to the closest twenty-four-hour convenience store.

I shake my head, wishing we could move this party inside. Or anywhere with the proper supplies, because…

"Me either."

"Damnit," Phoenix whispers, and I feel his forehead roll back and forth over my skin as he shakes his head. "We need to stop then. It's not—"

"Fuck the condom," I tell him, turning in his arms to meet his eyes. "We can stop if it's really what you want, but you're not gonna catch anything from me. I'd never put you at risk."

His expression is filled with worry and unease. Doubt, even. And honestly, it's not unmerited given my reputation, even if it is a bit insulting.

"I swear it on my parents, Nix."

The way his eyes soften as I say those words tells me two things: One, he was definitely listening in the car that day while we drove down here, especially with the little hint of sympathy in his gaze resurfacing. The second is him taking my words at face value.

I'd never, *ever* put him at risk.

He works to swallow, nodding before whispering, "What about lube?"

I groan, my head falling back against the slats of wood.

Goddamnit.

The feeling of defeat slams into me, and I'm starting to think this really isn't meant to happen. That the timing is off, or the stars aren't actually aligned or—

A lightbulb flicks on inside my head, and before I can say anything, I'm sliding past Phoenix and out of the enclosure.

"Where are you—"

"I have an idea," I tell him, and I'm back less than thirty seconds later with a solution I'm praying will work. But as Phoenix stares at what I'm holding in my hands, I can tell he's more than a little apprehensive.

"Is that—"

"Aloe, yeah," I say, breaking open the skin of the plant.

Even as the clear gel starts revealing itself, the wariness on Phoenix's expression doesn't dissipate.

"You're *sure* this is aloe?"

"I watched Theo use it yesterday on his sunburn, and he's still alive," I answer, crushing the gel in my fist so it will spread better. As I go to smear it over his shaft, he steps away from me.

"His shoulders are completely different than my dick."

Fair enough, but I don't see him coming up with any other options.

"It's this or nothing, Nix. I'm fine with whatever you want, but this is our best bet."

Meeting his eyes in the dim light, I offer him an understanding smile. If only to let him know that I won't be pissed if he ends this here and now.

Well, I won't be pissed at *him*. Just maybe in general.

I watch the gears spin in his head, no doubt working through his thoughts or whatever he does when he retreats inside himself like this. But if his stepping toward me is any indication, the pros must've outweighed the cons.

Tentatively, I reach out and grip him in my fist before covering his length with the gel, paying extra attention to the red, angry tip.

"This is so fucking stupid," he mutters, but at least he's arching into my touch as I work him over.

"Probably," I agree. "But I honestly don't care. I don't care if it's raw or painful or stupid. I just fucking want you."

His eyes meet mine, and something in his expression changes. The resolve that was lingering there melts away in front of my eyes as he takes some of the aloe from my palm before urging me to turn back around. My chest presses into the bamboo again while he spreads the makeshift lubricant down my crease, and I arch into his touch on instinct when he works the gel past my rim.

Seeking more friction, more pleasure. Just *more*.

My heart rate spikes when I feel the head of his cock nudge against the tight ring of muscle, but it's nothing compared to how it leaps out of my chest the second he breaches me.

"Holy shit," he rasps, his breath hot on the back of my neck.

A sharp gasp slips out of my mouth as he continues tunneling inside me, inch after agonizingly slow inch. The initial burn of his intrusion is cooled by the aloe as his cock slides in deeper, the pleasure so powerful I might combust from it on the spot.

It short-circuits my brain, stealing the air straight from my lungs.

It's only when he's seated all the way to the hilt that I can finally breathe again.

"Oh, hell," I say on a rough exhale as he pauses, letting my body adjust.

Phoenix lets out a low sound—some mixture of a moan and sigh—as he trails bites and kisses over my neck. His fingers dig into my hips to nearly the point of pain while his mouth explores my skin.

I feel him everywhere. Not just where he touches me either.

Every atom in my body is attuned to him.

He starts moving slowly at first before picking up speed, becoming harder and more punishing. I feel his anger as much as his desire, and I welcome it. Crave it, even.

"Fuck, baby," he groans. "Your ass feels like heaven."

His hips slam into me relentlessly, and I press back into him, impaling myself on his cock as much as he pistons it into me. Meeting him thrust for thrust as we climb this mountain together. Bringing each other higher and closer to the peak of ecstasy, ready to jump into the freefall.

One hand leaves my waist and wraps around my shaft, and the dual sensation of his cock and fist fucking me sends me sky-high, straight into bliss.

Into outer-fucking-space.

My fingers dig into the wood, clawing at the smooth surface as if it's the only thing keeping me grounded. Like if I let go, I'll be lost to gravity and float right off the face of the planet.

"I'm close," I pant, the tingling feeling of impending release rippling through my extremities.

"Good," he rasps in my ear. "Get there for me, baby."

The head of his cock swipes over that spot inside me, lighting me on fire from the inside out. Desire races through my veins like a train off its tracks—uncontrollable and potentially devastating. Hell, I'm not sure either of us will be more than a puddle of goo to be washed down the drain with the water still pouring over us when it's all said and done. And honestly, I couldn't give a shit if that's the case.

Nothing—and I mean fucking nothing—matters besides the feel of him inside me.

Taking me, claiming me.

Owning every inch of my being.

"Nix."

His name leaves my lips with a guttural moan when he pegs my prostate again, causing me to see stars. Release slams into me like a tidal wave, the force nearly enough to knock the wind straight from my lungs while my ass constricts around him like a vise. I bear down on his cock, feeling myself clamp around him as cum spills from my own through his fingertips before disappearing down the drain at our feet.

His thrusts become quicker and more erratic, signaling he's right there with me.

"Where—"

"Inside," I pant, unable to get more than that single word out.

He must understand what I mean, though, and his hips pound against my ass until his release fills me. Every clench and squeeze my ass makes around him draws out his orgasm, and I almost come all over again at the sharp bite of pain in my shoulder as his teeth sink into the flesh there.

Cum spills from my ass and drips down my leg when he pulls from my body, still gasping for air. His breath is a whisper across my heated skin, and it sends shivers down my spine. A feeling only amplified when he presses a kiss to the spot where his teeth marked me.

No one has ever made me feel this thoroughly owned.

Honestly, I don't think anyone else ever could.

I'm caught somewhere between the high of my orgasm and utter exhaustion as I turn in his arms. Ready to collapse into a sweaty, sated heap right here on the ground and not move until morning, yet also wanting to drag him to one of those pool loungers and go for another round.

His eyes meet mine, and I swear, he can read every thought running rampant through my head. It makes my body tingle, a buzz coming from more than just the alcohol still coursing through my veins.

I'm high on sunshine, tequila, and him; a combination sure to decimate the willpower of even the strongest of men.

Something I've never been, nor will ever claim to be.

I reach up, my fingers curling around the nape of his neck when I press my forehead to his. The pounding heart inside my chest shows no signs of slowing, even as seconds turn to minutes while we come down from the high—a feat nearly impossible when I'm still in his proximity.

Something about him just…gets to me. Messes with me in ways I can't quite comprehend.

"You fuck me up, Nix."

The words fall from my lips without warning, and I'm helpless to stop them. Helpless to keep fighting this when he has a way of turning my entire world inside out with a single touch.

It's why I should break away. Go inside, crawl into bed, and put this whole night behind me without batting an eye. But it's easier said than done when no part of me wants to leave this spot.

The second we do—the moment I can no longer feel his skin against mine and breathe in his scent—the spell will wear off.

And once it does, things will never be the same.

EIGHTEEN

Phoenix

The sounds of birds chirping and the ray of sunlight directly on my face are what wake me the next morning, groggy and disoriented. Even when I open my eyes, I can't focus—probably thanks to my brain pounding against the inside of my skull—the confusion only grows as I feel a breeze in places I most definitely should *not* be feeling it.

Why am I outside, naked?

My sluggish brain runs through the previous night, recollecting the events as fast as it will allow.

The face-off at the bar. The secrets in the pool.

The kiss leading to us naked in the shower—

I bolt upright on the lounger, panic and anxiety making an immediate appearance as I attempt to gain my bearings. The sudden movement effectively knocks Holden's arm from where it was draped across my chest, who is asleep—buck-ass naked—beside me on a lounger.

The same place we collapsed together last night in a satiated, exhausted pile of limbs.

"Shit," I hiss out the curse and immediately slide out from beneath him in search of my swim trunks, which I find in a pile with his next to the outdoor shower stall we—

Do not even think about what happened last night.

If I do, I might be sick. Or maybe that's the hangover talking.

Both our trunks in hand, I head back to where he's still slumbering and toss the stupid pink, banana-printed fabric at his face, where it lands with a damp plop. It has the desired effect, though, and he lets out a long groan before pulling them from his face.

"Good morning to you, too," Holden grumbles, sitting up and squinting at me.

"Seriously?" The words come out in a sharp tone. "That's all you have to say right now?"

"Calm down," he grumbles, using the trunks to shield his eyes. "It's too early to be this worked up."

"Calm down?" I ask incredulously while shoving my legs into my trunks. It's only when they're firmly around my hips again that I whirl on him. "Someone could have *seen us,* Holden."

A crease forms in his forehead as he rises off the lounger at a snail's pace, clearly still attempting to regain his equilibrium. But even in my anger and frustration with his lackadaisical movements and no-fucks-given attitude right now, I can't help staring at the lines and planes of his body. A body, just last night, I touched and licked and—

Goddamnit, don't go there.

Still, my sex-starved brain slips right back into lust. He's woken a beast inside me I didn't know existed, and now it's insatiable.

Holden watches me closely as he slips back into his trunks, those whiskey-brown eyes giving nothing away. "Would it have been such a bad thing? If someone would have seen us?"

And there's the bucket of cold water I needed.

"You're kidding, right? You're here *with Kason,* and you don't think someone walking out on us naked together in a pool lounger is a bad thing?"

He's gotta be insane if that's the case.

"Kason and I aren't together," he says, arms crossed over his chest as he frowns at me. "We aren't in a relationship, never have been. There's nothing monogamous about it, and if he wanted to see someone else or sleep with someone else, he's perfectly allowed to."

All I can do is stare at him. At this...*fuckboy.*

"What is wrong with you?" I snarl, stepping away from him. "You and Kason *are* together, and with him kissing you on the beach and groping you last night, everyone on this stupid trip knows it. So either you truly are fucking delusional, or—"

"Or I'm just fucking with him, right? Playing games like the asshole you've made me out to be?" His brows arch in amusement. "Think what you want of me, but neither of us asked for exclusivity in this. Both of us are unattached. It's not my fault if he didn't tell you that bit of info—"

"Don't even finish that sentence unless you want to be decked in the face." It's a threat as much as a warning. Because if he doesn't tread carefully, my composure will surely snap. It's already halfway there from waking up naked next to him as it is.

"You might not like it, but it's the truth. Maybe your bestie doesn't tell you everything." He shrugs indifferently. "Or maybe you've been too busy being pissed at me to listen."

No part of my mind can understand how Kason would just agree to a no-strings thing with Holden. There's a reason he was still a virgin before this whole flirtation began—because hc puts an enormous amount of stock in sex.

We both do, which is why I've been so protective. To prevent him from sleeping with someone who doesn't give two flying fucks about him, which is precisely what has happened to me with Holden.

Twice, now.

"Get outta your head," Holden utters, and I slide my gaze to his. "Get out of it and listen to what I'm saying."

"Listen to you?" I scoff. "Yeah, that's not happening. Besides, you've got no idea what's going on in my head right now."

"Considering you're as easy to read as an open book? I do." He's stepping in closer to me, the distance between us being erased with every step. He makes no sign of stopping either, not until he's got me backed up to the edge of the pool with nowhere else to go. "You're torn between regretting last night and wanting it to happen again. It's written all over your face and how you're looking at me right now. In how I caught you checking me out when I was getting dressed." He cocks his head, those analytical eyes flicking over my face. "You loved every second of what happened last night, and the only reason it's killing you inside is your loyalty to Kason."

My teeth bite into my inner cheek until the faint taste of copper fills my mouth.

Everything he's saying is true. And I hate it; the way he can see right through me like I'm nothing more than a piece of fucking cellophane.

"The only thing killing me inside is having to stand here and listen to your psychobabble bullshit when you have no idea what you're talking about," I seethe, shoving past him to head back toward the house. He doesn't let me get more than a step however, before grabbing my arm and reeling me in all over again.

And though our positions have swapped, I'm still trapped here at his mercy. No freedom in sight when his bare skin against mine sends my brain into overdrive. Especially after last night.

A fact that only serves to piss me off more, making my fists tighten at my sides.

"Let go of me."

The words come out slow and deliberate, leaving no room for debate. Except, it's clear my venom has no effect on him, so he simply blinks it off as he continues analyzing my face until he ultimately releases his hold.

"You can lie to me all you want, Nixy. But at the end of the day, you'll never be able to lie to yourself."

"Even if you're right, it doesn't matter," I mutter with a shake of my head. "Because this never happened."

His lips quirk and he lets out a breathy laugh. "Keep telling yourself that. Doesn't make it true."

"It never happened." I tell him again before adding through gritted teeth, "And more importantly, it's never happening again."

His proximity, paired with how he's looking at me, instantly ignites a fire inside me. An uncontrollable inferno of hatred, passion, and desire that's burning away the mask of indifference I'm trying so desperately to maintain.

If I'm honest, it's already nothing more than a pile of ash at his feet, ready to be kicked into the pool behind him or blown away in the breeze like it never existed.

"Eyes and mouth, Nix," he whispers, stepping in even closer.

I feel the heat of his chest against mine, the lust-filled wanting as it crackles between us. And once again, I'm ensnared. Captivated. Incapable of walking away or escaping this undeniable chemistry we've both been failing to fight.

Only, from the way he's looking at me...it seems he's done fighting it. He's just waiting for me to do the same.

"What's going on down there?"

The sound of Kason's voice sends ice rushing through my veins, and when I glance up, I find him standing on the balcony attached to the living room. He's shirtless, running his hands through his amber hair, likely just waking up.

"Just figuring some shit out," Holden says, and when I return my gaze to him, I find his never left me to begin with.

"Yeah, but we're done now," I grit out, painfully aware of Kason watching our every move.

"Not even close," he whispers just for me. "We've yet to resolve anything."

Maybe, but right now isn't the time.

"Get out of my face, Holden," I hiss. My fingers open and close at my sides, balling into fists like they'll help me gain a grip on my composure. "I'm not kidding."

"Just admit one thing to me first." There's a hint of amusement layered under all that lust when he utters, "Admit you want me."

"Not happening."

"You keep saying that, Nix, yet I don't believe you."

"You want *Kason*," I remind him, which in itself is a ridiculous notion. Nevertheless, if I need to remind him who he's here with—who asked him to come on this vacation turned hellhole—then I will.

My chest rises and falls quickly as his attention dances between my eyes and lips before fixating on the latter. Like he wants nothing more than to snag one between his teeth. "You need to walk away. Right now. Before you do something you regret."

"I never regret anything." His eyes flick back to mine. "Not last night. Not whatever happened back in May. *Fucking nothing.*"

I glance away and shake my head. "I told you, Holden. I'm not doing this with you."

"Or what?" His eyes dart down to my lips before colliding with my gaze again. "Because I don't believe you'll hit me for a second. Not in front of an audience. And especially when I know he's asked you to play nice while we're all here."

Damn him.

Damn him for reading me so well, for calling my bluff, for digging under my skin.

For making me want him, despite knowing I shouldn't.

My jaw ticks as we remain locked in this stare-down, our battle of wills.

The only thing to do now is fight fire with fire and be careful not to get burned.

"You're right," I find myself murmuring before my hands slide up his chest. His skin sears me where I touch him, the heat blazing as I look into his eyes. From his expression, he thinks he's won. That I've finally conceded.

How very fucking wrong he is.

His tongue darts out over his bottom lip before he smiles. "Glad you're finally starting to—"

He doesn't get to finish his thought, because I shove him backward, sending him straight into the pool. The loud crash of his body breaking through the surface isn't nearly as satisfying as I'd hoped, and I realize it's because it's too little, too late.

I'd have been better off doing this exact thing last night when I had the chance. If I had, maybe all of this could've been avoided.

Yet, if I've learned anything from the mistakes I've made with Holden Sykes, it's that I can't change the past. So rather than dwelling on it, I storm into the house without making sure he comes up for air.

NINETEEN

Holden

The entire day passes after Phoenix pushes me into the pool, and I haven't seen him since. Granted, he has to be here somewhere. The condo might be huge, but there are only so many places to hide for long.

I haven't gone looking for him, in any case. The last thing I want is to piss him off even more than I already have, so I'm giving him some time to cool down. But there's no way the conversation from this morning is over.

No fucking way.

After last night, there's no going back. Not to ignoring each other, and certainly not to enemies. No matter how hard he wants to try, this is one bell that can't be unrung.

"You ready to head out for dinner?" Kason asks, peeking around the corner into the bedroom we've been sharing. A circumstance that's grown quite stale since arriving here, but especially after waking up beside Phoenix this morning.

I'd be a liar if I said I wasn't interested in doing it again, yet another chapter in this series of unforeseen events.

"Ah, yeah," I say, grabbing my wallet from the dresser and slipping it into my pocket. "You got everything?"

Kason's footfalls on the wood flooring alert me of his approach before I feel the heat of his body behind me, let alone see his arms as they cage me against the furniture.

"I never had the chance to ask, but where were you last night?" he murmurs, his chin resting on my shoulder. "I was surprised you weren't in here when I woke up."

Something like guilt churns within me, and it doesn't sit well.

Even for me, what happened last night with Phoenix is a gray area.

While this thing with Kason has been fun these past couple months, it's never been anything serious. We've talked about it and have always been on the same page about that, exactly like I told Phoenix this morning. So there's no reason I should be feeling bent out of shape about this, considering this is just a situationship where we've barely so much as kiss—

"Earth to Holden?"

I blink up at him, realizing my mind went off in another world without answering him.

"Sorry, I didn't get much sleep," I tell him. And it's not exactly a lie. "Let's just say I wouldn't recommend passing out on one of those pool loungers. They might look comfortable, but I can assure you, they are not."

Not unless you have a six-foot-two, muscled baseball player to use as a pillow.

A small smirk curls his mouth up at the corner and he steps back. "You were pretty fucked up last night."

Except I wasn't. At least not by alcohol.

"Yeah, I guess," I say with a forced laugh.

"Probably a good thing you laid off the booze today."

That was the intention, though God only knows our bristly pal Phoenix is close to driving me to it anyway. Which he very well might before the night is over. Between the magnitude of what happened last night and his avoidance of the events altogether, the odds aren't in my favor.

I blow out a sigh and nod before we head downstairs, ready to head out for our last night here. It's supposed to be lowkey—grabbing dinner down at the boardwalk—seeing as no one wants to be hungover off their ass for the drive back to Phoenix's parents in Nashville.

The other guys are already waiting outside by the cars when Kason and I step out of the house, minus Theo.

That's when I get my first glimpse of Phoenix in nearly twelve hours.

His attention is thoroughly fixated on his phone while he leans against the Jeep, but I can tell from the rigid set of his shoulders, he knows I'm standing here. He can feel me, just like I can feel him. The only difference is, he's choosing to ignore it.

Ignore me.

Ignore everything happening between us.

My teeth sink into my cheek, biting back the irritation growing inside me like a cancer, and I force myself to glance away. Getting torn up about shit like this isn't me. If Phoenix wants to pretend it never happened, I shouldn't care. It shouldn't matter to me.

And yet it does.

I can feel this shift happening in the way he looks at me. How it lingers when I catch his gaze, and not only the heat from this insane lust, but also the emotion I see in it too. The unexplainable connection that truly makes no sense when I try to think about it logically.

As vexing as it might be, this thing with Phoenix defies everything I've known.

Theo draws my attention away easily enough when he comes barreling out of the house a few seconds later, slightly out of breath and full of energy. Then again, he's the only one not sporting a massive hangover today. I'm sure he still had one helluva headache last night, though, seeing as he was both DD out at the bar and then lifeguard once we got home—making sure none of our dumb, intoxicated asses drowned in the pool.

"Dinnertime," he says, a chipper spring to his step as he pulls open the Bronco's driver-side door. "Autobots, roll out."

The rest of the guys start piling into the cars, all opting to hop in whatever vehicle we made the drive down to Florida in…except Phoenix. He's getting in Theo's Bronco rather than jumping back in the Jeep with me, Noah, and Kason, apparently taking the extra step to ensure he puts as much distance between us as possible.

And I don't miss the glare he aims at me before he slams the door behind him, either.

Kason must notice too, because he glances my way and hitches up a questioning brow. "What happened this morning to make him so pissed at you?"

You mean besides him spending the night fucking me clear into next week, only to wake up with a head full of regrets?

"You know him better than I do," is all I say before throwing the Jeep into reverse.

I'd have no problem admitting what happened last night to Kason, and if this were any other situation, I probably would have here and now. But I don't have to be intimately familiar with Phoenix to know it's a terrible idea. Hell if I'm gonna give him another reason to hate me.

Not when I'm already dying for him to stop.

"Remind me again how I got talked into this?" Phoenix shouts over the pop music as he stands on the back deck of the boat, strapped into a giant harness.

"Because we're friends with a bunch of jackasses," Theo reminds him from where he's lounged on one of the bench seats.

"You're the one who came up with the idea," Noah reminds him with a *gotcha there* look.

"All I said was I wish we would've thought about going parasailing sooner in the trip," he rebuts, raising his hands. "You and Luca were the ones who called the place to book us in for tonight."

That's exactly what happened too. Theo saw these guys parasailing off the coast while we were devouring our dinner—the first meal all day, for those of us still a bit hungover—and mentioned something about going out on it. It was all Noah and Luca who pulled up the number on the sail and called to see if they could take us tonight.

"Who's going with?" one of the crew members asks, arching a sun-bleached brow after he finishes hooking Phoenix in.

Besides Phoenix and Kason, the rest of us have already gone up. However when I glance over at Kason, I know there's no way he's making the journey. Not when he's losing his dinner over the side of the boat.

Wyatt's nose wrinkles up in disgust, seeing as he's the closest to Kason while he tosses his cookies. "Told you that alligator was a bad idea, man."

"He's probably just hungover still," Luca concludes, though the slight green tint of his own skin tells me he's not faring much better.

I'm still in my harness, having just gone on the last run with Harrison, so…shit, I might as well.

"I'll go," I offer, hopping back up on the deck.

Phoenix opens his mouth to say something—no doubt to get out of going up there together—but the crew member is already clipping my harness back into the weird horizontal pole contraption used to keep us, along with the sail, connected to the boat.

"Well, I guess I was wrong about one thing," I say to Phoenix, completely ignoring the guy adjusting all the straps around my body.

Phoenix's eyes remain staring forward as he mutters, "Oh, I'm gonna love to see where this is going."

"You don't have feelings for Kason."

Between the music and the distance between us and the rest of the group, I sincerely doubt anyone heard what I just said. Well, except maybe the man making sure I don't plummet into the Gulf from unknown heights. Yet, from how Phoenix's head snaps to me, I might as well have shouted it through a megaphone.

"No shit, Sherlock," he hisses. "I told you that a month ago, and you're just now figuring it out?"

"Nah, I figured it out a while ago. Just didn't have complete confirmation until last night."

If possible, the irritation in his eyes flares even hotter. "We're not talking about that."

"So you are still pissed at me." It's not a question. There's no doubt in my mind from the way he's looking at me and the tone of his voice that he's angry.

Yet something in his eyes tells me I might be wrong. That he's really just trying to act indifferent—which is a huge step from actually *being* indifferent.

"I'm not *anything* at you," he mutters, glancing away. "Now, please, just drop it."

It's not in my nature to just *drop it*, and it's something he should be well aware of by now. But the crew member chooses that moment to give the boat's captain a thumbs up.

"Enjoy your ride," he tells us, before offering me a wink.

The carabiner keeping us clipped to the boat is released, and within half a second, we're flying backward into the air, slowly floating away from the boat. It's a spike of adrenaline, the moment solid ground flies out from beneath us with our bodies being pulled back by the wind inflating the sail. But the rush quickly evaporates when I glance over at the horizon, at the colorful glow of the sunset.

"Oh, holy fucking God," Phoenix mutters, and when I turn his way, I find him white-knuckling the vertical straps like he's hanging on for dear life.

From the looks of him, that's exactly what's happening in his mind.

"You good?"

"I, uh, maybe, but—" He shakes his head slightly, and I notice his skin has gone ghostly white. "No, I don't think so."

Well, shit.

"If you're afraid of heights, why did you agree to do this?"

Phoenix might not be a rocket scientist, but he is smart enough to know what parasailing entails, especially when he watched six of us go before him. So him being up here right now…well, the math ain't mathin' for me.

His voice comes out strained and anxious. "I wasn't about to be the party pooper of the group, and by the time Kason started blowing chunks, I was already clipped in."

Oh, you beautiful fucking fool.

I'm about to respond when the wind lifts us a bit higher and we hit the end of our rope, causing us to jerk slightly. The sudden movement has Phoenix drawing in a deep breath…and looking straight down at the water below.

"Oh, shit," he says, breathing heavily. "That's a long drop."

"Nix," I murmur, my best attempt to soothe him. "Nix. Hey, look at me."

I grab his hand from the strap to snap him out of it, and it's enough to wrench his attention off the water below. Those deep brown eyes look lighter in the setting sun as he gazes at me, more of a rich mahogany than almost black. And it's the fear in them that has me threading my fingers through his.

"You're okay," I tell him earnestly. "You watched all the rest of us do this and come out in one piece, right? Nothing bad is gonna happen."

"You don't know that."

Okay, new tactic.

My thumb traces over the back of his mindlessly. "Then just close your eyes and focus on the wind. How it feels against your skin and whipping through your hair."

Phoenix visibly swallows before his lids fall closed, listening to my request.

"Okay, now talk to me," I murmur. "Tell me what's going through your mind."

"I can feel my heartbeat all the way in my ass."

"That's probably just the way the harness is sitting."

"Holden—"

"Okay, okay, not helpful." I pause, wracking my brain some more. "Just think of it like a giant swing, then. That's where the wind is coming from."

"We're five-hundred feet in the air above open water—a drop we would not survive, by the way—and you wanna act like we're on a goddamn swing set?"

"Why not? It'll take your mind off it. C'mon, let's get married."

His eyes fly open despite the height, and he looks at me like I've just grown two extra heads.

"What?"

I arch a brow, giving him a dubious look. "Don't act like you don't know what I'm talking about."

"I can assure you, I don't."

"It's the thing you say when you're a kid on the swings and someone beside you starts swinging in sync with you."

A look of relief takes over his face and he starts laughing. Like a real, genuine laugh, and I realize this is the first time I've heard it.

And my God, if it isn't the most incredible sound on this planet.

Even if I have no idea why he's laughing in the first place.

"You're in my shower," he manages to say between chuckles.

My brows shoot up. "I mean, if we're really talking about this now, then yeah. I remember. Vividly. But I'm not sure what that has to do with—"

"No, no," he cuts in and laughs some more. "That's what we would say when that happened. We'd look at the other person and say *you're in my shower.*"

Now it's my turn to burst out laughing. *"What?"*

"Yeah," he says between chuckles. "And then we'd usually jump off right after."

"That's the most ridiculous thing—"

He shakes his head and rebuts, "No more ridiculous than proposing."

"I wasn't proposing. *We're married* is just what we said."

"Doesn't make it any better."

Okay, fair point.

I roll my eyes. "You probably call shopping carts a buggy and shit too."

"Abso-fucking-lutely," he says, a big smile on his face. "And all soft drinks are called coke."

"Soda."

He shakes his head and winks at me. "Not in the South, baby."

The term of endearment slips so easily from his lips, causing a strange sort of flutter in my stomach. It's different hearing it now, away from a moment heated with lust and desire.

If only he didn't clearly regret it leaving his mouth in the first place.

"I didn't...you know—" He lets out an uncomfortable sort of laugh. "Do me a favor and forget I just said that."

His cheeks have a pink tint when he meets my gaze, making me want to brush my thumb over them. Feel the heat of his skin radiating into my touch. Cup one in my palm as I drag his mouth to mine and make him forget the heights, the slip-up, his own fucking name.

Maybe that's why the words spill out of my mouth, low and husky, before I can even attempt to reel them back in.

"Kiss me, and I promise I won't remember a word of it."

Phoenix's eyes drop to my lips immediately, and I swear I'm watching the gears spin in his mind as he thinks about doing just that. And that's how I know he's in this just as deep as I am. There's no use in either of us denying it anymore. Not when proof of this chemistry—these feelings— are staring us straight in the face.

But it's clear he's still hell-bent on fighting this when the flush on his cheeks deepens to red, and he glances away.

"You have to stop looking at me like that."

My eyes follow the lines and planes of his face as I murmur, "I wish I knew how."

"Holden..."

"Phoenix."

"We're being pulled in," he whispers, keeping his gaze averted.

I glance out in front of us to find he's right. I was so focused on his face and mouth and just him, I barely realized the line attached to our sail was slowly getting shorter and shorter.

"Nix—"

"No." Our eyes meet, and I see the plea in his before he even speaks it. "Please, don't."

Blowing out a sigh, I focus my attention on the boat as we rapidly descend toward it.

"Stand up, stand up," the crew member calls as we close in on the boat, and just as quickly as the deck disappeared when we were first released, our feet collide with the surface again.

The guys on the boat whoop and holler, just like they did the first time I went up, and Noah goes as far as holding up eight fingers to give us a score for our landing.

"Well then, that wasn't so bad, was it?"

Not at all, even though I can't say the same for Phoenix, who is back to barely acknowledging my presence.

It's not until the harnesses are unclipped and we're ushered off the back deck that I realize I was holding his hand the entire time.

And I didn't want to let go.

TWENTY

Phoenix

We make great time returning to Nashville the next day, giving us the remainder of the late afternoon and evening to spend with my family. And all three of them are a welcome sight in the doorway after ten miserable hours in the car with Kason and Holden.

No amount of Netflix, Spotify, or reading could save me from the thoughts circling around the three of us and the fucked-up situation we've found ourselves in—one Kason is still wholly oblivious to. Or from looking in the mirror, only to catch Holden's gaze already on me, which was so much worse. Because every time our eyes collide now, there's a lot more depth in them. I don't know how to describe it other than that, and it's enough to have me looking away every time.

Just like right now, as he brushes by me to enter the house with the rest of the guys.

"Phoe Phoe!" Charlotte screeches, steering my gaze to her.

"Aren't you a sight for sore eyes?" I sweep her off the ground the second she's within reach and swing her around in circles, drawing out endless bouts of laughter and giggles.

"I miss you so much," she says, wrapping her arms around my neck in a bear hug.

"I miss you too, Bug," I tell her, squeezing her a little tighter than necessary. I didn't realize how much that was true until I was actually holding her in my arms.

"Did you have the best time?"

Her hazel eyes twinkle as she smiles at me, ready to hear all about our adventures. Ones probably far more epic in her head than in reality. Nonetheless, Charlotte's always had a massive love for the ocean, and in turn, any time we spend down at the condo. I think it's the place she's happiest, which is why the next words to come out of my mouth are nothing short of the truth.

"It was fun, just not as much fun if you would've been there."

If possible, her smile grows even wider.

She babbles on and on for a couple minutes about all the things that happened at school this term, and I probably only understand half of it because she's speaking so fast. But the animated way she talks and tosses her hands in the air while she does wraps a fist around my heart and squeezes.

Not as much as when she pauses and looks me dead in the eye to ask, "Do you really have to go back to college tomorrow?"

One single emotion slams into me at full force at her words. Guilt. It's all I seem to be feeling these days. Maybe it's because I feel like I'm constantly letting everyone down.

"You know I have to go back to school," I tell my little sister, hating the sadness on her face the moment the words leave my lips. "I would stay here with you if I could. You know that, right?"

She nods and quickly bounces back into more cheerful spirits when she remembers we have company. Lots of it.

"Put me down so I can go say hi to KK," she commands. "I didn't get to see him yet. Or anyone else. I want to meet all your friends."

Charlotte didn't see any of the guys when we passed through last week. She was already asleep when we got here on the way down, and with a heavy driving day the next morning, we left before she was even awake. So naturally, her FOMO is demanding she gets the chance now.

I laugh and, per her request, set her on her feet so she can find wherever Kason's disappeared to within the house. Probably in the room directly across from mine, where he's always stayed when he needed an escape from his own home.

"She's cute," a voice says from behind me as I watch her scamper off, instantly creating a warm, fuzzy sensation in my stomach.

I was so distracted by giving Charlotte my undivided attention, I hadn't realized Holden was still standing there. Hadn't felt his penetrating gaze boring into me, so I assumed he'd gone off with the rest of the guys to find a place to sleep.

"Yeah, she is." I peer down the hall where she disappeared before adding, "She's one of my favorite people on this planet."

In truth, I'm close to my entire family. It's not common these days, but we've always had a very tight-knit bond. Despite Dad's demanding career, he's always made time for our family, and it's something I'll forever be grateful for.

"I can see why." Holden gives me a soft smile that does something stupid to the organ in my chest. "She seems like a little spitfire. I wonder who she gets it from."

"Whatever you're implying, I can guarantee you're wrong."

"That your little sister is just like you?"

My eyes flash to him, and I murmur, "An impossibility, seeing as she's adopted."

Holden blinks, like he's not sure he heard me correctly. "What?"

"She and her parents were in a terrible car wreck when she was six months old. She lived, they didn't." I pause and clear my throat, trying not to let my emotions get the best of me. "Mom and Dad always wanted another kid, and when the opportunity presented itself, they took it. She might not be my blood, but she's my sister in all the ways that matter."

It's strange, sharing this bit of my family with him. The only person at Leighton who knows the truth about Charlotte's birth parents is Kason, and that's because he lived it with me. But as strange as it might be to give Holden this information, I don't have the power not to.

"I...I didn't—"

"I know you didn't," I cut in, letting him off the hook. "How would you have?"

His teeth roll over his bottom lip, worrying it in a way that makes me think I'm missing something, yet I have no idea what it could be. But then he just shrugs, throwing my thinking entirely off course.

"I guess you're right."

I don't have the chance to open my mouth because Charlotte comes running back down the hall.

"Phoe Phoe, this is your friend Holden, right?" she asks, still running toward Holden, making no sign of stopping until his hands land on her shoulder so she doesn't collide with his legs.

I open my mouth to speak, but Holden's charismatic charm takes care of it for me when he squats down, dropping to her level to speak with her.

"I sure am, but I don't think I've met you. What's your name?"

"I'm Charlotte Louise Mercer, and I'm six years old," she says, a big smile on her face. "But Phoe Phoe calls me Bug, and since you're his friend, that means you can too."

Holden glances up at me and lets out a fake little scoff before giving her his attention again. "You look more like a princess than a bug to me."

"Thanks, I think so, too."

He lets out a laugh, "And modest."

Charlotte's blonde brows scrunch together as she looks at me. "Phoe Phoe, what does that mean?"

I smile at her, not quite sure I'm ready to explain the inner workings of sarcasm to a six-year-old. "He's just being silly," I tell her.

She gives a little shrug before turning back to Holden, totally unphased. "KK said you have pictures to show me."

"KK?" Holden repeats, his eyes flicking up to me. "Seriously?"

"Judge the nicknames, I dare you," I warn, my brow arched in his direction. "Because I can easily get her to start calling you HoHo."

God only knows it would be fitting.

"Like Santa says!" she pipes in, and all three of us start to laugh.

I smile down at her. "Something like that, Bug. Now what do you mean by pictures?"

Even I have no idea what she's talking about, and from the looks of it, Holden doesn't either.

Charlotte is radiating happiness and joy when she peers back at Holden again. "KK told me you took pictures of Mingo, and I want to see them."

Confusion is written all over his face before glancing at me. And then, just like that, the lightbulb switches on.

"Charlotte, I'm more than happy to do that, but I need to tell you a little secret first."

Her tiny eyes widen and she nods quickly. "Okay. I can keep secrets."

"Okay, well…I called Mingo something else when I was there. Francesco. Is that okay with you?"

She giggles a little, her tiny nose scrunching up as she does. "That's a funny name, but I don't think Mingo would mind."

"Good, then where do you want—"

"Let's go!" Charlotte grabs his hand and starts yanking him toward the living room, breaking out into a run. A hilarious sight, considering he takes one stride for her three or four. Still, the sight of the two of them hand-in-hand also makes the organ in my chest stutter and stumble as it beats, especially when he glances over his shoulder and beams at me.

I've really gotta get a fucking grip.

I follow as she pulls him into the living room, only to find some of the guys already in there chatting or scrolling through their phones while we wait for the pizza Dad ordered for dinner. Charlotte isn't fazed however, dragging Holden over to the giant beanbag in the corner she's claimed as hers since the day we brought her home.

She plops down on the thing, and Holden carefully folds himself into it beside her and pulls out his phone. Together, the two of them swipe through whatever images are on there. A few of them I saw him take, like one with his duck on top of the flamingo's head or one with him sitting on the float, legs on either side of the neck, tossing a "hang loose" sign in the air.

They go on like that for twenty minutes before she's asking to start all over again.

"Let me see the duck one again," Charlotte says, drawing my attention back to them.

"Okay, okay." He chuckles and starts flipping through his phone again before showing her.

Giggles come bubbling from her lips, the sound music to my ears after the turmoil I've been feeling lately, and a sense of lightness settles over me for the first time in weeks. Being around Bug always seems to have that effect.

"More, more," she demands, while doing a little bounce beside him. Only, rather than waiting on Holden to do the swiping, she grabs the phone from his hands, clearly intent on doing it herself.

"Shi—oot, hold on," Holden mutters, grabbing his phone away from her. "There's a couple in here that shouldn't be viewed by innocent eyes."

"Better not show Kason, then," Noah says from across the living room, not even looking up from his phone.

"Ha, ha. Poke fun at the virgin because it's so funny," Kason grumbles from where he sits on the couch. He says it quietly enough not to draw Charlotte's attention, which is probably a good thing. I really don't need her going up to either of our parents tomorrow after we leave and asking them what a virgin is.

"Dinner will be here in a few," Mom's voice comes from beside me.

I smile at her and wrap my arm around her shoulder and squeeze, only to feel her return one around my waist.

"Thanks, Mom."

Our attention shifts to where Charlotte and Holden are when she lets out another fit of giggles. It amazes me how enthusiastically they talk between themselves. Like no one else is in the room.

You wouldn't know by looking that there's almost a fifteen-year age gap between them, because he treats her just like any of us. A bit softer, of course, since she is still a child. It's something in his tone of voice and demeanor; he is not handling her with kid gloves like most people do. Especially if they know about her being adopted.

"She's enthralled with him," Mom whispers, just for my ears.

My attention shifts, and I meet her amber eyes. "Yes, she is. Not something I expected, but it's cool, regardless."

"And he's good to Kason?"

The question takes me off-guard, and I force myself to whisper an answer I don't believe in. For so many reasons, I can't even begin to list them.

"They're great together."

"I'm glad. That boy's family, and Lord knows he deserves something good in his life." There's a hint of a smile on her face as she continues watching Holden with my sister. "I can see why he'd be just as captivated."

He's not the only one.

And the thought alone is exactly why I don't think I'll be able to last another full day in the car with the two of them tomorrow.

I see the way Kason looks at him; the affection in his gaze that's become so painfully obvious, it's almost sickening. Or maybe the nausea is because it's the same way I've caught myself looking at him, too.

He has a way of bewitching me and everyone else around him. I hate admitting it, even if it's just to myself, but I can't deny the truth anymore. Something about the guy draws me in, dragging me under his spell and twisting me up inside. Knotting up my intestines and coiling around my heart in a grip that continues tightening no matter how hard I try to escape.

But I have to.

If I know what's good for my friendship and my fucking sanity…I *need* to.

"What's wrong, honey?" Mom asks, and I realize I never responded to her.

I'm not the type to keep secrets from Mom or Dad. It might not be considered *normal* these days, but I firmly believe they're there for me no matter what. With advice, just a listening ear, or whatever it might be.

Yet I can't bring myself to talk about this right now.

"Just kinda out of it, I guess," I tell her, eyes focused on Charlotte and Holden. And once again, I have to ignore the way my stomach flutters and my heart races when I catch him smiling down at her.

It's a mental picture I plan to store in my memory bank for a long time.

Mom's always been able to read me like a book. It's one of the many reasons I'm so comfortable talking to her about things. And she proves her capability to read the situation and reach inside my mind hasn't waned with my going off to college when she gives me another gentle squeeze at the waist.

"Honey, you know you won't lose Kason just because someone else comes into his life, right? Your friendship is the forever kind. Whatever comes between you two, you'll come back together, stronger at the end. I have no doubt about it, and neither should you."

I give Mom a half-hearted smile, knowing in my gut that she's wrong.

Because after everything that's happened, there's no way my friendship with Kason will be the same. Not unless I figure out a way to turn these feelings for Holden off for good.

"What did your Mom mean by you staying here?"

The incredulity in Kason's voice is unmatched as the question leaves his lips, forcing my attention up from where I'm lounging across my mattress in my childhood room the next morning.

I shift into a sitting position, brows furrowing. "Um…exactly that?"

The decision was made early this morning to not drive back with the rest of the guys—opting to spend the rest of winter break here with my family instead. I hadn't realized how much I missed them, and it also gives me a little bit of reprieve from the weird, toxic cloud forming whenever Holden, Kason, and I are in the same confined space for too long.

Kason's arms cross over his chest. "So what am I supposed to do for the next week when I get back to campus?"

I know Kason means no harm by turning this around to how it affects him—after all, it's a valid point considering he'll be at the apartment alone—but it still gives me a weird feeling regardless.

Or not alone, if he decides to invite Holden over.

The thought only causes my temper to flare internally, and I let out a dry, "I'm sure you'll figure it out."

He just frowns at me, head cocked to the side, like he doesn't even recognize me. Hell, if he knew half of what's been running through my head or has been happening with Holden, he surely wouldn't.

"Why are you acting so weird?"

My brows collide in an effort to play dumb, all the while knowing it's getting a lot more difficult to do. Especially when I'm having a hard enough time maintaining eye contact. "I'm not acting any weirder than my normal level of weird, Kase."

"Yeah, you are," he says, crossing the room and taking a seat on the edge of the bed. "You've been quiet and distant as shit for the past three days. I don't think you even said a word all day yesterday. Even when Noah or Holden made some stupid comment while we were driving up here— and that isn't like you."

The mere mention of Holden sends a rush of heat flowing through my veins. Not the good kind of heat—the kind of lust and desire. No, instead, this is all shame and guilt.

I don't miss how the regret is lacking, though; that little fact only exacerbates this whole thing.

"I'm just tired," I tell him, yet another lie slipping off my tongue with ease.

There was a time in my life when I would've rather stepped on a Lego or shot myself in the foot than lie to Kason. When I would've gone out of my way to kick the ass of anyone who'd dare treat him poorly or hurt him. So the irony isn't lost on me that I'm doing all those things now, even if he doesn't realize it's happening.

"You're tired?" he repeats, brow hitched up in a *you're kidding me* kind of way.

"You know the beach always wears me out," I try reasoning, though it comes out apathetic at best. "All the salt and sand and sun is draining after a while. I need some time to recuperate."

His eyes continue raking over my face, a clear attempt to read between the lines. "And somehow that equates to you staying here instead of coming back to Chicago with us?"

I can see it in his eyes as he gazes at me; he thinks I'm pissed at him and that's why I'm staying behind. Because he made me the third wheel by inviting Holden. Or because he knows I didn't want Holden and all the other guys to join us on our annual trip in the first place and could still be holding onto a grudge.

And yeah, he'd be right about one thing. I am pissed. Except it's not him I'm pissed at.

It's myself.

I shake the thought free from my head—not willing to unpack any of that with Kason sitting beside me—and do the only thing I can think of. The only thing I seem to be doing anymore.

I lie.

"I just want to spend the rest of winter break with my family." The words taste bitter on my tongue, as deceit often does, even if it is laced with the truth. So naturally, I double down with some more. "Plus, Charlotte asked me if I'd be going to her ballet recital, and I'd have felt like a shit older brother if I didn't stay for it."

Kason stares at me, probably measuring the honesty in my words. But either he's blind to the truth, or he's deciding not to fight me on this, because he only shakes his head in concession.

"Fine, just know you're leaving me alone with a couple of idiots the rest of the way home. So if I die without you there to keep them in line, that's on you."

I muster the best smile I can and shake my head. "I'm sure you'll be fine."

I'm just not so sure I will be.

There's a moment of silence between us, and for the first time since all this crap with Holden started, I feel at ease with my best friend. The tension has started to dissolve, leaving only the comfort I've always known his presence to be, to the point where I'm about to open my mouth and offer him to spend the rest of the break here too. Stay with me and let the other six go back to Chicago. Have some time for just us, like we've done for the past two years.

But Kason blows that little idea to smithereens when he sighs and says, "Okay, well, before we head out, I do need some advice."

"Sure, man. What's up?"

"Well…" He blows out another breath and chances a glimpse my way. "It's about Holden."

My heart sinks, but I plaster on a smile anyway. "I'll remain as impartial as possible."

As if there's any remote possibility of it, to begin with.

"I think I'm starting to…"

Kason's tongue rolls against his cheek, and I can visibly see all the thoughts forming in his brain. The things he's wanting to say, but doesn't know how. Or maybe isn't ready to.

"You're starting to…" I hedge. All the while, my heart hammers in my chest, pounding like the hooves of a racehorse in the homestretch as I wait in agony for him to continue. All the while praying to any God that exists for me to be wrong about where this is going.

Please, don't say it. Please, please, don't fucking say—

"I think I'm starting to like him, maybe?"

A vise clamps around my heart so tight, it's a wonder I'm still alive and breathing. Nonetheless, I stumble through the pain and offer him the best response I can muster.

"I would have thought that was obvious, seeing as you invited him here."

Kason shakes his head. "Well, yeah. I just mean things between him and I have been going pretty slow. It's my own doing, and he's been fine with it. I think I'm ready to take a step forward now—maybe even ask for exclusivity once we take that step. But…" His eyes shift over to me, and I hate how much worry and anxiety I see in them. "I don't know, Phoe. I can't really explain it. He just makes me so nervous all the time. I feel like a bumbling fool around him, so I don't even know how to broach the subject."

I know what I want to say.

It should be easy for him to talk to the guy he likes, especially about something like this. The one he's supposed to be with will make him *more* comfortable, not less. But if either of those things come out of my mouth—no matter how true they might be—it will all feel tainted for my own personal gain.

I have to be the supportive best friend here. It's what he needs.

So despite my better judgment, I paint a picture for him with half-truths.

"Comfort will come with time and, more importantly, experience." I swallow past the knot in my throat and force out more words of reassurance. "Once things...*progress* between you a bit more, you'll become less jittery around him."

He shrugs, clearly disbelieving of my point. "It's been almost two months. You'd think I'd be able to act like less of a nervous wreck whenever he's within two feet of me." His head sinks into his hands, fingers raking through his auburn hair. "And I feel like the more I'm starting to feel comfortable, the more he's pulling away. Like, you saw it on the beach when I kissed him. He couldn't get away fast enough."

Because he's not meant for you.

But I can't say that. I can't possibly begin to explain how and why I know that, either.

So I say the only thing I can, instead.

"I'm sorry, Kase. I'm really fucking sorry."

TWENTY-ONE

Phoenix

January

The first day of the spring semester comes before I can blink. And with it, a change of schedule, a brand new set of classes, and plenty more sleepless nights of studying. But it also means my favorite time of year is finally here: baseball season.

Sure, Coach wants us in the weight room during the off-season, but starting today, we're officially adding the cages and fielding drills to the mix. It's the normalcy and peace I've been craving for months, even if it means I'm rarely home.

Though that fact is more a blessing than a curse right now, seeing as I don't have the heart to look Kason in the eye anymore.

He was asleep when I got in from Nashville last night, and I made sure to leave for my morning lifting session before he woke—still not ready to face him. Avoiding him won't work forever, though it's what's necessary until I figure out how to navigate this friendship after what I've done to betray him. Especially when he texted me a few days ago with the news that Holden had cut things off with him.

I think we're better off as friends, is what Kason relayed to me—and like the asshole I am—I told him he'd find someone twenty times more deserving of his time.

My stomach swirls as the sordid events over the past few weeks replay through my head, the memories threatening to have my breakfast make a reappearance right in the middle of this lecture hall.

I'd thought Holden ending things with Kason would make me feel a little better about everything that happened between us in St. Pete's, but I was wrong. The guilt has only grown. To the point of festering, and I might as well be eaten alive by it.

At least I don't have to see either of them anytime—

"Is this seat taken?" a familiar voice cuts through my thoughts.

My eyes sink closed, and I bite my tongue to keep a string of expletives from slipping free. All in the hopes that when they reopen, the sound of Holden's voice would only be a figment of my imagination rather than a reality.

But the illusion is rapidly shattered when he says, "Just because you close your eyes doesn't mean I'm going to disappear."

"I was hopeful," I mutter, lifting my lids to find him staring down at me only a few feet away.

He's still his sinfully good-looking self; same as he was before everything that happened in Florida. But something about the look in his eyes has changed. The mischief and playfulness have dulled, enveloped by a tinge of sadness.

A strange sight on him.

"I'm surprised you even waited to sit down," I catch myself saying as

I stare up at him, still analyzing his features. I've been learning to read the lines of his face for the past few months, though all that time of digging under his skin and messing with him isn't enough. No matter how hard I try, I still can't get a read on him.

The corner of his mouth lifts, the tiniest amount of his playfulness shining through the sorrow. "Last time I did that, I was called a douchebag."

"Wouldn't be the first time, probably won't be the last."

His grin grows, curling into a real smile now as he lets out a soft laugh. "Well, let's just say I'm trying to turn over a new leaf."

If he was trying to pique my curiosity with his statement, he succeeded. But not enough to erase the plethora of emotions swirling through me thanks to his presence, specifically when he drops his bag to the ground and sits beside me.

I glance toward the front of the room, wishing like hell to be anywhere except here. I'd rather be stuck in a room with Kason, forced to tell him every damn thing that happened in Florida, than suffer through the next fifty minutes with Holden silently sitting next to me.

All while feeling the heat radiating from his skin and smelling the muskiness of his cologne.

It's the worst form of torture.

"Why are you here, Holden?" I ask softly.

He remains quiet until my attention shifts back to him. "I'm in this class."

"I meant next to me." I raise my brow in a *c'mon now* look. "You know, when I told you I had nothing more to say to you?"

His shrug doesn't quite match his demeanor, nor the way he says, "I saw a friendly face and figured I'd sit with you."

"We aren't friends," I whisper. "And we never will be."

Not when I think about the way your ass clenches around my dick when you come every time I look at you. Or the way my stomach does more flips than a gymnast when you're around.

He huffs out some combination of a scoff and a laugh. "Glad to see you're, once again, making decisions for the both of us."

"What is that supposed to mean?"

"Forget it." His eyes flick to the front of the room. "But for the record, I didn't just sit here to talk to you. If you say we're done talking about what *didn't* happen, then we're done."

"Good."

"Good," he repeats, a little smirk on his face. "Now, you should probably shut up and pay attention."

Holden's version of *paying attention* lasts a whole twenty minutes into the lecture before either boredom or disinterest takes over. By a third of the way through, he's fully engrossed in his phone; probably scrolling through social media or texting God knows who.

Maybe even swiping on Toppr—the currently trending gay hook-up app—yet I try to not let that thought linger too long.

Whatever. It's his eligibility on the line come the fall term, not mine.

My phone vibrates in my pocket, momentarily pulling me from my silent musings to check the screen.

Unknown: You look pissy.

You've got to be kidding me.

I veer my focus over to Holden, who is still playing on his phone. There's a small likelihood it could be someone else in this class, but...

Unknown: C'mon, don't ignore me. I literally saw you read my text.

Unknown: If you're going to verbally ignore me when I'm sitting

right beside you, the least you could do is acknowledge my existence via text.

I try not to fixate on the irony, seeing as I know exactly what it's like to have the roles reversed. Plus, who knows, maybe it would serve him right if I continued ignoring him—even though I now know he has zero recollection of our night at Kappa Sig.

But I'm smart enough to realize how tenacious Holden is, and if I don't give in and text back now, he'll only keep blowing up my phone. A fact that's confirmed when I see the three bubbles pop up while I'm still staring at the screen.

Holden: Typing back isn't hard. Just tap your thumbs on the little glass screen where the letters are.

Me: You're so annoying.

Holden: You did it. Gold star for Nix.

I roll my eyes, not at all amused with his...flirting? Teasing? Torment? I can't even tell the difference anymore, and it's making the mess inside my head all the more confusing.

Me: How did you get my number?

Holden: You're not the only one good at stealing your roomie's phone.

My teeth sink into my cheek as I sigh, knowing exactly who he's talking about.

Theo.

Me: I suppose I should be flattered you'd go to all that trouble, but I'm trying to pay attention if you hadn't noticed. Unlike you. Now stop texting me.

Holden's phone vibrates in his palm a second later, and I watch his eyes move over the screen before they swing back to me.

There's a subtle arch to his brow as he gives me a *you're serious* look, and I nod.

A slight frown forms on his lips, drawing the corners down in a way that definitely shouldn't be as attractive as it is.

Jesus Christ.

I mentally slap myself, locking away those thoughts in a box with the security of Fort fucking Knox before shifting my focus back to the lecture. The last thing I need is to start thinking about his lips or mouth and all the wonderfully wicked things he can do with them.

Another ten minutes pass with no new notifications on my phone, and I'm relieved that Holden hasn't texted me back again—

My phone buzzes, and I silently curse as I flip it over to check the screen.

Holden: This silence is driving me insane.

Me: We're in a lecture. The only person talking should be Professor Fredricks.

Holden: Playing coy isn't cute anymore, Nix. You know exactly what I'm saying.

Me: I've already told you we've done enough talking.

Holden: We haven't even scratched the surface.

My blood heats as I read his text because, apparently, the head in my pants has decided his sentence is a double entendre for all the dirty things we could still do to each other.

I'm so fucking fucked.

Me: Like I said. Not happening. I've said all I have to say.

Holden: Well, that must be nice, but I haven't.

I'm in the middle of telling him *it sucks to suck* when another text pops up.

Holden: I haven't stopped thinking about you.

Goddamnit.

A knot forms in my throat as I reread the message more times than I should, before typing out a response.

Me: I see through your bullshit. Your lines aren't going to work on me.

Holden: They aren't lines when it's the truth.

My lips roll inward, forming a tight line as I process his text.

There's a huge part of me that doesn't believe a word he's saying—at least the part about him not using lines on me. This is Holden, after all. And for as tenacious as he is, he's equally smooth.

It's a deadly combination, and I can't keep allowing myself to be drawn in by him.

My phone buzzes in my hand as two more texts rapidly pop up.

Holden: Talk to me, Nix.

Holden: Please.

As if to drive the point home—to make me feel his plea instead of just reading it—he presses his knee against mine.

I feel the electric jolt of heat through both our jeans, creating an ache in my chest like I've never felt before.

I can't do this right now.

Shaking my head, both answering him and trying to hold it together long enough to pack up my things as quickly and quietly as possible.

"Nix," Holden whispers beside me as I finish zipping my bag closed and stand up. He utters it again, and even goes as far as grabbing my hand when I climb over my seat. But after finding a clear path to escape in the row behind us, the last thing I'm gonna let him do is hold me here.

I slip my wrist from his grasp with a quick yank, and within ten seconds, I'm in the empty corridor. Shouldering my bag, I set off toward the exit, a frantic need for as much space as possible between Holden and me acting as my driving force.

Except once again, I underestimate the guy and how relentlessly stubborn he is.

Which is why I know whose hand catches my elbow before hauling me through a door and into a dark room. The electricity coursing through his skin into mine was a dead giveaway the second he touched me. Instantly confirmed when the light is flicked on, illuminating the empty classroom.

Only one person makes my body react this way, and it's the very person I'm trying to evade.

"Walking out of class now, Nix? That's what it's come to?" Holden doesn't even try to hide the hurt in his voice when he adds, "That's how much you don't want to hear what I have to say?"

A growl of frustration rips from my chest as I yank my arm free from his grasp and glare into his whiskey eyes. "Give it a rest. There's nothing to talk about."

"You know we need to talk about this, or it's only going to get worse," he whispers.

The frustration evolves into anger as I move past him toward the door. "I don't fucking know anything right now other than I can't be here. I can't do this with you. So please, Holden. I'm begging you, just leave me alone!"

The plea rips from my throat in a cry—something between agonized and feral—and I think the sound alone keeps him from chasing after me this time.

Only Holden doesn't need physical contact to have a hold on me. To keep me here, once again trapped and desperate for freedom. He can stop me dead in my tracks with a simple sentence alone.

"I ended things with Kason."

I spin on him, not just angry but entirely pissed off now that this man—this exasperating, unrelenting man—is capable of twisting me into a person I don't even recognize. Into a man who would put my own selfish gain over the happiness of the one person who I care about most.

"And that's supposed to make what we did less fucked-up, right?" I snap. "We're suddenly absolved of our sins now that you're free to screw whoever you want?"

"I always was, but that's not what I'm—"

"Really? Because it sounds to me like you're ready to hop from one guy's dick to the next." I toss my arms out to my side, unleashing all the guilt and resentment from my body in vicious words. "Newsflash, Holden, we've already had sex. Twice, now. So I don't see the need for another repeat, considering you've already stopped at this stone on your path to sleeping through half the student body before graduation."

Holden doesn't so much as wince at the venom I'm spewing. Rather, he simply crosses his arms over his chest and leans back against the wall—taking all my animosity at full force.

"Honestly, I don't even know why you want to talk to me at all. You've been known as *Mr. Love 'em and Leave 'em* since freshman year, and I doubt that will change anytime soon. So really, Holden, what makes me different? Why am I *suddenly* so important to talk to when no one else ever has been before?"

My chest heaves as the final words leave my mouth, only some of the anger vanishing after my outburst.

But to his credit, Holden remains motionless and silent, simply watching me with curious eyes until I finally catch my breath.

"You planning to let me talk now?"

I honestly don't want to. God knows there are a million things I'd prefer to do, but if we get this over with now, then we never have to do it again. We can move past it, call it a mistake of the past…and be done with each other. For good, this time.

So rather than fighting it, I concede with a nod.

"About fucking time," he gripes with a shake of his head. "You really think you have this shit all figured out, don't you, Nix?"

I toss an unamused glare at him. "Stop calling me that."

"No." He pushes off the wall and walks over to me. "Because you like it when I call you that. I see it all over your face. In the same way I know you don't regret what happened between us. Kason or no Kason, it doesn't fucking matter."

Is he deluded?

"Of course it matters. You know—"

"I get he's your best friend, I do. But are you seriously planning to let his happiness dictate your own for the rest of your life?" Holden's head cocks to the side as he stares at me. "Because if you wanna talk about the paths we're both on? Then that's yours."

"Awfully bold of you to assume you're something that makes me happy."

"Is it, though?" Those golden eyes narrow on my face, studying and analyzing me the way I was him earlier. Except, from the small hint of victory there, he's having an easier time than I was.

Because—on some fucked-up level—he's right. Even if I wish he wasn't.

So rather than face it head on, I deflect.

"I don't know what you're trying to accomplish here."

His response is immediate. "I want you to give in to this, Nix. The way I know you want to."

My jaw ticks with effort, and I taste the lies on my tongue when I utter, "You're wrong."

He's asking for the one thing I can't give.

"Except I'm not." He takes another slow step toward me, closing the distance between us until I'm backed into the wall. Placing his hands on either side of my head, he cages me in like he always seems to do; close enough to touch but still so far away.

The inches feel like miles when he's in my space like this.

Breathing my air. Intoxicating me the way only he can.

"I'm not wrong," he whispers, "and we both know it."

The back of my head collides with the wall, and my eyes fall closed as a secret spills from my lips. A secret I've been trying to hang onto like it's my last thread of sanity.

Except now, it's lost in the wind.

"I don't *want* to want you."

"I know."

Eyes still closed, I shake my head. "It's not fair to Kason."

"I know. But it's not fair to you either."

"We should…" I trail off, torn between what feels right and what I *know* is. "We can be friends, but I can't do anything more. I can't do that to Kason. I just…"

I can't.

Holden shifts in front of me, and the sudden heat of his palm cupping the back of my neck sends my eyes flying open.

Only the second they do—my gaze colliding with his once again—I realize my mistake.

Because now I can't unsee the look in his eyes. The honesty and vulnerability in them is disarming.

"And I can't just be your friend, Nix. I don't know how."

His attention dips to my mouth for a moment before resting his forehead against mine. The hand curled around the back of my neck tightens, like the tiny hold on me is the only thing keeping him grounded.

"Let yourself be selfish," he murmurs, lips a breath away. "Even if it's just this once."

My fingers dig into his forearm as the war between desire and loyalty rages within me, each trying to gain the upper hand. I'm not even sure which side will prevail, only that the battle is tearing me apart from the inside out. Ripping my soul to shreds until there's nothing left.

The tip of his nose brushes over mine with a gentleness nearly capable of bringing me to my knees.

"Nix."

My name is a plea on his lips. For concession. For reprieve.

And it's then I realize I'll never be strong enough to withstand him.

So I stop trying…and I crush my mouth to his.

It's far from the first time we've kissed, and it still isn't even close to guilt-free, but it creates a sense of peace I've been craving regardless. The fury and passion in every press of his lips and sweep of his tongue work together to set my every atom and cell ablaze.

It fills me with a need like I've never felt. A desire so potent, I doubt I'll ever be satiated.

Holden shoves me back against the wall, his tongue seeking entrance as our hands search for skin-on-skin contact. His tongue slips past the seam of my lips while I roll my hips against his, eliciting an animalistic moan from him that I swallow down like a man starved.

I'm going to Hell for this.

But fuck, the road to Hell has never tasted so sweet.

TWENTY-TWO

Holden

Phoenix pinned against the wall, his hard body rocking and arching into mine as he seeks out my touch, has to be the foundation of all my recent fantasies finally coming to life. His soft moans against my lips being swallowed down, my touch creating a feral need he can no longer fight. It's everything I've been craving since that night in Florida.

Even my wildest imagination couldn't hold a candle to the real thing, though.

"We shouldn't do this here," he pants into my mouth. "We shouldn't do this at all."

I agree with him about the first point—there's a good chance someone could walk in this room at any time only to get an eyeful of two guys going at each other like animals in heat.

But the second point, we'll have to agree to disagree.

I just wish he'd stop fighting this.

"If this is wrong, then why does it feel so fucking right?" I ask, my hands slipping under his shirt. Hard, smooth skin waits for me beneath the hem, and my fingers dance across the bumps and ridges of his abs before grabbing the waistband of his jeans.

His breaths are harsh against my lips as he mutters, "Being that your morals and loyalty are questionable at best."

"Loose morals make for good stories," I remind him, my mouth moving to his throat to bite and suck at the skin there. "But contrary to what you might think of me, I'm as loyal as they come."

He shakes his head, and I'm not sure if it's in disagreement with what I said or something else. But he clearly has no intention of voicing the reasoning, because he just claws at my jeans some more and murmurs against my lips.

"Would you just stop talking and take your clothes off before I change my mind?"

"We both know changing your mind is out of the question, Nix," I murmur, licking at the seam of his lips. "We're both in far too deep for that."

The flare in his eyes as he pulls back to look at me reveals he knows it's the truth. This thing between us might not be what we expected. Hell, it might not even be what we wanted to happen, either. But there's no way we can stop it now.

His teeth sink into his lower lip before whispering, "Then strip."

I shake my head before resting it against his. "Absolutely not."

"Are you kidding—"

I cut him off with a kiss, hoping it's enough to rein in the ire. Or better yet, for him to channel it into me. Thankfully it works, his lips melting into mine as our tongues flick and roll against each other in slow, tantalizing perfection.

"I'm not kidding," I murmur into his mouth when I break away. "As much as I want you to fuck me here and now, I'd really like to prevent someone from hearing us and walking in."

"I don't care about getting caught," he pants, hips rocking forward into mine.

A soft laugh leaves me as my mouth trails over his jaw all the way to his ear. "And here I thought you said you *weren't* an exhibitionist."

He lets out a low growl at my taunt, and if his mind is anything like mine, he's thinking back to that sinful moment at the condo where I watched him fall apart from my touch.

A different room, a different locked door, but all the same risks.

Heat flares in his eyes as he swaps our positions, my back colliding with the wall as he presses his entire body against mine. I can feel him everywhere—every hard, muscled inch of his body—as he cages me in the way I love to do with him.

He doesn't stay there long, though, instead opting to take this sordid encounter a step further by dropping to his knees in front of me.

"If you're not gonna give me what I want willingly," he whispers, deft fingers working open my belt with ease, "then I'm gonna have to be forced to take it."

My jeans and boxers are shoved down just past my ass, and my God, the sight of him wrapping his hand around my cock while on his knees is nearly enough for me to come undone on the spot. But it's got nothing on the pure bliss that encompasses me when his lips wrap around the head of my cock instead.

"Oh, fuck, Nix," I groan, my head falling back against the wall as I close my eyes.

He lets out a low, appreciative hum as he takes me deeper, letting my shaft slide in and out of his mouth with ease. His tongue flicks around the crown of my cock each time he pulls back, playing with the sensitive bundle of nerves below the head before diving back in again. Taking me to the back of his throat, he lets out another hum, and it sends waves of lust zapping down my spine, straight to my balls.

I moan, my hand sinking into his soft, brown locks. "Your mouth is something straight out of heaven."

His lips tighten around my shaft, and when my eyes open to look down at him, I find the asshole *smiling* around my cock. Like a kid with a lollipop in his mouth.

Oh, hell.

He keeps working me over like that, taking me deep enough for his nose to brush my pelvis before retreating to just the head. It's slow and tortuous, but also deliciously addictive. But if there's one thing for certain, he has every intention of drawing this out. Of making me suffer in pleasure before finally allowing me release.

If he allows it.

He pops off my cock, his hand taking over where his mouth just was.

"You gonna come down my throat, baby? Because I'm dying to taste you again."

I don't miss the way he said *again,* and seeing as I can't remember this man getting on his knees before now, I can only assume he's talking about the first night we were together. The one I can't remember.

So I put a pin in that thought for later and move my hand, curling it around the back of his neck.

"Depends if you're gonna let me return the favor. Because you know I'm a tit-for-tat kinda guy."

His grin is downright devious when he leans forward, brushing his lips against the head of my cock. "Nah, I think it's my turn to have all the fun."

I think not.

He's about to dive back in, licking and sucking my dick like a popsicle all over again, when my fingers tighten in his hair and halt him from moving. And the glare he shoots my way because of it could melt ice and make the devil weep, but I don't care.

I want my hands on him. Now.

"Get up here," I snap, grabbing him by the arm and dragging him back to his feet. "If I'm coming, so are you. Now take off your fucking pants."

There's a defiant glint in his eye as he stands in front of me, and I swear, it might be the sexiest look of them all. Specifically when it's aimed at me while he slowly lowers his zipper.

"Do what you want to me, baby. Do your fucking worst."

It's clear he thinks I'll be dropping to my knees in return, but little does he know, I have very different plans.

Reaching out, I grab the collar of his shirt and reel him back to me, our mouths colliding in an addictively furious kiss. One full of pent-up lust and desire, making my toes curl as I swap our positions again. His back hits the wall behind him with a louder thud than intended, and I send up a silent prayer that no one is in the room next door. Or at least, no one who cares enough to come and check.

My hand slips between us, and I quickly shove his pants down past his ass—just enough to pull his cock free. It's hard and swollen, the red, angry tip already glistening with precum that makes me want to change my mind and drop to my knees. But I shove the thought away and press into him so our dicks perfectly align.

I spit in my palm a couple times before wrapping my fist around both our lengths and giving us a nice, slow tug.

Phoenix's eyes roll back in his head before he lets out a low groan, the sound going straight to my already aching cock. His hands skate up my back to my shoulders while I work us over, and from the way they grip my deltoids tightly, he's barely keeping it together already.

I stroke us from root to tip, rolling my fist over our heads and drawing out more precum to coat our shafts. His hips arch into my touch, seeking more of the friction I'm providing.

"Fuck, baby," he rasps, those dark brown eyes now black with lust. "Don't stop."

I have no intention of stopping until we reach that peaceful oblivion and are both wrung dry of cum, barely able to stand, let alone walk out of here.

My tongue licks a path up his throat from his collarbone to his jaw, and a groan rumbles deep in his chest. His hands grip me tighter, like he's holding on for dear life when I want him to let go. To be taken over by pleasure, only to be lost to the world.

To anything except me and him and this and us.

I pick up speed, my hand moving quickly over our shafts now. The bump and grind of our heads creates the perfect kind of friction, and it's got my cock twitching in my palm. From the soft groans and precum seeping from his slit, he's feeling the same way.

"You're so fucking perfect," I murmur in reverence, loving every movement and sound he makes.

My lips brush against the skin of his throat before placing a kiss to his pulse point. I keep working them over his heated flesh, making my way toward his mouth as his hips start rolling in time with my hand.

A moan drags from his throat when my mouth skims over his, not in a kiss but in a whisper of a caress. One as seductive as it is taunting.

"Kiss me," he pants, but rather than waiting for me to do it, he grabs the back of my neck and draws my mouth to his.

His tongue spears between my lips, taking what he wants as I push us closer and closer to the impending bliss. He must be close too, because he starts thrusting up into my palm, and each one drives me closer to the edge of insanity.

Release is right there for the taking; I can feel it all the way down to my toes. And when his teeth sink into my lower lip, tugging at it to the point of near pain, I fall off the cliff into ecstasy with a low moan.

Cum spills from my cock, the liquid coating my fingers and spreading down our lengths as I continue jacking them together. I need him there with me, though. I want him thrown over the cliff into freefall right beside me.

"Fuck, Nix," I pant as I shuttle my fist over us faster. "Come. Give it to me."

As if my words alone were enough to push him over the edge, Phoenix's cock pulses against mine and his release spurts free. It drips down our shafts, mixing with mine as I continue working him through his climax. His teeth sink into his lower lips as he tries to stay quiet, but the moans and pants are too much for me to withstand, so I haul him closer and seal my mouth over his.

I swallow down those little sounds, taking them for myself. After all, they belong to me.

He belongs to me.

His grip on my shoulder lessens before his arm falls to his side, but the one wrapped around my neck remains as he takes our kiss from frantic to languid. Every soft, slow sweep of his lips on mine has my heart racing faster than my orgasm slamming into me at full force.

"Holy shit," he murmurs as we both come down from the high of our climax. But when a smile forms on his lips while they brush mine, the same fluttering feeling hits me all over again.

Everything about this guy turns me inside out before twisting me in knots.

I release our cocks and pull my shirt over my head to use the fabric as a cum cloth. Not exactly ideal, though it's the quickest, easiest option to get us cleaned up. We've already chanced this encounter enough, and as much as I'd like to curl up in a cum-soaked heap on the ground, the likelihood of us getting caught here with our pants literally down only gets higher the longer we stay.

Phoenix's eyes never leave me as we right ourselves, and once he's completely redressed, he digs through his bag until he pulls out a Leighton Baseball hoodie.

"Here," he says, holding it out for me to take.

My throat constricts as I shrug into it, becoming enveloped in his scent, and God, if it doesn't do something strange to my heart. It feels like he has his fist wrapped around it, and every time I catch sight of a new or innocent piece of him, he squeezes it a little harder. Claims it a little bit more.

And that's how I know I'm well and truly fucked here.

But not as much as when his eyes slide over my body while wearing his hoodie, before he cups the back of my head and draws me in for another kiss. One that's not remotely sexual or seductive, just a simple press of his lips to mine. Soft, sweet, and painstakingly slow.

Correction: now, I'm fucked.

His brown eyes bore into mine when he breaks away, and when his fingertips scrape against my skull, I have to fight the urge to lean into his touch.

"You still wanna talk? Now's the chance."

"*Now?*" I ask, my brow lifting in surprise.

"No time like the present," he counters. "Or did you say everything you had to when you cornered me in here?"

I have so much more to say, it's not even funny. And on top of that, a mountain of questions that only pile higher every time the two of us are alone. Or when we end up naked and coming.

However, the last thing I want is to ruin this moment by pissing him off. Or worse, sending him running for the hills, only to avoid me for weeks on end all over again.

"What does this mean?" I whisper, my nose brushing against his. "Because this is all new to me, Nix, and I have no idea what I'm doing. I don't know…"

"I don't know, either." He presses his forehead to mine. "I just know I don't do casual, and I don't share. I'm not built for it. So if you can't do that, then—"

"Done."

A soft chuckle escapes him. "Do you even know what that means?"

"I think I have a pretty good idea."

His forehead rolls against mine when he nods, finally accepting whatever this is between us as something he can no longer fight. "We can't tell anyone. No one will understand. Especially Kason."

"Okay." At this point, I'll agree to whatever terms he lays out for me without question. "Whatever you want, as long as that happens again really fucking soon."

"You could've had even more, but you said no."

"There's always time for round two if you come over after practice," I remind him.

He chuckles again as his fingers scrape and rake through my hair some more. "God, I really am going to Hell for this."

My mouth curls into a grin against his lips. "That's okay. I'll meet you there."

TWENTY-THREE

Holden

Only a couple of weeks have passed since the start of the new semester, and Phoenix has already been buried alive beneath a mountain of classwork on top of his practice schedule. A fate I'd never wish on my worst enemy. Which, funny enough, Phoenix used to be.

The only positive thing coming out of this is it gives me a reason to crash his cram sessions; meaning I get to spend more time with him, all under the guise of doing my own work. And it definitely is a guise, seeing as the only thing I can focus on studying is the way his teeth sink into his lower lip when he takes notes. I'd love to bite it for him, if he wasn't so intent on actually using our time in one of the library's study pods for actual work rather than other much more fun activities—

"You're staring."

I smile. "You're distracting."

His attention falters and he peers up at me, brows furrowed in confusion. *"How?"*

Before thinking better of it, I reach over and trace my thumb over the little swollen patch of his lip, the brush of his skin electric beneath my touch.

"I can't think when you bite your lip like that."

Heat flares in his eyes, but he sits back in his chair, forcing my touch to fall away. "You're the horniest person I know."

"Guilty as charged." A smirk lifts my lips. "Don't try acting like you don't enjoy it, though."

As if to prove his point and my own, I slip my hand beneath the table and trace a daring path up his jean-clad inner thigh. And just like I thought, his lips twitch before rolling inward, only parting again when my fingers graze his cock through the denim.

He groans before catching my wrist, eyes as dark as a starless night when he stares at me.

"You're trouble," he whispers, voice gruff and full of lust.

"The best kind."

His teeth scrape over his bottom lip in a move far sexier than it should be, especially if he's asking me to keep my hands to myself. "Sometimes I'm not too sure about that."

"Eyes and mouth, Nix."

Some mixture of a scoff and a laugh leaves him, and he lowers his gaze back to the book while shaking his head.

We've been careful ever since that day in the empty classroom, ensuring to keep any and all hook-ups behind closed, locked, *private* doors. If we're keeping this a secret the way Phoenix wants—at least from Kason—then having someone walk in on us is pretty much the worst thing that could happen.

After all, people talk, and word spreads fast. Even at a college Leighton's size.

But moments like this? When we're alone and I make the mistake of touching him, or he catches me staring? Fuck, they make it hard to remember why we're supposed to behave.

"Stop. Staring," he says, his tone flat and direct while his eyes stay locked on his notebook as he continues writing.

"Stop. Being. Sexy."

"Kinda something I can't control, considering I'm not even trying," he retorts.

"Mmm, yeah, you're right. This is one of those *maybe he's born with it* moments."

His gaze lifts from his notebook again. Slower this time, before he cocks his head and blinks at me. "Did you just *Maybelline* me?"

My lips lift in a grin. "Maybe."

"You're ridiculous, you know that?"

I hold my hands out to my sides in a *what can you do* shrug. "Hey, at least I'm entertaining. There's nothing worse than a boring study partner."

"Actually, there's nothing worse than a partner who just doesn't study."

Touché, Nixy.

I don't have a rebuttal, so I just laugh and go back to reading about the fall of the Qing Dynasty. But every time I look up, there's Phoenix with his teeth in his lip all over again. I swear, he's doing it on purpose now, but...fuck.

"Keep biting your lip, and I'm gonna bite it for you," I warn him.

From the little smirk that forms as he releases it, he's definitely doing it on purpose now. One of the many ways he drives me crazy.

Over the past few weeks, I've discovered this chemistry between us is indescribable. It's unlike anything I've ever felt, and it makes me wonder if it was similar the first time we hooked up. The night, no matter how many times I ask, I still know nothing about.

At this point, it's become a game to him. So while I know him telling me what happened—in every glorious, explicit detail—won't bring back my memories, part of me still wants to know.

But then again, maybe what happened isn't the question I should be asking.

I watch him as he's writing dates for something, and then the words fall from my lips before I realize it.

"Why didn't you tell me about the night at Kappa Sig sooner?"

Phoenix's pen pauses on the paper as he looks up at me. His eyes search mine momentarily, his face taking on an indecipherable expression that quickly turns to something like…shame? Guilt, maybe?

"I didn't know you were so drunk that you wouldn't remember," he says, casting his eyes down again. "It wasn't until you brought it up at the bar in St. Pete's that I realized it. Up until then, I just thought you were an asshole and wanted to pretend we'd never slept together. Or it was so unmemorable, you…"

He doesn't need to finish his sentence. I have a pretty clear idea of where it was heading.

So unmemorable, I didn't realize he was the person I'd slept with.

An ache emerges in my chest from an onslaught of emotion—one I've been feeling a lot more lately when it comes to him.

Regret.

Not for sleeping with him—but for ever making him feel like that. As if he could ever be unmemorable or lackluster or anything other than fucking amazing.

I shake my head vehemently, rejecting the idea that could ever be the case.

"I didn't remember. I still don't."

"I know, I believe you. The constant badgering about the details kinda gave it away." He offers a wry smile before his expression sobers a bit. "But at the time, I wasn't about to give you the satisfaction of knowing I was thinking about it. If you were hell-bent on acting like you'd never met me or it never happened, then I was too."

"Spiteful," I point out, with a smirk. "How very on-brand of you."

He lets out a soft laugh and shakes his head. "You definitely brought out the worst in me at some points."

I don't miss him saying it in past tense, and it sprouts something within me. Something resembling hope. Like maybe he and I are done with that part of our story, and now we can focus on bringing out the best instead.

I reach my hand over the table and grab his. "Nix, about that night—"

He shakes his head. "You don't have to explain. It's fine."

"I do, though." I glance down to where my fingers trace over his knuckles, working up the courage I need to give him this piece of me. It's only when his hand shifts to lace his fingers with mine that I find the words. "The night of the finals week party was the anniversary of my mom and dad's death."

Phoenix's fingers tighten around mine imperceptibly as he lets out a soft curse. "Shit, Hold. I—"

I wave him off. "You don't have to apologize. Seriously. It's been...God, almost six years now. I should honestly be a lot more adjusted than I am."

"You're doing the best you can." His thumb rubs the back of my hand in soft, soothing motions, and I sink into the familiarity of his touch. Even if it's just that singular spot, it's the kind of grounding pressure I've been missing for years.

"Yeah," I whisper, my voice coming out on shards of glass.

Looking up at him, I find sympathy in his eyes as he watches me. But as I look closer, I realize it isn't the kind I hate, the kind filled with pity. It feels different, yet I don't know why.

"I haven't told many people this, but…my parents who died weren't my birth parents."

His brow arches imperceptibly, and it's like something clicks together in his brain when he murmurs, "You're adopted."

I swallow roughly and nod. "Yeah, they adopted me from birth." My focus shifts over to the door of the room, finding it easier to tell him this without looking at him. "I guess my birth mom was a teen girl who didn't even know who my father was. And the couple who adopted me—my parents—couldn't have kids of their own, and by some divine intervention, they found my mother a few months before I was born."

Phoenix's hand squeezes mine, and I focus on his thumb still circling over the back of my hand before continuing.

"My parents were never secretive about my being adopted. I've known for as long as I can remember, and they always answered any questions I had about my bio mom. They even offered to contact her so I could meet her, if that was what I wanted. But to me, *they* were my parents. I didn't know anything else, and even though I had my curiosities, I didn't feel like I was missing anything by not knowing her."

"Have you thought about reaching out to your birth mom since they passed?"

"I can't," I whisper. "She died when I was twelve from a drug overdose."

Pained doesn't even begin to describe Phoenix's expression when I finally glimpse at him. But again, it's not in sympathy. It's like he's feeling all the emotions I am. Like he's taking them for himself, so I don't have to carry the burden alone.

He licks his lips and exhales a heavy sigh. "I know you don't want apologies, but I'm sorry you no longer have them. All of them. I know it can't have been easy to go through all that loss."

My throat constricts, and I nod. "At least I had Gran. But no matter how glad I am to have her, it's not the same, you know?"

A sad smile curves the corner of his mouth. "I get it."

Emotion lodges itself deeper in my throat, and I let out a rough laugh. "She'd like you, though, with how you're always putting me in my place and giving me shit."

"Someone has to do it."

I'm starting to realize there's no one else I'd rather have doing it—only him.

"I'm not telling you this to make excuses for how I acted that night. I'm well aware I'm an adult and can only blame my decisions on myself. But you deserve to know why I wasn't entirely myself. So if I did or said anything to make you hate me—"

"You didn't. And I'm sorry for not—"

I shake my head, cutting him off before he can get the rest of the apology out. "Water under the bridge." The corner of my mouth lifts, and I raise a brow. "Unless you want to fill me in on the details. That I wouldn't mind rehashing."

His head drops, and he lets out a low chuckle before looking back up at me. "You're relentless."

"It's one of my more endearing qualities."

"Says who?"

"I dunno. Someone, I'm sure." Resting my chin in my free hand, I gaze at him expectantly. "So, you gonna finally spill the tea?"

His lips twitch, and I can tell he's trying not to laugh. "Maybe another time. After you actually do some studying for a change."

"Studying is for the weak," I tell him, and this time, he can't control the laugh from slipping free.

"How do you still have eligibility?"

"You really wanna know?"

He shoots me a dubious look. "Please tell me you don't pay someone to do your work for you, because that's illegal as shit."

I squint, my lips rolling in a line as I let out a low hum. "Pretty sure it's just frowned upon."

"Oh, my God," he says with a shake of the head. "And now you've just made me complicit by telling me."

"Always expecting the worst in me," I say with a playful scoff. "I don't actually pay anyone. I have a photographic memory."

Phoenix blinks at me, waiting for the punchline. But when none comes, his eyebrows shoot to his forehead. "You're shitting me."

"Not at all."

He gapes at me ridiculously—literally mouth ajar—and I reach over and snap it closed playfully. But all light-heartedness vanishes quickly, and I realize touching his face is my first mistake. An epiphany made a tad too late to be helpful.

My skin flares, breaking out with heat where it brushed against his, causing me to reel my arm back to my side of the table. Only the damage is done, and now I can only think about touching more of him. Dragging him in for a kiss and devouring his mouth until we're forced to come up for air. And if we're feeling frisky, maybe even make damn good use of the soundproofing walls in these pods.

From the intensity crackling between us as we lock eyes, I'm pretty sure he's thinking along similar lines.

"I, uhh…" He clears his throat and breaks eye contact in favor of the textbook in front of him, "think we should get back to work."

Studying doesn't last more than another twenty minutes, though not for lack of trying on Phoenix's part. It's the sexual tension filling the air of the tiny room with an electric charge set to ignite with a single look. Staying in there any longer would have only ended with the two of us naked and going at each other, so it was probably for the best anyway.

I'm amazed when he doesn't say anything as I fall in step beside him, choosing to walk with him to practice rather than hop in my Jeep parked outside the library. Although at this point, I'll take any spare minute I can with him, especially if it means tossing some snark back and forth.

Or better yet, stealing a kiss or two.

I might even enjoy the comfortable silence stretching between us as we walk side by side the most. Just being in his presence has this strange sort of calming effect on me. One I haven't felt with anyone except my parents, honestly. And my Gran.

Our gazes collide every once in a while as we cross campus—more me catching him looking my way—and I smirk.

"Now who's the one staring?"

I expect him to tell me to fuck off or shoot some variation of snark my way, but instead, he just sinks his teeth into his goddamn lower lip. Not in the sexy way he was in the study pod earlier. More in a nervous fashion, like he's trying to keep errant thoughts from spilling free.

"What's up?" I ask, canting my head to the side. "You look like you've got something eating away in that mind of yours."

He nods, gnawing on his lips a bit more before asking, "I have a question to ask you, but I know I might not want the answer to it."

I frown a little, wondering where the hell he could be going with this. "Okay."

"I know it's none of my business. I promise, I do, so you can tell me to—"

"Spit it out, Nix."

"You and Kason didn't..."

"Sleep together?" I finish for him, brow arched. "No, we didn't. But I have a feeling you already had that bit of information from Kason, so what are you really asking?"

"I..." He blows out a breath. "I guess I want to know why."

I reach out and grab his arm, halting him in his tracks before pulling him away from the doors to the baseball team's practice facility. "I would've thought you'd be happy to know I stayed true to my word."

"Your word?"

A sharp laugh leaves me. Of course, he'd want me to spell it out for him. "You told me you didn't think I could go without sleeping with him, so I didn't."

Confusion mars his features, drawing his lips down in a frown. "Really? That's why?"

"Why do you look upset?" I ask with a laugh. "Are you disappointed I was able to overcome my man-whore ways and behave?"

"No, I'm just surprised. I would've thought with you two sharing a room down in St. Pete's and..." He trails off and shakes his head before rolling his shoulders. "I just thought you would've. If not sex, then *something*."

"Nope," I tell him, stepping closer. "I might be a slut, but I respect boundaries. And I wasn't just taking things slow because you didn't think I could—even though my desperation to prove you wrong was one helluva driving force. Kason set a pace from the beginning, and I was fine with following it. Besides, I was being honest when I said things with us weren't exclusive. It was just a..." I pause for a second, searching for the right word.

"A situationship?"

"I think so, yeah. We were friends who were interested in each other but not truly acting on it. And I think that's because we both knew it wouldn't have worked out anyway."

Phoenix looks away, his mouth drawn in a tight line. The same expression someone has when they know something and are caught between spilling the beans and keeping it to themselves.

"What aren't you saying?"

"He told me he was developing feelings for you."

I frown, not expecting this turn of events. "When?"

"The morning you left Nashville to come home."

"I ended things that night when we got back."

"Yeah, I know. He texted to tell me," he murmurs. "And the guilt has been eating me alive ever since."

I'd have to be downright stupid to not know this thing between us has been wearing on him. Which is why I'm more than happy to tell Kason what's going on, even with the new knowledge of his developing feelings.

Still, I know if I push for that before Phoenix is ready, I could very well lose him. Which isn't a chance I'm willing to take.

"It's not like I planned this," I whisper, my fingers tracing the lines in his forehead, desperately wanting to smooth the worry away. "But there's something about you that I can't stay away from. Something I just can't…" Words escape me, and I shake my head. "It doesn't mean I wanted to hurt him, though."

Phoenix gives me a sad smile before whispering, "Did you have feelings for him at all?"

I roll my lips inward for a second, giving myself a moment to think. The last thing I want is Phoenix feeling more guilty because of *my* actions.

"I did, just not the way you're asking about. As a person and teammate? Of course, Kason's a great guy, and I care about him. And yeah, I'd have to be blind not to think Kason's attractive." I pause, continuing to measure my words carefully. "But it didn't take a rocket scientist to figure out that's all I was chasing with him. Attraction. He just didn't light me on fire or get under my skin or make me feel like I can't breathe unless I'm near him."

I keep the words *not the way you do* off the end of that sentence, though I think we both can hear them in the silence between us.

"So you ended things with him when you realized that…and not because we'd slept together?"

"It blurred the lines for me, but it wasn't the reason why. And if he felt something, wanted more, or was ready to take another step, he never said anything about it. Not to me."

He nods, accepting this before asking, "And you were straight with him the whole time?"

"I never promise someone something I can't give." My hands shift, wrapping around the back of his neck. "I told you, I always make sure the score is known."

"Then what's the score with us?"

"You tell me, Nix," I murmur, my attention darting between his eyes and lips. "Because from our conversation in that classroom, I'm under the impression we're doing this your way. You're mine, and I'm yours, and that's the end of it."

"Glad to see you were listening."

There's a small smile lifting his mouth at the corners—equal parts innocent and sexy—and it takes everything in my power not to kiss him breathless right here outside the practice facility. But I can still see his hesitation, paired with the worry in his eyes. And my only thought circles around erasing it. Even if for a moment.

"Do you have a game on Friday?"

He shakes his head before leaning back against the wall. "Season officially starts at the end of next week."

Perfect.

I take a step away, a smile on my lips. "Good. Then I'll pick you up at five."

A line forms between his brows. "For what?"

"Our first date."

TWENTY-FOUR

Phoenix

I snap a photo of The Peach Pit's marquee sign listing Icarus Ignites as the headliner for tonight's sold-out show and send it off to my father with absolutely zero context. Then I send another for good measure, this one of the VIP pass hanging from the lanyard around my neck before looking around at the scenery.

We're at one of Chicago's oldest music venues—one I've never been to in my three years at Leighton—and it's near the heart of downtown, surrounded by massive high-rises, condos, and office buildings that dominate the skyline. Despite being a smaller venue with standing-room only, it still retains a lot of notoriety for bringing in some of the best acts to the Chicago metro area—a bit like the Opry does for country music back home. It's one of the many reasons I'm excited to finally be here.

My phone buzzes in my hand, alerting me of my father's text, and I check the screen.

Dad: Have fun. Let me know if they're any good. Might have to sign them. ;)

I let out a little laugh, seeing as he knows damn well how good these guys are. Even if their lead singer can be a tad bit problematic.

"You look like a kid in a candy store," Holden says suddenly, amusement laced in his tone.

I glance up to find him watching me from where he's leaning against the wall. He's looking sexier than should be allowed in a fitted black long-sleeve shirt—one he's bound to be dying of heatstroke in later—and a black snapback sitting backward on his head.

"What makes you say that?"

"Don't act like you weren't just snapping pics of the sign and sending them off to your dad." He glimpses at my phone, leaning toward me and pretending to look at the screen. "What'd he say, by the way? He said I did good, right?"

Pocketing my phone, I frown. "He said nothing about you, actually."

Holden narrows his eyes at me. "Only because you didn't tell him about the super awesome, ridiculously hot guy who's taking you to see one of the best up-and-coming bands in metalcore, right? Even though he and I are best friends now?"

I laugh softly at the *best friends* comment, knowing it might not be that far off.

When he wasn't entertaining Charlotte with those ridiculous photos of Francesco the Flamingo, Holden spent most of our night in Nashville last month chatting with my dad. Mainly about his job in the music biz; something Dad is more than happy to go on about for hours. And to his credit, Holden was thoroughly engaged in the entire conversation, even asking him things I never thought to ask as his own kid. Like why he started in the business or why this particular genre of music.

Not sure if that merits the title of best friend, though I could tell from the smile on my father's face, he really enjoyed talking with Holden.

I cross my arms and arch a brow. "You wanna know what he would say if I told him about the super awesome, ridiculously hot guy who took me to see Icarus Ignites for a first date?"

"What?"

"He would've said it's too bad he wasn't told ahead of time, because he could've gotten us backstage."

He rolls his eyes. "Fair enough. But I bought these tickets months ago during the artist presale, so I figured we might as well use them. Even if backstage passes would have been a lot more fun."

"Artist presale?" I ask with a laugh and a shake of my head. "You really are a closet emo, after all."

"I just have good taste in music," he says, brow lifted in a defiant way I find oddly sexy. Funny, seeing how a couple of months ago I would've only found it irritating instead.

"I don't buy it. I think you're afraid for the world to find out the golden retriever is really a black sheep."

His lips quirk up in amusement. "Black sheep? Really? I think you're projecting a bit there, Nix."

"Mmm," I hum while walking toward him. "And I think you're just wearing a mask of the popular playboy when you're really just as sad and lonely as the rest of us."

He kicks a brow up, even more amused now. "Well, if that's the case, I don't feel very sad or lonely right now."

God. I don't know what to say or think when stuff like that comes outta his mouth. But I do know it makes my stomach twist and swirl with a strange feeling I can't decipher.

As I approach, he slides his feet apart, leaving space for me to stand between his legs that I'm more than happy to occupy. My hands land on either side of his head, caging him in the way he has me so many times before. From the bright smile taking over his face as his arms wrap around my waist, he's thinking the same thing.

He links his fingers at the small of my back, holding me against him. "What the hell am I gonna do with you, hmm?"

"You know, I've been asking myself the same question for weeks now."

"Oh, yeah? Well, if you've come up with any answers, please do feel free to share them with the rest of the class."

My head dips and I whisper in his ear. "Why would I do that? You're the one with the photographic memory. Surely you can figure it out."

His soft, throaty laugh sends my heart bouncing through my chest cavity like a pinball, but not as much as the brush of his lips against my jaw.

"And you said *I* was trouble."

There's nothing I want more at this moment than to show him just how much trouble I can be. Lay one on him right here and now with countless people around us; be freely affectionate without worrying about it somehow getting back to Kason. It's more than tempting.

My phone vibrates against my thigh, and when I check the screen, I expect it to be my dad again. So when it's not, and I see the name, my stomach drops instantly.

Kason: What are you doing?

Swallowing harshly, I lift my phone between mine and Holden's body and type out the most watered-down response I can think of without lying to him.

Me: On a date.

His response is almost immediate.

Kason: Wait, since when are you dating someone?

I'm painfully aware of Holden's eyes on me while my fingers hover over the keyboard, not entirely sure what to say.

Me: It's new. A first date. Nothing serious.

My own fucked-up version of two truths and a lie.

The first two sentences aren't a lie at all. This is Holden's and my first date. And new…well, I guess it depends on what we're defining. The feelings rapidly developing for him since we got back are undeniably new.

Still, the part about it not being serious? Shit, I know deep in my gut it's a lie. Nothing about this thing with Holden feels casual anymore. In truth, it hasn't since the moment I cuffed him to his bed before we ever went to Florida.

I watch as the three little dots move while Kason types out a response, feeling a mixture of relief and shame as I read his final text.

Kason: Oh, okay. Well, have fun. Let me know if you need me to call with a fake emergency like they do in the movies. ;)

Groaning softly, I shove my phone back in my pocket before gripping Holden's waist and resting my forehead in the crook of his neck. His fingers scrape against my lower back in a soothing caress, and I feel him brush his lips over the spot above my ear.

"Nothing serious, huh?" he murmurs, and even though I hear the playfulness in his tone, I don't have it in me to look at him. Probably because I'd be forced to acknowledge just how false my statement was, and that's not something I'm ready to do out loud.

"What else am I supposed to tell him?" I whisper.

But I don't even need to ask. Just like I don't have to look at his face to know exactly what he thinks I should have told Kason.

The truth.

"I stand corrected," Holden says from beside me, knocking his shoulder against mine as we stand at the barricade between the last opener and the headlining sets.

"About?"

"*Now* you're a kid in a candy store."

I grin over at him, too high on the music to argue differently. Both of the opening acts killed their sets, and the energy radiating through the crowd as we're waiting for the headliners to take the stage is top-notch. The VIP meet and greet was also cool, despite having already met the band when they first got signed. Add in how the vibe between Holden and I is still playful and fun—even after Kason's momentary interruption—and the night has been nothing short of exhilarating.

And though it's nowhere close to over, I think this is probably the best date I've ever been on.

As if reading my mind, Holden leans in closer to murmur, "Pretty good first date, right?"

"You honestly need me to boost your ego?"

He lets out a low chuckle, the decadent sound floating over my skin like satin. "I just want to know you're having fun."

"Oh, I can assure you, I am." I lift a brow. "The question is, are you?"

"Yeah, it's been great," he responds, though it comes out a little too quickly. Then a frown forms on his lips before he adds, "Why would you think I'm not?"

I turn his way. "Because you've been antsy as shit the entire time."

An embarrassed grin takes over his face, telling me he was aware of it as well, but probably hoping I wouldn't notice. It becomes even more evident when his cheeks take on a pink tint I know isn't from the heat of all these bodies jam-packed together like sardines.

"You're about to judge me so hard for what I'm about to say," he starts, a wry smile still in place. "I normally like to be in the pit for the heavier songs."

"Black sheep," I mutter immediately.

Some mixture of a sigh and laugh leaves him, and he shakes his head. "See. Judgment."

"It's not, and even if it was, don't pretend you don't enjoy it." I tilt my head to the side, studying him. "So, why haven't you gone back there yet?"

One brow hitches up as he looks at me, his tone is laced with sarcasm when he replies, "Probably because I didn't wanna be that asshole who leaves you on the first date to go get thrown around by other dudes."

"Hey, if that's what gets you going…"

"You're right, it could be a fun form of foreplay."

A bark of laughter leaves me. "You're unbelievable."

The crowd erupts as the band members take the stage one at a time in the darkness. First is the bassist, Saint, and then the lead guitarist, Bishop, and the drummer, Rio, comes out next. I swear the anticipation is palpable; shouts and chants echo through the venue, bouncing off the walls in a chorus as we wait for the final member to take the stage.

And the second Nash Kaelin appears at the microphone at center stage, the whole place detonates all at once in a singular, feral scream.

The heavy drums and bass kick into their first song, and the crowd only gets wilder. The initial push forward from the pit presses the middle of my torso against the rail, and I instinctually grab for Holden so the bodies cramming together don't separate us.

He must have the same idea, because I don't have the chance to make contact with him before his hand is at the small of my back and fisting into my shirt.

"You're not going anywhere," he shouts in my ear, and when I glance over at him, I find a devious smile painted on his expression. One that looks a lot more devilish than any demon in the song Nash is currently screaming into the mic.

The first two songs they play showcase not only the entire band's artistry but also the vocal range Nash was seriously gifted with. From hitting high notes most opera singers would be jealous of, to letting his demonic scream rip from his chest, the man can do it all.

And he does it with ease, stepping onto the riser and showing the crowd why he was born to perform.

The band closes out their third song moments later, and the crowd goes nuts as both Nash and Saint start stripping down to thin tank tops. Miles and miles of inked skin are revealed between the two of them, and honestly, I understand the hype behind the man himself too.

"Nash Kaelin is a fucking god," I shout in Holden's ear over the roaring fans. "It's the only explanation why he can look like that and also sound the way he does."

Holden turns to speak directly into my ear, his lips brushing the shell as he says, "Is this you trying to make me jealous? By fawning over another man in front of me on our first date?"

It wasn't, actually. It's just a fact. For him to have those looks paired with his vocal abilities? There's no way he's human. And if he is, then he's also living proof that God plays favorites.

"Not at all," I say, shaking my head.

"Good, because you've gotta know as well as I do that his reputation is far, *far* worse than mine will ever be." He nips at my ear before murmuring, "And just so we're clear, Nash Kaelin might be a god amongst men, but all that means is he'd never get on his knees for you the way I do."

I smirk to myself, enjoying the hint of possessiveness in his tone. It's a different side of him I've yet to see, and I don't hate it. Not one fucking bit.

Something to keep in mind.

"It's probably just the tattoos." I peer over at him, my eyes tracking down all the clean, visible skin of his forearms. "You'd look hot with ink, too."

He lets out a sharp laugh before brushing his lips over the shell of my ear. "Your fear of heights is my fear of needles, so it's not happening in this lifetime. But we both know I look hot, regardless."

Ain't that the truth.

Bishop starts a riff into their next song—this one I recognize as one of their heaviest—and Nash hops onto the riser at center stage to watch the crowd. There's a hellish smile on his face as he scans the room before pointing out at the center and making a slow circular motion, a clear call for the pit to kick things up a notch.

He doesn't have to speak his request; the fans are already on it, growing the pit to nearly double the size it was before by the time the drums kick in and Nash hits us with a growling scream that would make Satan quake in his boots.

Holden taps me on the shoulder, and I find him pointing back toward the pit.

I smirk and nod, knowing exactly what he's saying, before holding out my hand to take anything he doesn't want to lose or break while getting tossed around. He sets his phone and keys in my palm before placing his hat backwards on my head with a wink.

"I'll be back in a bit," he shouts. Then with a press of his lips to my temple, he's off, squeezing his way between people. I watch as he bobs and weaves his way through the crowd, but the pit is back far enough from the barricade that he disappears from sight well before he hits the edge of the circle.

Even with him gone, I can still feel the heat on my skin from where his lips brushed it.

Sometimes I don't know what to do or think of the easy affection that seems to come so naturally to him. As simple as breathing. And whenever he gives it—a soft sweep of his lips and arms wrapped around my body—I feel this whole thing between us becoming more real by the second.

I feel myself falling—harder and deeper.

Shoving the thoughts away, I return my attention to the stage and let the music flood my mind and senses instead.

The band continues blasting through their setlist, sounding absolutely incredible on every song they play. I rock out with the girl next to me, singing and screaming and banging our heads along to every song without a care in the world about who might be watching.

That's the beautiful thing about the metal community. Nothing matters once the artists take the stage, because you become one with the crowd, the music, and the experience.

We're about halfway through the set when Nash hops up on the riser at the front of the stage again and squats down to talk with the crowd about their newest album charting.

"Hey, watch it!" I hear shouted behind me, and I swear I hear my name called.

No, I *definitely* hear my name called.

"Nix!" Holden shouts. I turn in time to catch his head bobbing up and down about halfway between where I am and the pit, and it's clear he's still looking for me. I raise an arm for him to find me, which he spots quickly and starts working his way back up through the crowd with ease.

That is, until he reaches a couple who give him the glare of death about three people behind me.

"I'm with him," I catch Holden say, pointing to me. "I'm just trying to get back to him."

I don't fully hear what the guy says, but from the bitchy look on his girl's face and the shake of his head, I don't think it's going well.

Damnit.

I give the few people behind me an apologetic smile before slipping between them to get back to where Holden is being held up.

"I understand," I hear Holden saying as I weave through another set of people. "And I'm sorry your girl is getting shoved around too much. It happens at shows like this. But I'm just trying to get back to my guy."

The other dude shakes his head and holds his hand out in front of him, motioning to the people crammed together like a can of sardines. "With what room? The way the pit's been moving, there's nowhere for you to go."

I curse silently as I slip past the two girls separating me from Holden and grab the lanyard around my neck.

"He was up here," I tell the guy, showing him the VIP pass that matches Holden's. "He just went back to the pit for a while."

Dude doesn't even look at Holden, just shrugs and says, "Yeah, and now he can stay back there 'til the show is over."

"C'mon, man," I try reasoning. "You see his pass. Just let him up here."

Too bad my words fall on deaf ears. Literally, because the band chooses the same moment to kick into another heavy song, and from the look Holden and I share, we know any conversation we could've had is now over.

So I do the only thing I can think of—I reach around the guy's side for Holden to grab my hand so I can pull him through. Yet, the moment my fingers latch onto Holden's, the guy breaks our hands apart with his forearm.

Even over the bass and the drums, I can hear the guy shout, "I said, stay the fuck back," directly in Holden's face, right before he shoves him in the chest.

And I see red.

The thing about venues with standing-room-only…things are bound to get rough. Rowdy, even, and sometimes that can lead to conflicts. I've seen it firsthand at shows myself, though they are often few and far between. Usually, it's just verbal—someone knocking someone else a little too hard in the pit—or a couple girls getting catty because one is too drunk or even too high to act right.

I'd be willing to bet my career in baseball that ninety-nine percent of the time, it never escalates to physical blows.

But when the jackass shoves Holden again—this time, hard enough to push him back into the girls behind him—I have no fucking problem being in the one percent.

TWENTY-FIVE

Holden

"Y ou're sure it's okay for me to come in?" I ask, glancing over at Phoenix while he unlocks the door of his and Kason's apartment. "I know you don't want him to know anything, so I can go—"

"You're fine," he says, shoving the door open into the dark living space. Light illuminates the apartment seconds later, and Phoenix turns to me. "Kason's back home for his grandad's eightieth birthday this weekend. We've got the place to ourselves."

I try not to let my mind go anywhere crazy with that knowledge, instead letting the door fall closed and locking it behind us.

Phoenix is already in the kitchen grabbing an ice pack from the freezer when I slip out of my shoes and join him.

"I'm sorry I ruined our date," I murmur before jumping up on the counter.

"You didn't, I swear," he says, flexing his left hand. "It was that asshole's fault, not yours."

"Still, if I hadn't gone in the pit…"

"Hey, it's fine. I promise." He steps between my legs while pressing the ice to his hand, and I can see him trying his best not to wince when it makes contact with his busted skin. "It's not on you when other people are dicks."

He's right, obviously. Though I still don't like ending up here—my actions being the catalyst for this outcome.

"We can always catch another show."

A small smile creeps over his face. "Yeah, but let's go backstage next time."

I laugh, shaking my head. "Yeah, probably a good idea. Don't need you throwing punches more than necessary."

When my eyes rise to find his, there's something different in his gaze as he looks at me. Something I can't quite place, despite it being right there under the surface.

My hand moves without thought, lifting to his face and brushing away an errant strand of hair flopping over his forehead. I map his expression as I do this, as if that would be enough to get inside his head and see what he's thinking.

"I really am gonna make it up to you with an equally-as-awesome second date, though."

The smile he gives me makes my heart lurch. "You're taking this seriously, I see."

Hell yeah, I am. If this thing between us isn't going to work, it's not gonna be for my lack of effort or dedication to trying. I'll do everything in my power to keep this guy exactly where I have him.

"I told you I would. You're not the only one who can be true to their word, you know," I whisper as my hand drops back to my lap. My eyes shift down to where he's holding his iced hand. "How's it feeling?"

"Like I decked someone," he mutters dryly, even though there's a small smirk still on his face that ties my stomach in knots. I'm still getting used to him looking at me like that.

With affection, rather than animosity. Like he actually...likes me.

"Understandably so," I say with a low chuckle. "Weird way for me to find out you're left-handed, though."

He blinks. "Playing an entire game of beach volleyball—where I served and hit with my left hand—didn't do that?"

"You were the one who told me to stop looking at you," I remind him.

A sigh leaves him. "Okay, fair enough."

I smirk while wrapping my fingers around his wrist to gently lift his hand. As carefully as possible, I remove the ice, noting the busted-up skin hidden beneath. "I thought bloody knuckles only happened in movies."

"Must've not landed the punch right," he says, wincing as he flexes it again in my hold.

"Oh, since you have so much experience with it, right?" I utter sarcastically, rolling my eyes for good measure. "But you definitely need to get this cleaned up."

He doesn't say anything; he just nods, bites his lip, and steps out of my space. Except something about his facial expression snags my focus, and I follow him as he heads to the bathroom down the hall.

"Wait. *Do* you have experience with punching people?" I ask, leaning against the doorframe.

Phoenix remains silent and focuses on rooting through the linen closet for a washcloth before pulling one free. Which only makes my spidey senses tingle more.

"Nix."

His eyes flash to me as he wets it in the sink. "Yeah, okay? I've been in fights before."

I'm floored by this information. Totally fucking bamboozled. Phoenix is no pacifist like Oakley claims to be, but I'd never take him for the knock-down-drag-out type, either. He seems more the type to fight with words over fists.

"Seriously? Why?"

His eyes stay fixed on the rag, wringing the excess water out before muttering, "Kason."

What?

"You've punched Kason?"

"What? No." He glances up from what he's doing, meeting my eyes in the mirror. "I punched people *for* Kason."

"We're talking about the same guy who looks like he could snap both of us like a twig?" I ask, not bothering to hide the incredulity in my tone.

Phoenix rolls his eyes, not at all amused with my antics. "All through middle school, he was actually a lot smaller than me, and that made him a target. He was still sort of new, too—having just moved to Nashville in sixth grade—and he wasn't exactly making friends. I was pretty much it, and I was the only person who'd stand up for him."

"So what changed?"

"The summer between eighth grade and freshman year, he grew four inches and bulked up overnight, making me look like a pipsqueak." He lets out a soft laugh. "Then he joined the football team after and ended up being really good at it. Between all that, no one even bothered messing with him again. At school, or at home, though he didn't spend much time around his parents by then as it was."

A wave of understanding crashes into me, and though Phoenix is clearly leaving out some details, it doesn't take a genius to fill them in on my own.

The words leave my mouth before I realize they slip free. "So you were his protector."

He rolls his lips inward and nods, not meeting my eyes. "I always have been."

I knew his more-than-overbearing nature was a big reason he never wanted Kason and I together. It was obvious from the very first time Phoenix stopped me from taking Kason home—even if there was another major reason that had nothing to do with his best friend.

Phoenix clears his throat and lifts his gaze. I can tell there's plenty more to this story of Kason and him. More truths not his to tell me, nor are they mine to ask for.

But one thing is for certain: I had no idea how deep this loyalty ran until now.

And as if reading my thoughts, he quietly adds, "I'll always protect the ones I care about. However I can."

All the oxygen might as well have been sucked out of the room as I do my best not to let my mind run rampant with ideas it has no business thinking. Like how his sentence could apply not only to Kason, but to me too. Because this is new and fun, even if it is on his terms of exclusivity. There's no reason my heart should be stumbling over the thought of Phoenix not only caring for me but caring enough to fight for me. Not yet, anyway.

So yeah, my brain should stay far, far away from those thoughts.

Yet no amount of mental fortitude is enough to stop them from sneaking through the cracks.

Licking my lips, I let out a soft laugh and attempt to defuse the emotion and tension flowing between us in an electric current. Lord knows what might happen if I don't.

"I guess I should be honored that you'd punch someone for me, then."

A half-hearted chuckle leaves him. "Yeah, you should be, considering my coach is probably gonna kill me for it."

From the looks of it, he'll be fine in a few days. I doubt his coach will even notice.

"Just don't turn into Quinton de Haas on me, okay?" I say lightly, poking fun at the hot-headed winger Oakley's been at odds with for years now.

His nose wrinkles up as he puts his hand under the running water, only to pull it out immediately when it stings. "Yeah, I've got no intention of that. I forgot how much the aftermath sucks."

Rather than letting him do the punching *and* the cleanup, I grab the cloth from his right hand before he goes back to work on the cuts. My body slides between him and the sink, and I take his hand to slowly begin dabbing away the now-dried blood, careful not to reopen the wound already starting to scab over.

He lets me work in silence, though I can feel the heat of his stare on my cheek as more and more blood wipes away from his skin and disappears down the drain as I rinse out the towel. It doesn't take more than five minutes total, but it might be one of the most intimate moments we've shared together.

Just…comfortable silence while I take care of him.

"They look small enough that you shouldn't even need bandages," I say softly once I've finished, setting the washcloth down over the faucet behind me. "But I can wrap it if you want. Just tell me where the gauze is."

He holds his hand up, clenching and unclenching his fist to check for bleeding. "It looks fine, just gonna be sore for a bit."

His attention shifts from his hand to me, and once again, I see the same emotion as earlier swirling in his dark irises. Maybe that's what possesses me to grab his hand again and lift it to my lips, brushing a feather-light kiss over each scrape and scratch. Like he's a kid all over again, and a kiss can make anything better.

His stare is red-hot on my face as I do it, eyes never once leaving me, even as I release him. And though it might be crazy, I hear his words in my head well before he actually says them aloud in his gruff whisper.

"Thank you."

Swallowing, I lower his hand back to his side despite the parts of me begging not to. Despite my body screaming to hold him tighter, closer, longer.

To never fucking let go.

"You don't have to thank me." The words come out gentle, barely more than a whisper. "I should be the one saying thank you."

"For punching someone out?" When I nod, he lets out a little scoff. "I hardly think that merits it, but you're welcome."

The consuming need to touch him roars back to life—the bone-deep urge too great to withstand anymore—and my hands trail down his back without warning. They coast over the fabric of his shirt until reaching the hemline, where they finally slip beneath the cotton and find his skin.

It's on fire beneath my fingertips.

"Well, I do." My voice is thick with lust and heightened emotion when I meet his eyes. "So, just let me thank you."

I'm not sure which of us moves first, only that our mouths collide seconds later in a kiss equal parts sensual and desperate. As seductive and provocative as it is frenzied.

My palms skate up the smooth muscles of his back while he grips the bottom of my shirt, shoving it up until we're forced to break apart so he can pull it over my head. His shirt joins mine on the floor soon after, and our lips come crashing back together.

The second they do, something inside us both ignites.

Hands grasp bare skin, our hips rocking into each other of their own accord—both of us painfully hard behind our zippers. His tongue licks at the seam of my lips in a taunting, wicked caress, leaving me no option other than to open for him. It flicks and rolls against mine, exploring my mouth slowly, all-encompassingly. Like it's the only thing in the world he wants to be doing.

Like he could spend the rest of his life doing it.

A moan breaks free when I cup his length through the denim, and I greedily drink it down. The taste of his unfiltered desire only heightens my own, adding to the feral, uncontrollable need burning between us.

Phoenix rips his mouth away and presses his forehead to mine, his breathing coming out in harsh pants. "You wanna thank me, baby?"

I nod, my forehead rolling against his. "Yeah, I do."

He smiles against my mouth before brushing another kiss over my lips. "Turn around. Hands on the counter."

My heart ratchets some more at the husky cadence of his command, and I spin in place before pressing my palms to the cool surface of the vanity. But the pounding against my ribs shows no sign of slowing as I watch him step up behind me in the mirror.

His eyes, dark with hunger and desire, meet mine before he brushes his lips across my shoulder. He works his way toward my neck at the same time his deft fingers flick open the button of my jeans and draw down the zipper. Desire ripples down my spine, following the path his mouth takes as it skims over my back until his knees hit the ground. And then his fingers hook into the waistband of my jeans, dragging them and my boxers down with him, leaving me completely naked.

Kiss after kiss is pressed to my heated skin. First on my hip, then my ass, before his teeth sink into the firm muscle. They bite the flesh there hard enough to draw a moan from my lips, and my hand reaches around to grip his hair.

"On the counter," he murmurs, his hand returning mine to the vanity.

Goddamnit.

"What if I want to touch you?" I rasp, my fingertips clawing at the counter as I try to keep them to myself.

Touching him is all I want. All I need.

It's a craving at this point. An addiction I'm desperate for a fix of.

I glance behind me to find him smiling against my skin, eyes locked on my face.

"You'll have to be patient."

It's a difficult task when one of his hands slips between my legs, heightening my anticipation to unbearable lengths. And it only gets more excruciating as his hand travels up my inner thigh, inching toward my cock at an agonizingly slow pace. Except his intention isn't to bring me pleasure. No, he's trying to kill me on the spot by removing his touch entirely.

"Oh, my God." A small bout of irritation slams into me as I turn and glare at him. "Are we playing this edging game again?"

His raspy laugh sets my nerve endings on fire when the heat of it floats over the back of my thigh. "Relax, baby. I promise, I'm not."

I track his movement as he reaches for the cabinet below and pulls out a bottle of lube.

Oh, thank fuck.

There's an amused arch to his brow as he flicks open the cap and douses his index and middle fingers in the liquid. "Are you done complaining now?"

"Not a chance until you—"

All words leave my vocabulary as his fingers slip up my crease and press against my hole. They cease to exist as he massages the tight ring of muscle, the pressure drawing my balls up with desire.

A single digit breaches me, and I gasp at the intrusion, the sound turning into a savage groan as he continues biting and nipping my cheek while kneading the other in his palm.

His soft laugh floats over my skin when more unhinged noises come from my throat at his torment. "You were saying?"

Was I saying something? I don't think I was. Then again, it's hard to think about anything other than the way he keeps swiping his finger over my prostate like a fuckboy on Tinder.

He presses another finger inside me, the extra stretch drawing a chain of expletives from my lips. "Holyshitmotherfuck."

I start pushing back into his touch, desperately seeking more of what he's giving me while his lips trail over my ass. Every sweep and brush against my skin is timed with a press against that spot inside me, and the dual sensation has me needing more.

Anything he's willing to give.

I'm aching for him in the most desperate, primal way.

"God, Nix," I groan, as he switches back to little bites and nips on my cheek instead. "Need you."

His low hum goes straight to my balls, causing goosebumps to break out across my flesh. And with a final press of his lips to my ass, he rises to stand behind me. The solid planes and muscles of his body crowd mine against the sink, and my cock pleads for attention when I feel his own nestled in my crease.

"Look in the mirror," he whispers, his hot breath coasting over my shoulder and throat.

My eyes flick up to our reflection, only for them to meet his gaze while he slips out of his jeans and underwear. It immediately takes me back to the car ride from hell, his death glares directed at me through the mirror whenever the opportunity presented itself. Nevertheless, the look in his eyes as the head of his cock slowly presses inside me is nothing like the ones he's aimed at me before.

There's no anger or irritation in them. Only reverence.

A low sigh slips past my parted lips as he slides in further, every inch of his cock filling me to the brim. Owning me, the way only he can.

I bite down on my bottom lip to keep from moaning when he bottoms out entirely, and my head drops toward the counter as I wait for my body to adjust to his intrusion.

He peppers kisses across my shoulders and upper back, his hands coasting up and down my sides as he does it. It's almost like he can't stop himself from touching me. Feeling me. Tracing every inch of available skin like he's mapping them to memory.

It doesn't take long for him to start moving. Pulling his hips back so just the tip is still lodged inside me before pushing in again with another long, slow thrust.

"Watch me fuck you, baby," he rasps between another achingly slow thrust. "Watch yourself take every inch of my cock."

My head lifts, and fuck, it's a sight to see; the two of us in the mirror while he pistons in and out of me. The lust simmering in my eyes, along with the intensity in his as his gaze meets mine. The way he bites his lip when his pelvis meets my ass or the way his mouth parts slightly when he starts picking up the pace.

It's deliciously, sinfully erotic.

"I love taking you from behind like this." His teeth sink into his lower lip as two fingers trace down my spine in a way that has goosebumps breaking out over my skin again. "Your ass is a thing of perfection as it is, but it's even better when I watch it swallow my cock."

"Is that what you did our first time? Took me from behind?"

His attention flicks up, meeting my gaze in the mirror as his fingers reach my crease. There's a slight twitch to his lips—like he's trying to keep from smiling—before his tongue swipes over his bottom lip.

"Nope. But nice try."

My pants mix with a gasp when he slides his finger in beside his cock, and I barely choke out, "A for effort, I guess."

The extra stretch sets my skin on fire, sweat breaking out along the surface as he continues slowly fucking into me with deep, measured thrusts. It makes my balls ache, my cock throb, and there's a good chance I might combust on the spot.

There's no way I'll ever tire of this.

Pushing back, I take him to the hilt over and over again. Every press and grind of our bodies together sets off fireworks inside me, only getting brighter and more explosive as his crown swipes over my prostate. The little button inside me might as well be a set charge ready to detonate, and he's coming awfully close to making that happen.

"I'm close, Nix," I groan, my teeth sinking into my lower lip. "I'm really fucking close."

"Get there for me," he manages between pants. "Fuck your fist. I wanna watch while I'm deep inside you."

Doing as he says, I grab the lube on the counter and douse myself haphazardly before I start stroking my aching cock like my life depends on it. I time it with his thrusts, rolling the head in my palm when he's fully seated inside me.

He removes his finger, and the extra space allows him to slide in with even more ease than before. Maybe even deeper, because I swear I can feel him all the way in my chest.

Or maybe that's the vise-like grip he has around my heart.

Regardless, I can't help the moans falling from my lips or the shameless way I keep pushing back onto his cock. Taking as much as he's giving. Craving the pleasure his body is providing. Nothing else matters besides that.

It's just me and him and the way he's sending us both straight to high fucking heaven.

Harsh pants and the smell of sweat and sex fill the bathroom while he pounds into me, the pace now increasing relentlessly when both of his hands grip my hips. The blunt ends of his fingertips dig into my skin, and between that and the sight of him truly coming unglued in the mirror, I find release.

"Fuck, Nix," I moan as cum floods my palm and drips to the floor. My ass squeezes around his length, bearing down on him while I jack myself faster through my orgasm.

"That's it, baby," he murmurs against my skin. "Just like that."

His hips continue snapping forward with every thrust, impaling me on his cock while he chases his own climax. It's short to follow, his head falling to my shoulder as I feel the warmth of his release fill me.

"Oh, God." His teeth bite and nip where my shoulder and neck meet—some of them hard enough to surely leave marks—but I don't care.

Let him mark me, brand me, stake his claim.

I'm already his.

I have been since the night I laid eyes on him—maybe even before then. All I know is it's been far longer than either of us realize.

His movements slow as his orgasm wanes, only to fully stop when he wraps his arms around my waist while still lodged deep inside me. My hands cover his on instinct, and together, we float back to Earth.

He presses a kiss behind my ear and nuzzles his nose against my throat before whispering, "That was…"

"Yeah," I say, letting out a breathy laugh. "That was."

With a final kiss—this one to my jaw—he pulls from my body and steps away to grab a towel to clean us up. But the sudden emptiness creates a hollow feeling in my stomach, and it's unexpected.

What the hell is he doing to me?

I watch him in the mirror, but my gaze quickly snags on my reflection instead.

A man I hardly recognize stares back at me, and the craziest part is, it's not a bad thing. Because the guy looking at me, the guy searching out Phoenix in the mirror, has changed. Has grown and evolved into someone I didn't think myself capable of being.

And it all happened because of Nix.

He returns to me a moment later, towel in hand and oblivious to the epiphanies floating through my headspace. Squatting down behind me, he starts to wipe up the mess he's made, except something stops him.

"That's one sight I'm never gonna get sick of," he murmurs, and I turn my head to find his eyes locked on the cum seeping from my ass and dripping down my leg.

The corner of my mouth lifts in a half-grin. "You're a possessive one, aren't you?"

I think he doesn't hear me at first, since his attention stays fixated on where his release coats my skin. It's only after he wipes the cum up slowly with the towel, taking great care in making sure I'm thoroughly clean, that he responds.

"I just take care of what's mine."

His gaze lifts, colliding with my own, and my stomach instantly twists into all kinds of knots. It's like he just reached into my mind and pulled out the thoughts I've yet to share aloud. Ones…I'm a little afraid to, if only because I have no idea how he'd react to them. Both with how new this is, but also because of Kason.

Roughly swallowing, I bend to grab my underwear before shoving my legs through them. Phoenix does the same, but he halts me from picking anything else up off the floor. Instead, he takes my hand in his and silently leads me out to the hall and to his bedroom.

I've only been in it the one time he stole my clothes, yet him bringing me here of his own accord somehow feels different. Like he's sharing another little piece of himself with me.

The thought tightens the vise around my heart even more.

He pulls me further into the room, the only light illuminating our path coming from the moon streaking through the window. I swallow, emotions clogging my throat as he drags me down onto the bed with him before wrapping his arms around me again. Chest to chest this time, our legs becoming a tangled web of limbs.

I do the same in return, and the heat of his body radiating straight into my skin creates a calming serenity that, if I'm not careful, I could quickly become addicted to.

Who am I kidding? I already am.

His fingers skim up and down my back as we lay there in silence, only to be broken when he whispers, "Do you have any plans for the rest of the night?"

All I can do is shake my head in response.

A sharp inhale comes from him, almost like he's steeling himself to say what he wants to next.

"I think you should stay here."

The declaration surprises me, but not as much as the realization that...I want to.

Sleepovers are—*were*—a big fucking no for me in the past. But I know I've also been craving waking up beside him since the morning I did in Florida, even if it didn't end well.

I want a do-over. I just haven't known how to ask for it.

"Really?"

His nose brushes mine when he nods. "Yeah, baby."

The organ in my chest squeezes for a moment, more emotions slamming into me at the nickname. It's not the first time he's said it—not even the first time tonight—but it's not the same when we're curled up like this.

"I don't have clothes, though," I murmur, my lips a whisper over his. "Unless you stole more and have them stashed in the back of your closet again."

His chuckle against my mouth sends my stomach into backflips. "I haven't made that a habit, sorry to say. But you've already worn my hoodie once. I don't think it'll kill you to do it again tomorrow."

"Fair enough," I whisper. "Then I'll stay."

Because I wanna be with him. As much as possible. Even if it means breaking more of my rules.

The smile I felt against my lips only grows at my agreement, yet what really does something stupid to the slab of meat in my chest is the way his hand curls around the back of my neck and he kisses me.

As if all he wanted was a yes.

As if all he wants is me.

TWENTY-SIX

Holden

February

"**Y**ou don't look like you're studying."

I glance up from where I'm lounged across my stomach on the rec room sectional in our basement, using my textbook as a pillow. A very uncomfortable one, but then again, it's not their intended use, so I can't necessarily complain.

"I am studying," I mutter, eyes tracing his long, muscled body sitting on the floor while he leans against the other half of the L-shaped couch. And then I promptly drop my head back on the smooth, cool pages.

The decadent sound of Phoenix's laugh floats over my skin like warm satin. "Last time I checked, you can't learn through osmosis. Even if you do have a photographic memory."

"Well, you should be able to."

"You do realize the sooner you read, the sooner you can take an actual nap?"

"I'm tired *now*." My head lifts and I catch his gaze. "Any guess as to whose fault that is?"

Because the blame for my state of exhaustion lies firmly in his hands. After all, he's the one who wrung not one but two orgasms out of me less than twenty minutes ago. He's lucky my brain is even functioning at this point.

Phoenix drops his pen into the spine of his own textbook, both amusement and annoyance written on his handsome face. "You only have yourself to blame, considering you wouldn't even let me set my backpack down when I got here before you were stripping my clothes off."

I sit up and glare. "You agreed we would exchange a study session for sex."

"I was thinking we'd have sex *after* studying." One of his dark brows arch before he adds, "You know, as a reward for you actually doing what you're supposed to be doing?"

I arch a brow right back, a victorious feeling spiking through my veins. "And why do you think I mauled you the second you walked through the door?"

Phoenix opens his mouth, but he must not have a rebuttal ready since only a moment goes by before he closes it again.

"Gotcha there." I shoot him a playful wink. "When are you gonna learn, you can't outwit me?"

I don't have a chance to think, let alone catch the pen he launches at my chest. It smacks me straight in the pecs, the plastic stinging on impact.

"Ow. Asshole," I say with a laugh as I rub the spot.

"Aw, poor Holden," he says dryly, sarcasm dripping from his tone. "Do you need me to kiss and rub it to make it all better?"

There's a hint of desire mixed with the playfulness in his gaze, and it makes my stomach do more cartwheels than the Leighton cheerleading squad. But I play it off and toss the pen back at him. Which he catches.

Damn.

"I'd prefer not to be used like some piece of meat."

"Seriously, you wanna go there?" He tosses the pen at me again, then reaches into his bag and throws three more. "Do I need to remind you *again* about which one of us did the jumping when I got here?"

He keeps throwing pens my way and laughing while I shield myself with my textbook from the onslaught of projectiles flying at my face. "Jesus, how many pens do you have?"

He chuckles some more when I peek out from behind the book and tosses two more. "I have a whole bag."

"Why?"

"Because assholes like you who never come to class prepared always ask to borrow one and then never give it back." Another pen smacks against the textbook. "So I have a stockpile now, and apparently it's coming in very handy for situations when you're being a dick and the uncontrollable urge to pelt you with them—"

His words cut off when I bolt straight at him from my spot on the sectional. I land half on him, half on the couch, and I quickly make a grab for his ammunition—ready to take matters into my own hands. He's quicker though, and yanks it from my grip, effectively pulling me off the couch to the ground.

After that, it becomes an all-out wrestling match, each of us getting the upper hand for half a second before the other takes control again. But he doesn't know I did a little bit of wrestling back in the day, and the second he gives me the right opening, I put him flat on his back with both his wrists in my palms. The only issue is the sudden movement has the bag—and all the pens—flying in every direction.

On instinct, I hunch down over him to cover both our faces as they all fall to the ground around us, not wanting this to literally be one of those *it's all fun and games until someone loses an eye* moments.

We're both a little breathless when I lean back enough to look down at him, his wrists still in my hold.

"Well, this is awfully familiar," I rasp through my panting. "You were saying?"

"You're crazy. Like, literally lost your mind," he says, yet the throaty chuckle has me thinking maybe he likes it that way.

"Just a little." I loosen my hold on him and roll away, landing on my back beside him. "But circling back to me jumping you...in the other way. You know you can always say no."

"Oh, sure. And I'm also the Queen of England, right?"

"Nix, I'm serious," I murmur, rolling to my side and propping up on an elbow. "Yeah, I have a high sex drive, but I'm fine. I wouldn't ever want you to feel pressured."

His head turns and he gives me a dubious look, brows arched in disbelief. "So if I told you I wanted to stop having sex, you would be fine with that?"

My brows kick up in surprise, not expecting the conversation to take this turn. "Is that...what you want?"

His eyes roll. "No, it's not. It was a hypothetical."

I let out a dramatic sigh of relief, and thankfully, he cracks a smile.

"Well, for the record, if you wanted to stop having sex, I'd respect your wishes." I pause, leaning in to whisper in his ear. "But after what happened earlier? I certainly wouldn't be happy about it."

His eyes flare with heat, clearly recalling the way we put those handcuffs he left in my room to good use; first while he took me down his throat until I couldn't think straight from wanting to touch him, and then when he fucked me mindless after sucking my brains out through my dick.

It was sexy and addictive, but it was insanely fun too, and I think that's a helluva lot more important.

I don't think I've ever laughed as much in bed as I do with him, though that's probably because we're constantly bickering and challenging each other. For good reason. It's a little tricky to keep a straight face when you're naked and arguing about who gets to suck who's dick first.

"You'd probably go find someone else to get off with in the meantime, right? Revert back to your slutty ways of one-night stands and meaningless sex?"

The words come out with all the snarkiness and sarcasm I've come to expect from him, and usually, I'd toss it right back to him in kind. But there's something in his eyes that gives him away. Like he thinks it's actually a possibility.

As if he hasn't completely flipped my entire world upside down.

"In the past, yeah. Maybe I would have. But I really hope you're starting to realize I'm true to my word," I murmur, my hand reaching out and brushing through the silken brown locks on his head. But the heaviness of the conversation is a bit too much, so I make an effort to lighten the mood. "Because, believe me, Nix, you're the only one I'm interested in getting naked with."

He laughs, another one of those genuine ones, and my heart stumbles in my chest.

"Well, that's a relief," he says, rolling over to mirror my position. "I was getting really worried there for a second."

I smirk, the sarcasm lacing his tone now back in spades.

My level of comfort around him has increased dramatically over the past few weeks, and it's showing no signs of stopping anytime soon. Even in the silence—like right now—there's a sense of calm and familiarity I've begun to crave when he's not around.

Which, truthfully, isn't all that often anymore.

My free hand reaches out on impulse, coasting up and down his arm. I feel his eyes locked on my face while my fingers dance over his skin, tracing the network of veins beneath the surface.

"Since we're on the subject of one-night stands," I murmur, focusing on the heat of his skin beneath my touch, "Was I the last person you slept with? Before Florida happened, I mean?"

"Are you gonna judge me if I say yes?"

"I definitely could since you love judging me about my sex life." A soft smile forms on my lips as I gaze at him. "But no, not at all."

"You were," he says slowly, his nose scrunching up a little before he asks, "Am I that out of practice for it to be obvious, or—"

"Absolutely not," I cut in, not daring to let him even entertain that idea. "I promise, you're not."

"Then what made you ask?"

I lift my shoulder in a shrug. "You know all about my promiscuity, so I just wanted a little insight into yours."

He lets out a long, deep sigh. "Well, I was dating this one guy for about six months last school year, but he broke things off at the end of April because he 'wasn't feeling it anymore.'" He does little air quotes around his ex's words before continuing. "Besides him, there was only you."

The revelation of being one of two people to have him this way is intoxicating, but I'm more interested in the timeline he just laid out for me.

"So it seems I wasn't the only one looking for an escape that night." My hand halts over top of his, and I lace our fingers together.

"You'd be right," he whispers, his thumb brushing over the back of mine before he meets my eyes. "And before you even ask, no, I'm not gonna tell you what happened."

Damn.

"Are you ever gonna tell me?"

"Maybe one day. In the far-off, distant future."

I shove him away from me and laugh. "Jackass."

"Gotta keep you interested somehow," he says with a sexy little wink.

"Oh, you've already got that covered, Nix." A smirk curls the corner of my mouth. "So unless your relationship with fuck-knuckles started the same way, I was your first one-night stand?"

He nods, his teeth sinking into his lower lip. "First and only."

Somehow, that fact fills me with pride. No matter how misplaced it might be.

"Well, you're the only blackout hook-up I've had, so I guess we both had firsts together that night."

"You're telling me you've never blacked out with anyone besides me?" He raises a disbelieving brow. "Seriously? With how much you sleep around?"

"There's that judgy tone again," I say with a laugh. "You might be worse than Oakley. And for the record, I'm not nearly as bad as everyone makes me out to be. I just have rules."

Had, a little voice reminds me. *You* had *rules.*

They don't really exist anymore, seeing as Phoenix came into my life and blew every single one of them outta the water. He can't even be classified as a one-night stand anymore unless we're talking about how epically it failed to be just a single night.

Or how I failed to remember it.

"I just don't get it." He disengages his fingers from mine and takes his turn mapping the veins in my arm. "So it's not so much judgment as not understanding."

"There's not a whole lot to misinterpret about the hook-up culture, Nix," I point out.

"I just don't get *how* you can have all these meaningless flings. My brain can't comprehend how it's enjoyable for you, sleeping with random people at any given time." His attention flicks up to my face briefly before he continues. "Wouldn't you rather sleep with the same person a ton, especially if you have good chemistry with them? Quality over quantity kinda thing?"

"Spoken like a true serial monogamist."

His teeth sink into his bottom lip the way it does when he's both focused and anxious. I hate knowing this situation is probably the latter.

"I'm being serious," he whispers.

"So am I." I reach up and brush my thumb over his bottom lip, pulling it free from where his teeth have captured it. "And yeah, quality over quantity is a very valid point. It's one of the many, *many* reasons why I agreed to do this your way. Because the way we are together…" I trail off, not having the words to describe what it's like.

It exceeds everything I've ever known before him.

"Yeah, I get it," he says before pressing a kiss to the pad of my thumb. "Even if I don't understand how this happened, I know what you mean."

"It's because, deep down, you like me," I tease. "You *really* like me."

"At this moment, I really fucking don't."

I hike up a brow. "Oh, if that's the case, then why did I come out of class to a duck on my driver's side handle?"

He blinks at me, the picture of innocence. "I have no idea what you're talking about. You and your little Jeep cult can do your own thing, but I want no part of it."

"Really? That's the story you wanna go with?"

"Yeah…" he says slowly.

Oh, you're so full of shit.

I shift to dig my hand into my pocket and pull out my phone. It doesn't take more than three seconds to swipe open my photos and find the image of the little duck left on my vehicle today. It's a little white duck wearing a leather vest with an orange mohawk on its head and barbed wire tattoos on each of its wings. And while it's one of the most ridiculous things I've ever seen, I'd be a bold-faced liar if I said finding it today didn't give me the biggest smile.

Flipping my phone screen to face him, I say, "You're gonna tell me some random ass person happened to have this duck on hand to put on my Jeep? And it has nothing to do with us going to see Icarus a couple weeks ago?"

Phoenix bites his lip as he looks at the screen before shrugging. "Nope. Not me. But maybe they saw Jerry and thought he needed a friend."

"Mhmm," I mutter, watching his features closely before pocketing my phone again. "I'm sure that's exactly what *they* were thinking."

"I'd bet my life on it," he simply states, but I don't miss the little twinkle in his brown irises or how they crinkle just a little more around the edges when he smiles.

It's always his eyes that give him away.

TWENTY-SEVEN

Phoenix

If there was a photo beside the word *regret* in the dictionary, it would be of me right now; sitting on the couch in the townhouse, watching the stupid Super Bowl, all while two idiots constantly banter back and forth for the entire game.

A game well into the third quarter at this point, and I don't think they've stopped for more than five minutes.

"E-Trade always has the best commercials."

Luca looks over at Noah like he's just lost his marbles. "You're off your rocker, man. It's always Budweiser. Hands fuckin' down."

A snort leaves Noah, and he shakes his head. "Yeah, if you like to cry, maybe."

"It's called *ethos*, Noah. Not that you'd understand what it even means, seeing as you're a sociopath allergic to all human emotion."

"Aw, you noticed. How sweet of you," Noah snarks back before tossing a chip at Luca's face.

I think I'm about to lose my fucking marbles if I have to listen to this any longer.

"Oh, my God, do they ever shut up?" I mutter to Theo, who is sitting beside me on the couch.

He lets out a scoff. "I'd have thought you would know they don't after spending ten days with them in Florida."

Touché, my friend.

"Wishful thinking, I guess," I say with a sigh.

I'll admit the game itself has been somewhat entertaining up to this point, despite those two bickering like an old married couple. Nashville and New England have been going back and forth with the lead, and the wide receiver named Grady caught a bomb in the endzone to put them ahead by two points.

But the half-time show was abysmal at best, which I shouldn't be surprised about. I think the only way I'd ever be hyped is if they put some sort of metalcore band on stage—or even alternative or punk, like Fall Out Boy.

My phone vibrates in my palm, pulling my attention away from the two idiots still snapping at each other to check the incoming text. And I can't help the smirk curling my lips when I read it.

Holden: Aren't you happy I convinced you to come? This is fun.

Convince?

He must be trying to rewrite history because, from my view, it was more like kidnapping me from my apartment after blackmailing me with threats of a sex-ban if I didn't come with him.

Me: Yeah…not in the slightest. Noah and Luca are driving me to the brink of insanity. I could be at home watching porn instead. All

alone. In peaceful silence.

Holden: That does sound enticing, but football is sexier than porn, and you know it.

Instinctually, my eyes flick over to where Holden sits at the other end of the sectional. He must feel my gaze on him, because his focus slowly shifts my way.

Holden: Look at me like that again, and I'm gonna need to borrow the pillow beside you.

Me: I have no idea what you're talking about.

Holden: Mhmm. Sure, you don't.

Holden: Oh, and for the record, baseball players are hot too.

The smirk lifting my lips can't be helped as I send him a text back.

Me: If that's the case, maybe you should attend a game or two this season.

Holden: I don't know if they're THAT hot. I mean, nine whole innings and no one hits each other?

Me: All they do in hockey is hit each other, but I don't see you heading to the rink anytime soon. Not even for your best friend.

I glance up and wait for Holden to read the text, only to arch a brow at him when he looks up at me. His smile is instant, and I watch him type out his response.

Holden: You make a fair point, Nix. Care to make a deal with the devil?

Me: Tempting. What are the stakes?

Holden: A trade. I'll come to watch you play as long as you're in MY jersey next season.

Me: Awfully possessive of you. But I think those are agreeable terms.

I watch as Holden starts typing out his response, only to be distracted by Nashville rushing up the middle, the running back somehow sneaking through before barreling down the open field. The townhouse front door opens as the player sprints toward the end zone, but almost everyone here is too engrossed by the scene on the television to notice what's happening in real life.

Not me, though. I'm thoroughly aware of who just walked through the door, and it has both my heart and stomach-dropping clear out of my ass.

"Kason, no!" Noah shouts, jumping to his feet before looking at my best friend in the doorway. "You need to turn around and leave, right now."

Kason's eyes widen as he slowly takes a step back. "Why?"

"Because Nashville just scored again on that rush," Luca pipes in with a sigh. "And he seems to think Mercer, and now you, are putting bad juju on New England by being here."

Confusion is written in Kason's expression as he scans the room, only to get all the more confused when his eyes land on me. Anxiety wracks my nervous system, and I give him an awkward wave before pulling out my phone and texting Holden.

Me: I thought you said he wasn't coming?

Holden: He said he wasn't! Can't fault me for him changing his mind.

Not helpful, Holden.

I'm not so irrational to realize this isn't his fault. He was telling the truth with the information he had at the time, and there was no way he could predict Kason changing his mind and showing up with only a quarter left in the game. But it doesn't make the reality of it suck any less.

My phone buzzes in my palm when another text from Holden pops up on the screen.

Holden: You're so tense, you're giving me anxiety from all the way over there. Just relax. He's not gonna know you're here with me.

I glance up to where Holden is seated, only to find his eyes already locked on me. His brow gives a subtle arch, as if begging me to disagree with him, and I return it with a dubious *you're joking me* look.

Blowing out a silent breath, I send him my reply.

Me: He will if you keep watching me.

My phone buzzes in my palm again almost instantly, and I'm fully prepared for it to be Holden's name on the screen. Only, it's not him.

Theo: Does he know?

My eyes shift to my teammate sitting directly beside me, who quickly glances at me before looking back down at his phone.

Theo: Don't act like you didn't just enter full-blown panic mode when Kason walked through the door, Merce. I can read you better than that.

Me: Are you also reading my texts over my shoulder?

Theo: Oh, please. I don't need to. You and Holden are as subtle as a hippo in a pet store. And you forget I share a floor with him in this house. It's not hard to put the pieces together.

I blink a few times, wondering where the hell he'd ever heard that kind of saying before. But seeing as it's not the important topic of discussion, I circle back to his question.

Me: No. He doesn't, and we're trying to keep it that way.

Theo: Keeping it a secret is only going to blow up in your face...

Me: I don't know how to tell him. Not now.

I catch the subtle shake of his head beside me before his next text comes through.

Theo: I hope you know what you're doing.

My gaze lifts to find Kason and Holden chatting over in the corner. Even from here, I can see a small mixture of sadness and longing in his eyes as he watches Holden speak, and it's enough to have me slamming the rest of my drink on the spot.

Rising from the couch, I head into the kitchen for another. The beer is pretty much the only thing getting me through this shit in the first place, and with Kason here now, the alcohol is really fucking needed. I pop the cap off the bottle and take a long swig, but the icy liquid does nothing to temper the rush of anxiety running through me faster than a receiver toward the end zone.

An arm reaches under mine to grab the bottle opener I was just using, and I'm about to move out of the way when the scent of Holden's cologne wafts over me.

"Excuse me, but I need this," he says in a soft, seductive cadence that goes straight to my dick.

"Of course you do," I say, feigning annoyance despite the smile I'm desperately trying to hide. One he must pick up on in my voice, because he steps in closer to me, his chest brushing against the back of my shoulder.

"You're playing a dangerous game here," I murmur, keeping my eyes locked straight ahead.

The hand that's hidden from view of the living room traces a feather-light trail down my spine, and I fight my urge to lean into his touch.

"Don't pretend you don't like it."

I laugh softly and shake my head before stepping out of his grip. The last thing we need is to get too into our little game of back and forth with half the football team here—Kason included.

Too bad for me Holden has no intentions of letting me slip away easily. His palm wraps around my wrist, and he drags me down the hall toward the back door, just out of sight from the rest of the group. He wastes no time backing me against the door either before his lips begin a slow, seductive descent down my throat.

"You're just asking for us to get caught right now," I murmur, even as I arch my neck toward him. "Is that what you want?"

"Stop being so tempting and I wouldn't have to risk it."

"Have some self-control, and it wouldn't matter how *tempting* I am," I counter.

"I feel like we've had this conversation before." He pulls back, his brow lifting playfully. "But in case you need a reminder—"

"I'm good," I say with a laugh. Lord knows I don't need him doing something even more obscene—like dropping to his knees—here, where anyone could find us so he can prove his point.

"Thought so."

He leans his forehead against mine, and I can't help breathing him in. The scent of his cologne mixed with whatever body wash still lingers on his skin is just as potent as his presence. Intoxicating, which is why I understand what he means about being tempted.

But what just about brings me to my knees is when his nose brushes back and forth against mine in a way that simultaneously makes my stomach swirl with lust and my heart constrict with emotion.

"I'm glad you decided to come," he says softly before pulling away. His whiskey eyes lift to meet my gaze, and I can't quite place the emotion I see in them. "I know it's not exactly what you were planning, but I hope you're having *some* fun."

Besides Kason's unexpected presence and the constant bickering between Luca and Noah, it's been fine. Truly. Don't get me wrong, it'd be a bit better if it was for the World Series, but beggars can't be choosers.

"I am, I guess."

"Don't sound so enthused." He rolls his eyes. "I'd think with it being your hometown team, you'd be a little more invested than normal."

"And I'd think with you being from California, you wouldn't give two shits about who wins tonight."

"Oh, I give no shits about who wins tonight, Nix."

I blink at him. "Then why are we here?"

He cocks his head, staring at me like I've grown three heads. "It's football."

Oh, right. My bad.

I don't have the chance to respond, because a commotion breaks out in the living room before Noah starts calling out at the top of his lungs for his teammate.

"Holden, where did you go? Hurry your ass up! It's third and long, and New England only has time for one more play!"

Who knew watching football on TV required so much shouting? Or nervous pacing, from the way Noah and Luca were both bouncing and walking around the living room earlier like they're the ones playing in the damn Super Bowl.

"You're being summoned," I murmur with a grin.

"Oh, am I? I hadn't noticed." He leans in, his mouth trailing over my jaw. "I'm a bit preoccupied—"

"Holden, get *in here*!"

"I swear to God," he curses with a laugh, his forehead colliding with my shoulder.

It takes every ounce of my willpower to not wrap him in my arms and just inhale him. "Just go. He's not gonna stop until you're in there."

As if on cue, Noah shouts again.

"HOLD—"

"I'm coming!" Holden turns and shouts at his teammate.

The words leave my lips on impulse, before I can even attempt to rein them in. "Oh, are you now? Doesn't look that way to me."

"Someone's mind is in the gutter tonight." He looks back to me, a dirty grin plastered on those sinful lips. "Is it all the sexy football players you're watching on television? It's okay if you say yes. I know they're pretty irresistible."

More like the one currently pinning me against the wall.

My mouth curls up in a smirk. "It's more like what happens when I'm forced to hang around all you Neanderthals. Makes my brain revert back to the baser instincts."

He shakes his head with a soft laugh before pressing his lips to mine in the briefest kiss. Like it's natural—a habit, even, before he steps away and heads back down the hall.

I wait a few seconds before following, and the second I step out of the hall, the entire living room erupts in cheers. Shouts and hollers and even a few ass smacks are exchanged between the group, and I realize it's because the game is over.

"I take it New England won?" I ask Wyatt, who is standing in the kitchen watching this group of idiots act like…idiots.

"Yep," he says with little to no enthusiasm. "Apparently Nashville thought the QB for New England was gonna go for a Hail Mary, but he threw a short pass to one of his receivers. The same one from earlier—Grady. He caught it and ran it in for the winning touchdown." He blows out a long breath and shakes his head. "Football is fucking weird."

"Football *players* are weird," I correct him, watching them all celebrate a team that isn't even theirs. Nevertheless, I can't help smiling when I see the big grin on Holden's face.

Unfortunately, my best friend chooses the same moment to step into my view, blocking Holden from sight.

"Hey, I didn't realize you'd be here," Kason says with an awkward chuckle. "Not exactly your scene, but I would've caught a ride with you had I known."

Well, damn. The guilt sure didn't take long to join the party with his arrival.

My teeth roll over my bottom lip and I glance over to Wyatt, hoping to possibly find a way out of this conversation. But he's already slipped out of the kitchen to rejoin the rest of the group.

Shit.

"I didn't even think about it, honestly. Theo invited me over, and I figured…why not, ya know?"

Kason nods, but it's stiff and a bit jilted. I don't miss the way his attention keeps diverting over his shoulder to the living room as we stand here in awkward silence, either.

"This is gonna sound weird," he starts, still looking, "but is something going on with you and Holden?"

Panic hits me in an instant. "What? No, why would you even think that?"

"I saw you two talking a little while after I got here, which was strange enough considering the way you were at each other's throats the entire time in Florida. And with you saying you were on a date a couple of weeks ago…" He trails off, leaving me to fill in the blanks.

And I realize, this is it.

The moment of literal truth.

The one when I should finally come clean about the whole thing with Holden and let the chips fall where they may. And I want to—God, I fucking want to, because I'm sick and tired of drowning in guilt and hiding my feelings for Holden.

But even as the words form on my tongue, I'm helpless to let them slip free. Powerless to the fear of what will happen if they do, because the mere idea of losing either of them feels unbearable at this point.

"It wasn't him," I say quickly. "And as for us speaking...I guess ten days in the same house kind of makes you get over your differences."

Lie, lie, lie...like a fucking rug.

He must believe it, in any case, since he simply nods and accepts my words as the truth. However, it's the relief in his eyes that only makes the guilt churning in my gut grow to vomit-inducing, and it's then I realize two very crucial things.

Theo was right.

And I have not a damn clue of what I'm doing.

TWENTY-EIGHT

Phoenix

My mood has been shit since last week's Super Bowl party—all thanks to my inability to fess up to Kason about things with Holden—and the clouds of toxic doom around me have made no signs of lifting anytime soon. Though, there are moments when they break apart, and the sun shines through. Usually, in class, when Holden sends me a text message about something stupid that inevitably makes me smile while I'm sitting beside him.

I think my mood has even started infecting him, though. Which is exactly why I've decided to hole up in my room with my favorite episodes of *Friends,* hoping it might help a bit. And if "pivot" doesn't do the trick, I'm not really sure what will.

Or at least, that's the thought when my phone buzzes on my chest, pulling my attention away from my laptop screen.

Holden: Wydrn?

A little grin lifts my lips, having no idea what the acronym stands for.

Me: In English?

Holden: Are you eighty? I asked what you're doing right now.

I must be ancient, because I probably never would've pieced that one together.

Me: Nothing, why?

Holden: Really? You're doing absolutely nothing at all? Just staring at a blank wall?

Me: Ceiling, actually.

Holden: Pics or it didn't happen.

My smirk shifts into a full-blown grin, and I let out a little laugh. Never in my life did I think tossing banter and jabs back and forth with Holden would lift my spirits, yet here we are. The world works in funny ways sometimes.

Me: You're the definition of a man-child.

I find myself waiting and watching as the little bubble in the corner of the screen moves, indicating he's typing out his response, only to realize just how addicted I've become to talking to him. A fact that becomes all the more obvious when my stomach does a little flip after his message finally pops through, followed by a second.

Holden: So you've said before. But you can either send a photo of you clearly watching Friends on your laptop (not nothing, by the way) or come open your window and let me in.

Holden: Unless it's porn. Hard to tell from here. But if that's the case, then you do your thing, and I'll stay out here and watch.

My brows furrow as I reread the texts several times, still not entirely understanding what he's saying.

Open my—

A gentle tap at my window scares me shitless, causing me to drop my phone to the floor and jump clear off my bed. My eyes flash to the window, and sure as shit, there's Holden fucking Sykes standing on the fire escape.

Rushing over, I quickly unlock it and slide the pane of glass up and out of the way.

"What the hell are you doing?" I whisper-shout at him, a mixture of fear and adrenaline rushing through my veins like a rip current. "Are you trying to get caught?"

Holden smirks as he slides through the opening and steps into my room. "No, but I *am* rescuing you from a lame and boring night." His eyes shift over to my laptop and he frowns. "But I take it you weren't watching porn, after all."

Jesus Christ.

"Why would I need porn when I'm sleeping with you?"

A thoughtful look crosses his face before he nods. "Fair point."

He kicks off his shoes and pads over to the door before clicking the lock in place. Then he drops to my bed, making himself comfortable, and it only adds to my confusion about why he's here.

"I thought you said you were rescuing me?"

His brow arches playfully as he settles in amongst the pillows on my bed. "Yeah, I am. From having a lonely night here all by yourself when you could have a date-night-in instead."

"So you're not trying to drag me out into society right now?"

"I'm capable of being low-key too, you know. We don't need to go all *Fight Club* at a concert every date night to keep things spicy."

"There will be no spice, and you have to be quiet," I tell him with a pointed stare. "Kason's down the hall."

"Fine, then get over here," he whispers, motioning to the bed. "We're gonna Netflix and chill. But without the chill, since you insist on living up to your reputation as a human chastity belt."

I roll my lips inward to keep from laughing too loud as I cross over to the bed.

This guy.

Something about him lightens the air around me. Makes me feel like I can breathe again, even through all the shit plaguing my thoughts.

As quickly and quietly as I can, I climb in beside him and situate the laptop between us. Which Holden seemingly has a problem with since he grabs it, puts it over to his other side, and drags me toward him until my head is resting on his pec.

"So you're a cuddler, huh?" I murmur before wrapping my arm around his waist.

"Just with you," he whispers, his eyes still on the screen while he hits play. "But don't let it go to your head."

Except it does. Every time he says something sweet or even a bit corny, it sends my head straight into the clouds, at the same time vines of barbed wire wrap around my heart.

We settle in after that, silently watching a few episodes of the craziest friend group to ever grace television. His calm breathing and steady heartbeat beneath my ear ease some of the tension coiled inside me like a snake, and the deep rumble of his chuckles creates more butterflies in the pit of my stomach.

And it's being wrapped up together like this that brings the sense of peace I've been craving all week.

Holden presses a kiss to the top of my head halfway through our fourth episode before shifting his position, sliding down flat on the mattress and rolling to his side to face me.

"You're bored already?"

"A little." A small smile works its way on his lips. "But in my defense, the show is older than we are."

My mouth drops open. "It's a classic."

"Doesn't mean it's good," he murmurs, and from the way his lips quiver, he's just trying to poke fun. A feeble judgment call on his part, especially since it happens to be my favorite show of all time. But regardless, I slide down lower too and mirror his position, only for him to make my stomach somersault when he drags me straight into his chest.

My eyes sink closed, and I let the steady thud of his heart ease the rapid beating of mine.

His fingers dance up and down my spine in relaxed, soothing patterns that could very well put me to sleep if he didn't bury his nose in my hair and whisper, "Where have you been lately?"

"Gym, practice, class—"

"Not what I meant, Nix," he murmurs. His hand reaches up and he rakes his fingers gently through my hair a few times before lightly tapping the index one against my temple. "I mean in here."

My throat constricts, the question taking me more off guard than anything. He never fails to surprise me with how much he notices. All the little ticks or quirks or comments that no one else ever picks up on, he does.

But it also makes it impossible to hide things from him, because he just sees right through it.

So I don't bother trying anymore.

"Lost," I whisper, pressing my forehead against his chest. "Really fucking lost."

His hand traces up my back until it wraps around the nape of my neck, and I'm met with his imploring gaze capable of staring straight into my soul. There's tenderness in his gaze—something I've seen a lot more of lately.

And I recognize it, since it's the same way I've caught myself looking at him too.

"I can help you find your way out, but you have to let me in first."

If only it were that easy.

I press my forehead harder against his chest, as if the act will somehow allow me to burrow inside him for the peace and safety I'm desperately seeking.

"It's Kason," I whisper before attempting to swallow down the knot lodged in my throat. "Lying to him has created this guilt that's gnawing away at me...like a rabid animal or something. And I'm fighting and trying to keep it at bay, but it's exhausting."

I don't think I fully grasped the truth in that statement until I finally spoke it aloud.

I'm exhausted from keeping up with all the secrets without tacking all these lies on as well. Ones only growing in size as time goes on. It's draining—suffocating—looking into the eyes of someone you care about and knowing you're hurting them. Even if they aren't aware of it themselves.

Holden's voice is soft and gentle when he murmurs, "Then you need to tell him, Nix. For your own peace of mind."

The idea alone makes me want to vomit. For so many reasons, but I choose to speak on the one at the forefront of my thoughts.

"Hurting him just to ease my own guilty conscience isn't high on my list of priorities."

"Well, it should be."

My eyes widen in shock, and I pull back to look at him. "You can't be serious."

"Except I am." He exhales in a long, deep sigh before shaking his head. "I know I'm probably going to sound like an asshole for saying this, but fighting for your own happiness should always be your priority."

My teeth bite into my cheek, hating how wrong and selfish it feels to even consider that an option.

He skims my face, and it's moments like this when I wonder if he's got laser vision capable of burning right through my skull until he reaches my brain. It's the only explanation for why he seems to pluck thoughts from my head at the drop of a hat.

"You're allowed to be a little selfish sometimes, baby. It doesn't make you a bad person."

I'm not sure if it's his words or just the one in particular that makes my throat suddenly clog with emotion. All I know is I might as well be choking on it when I go to speak.

"Then why does it feel that way?"

"Because he's your best friend, and no one likes hurting someone they care about. Yet from what I can tell, you've lived through this whole friendship putting Kason first, and that's not normal. Sure, doing what you can for him to be happy isn't necessarily a flaw, but it is when it's completely at odds with what you want for yourself."

Holden's hand moves up to cup the side of my face, and I subconsciously lean into his touch, letting the heat of his skin against mine soothe the anxiety roaring inside me as he continues to speak.

"Kason told me you ended up coming to Leighton instead of heading out west for school because he asked you to. Was that the only reason you did?"

Yes.

"I mean, it's closer to home," I murmur.

The gentle curve of his lips tells me he knows I'm full of shit. "Okay, then what about you agreeing to let not just me, but also Harrison, Luca, and Noah come down to Florida over break? I can guarantee it only happened because you didn't want to be the bad guy or let Kason down, even if it wasn't what you wanted."

Well, shit. He's got me on that one. "Okay, maybe I do things for him, but I don't see how it has anything to do—"

"Because you're living for him and *his* happiness, Nix. Those might be only a few examples, but knowing you, I'd almost guarantee there are thousands more. And I want to know, when will you start choosing yourself?" There's a pleading look on his face, like watching me go through this pains him just as much as it does me. "You're so sure you'll regret hurting him by saying something, when in the long run, you'll only have regrets when you're not living for yourself."

"I'm all he has, Holden. His family life is…" I trail off, shaking my head. It's not my place to tell Holden the things that happened behind closed doors in Kason's childhood. The trauma rooted in his upbringing. "My parents didn't legally adopt him or anything, but they might as well have with how much he was with us to escape the horrors that awaited him at home."

Understanding swirls in his whiskey eyes as he murmurs, "The kids at school weren't the only ones to…"

He can't even finish the sentence, and no part of me wants him to. Not when the bruises and cuts I witnessed over the years are burned into my retinas for the rest of my life.

I nod, doing my best to ignore the gut-wrenching feeling swirling inside me. "He became my family the moment he walked into my life. So I don't know how not to feel guilty for being just another person to hurt him."

"By telling yourself the facts of how this all happened. From where I'm standing, the only thing that we've done wrong here is keeping this and our history a secret from him." His eyes are warm, filled with compassion, as his skin swipes over mine. "You know just as well as I do that Kason and I were never serious. Not down in Florida, and definitely not before then. No rules, no exclusivity, nothing. So even if he did start getting more of a crush and feeling things I wasn't on that trip, it's not going to devastate him the way you're thinking. He'll be mad, sure, but he'll forgive you."

My teeth scrape over my bottom lip, worrying the flesh before whispering, "And what if you're wrong?"

"I don't think I am, Nix. Not when it comes to this." His thumb shifts over, pulling my lip free before he presses a kiss there instead. It's soft and gentle and makes the vise he's placed around my heart clamp even tighter, but not nearly as much as the way he brushes his nose along mine.

Silence falls over us while his hand gently sweeps up and down my back. The only sound comes from the episode still streaming from my laptop, but eventually, Holden interrupts Monica's dialogue with his own. "I hope you know I'm not trying to pressure you into this, but I want you to know it's an option. We can take baby steps toward it in the meantime, and when you're ready, we can sit him down and tell him everything. I can even do the talking, if that makes it easier. Anything to get this weight off your chest."

I can tell from his tone, he means it. Hell, I bet he'd be more than happy to go into Kason's room right now, hand in hand, and come clean if it finally eased the guilt warring within me. After all, keeping this a secret wasn't Holden's idea. *I'm* the one who insisted on this remaining quiet—at least where Kason is concerned.

And I want to tell Kason. No part of me likes the sneaking around, the secrets, and the God-awful churning in my gut when I think about how much of a hypocrite this makes me.

But I just can't bring myself to look him dead in the eye and say the words, knowing they could very well be the end of our friendship.

"I don't know what to do," I mutter, my voice sounding like it's been grated over shards of glass.

"Eyes and mouth, Nix." His attention flicks between the two before settling on my lips. "Choose you."

He doesn't give me a chance to respond, instead kissing me softly all over again in a way that has my stomach doing little flips. I can hear his words loud and clear in my head after we break away from one another.

Choose you.

His nose brushes against mine when he murmurs, "Am I allowed to stay tonight?"

My immediate thought is, yes, that I want nothing more than his presence and reassurance and gentle touches to continue calming the chaos in my head. But Kason is right down the hall, and I know there's not a chance I can explain this away if he finds Holden here in the morning.

So logic wins out.

"It's probably not a good idea."

He nods, and even though I can tell he's disappointed, he starts shifting away from me to rise off the bed. "Then I can go."

Instinct has the arm slung over his body tightening, and I shake my head. "Just not yet."

There's another smile on his lips as he settles in beside me again, and if possible, he pulls me even closer to his chest before his lips sweep over mine in a whisper of a kiss.

"Okay. I'll stay as long as you want me."

I'll always want you.

The thought is immediate, and it only makes me feel more helpless. I don't know how, in this short amount of time, Holden's made himself an intrinsic part of my existence. I don't know what my reality is without him anymore, either. More importantly, I don't want to find out.

Silence descends again, and though I told him he couldn't stay, Holden falls asleep before the episode playing behind him ends. I don't have it in me to wake him so he can leave, and honestly, I don't really want him to as it is. Which is why I set an early alarm for him to sneak out before settling deeper into his embrace, all the while trying to ignore the niggling feeling in my gut that tells me this is wrong.

His words are still clear as day in my head, rolling around in my thoughts while they attempt to find a place to finally penetrate into the depths of my brain.

If I'm being honest with myself, I know I've been enabling Kason. Being a place of solace and home and comfort for him was as easy as breathing, despite the way it overshadowed my own happiness at times. But it was never something that mattered until now.

Now, it might matter more than ever.

Which is why I know Holden is right, and though it might be hard and painful at first, I have to start choosing myself. Because if I'm sure of anything, I don't want to live with regrets. Especially when it comes to this.

Though the fear of the unknown is still there, the pressure on my chest lessens, if only slightly. But it's progress, and that's more than I could ask for earlier tonight.

Baby steps, Holden had said. And he's been right about so much of this in the end, I have to believe he's right about this too.

There's just one part of this that feels wrong. One thing he told me that...I just don't see as a possibility. And it's a concern I whisper aloud, though I know he's not awake to hear it.

"I don't know if he'll forgive me for falling in love with you."

TWENTY-NINE

Holden

The last thing I expected from the townhouse meeting I called was the tables being turned on me and my fuck ups. After all, the entire reason I called this little meeting in the first place was because Oakley's been so MIA lately; the only reason we knew he was alive was because Cam let us know he was still showing up at the rink.

Discussing my love life was never meant to be on the table, yet in true Holden Sykes fashion, it seems like that's exactly what's happening.

"You in or you out?" Oakley asks, glancing between Theo and Camden.

"No, don't come in here acting like you give a shit now, Oak. It doesn't fucking work that way," I say before sinking back into the couch.

Oakley gives me an apologetic look, his eyes softening around the edges. "Except I do care, and I'm sorry I made you feel like I didn't."

I can tell he means it from his expression alone. Don't get me wrong,

I'm still irritated as hell that he hasn't been around, but I need to talk to him. For him to help me get my head on straight with all the secrets and the feelings I don't know what to do with. Otherwise, I'm liable to screw this all up more than I already have, especially with the way I found Phoenix last night when I snuck into his room.

I shake my head, unable to help the hint of a smile forming at the corner of my lips. "Fucking dick."

"Aw, look at that. Mom and Dad made up," Camden says with a laugh.

Theo's attention flicks between me and Oakley. "Which one of them is Mom?"

I open my mouth to rebut—Oakley's obviously the mom—except he takes the opportunity to steer us back to the subject at hand.

"So what happened?" he asks, brow arched.

The smile working its way onto my face falls, the question sobering me instantly. "Like I said, I fucked up. All there really is to it."

"But how?"

"Does this have anything to do with what's going on with Phoenix and Kason? Because those two are thick as thieves, and they haven't spoken in weeks," Theo muses, eyes locked on me.

If looks could kill.

He knows damn well this is about them. He might not have all the details, but he's far more aware than he lets on. I'd bet anything he's already pieced this together a while ago and just hasn't said anything. Then again, I'm sure Theo sharing the basement floor with me only leaves so much to the imagination.

The only thing he doesn't know is that through my original pursuit of Kason…I ended up falling in love with Phoenix instead.

The thought causes my head to drop to my hands, shoulders slumping in defeat before repeating myself. "Like I said. I. Fucked. Up."

"Well, now I'm intrigued," Cam says, shifting on the couch beside me. "Theo, go grab the popcorn. We might be here a while."

I hear Theo rise from the couch, his footfalls retreating away and—

Is he actually getting fucking popcorn right now?

Fuck, I'm ready to abort this mission. The messed-up status of my love life really isn't what I want tonight's entertainment to be. No matter how much I could use even one good piece of advice.

"Guys, seriously," I tell them. "It's a saga, and not a good one."

"But Theo's already getting the popcorn," Cam counters. "And besides, I've got some time to kill, so might as well get it off your chest."

I shift, my back hitting the leather as I stare up at the ceiling. "How much time you got?"

"However much time it takes," Oakley murmurs.

I glance over to him and give him a playful shove. "You sure you don't need to go hang out with your other friends?" But what is meant to be teasing quickly becomes me realizing I just shoved the shoulder Oakley hurt in his game earlier tonight.

My eyes widen, about to start apologizing profusely when he starts *laughing*. Sure, it's laced with a bit of pain, but it's laughter, regardless.

"Now you're lucky if I'll listen at all."

I roll my eyes, because clearly, he's fine if he's gonna start getting snippy with me while I'm ready to have a full-blown meltdown.

"So fucking dramatic tonight. You're definitely the Mom," I gripe before turning and calling over the couch. "Theo! Bring an ice pack while you're at it!"

Barely two seconds later, he's tossing one of our many communal ice packs at Oakley. Probably not the smartest move to make while he has a shoulder injury, though somehow, he manages to catch it and settle in on the couch.

Theo vaults into place over the back of the couch not long after with a giant bowl of popcorn in hand that he sets on the table. "Snacks have been taken care of, so now you can tell us exactly how you fucked up."

I blink at him, having no idea why he or Cam has any desire to be part of this. But while I'm not gonna hold my breath, I might as well spill my guts and pray—by some miracle of God—they have some insight for me.

Otherwise, it's all on Oakley's one good shoulder.

Blowing out a breath, I mutter the single sentence that started this entire mess.

"I slept with Phoenix."

The entire room is so silent you could hear a pin drop. Even their munching on popcorn halts as they let this bomb sink in.

"Okay, well, I already—"

"Yeah, I know," I snap at Theo, cutting him off. "We don't need to rehash all the shit you're aware of that you don't need to be."

"So he's the one with the handcuffs, huh?" he says with a laugh before popping another kernel in his mouth. "Didn't see that coming."

"Wait, back up for me here. We're still talking about Kason's best friend, Phoenix?" Oakley asks, which I confirm with a solemn nod.

Camden's brow furrows, and he glances over at Theo. "And also your teammate, Phoenix?"

"Yeah," I answer for Theo, eyes still locked on Camden. "We've been seeing each other in secret since coming back from Florida."

Cam's silent for a moment before responding with, "Well, I don't get what the big deal is."

"Were you not listening to the part where Phoenix is Kason's best friend?" Theo chides. He reaches into the bowl of popcorn and tosses a few pieces at Camden's face. "Pay closer attention."

Cam falters for a second, clearly trying to process, before nodding. "So you were seeing Kason, only to end things so you could pursue Phoenix?" It comes out more like a question than a statement.

"Yes, but no." I lean forward, elbows on my knees, and drop my head to my hands. "There's a bit more to it. As it turns out, Phoenix and I hooked up at a party back in May, which was well before I ever knew about Kason's sexuality. I just…" The words catch in my throat, guilt clogging them there. "I don't remember anything with Phoenix happening."

"Fucking hell, Hold," Oakley mutters, and I glance up to find him shaking his head.

If I didn't know how much these guys care about me, I'd really be questioning if I'm completely alone in this pile of shit I've landed in. Which is fucking massive.

"Wait a minute," Theo says, and when I glance over, he's studying my face intently. "You don't remember it at all? Like…none of it?"

I shake my head and rake my fingers through my hair. "I remember nothing between Oakley leaving to go home and waking up naked and alone the next morning in some random bed in the Kappa Sig house."

"Sounds like a typical weekend," Cam chimes in, and I glare at him.

"Funny, seeing as you rival me in notches on *your* bedpost."

"Cool it. Both of you," Theo says, his gaze snapping between the two of us before landing on me. "So if you don't remember, how did you find out?"

I stare at him. "You're the one who told me."

His eyebrows might as well hit the ceiling. "When did I—"

"At a gas pump somewhere near the Illinois and Kentucky border."

From the look on his face, the lightbulb has just flicked on. "Oh, shit."

304 | CE RICCI

"This is getting good," Cam says as he reaches back into the bowl of popcorn for another handful.

"I know," Oakley muses, and I don't miss the smirk on his lips as he pops a kernel in his mouth. "Good thing Theo got snacks."

I roll my eyes, ignoring the two assholes sitting here, and ask, "So you wanna tell me how you knew, but I didn't?"

"You mean apart from you being obliterated?" he asks with a scoff. "It's because I saw you, jackass. I was the one he was talking to before you so rudely interrupted, all so you could slam him against the wall and make out with him."

"Damn," Oakley mutters under his breath. "That's ballsy, even for you, Hold."

Uh, yeah. I'd say so.

My attention shifts back to Theo. "Then why didn't you say anything the next morning?"

Theo shifts in his seat, and for the first time all night, he looks a little uncomfortable.

"I didn't know you blacked out. None of us did." Theo glances over at Cam and Oakley, both of whom have sobering expressions on their faces. "And to be honest, man…if you wanted to forget that night, we weren't about to make you remember it."

I should be grateful for friends and roommates who'd look out for me. Who'd let me chase my demons away in peace and without judgment. It's the kind of friendship I never thought I'd find coming to college. But if I'd have known this information six months ago, who knows where this fucked-up situation between Kason, Phoenix, and I would be.

And that makes it really hard to feel anything except frustration.

Oakley lets out a low whistle as he settles back in his seat, wincing when his shoulder injury twinges slightly. "Well, this certainly explains the cock-blocking you received earlier this year."

"Thanks, Captain Obvious," I retort, but the snark doesn't quite hit the way it's meant to.

"Okay, so don't kill me, but I still don't see the problem here," Cam says slowly.

My hands rake through my hair. "The problem is Phoenix doesn't want Kason to find out."

"And you do?" Theo asks.

I nod. "I've wanted to since the beginning, but I agreed to the rules Phoenix laid down for me, so it feels like my hands are tied."

Camden frowns. "So why wouldn't you just tell Kason yourself? Like a double secret?"

"You can be so thick sometimes, Cam," Theo mutters with a shake of his head. "Phoenix and Kason have been best friends for half their life. So is it really so difficult to understand that Phoenix is keeping it from Kason because he doesn't want to hurt him or risk losing his friendship over a dude?" His eyes shift to me. "Am I close?"

Spot-fucking-on, actually.

"Add in the fact that all the lying he's been doing to his best friend is tearing him apart, then yeah. You're close." My head hangs, and I drop it to my hands. "I didn't know this would happen. But the whole time I was supposedly *with* Kason, I felt this pull to Phoenix. It was magnetic, and I couldn't explain it, let alone stop it. Couldn't keep myself from wanting him, despite knowing full-well the situation I'd be putting the both of them in by acting on it. And now, I think it's too late. We're in too deep." Swallowing hard, I fight the emotion that might as well be suffocating me. "I'm the rift between them, and if it's big enough for him to lose Kason, I don't think Phoenix will forgive me."

Theo cocks his head and asks a question I honestly hadn't even thought of.

"But what about you, and what you want?"

"I…I don't want to lose Phoenix," I answer truthfully. "But I can't keep going on like this either. I can't keep watching as the guilt eats him alive."

"Double-edged sword," Cam murmurs quietly to himself while nodding. "I'm sorry, man. That's tough."

"Thanks," I whisper, before my eyes shift to Oakley, who has been uncharacteristically quiet since the heavy emotions started becoming involved. Yet as his eyes study my face, understanding dawns on his.

"You love him," Oakley says, a hint of awe in his voice. "Don't you?"

Leave it to my best friend to see right through me like I'm nothing more than a piece of glass.

I bite the inside of my cheek, and before I realize it, I nod. "With every inch of me."

The admission produces a silence that hangs in the air like morning fog, and it's deafening. It leaves me to drown in my own thoughts and worries, not knowing where to go from here.

All I know is…I love him.

I've known it for a while now, even if I wasn't ready to admit it to myself, let alone anyone else.

"Didn't have that one on my bingo card for the year," Camden says, popping a few more kernels in his mouth.

"That's it," Theo snaps, turning to Camden. "If you can't be helpful or be quiet, you can leave." His tone leaves little room for debate, shocking us into silence as his focus shifts back to me. "But back to more important matters, have you told him you love him? Or how you're feeling about all this?"

I sigh and give him a worthless shrug. "Of course, I've thought about it. On both accounts. Only, at this point, saying anything at all feels like it'll just make things worse."

"You don't know that," Oakley says quietly. "There's no way of knowing either. So the real question is, are you willing to take the risk that this won't pan out the way you want it to?"

"You mean put my heart on the line and hope he doesn't use it for batting practice?"

"Pretty much, yeah," Theo answers. "Or you walk away. And from how things seem, that really isn't an option for you."

I shake my head. "Not at all."

There's no way in hell, actually. I'm not strong enough to be a martyr, and I'm far too selfish to give him up.

Theo nods. "Then you gotta fight for him 'til you can't anymore. Show him you're not going anywhere until he tells you otherwise."

Fight for him I can do. There's no doubt in my mind. I just don't know how. Not when it feels like he's slowly slipping away from me, even while he's still in my grasp.

I have to find a way to bring him back to himself. Make him smile and laugh the way he does when we're just us. When all the shit with Kason doesn't infiltrate his mind and weigh on him like an anvil.

"You could always do a grand gesture or a big showy love declaration like in the movies." This comes from Cam, whose eyes flash to Theo nervously. "I feel like that was helpful."

"It is, actually," I murmur, more to myself than anyone. But the issue still remains… "I just can't see him choosing me over his best friend when all's said and done. Grand gesture or not. His loyalty and protectiveness are unmatched, so the *bros before hoes* code is one I'm sure he'll uphold 'til death."

"I refuse to believe that shit applies to the one person who's gonna be the rest of your life," Oakley says with a shake of his head. "When it's your forever on the line, all the codes and rules go right out the damn window."

There's a firmness in his tone, and it feels slightly misplaced. Like he's almost speaking from experience. Still I don't waste time dwelling on it and look around at my roommates.

"Thanks for being in my corner, guys."

"I still don't think you fucked up all that bad," Cam says in a whisper that's a bit louder than he probably intended.

"And I'm done," Theo mumbles as he picks up the entire bowl of popcorn—or what's left of it—and dumps it over Camden's head before dropping the empty plastic on his head.

"I did absolutely nothing to deserve this," Cam chirps, the sound muffled by the plastic.

"Oh, but you did," Theo grumbles as he shakes his head.

"You do realize one of us has to clean this up, right?" Oakley says, thoroughly unamused by Theo's little stunt.

All he does is shrug before heading toward the basement stairs.

"Leave it for the dunce."

THIRTY

Holden

March

"This place is nice," Harrison mutters as we leave the main concourse of St. Sebastian University's baseball stadium to find our seats in the outfield.

It wasn't hard to convince him, Noah, and Luca, to drive down to Nashville with me so we can support Leighton's baseball team in their duel against St. Seb's this weekend. In fact, they were more than happy to make the trip; though I think most of their eagerness was due to the nearly seventy-degree weather promised the next two days, which is way better than the frigid, windy tundra Chicago is in near the end of March.

But I also think, after spending so much time with Theo, Wyatt, and Phoenix on our trip to Florida, they've become sorta tight with the guys. Not the way Theo and I are as roommates or Phoenix and I are as... whatever we are. Enough to consider them friends, in any case.

"Makes you wonder what their football stadium looks like," I muse, my eyes catching on the view of downtown Nashville off to my left as we climb the stands to our seats.

I chose left-center for the four of us, seeing as those are the ones closest to where Phoenix plays. I'd have preferred seats directly behind him—mainly to have an excuse for staring at his ass the entire time—but the damn scoreboard ruined that little plan.

Plus, Theo and Wyatt both play on this side of the field too. At least, that's what my Google search of baseball positions told me when I did my best to brush up my limited knowledge on the sport.

"I think I see them, but I can't tell. None of their jerseys have names on the back like ours," Noah says, shielding his eyes from the sun as he squints out at the field. "You said Theo plays…where?"

"Shortstop," Harrison pipes up before his lips draw down in a frown. "I think."

"Wait, which one is that?" Noah asks.

"The one next to Wyatt at third base," Luca says, pointing to the position where Theo is currently scooping up balls from the ground and throwing them across the field to the guy at first.

Noah's nose wrinkles. "That's stupid. Everyone else's position is called whatever base they're next to. He should be second base."

Luca's brows furrow. "There's already a second baseman on the other side of the bag."

"So? Why can't there be two? There are two wide receivers on the football field at the same time."

"Sometimes I swear you don't think about the words that come out of your mouth before you speak," Luca says with an eye roll.

Maybe this wasn't as good of an idea as I thought it was.

Luca's the only one of us with a clear understanding of baseball, the rest of us having limited knowledge from way back in our tee-ball days. But pair Luca's competence with Noah's endless questions, and Harrison and I might be in for a whole afternoon of listening to the two of them bicker back and forth.

Yeah, definitely didn't think this through.

"Oh, hey," Harrison says, leaning forward in his seat. "I think that's Phoenix."

My heart lurches at his name, and I'm starting to see I really am fucked when it comes to this guy. Head over heels, nothing-and-no-one-compares level fucked.

All it takes is one glance; even at a distance, I know it's him. I'd know that sinful, uniform-clad body anywhere. But the twenty-one on his back is also a dead giveaway, as it matches the jersey *I'm* currently wearing.

I pat Noah on the shoulder and rise out of my seat. "I'm gonna leave you to debate the inner workings of baseball and go talk to Nix for a minute."

Noah and Luca don't even hear me while they continue bickering, but I catch Harrison shooting a glare my way. "You're an asshole for leaving me alone with them."

I don't bother responding and instead give him my brightest smile before heading down the stands. They only go so far into centerfield, so Phoenix is still a good twenty yards away when I reach the corner closest to him and lean against the padding on top of the wall.

"Hey, Mercer!" I shout, not knowing any better way to get his attention. "Get your ass over here!"

Phoenix turns around the second he catches the ball his right fielder just threw him, and I watch as he squints at the stands.

"Holden?" he calls out, and I hear the uncertainty in his tone.

My grin is instant when he takes a tentative step toward me. "I said get your ass over here."

Phoenix picks up into a jog, only slowing to a stop when he reaches the base of the wall. "I don't have long, but what are you doing here?"

"We came to support our guys."

Well, I wanted to support *my* guy. *The others were just along for the ride.*

"We?" Phoenix asks, but where he's standing doesn't allow him to see anything more than straight up at me. "Who else is here?"

I nod over to the three idiots I just left behind. "Luca, Harrison, and Noah are over in the next section."

There's a little smirk of amusement on his lips when he says, "Careful there, Sykes. You might make your teammates change their tune about baseball after all."

Yeah, so not happening.

"Considering Luca and Noah are currently bickering about whether or not baseball should have also called the shortstop a second-baseman, I think I'm safe."

One of those genuine, sinfully addictive laughs leaves him, and he shakes his head. "Probably makes you regret inviting them already."

I let out a low hum. "Mmm, more like Harrison is regretting it, since he's the one currently dealing with them."

His lips lift in a small smile. One that makes me wish I could jump down into the field right now and kiss it clear off. "Well, I'm glad you're here regardless."

"Me too." My gaze flicks over his face, noting the smear of black on each of his cheekbones. "You know, eyeblack has no reason for being that sexy."

"Unlocking a new kink, are we?"

I bark out a laugh. "What can I say? Apparently, I'm a sucker for a guy in uniform."

He scrapes his teeth over his bottom lip, his eyes raking over my upper body. "Yeah, I've gotta agree, especially when it's you in mine. Though I am curious how you got it in the first place."

"Theo," I tell him with a soft laugh. "Guess we're not the only ones capable of stealing stuff from the locker room without someone noticing."

A scoff leaves him. "Glad to see whose team he's really on here."

"I mean, I'd say he's on *our* team."

His head cocks to the side. "So I take it he told you he knows about us," he muses.

My brows shoot to my hairline. "Wait, *you* know he knows?"

All he does is nod, and I wonder how neither of them let *that* little piece of information slip.

Unless...

"Does he know you know he knows?"

Phoenix nods again, this time with a light laugh. "God, this feels a lot like that one episode of *Friends.*"

I roll my eyes at his incessant love for the show. But his reference to the episode triggers something in my mind, if I'm remembering it correctly.

"I doubt he'd be the only one on our side, you know."

His brows draw down beneath the bill of his hat. "What do you mean?"

Licking my lips, I utter some of the most dangerous words I've dared since the night I snuck in his room. A subject I haven't touched in over a month.

"Theo isn't the only one who cares about both of us. And he certainly can't be the only one who'd want both of us to be happy."

"There you go again, assuming you could ever be the thing that makes me happy," he notes with a tiny smirk.

I'm not sure what I was expecting his reaction to be, but that certainly wasn't it. Neither is the twinkle in his eye. Nonetheless, if he wants to play a little game of back and forth, I can do that. Especially when we both know he's full of shit.

"Oh, Nix. You win this game, and I can promise you, you're gonna be really, *really* fuckin' happy afterward."

His smile is an all-out grin now, and my God, it does something to my heart that I can't control—not that I even want to. In fact, I want to lean into the feeling instead. Let the words on the tip of my tongue roll right off, right here and now.

Lay all the cards on the table for him to see and hope he feels the same way.

After all, it feels like Phoenix is finally taking the steps he needs to make the things he wants for himself a priority. I hope that's the case, and all the worries and concerns I word-vomited to my roommates last month were unmerited. Yeah, we still haven't told Kason about us, but clearly, his reaction makes it seem like he's not opposed to the idea anymore.

Or I'm reading far more into things than I should be.

I'm all for taking baby steps; the biggest is him letting go of the guilt eating at him for allowing his happiness to come first for once. Telling Kason will happen eventually.

Yet despite the progress he's seemingly made, the last thing I want to do is rock the boat while we're gaining a solid footing. So I swallow down the words I so desperately want to say in favor of some much more logical ones.

"You better get going."

He nods, tossing a glance over his shoulder before looking back at me. "I'll see you after the game, right?"

The grin I give him is instant. "Can't get rid of me if you try."

"So you've proven," he says with a laugh as he walks backward. "I'll see you later, baby."

God, I'm never gonna get sick of hearing him call me that. Or ever get sick of him in general.

He's everything I didn't know I wanted, and now I doubt there will ever be a day when he isn't.

The door to the hotel room Phoenix and Theo are sharing isn't even closed when I start ripping clothes from Phoenix's body. In fact, he doesn't have time to think or breathe or drop his bag to the floor before I'm peeling his suit jacket off his toned, muscular shoulders.

"Someone's eager to make good on their promises," he murmurs with a low chuckle.

Eager? Try fucking desperate.

"I've been waiting hours. Can you honestly blame me?"

They say football games take forever, but the whole *nine-innings* shit really takes an eternity. Especially when they're the only thing standing between you and the guy you love spending the night getting hot and sweaty between the sheets.

"I'm certainly not planning to complain."

"Good. Then get naked," I demand while working the buttons of his shirt open; the slow and tedious process making me want to rip the damn thing off instead. Yet eventually, I'm able to free it from where it's tucked in his pants and drop it to the ground.

"Mmm," he hums as he unbuttons the jersey I'm wearing, only to leave it hanging open down the center once he does. "You look so fucking sexy in my jersey. I almost don't want to take it off you."

Running my tongue over my bottom lip, I whisper two words sure to bring his fantasy to life.

"Then don't."

Phoenix's eyes flare with heat and desire as he stares at me, burning with an intensity they never have before. Like all coherent thought has left, leaving behind nothing but primal urge and carnal lust. Like the mere thought of owning me this way is everything he's ever wanted.

That look alone spurs me into action, and I shove his pants to his ankles. He does the same, peeling the layers of clothing from my body one by one, but far, far slower than I'd like. Especially when all I want is the both of us naked and on his bed.

My wish that's granted moments later when the two of us blindly fall to the mattress in a messy tangle of limbs and tongues—both of us stripped bare save for his jersey still hanging open over my torso.

Phoenix rolls on top of me before sliding his hand into my hair. Gripping the strands in his fist, he pillages my mouth some more, coaxing my tongue to battle with his. The aching throb my cock makes has me ready to plead for more friction than just the slow grind of his hips against mine.

I need all of him.

"How do you want me?" I pant into his lips when I break away for air. "Because I'm dying here, Nix."

"Maybe that's exactly what I want," he muses, lips traveling the length of my jaw before reaching my ear. "You ever think about that?"

"You're far more demented than I realized if that's true."

"In that case..." A filthy grin pulls at his lips, and I think he's about to continue with his torment when he whispers, "On all fours, ass up."

I don't think I've ever moved so fast in my goddamn life, flipping over in front of him so my knees and elbows are pressed into the mattress.

A low groan leaves him as his hand pushes down on my back where I'm donning his number.

"Fuck, baby," he whispers before a lone finger trails down my crease. "You've never looked better in your life. Ass in the air, my number on your back. It's a sight dreams are made of."

I bite my lip to keep from grinning when I look over my shoulder at him. The primal heat in his gaze is incinerating as he drags it over my body, leaving no inch untouched by it.

It didn't take long to learn that fucking me from behind is Phoenix's favorite position, and there's no doubt it's one of mine too. The way his cock fills me, sliding in impossibly deep with every thrust, is something I've begun to crave. Same with his fingers, which is precisely what I'm anticipating when his hands part my ass after he slides between my parted knees.

So when I'm greeted with the warm swipe of his tongue down my crease instead, I can't help but lurch forward. Mostly because I had no idea this was on the table for him. But hell if I'm about to try and stop it. Not when I'm in straight-up filthy heaven as he takes another languid pass over my puckered rim.

His grip on my ass tightens as he continues lapping at me, drawing out a tortured groan from deep within my chest.

"Oh, fuck," I mutter, fisting the sheets in my palm as my forehead drops to the mattress.

I feel him fucking everywhere.

His tongue trails down over my taint, causing my body to break out in goosebumps before he circles my rim again with the tip. One of his hands reaches between my legs and wraps around my cock, giving me a firm stroke that, paired with his talented tongue, has me primed and ready.

"Need you, Nix. Please," I pant, and I don't care if I'm begging.

There's the teasing kind of torment, and then there's pure torture, and what he's doing to my body is edging toward the latter.

All I get in response is a low hum before his mouth moves to one cheek, where he nips at my flesh. Then he sinks his teeth into my skin, hard enough to leave a mark this time, only to soothe the bite with gentle swipes of his tongue before moving back to my hole.

His hand moves quicker around my length now, jacking me while he continues exploring every intimate inch of me, and it's like my entire body has been lit on fire. Engulfed in flames, incinerated on the spot.

It's not long before I'm rocking with his ministrations, pressing back against his face before rutting forward into his hand. The friction is everything I need, and I feel myself getting closer and closer to impending bliss.

"Fuck, Nix. I…I—"

"Don't come," he demands, his hand working the sensitive crown of my cock. "Not until I'm buried inside you."

A shudder has me trembling where I kneel before him, and I don't think there's a chance in hell of me holding on until then. "Then you better get to it, because I can't—"

"You can, and you will." His voice is raspy, tainted with hunger and desire. "After all, you want to make me happy, don't you?"

More than fucking anything.

Something I think he's all too aware of. Knowledge he's using to his advantage now as he continues with more wicked, languid swipes of his tongue. Saliva drips down my crease and over my taint, and it sends a bolt of lust zipping straight to my cock.

I groan again, my release lingering right there. All he has to do is press against my prostate one time, and I'll shatter into a million pieces.

"I want you happy, but not at the cost of my own sanity, baby. And you're driving me straight to the brink of it right now."

A dark chuckle leaves his lips, vibrating against my skin before he finally has mercy on me.

"On your back," he murmurs, the quiet huskiness of his command sending another wave of goosebumps rising across my body.

I flip quickly; my eyes fixated on his sculpted ass while he searches through his duffel for—

"Should I be concerned about you carrying lube to an away game?" I muse, wrapping my fist around my length and stroking.

There's a gleam in his eyes as he turns around, already spreading it up and down his length. "There could be moments like this when I might unexpectedly need it."

"When someone surprises you with hotel sex?"

He shakes his head slowly as he kneels between my parted thighs. "When I need you too much, only for you to not be here, forcing me to take matters into my own hands."

The mere thought of Phoenix stroking his cock to thoughts of me is fucking intoxicating, but it's got nothing on the way he grabs my hips and drags me to him while staring down at me with lust-filled eyes. Though, I think I catch a glimmer of something else as well. Something deeper.

Reverence, maybe?

Whatever it is, it's far more potent than the desire darkening his gaze.

I'm in prime position for him to slide inside me with only the slightest press of his hips, but he chooses to run his hand up over my abs. Tracing the indents with his fingers between either side of his jersey.

"Fuck, baby," he whispers, eyes following the paths his hands have already taken. "I'm obsessed with you in this."

My lips quirk up in a devious grin. "Naked and at your mercy doesn't do it for you? You really want me wearing your jersey like some cleat chaser too?"

"I want you in all ways," he murmurs, a seductive tilt of his lips adding to his sinful aura. "But being inside you with my number on your back will, without a doubt, take the cake. So I really know you're mine."

My blood flares. "Possessive, are we?"

His nod is immediate before his words come out all grated and raw. "I wanna claim every part of you."

It's on the tip of my tongue to tell him he already has.

No piece of me doesn't already belong to him; my heart included.

Only I'm smart enough to know sentiments like that can't come now. Not like this—mid-fuck while emotions are heightened and meaningful words cease to mean a damn thing.

So instead, I scrape my teeth over my lower lip and make an offer I know he won't turn down.

"Then claim me. Own me. And if the jersey isn't enough, feel free to mark every inch of my body with your cum."

THIRTY-ONE

Phoenix

My brain can't help replaying Holden's declaration in my brain repeatedly while he stares up at me. The intensity in his gaze burns like a raging fire, speaking volumes about desire and lust. It's palpable. Intoxicating.

It's enough to spur me into action, gripping his waist and tunneling inside him with a single, powerful thrust. I bottom out, my hips pressed flush against his ass while a sharp gasp escapes him.

"Holy fuck," Holden pants before sinking his teeth into the plush bottom lip.

And holy fuck is right. Being inside him is nothing short of being sent straight into Nirvana, and the way he's clamping and squeezing around my length tells me this could all be over much sooner than either of us would like it to be.

I lean in, capturing his mouth with my own while I let his body adjust. My tongue prods at the seam of his lips before spearing between them, fucking and rolling against his in a seductive dance. Claiming it. Taking ownership of what's mine, just like he said I could.

My hips start moving of their own accord, pulling back so just the tip is still inside him before sliding all the way home. Nothing about this is slow or sensual, how things normally are. The way I fuck him with reckless abandon—now pistoning my hips relentlessly—is downright carnal.

I'm pounding into his ass like being inside him is the only thing keeping me grounded to Earth.

And honestly? It very well might be.

He's the first to break our kiss, letting out a breathy moan when I brush over his prostate, and the sound is music to my ears. All gruff and raspy as I drag it from his mouth the same way I'm pulling every ounce of pleasure I can out of him.

Taking it all. Leaving nothing left behind.

"Nix," he whispers, a plea that I steal straight from his lips.

I mold my mouth to his again, swallowing down every breath and sigh that dares to escape from where they're joined. His fingers claw at the back of my head, holding me there while our tongues and bodies meld together in a perfect rhythm.

One I've never experienced with anyone else, only him.

He starts meeting me thrust for thrust, arching up into me as I pump my hips forward at a haphazard pace. My self-control is hanging by a thread, and every moan Holden makes against my lips or squeeze of his ass around my length frays it by the second.

And though I'm desperate for release, I'm not ready for this to end.

Breaking apart for air, I rest my forehead against his and slow my movements slightly, giving us both a little time to breathe. Mainly because it feels like all the oxygen in the atmosphere has vanished with a single kiss. Except Holden's not having it, and his hands leave my hair in favor of my hips to draw me in deeper.

"Give me everything you have," he rasps, the blunt tips of his fingers digging into my skin. "All of it, Nix. All of you. No holding back."

His eyes might as well be two pools of molten gold as he stares up at me, want and desire bubbling at the surface. But I see something that feels more profound swirling in their depths too. Something eerily familiar to what I'm feeling now.

And though neither of us has said it to the other, I swear that's what it is.

I'd be willing to bet my life on it.

"I'll give you anything you want." My gaze flicks between his eyes. "Name it, and it's yours, baby."

It'd be impossible to miss the way his eyes soften, and I know without asking what he's thinking. And God, if I don't want to give him everything he could ever ask for. Even if it scares the living shit out of me.

But instead of bringing life to those thoughts, he asks for something else entirely.

"Then make me yours."

I can barely breathe past the knot in my throat as I close the distance between our mouths again, his words ringing loud in the recesses of my mind. And though he might want me to own and claim him here tonight, little does he know, he's been doing just that to me.

Has been for months now.

His hands find my hair again, yanking at the strands while his tongue flicks and rolls against mine. A firm grip keeps me locked in place, unable to escape the raw passion he's unleashing on my lips while I drive into him with zero control.

But I can't help it. The way he claims my mouth only makes the aching need for him grow.

To the point where I'm consumed by it. By him.

That tingling feeling of impending release gathers at the base of my spine, and I know I won't make it much longer. But I want to take him with me when the ground drops out from under me, and I'm sent into free fall.

"Need you there too," I pant before wrapping my hand around his length. I roll my fist over the head of his cock on every upstroke, paying extra attention to the sensitive spot below the crown. A mixture of pain and pleasure crosses his face as he arches off the bed below me, and I recognize it as the desperate need for more.

A sexy, tortured groan escapes from Holden's lips; the rolling motion of my hips allows my cock to swipe over the spot inside him that makes him see stars. Each pass takes him closer and closer to blissful ecstasy. Shoves him toward the edge of release. And from his euphoric expression, he's loving every second of it.

"That's it. Fuck, baby. Just look at you," I whisper in awe, my hand anchored at the back of his neck while I map his every feature. "You were fucking made for me. Meant to be mine."

It's not until the words leave my mouth that I realize how true they are. Until Holden, I'd never put much stock into the sense of possession. The ownership of another person—mind, body, and soul. But with him, I want it. Crave it, even.

I want him to be mine in every sense of the word.

And I'm not gonna stop until it happens.

"Shit. I'm close, Nix," Holden groans, his head sinking back into the mattress below him as his hand covers mine around his shaft.

A set of perfect, white teeth sink into his lower lip as his eyes slide closed, and I watch as the pleasure takes hold before shooting him sky-high. His release drags a long, guttural moan as cum spills from his cock, coating his stomach and our fingers with the milky liquid.

I slip my hand from beneath his, watching as he continues working himself through his orgasm. His ass clamps around my length, squeezing me to high heaven until it's nearly unbearable. But I hold on, still fucking into him frantically until he's completely wrung dry and panting below me. Only then does all the tension leave his body, that sated, blissed-out state taking over.

I'm left staring at him in awe, and I swear on my entire life, nothing is more beautiful than this man falling apart beneath me. It's a sight to behold, and I'll never stop wanting to watch it happen.

I could do this forever, and I'm not talking about just the sex, either.

I'm talking about all of it. All of him.

Everything.

Fighting, fucking, chasing, loving.

My throat constricts and my heart twists, the last word hitting me harder than expected. Probably because it's a feeling I never thought I'd associate with Holden, despite having felt it for weeks.

And yet, it's the only one that makes sense anymore.

I'm unsure if it's the thought alone, the way Holden's ass continues clenching around me, or some combination of both, but my orgasm slams into me like a ton of bricks only moments later. Cum bursts free from my cock, and I quickly pull from his body and coat his stomach with it. Mark his skin with my essence.

Claiming him as mine.

And the look on his face as I do is nothing short of untamed lust.

My pulse races, pounding beneath my skin as I stroke myself through the climax. A mixture of his cum and mine is painted over Holden's stomach and chest, and that feeling of pride—of ownership—causes my gut to churn and my heart to swell.

I trace my fingers through the sticky liquid, smearing it into his skin before dragging it down to his crease. A soft gasp leaves him as the digits breach him, pressing our essence into the tight heat of his ass and curling them inside him.

"There's no part of you that's untouched by me now, baby," I murmur between pants before withdrawing from his body. "No piece of you that isn't mine." Returning to the mess coating him, I spread the drops on his chest toward his heart and massage them into the skin over the prize I covet most. Emotion clogs my throat as I stake my claim to it, and I'm surprised when the last two words fall free from my lips. "Not anymore."

The same emotion clenching my own heart is evident in his eyes, and it's no more than a second before his fingers sift through my hair and he tugs me down to him for a slow, possessive kiss.

One that makes it clear while he might be mine, I'm just as much his.

He's the first to break for air, but not without brushing his mouth over my cheek, then my temple, before his arms wrap around my lower back. I press my forehead into the crook of his neck, whatever remains of our release smearing between our torsos while he holds me tighter against him.

Like it's enough to keep me there forever.

We take our time coming back to Earth, and the only thing I can focus on is the lazy paths his fingers trace up and down my spine. That is, until he breaks the peaceful silence lingering between us.

"I'm gonna say something that could possibly ruin all of this," he murmurs, one hand sliding into the back of my hair.

Swallowing roughly, I pull my head back to look at him and nod. "Okay."

His eyes search my face, the brown depths shimmering with little golden flecks as the light hits them just right. "I want to know just how far your promise goes. About you giving me anything I want."

I roll my teeth over my lip, knowing I should've seen this coming. How could it not after a declaration like that?

"You want to tell Kason," I say, and it's not a question. It's never been a question for him.

He nods. "I know I said we could do things at your pace and tell him when you're ready. But I don't wanna be your dirty little secret anymore, Nix. I can't be."

I want to love him out loud; I really do. Let every person on this planet know Holden Sykes chose me, and I'm never letting him go. If Kason wasn't an issue, there's a very real chance it would've already happened by now.

But that isn't the world we live in. And though I want nothing more than to let those three little words spill off my tongue the way they're dying to right now, I can't. Not when I can't guarantee he loves me back. Not when I have no idea if loving him in the first place will cost me my best friend.

And though I'm getting to that point with every passing day, I'm still not ready to find out either of those things yet.

"Baby, I—"

A loud knock comes from the other side of the door, and panic sets me on high alert. Thankfully, my rational side realizes it must be Theo, and that only causes irritation to lance right through me as I frown at it.

I told Theo I'd let him know when the coast was clear and it was safe for him to come to the room tonight. I told him *twice*.

But apparently it still isn't enough when the knocking comes again.

"Look at you. Saved by the bell," Holden muses, and I peer down to

328 | CE RICCI

find him smiling. Only the smile doesn't quite meet his eyes, and for once, I'm starting to see what he means by *eyes and mouth*.

Damnit.

"It's gotta be Theo," I mutter before brushing my lips against his throat. "Maybe if we stay quiet, he'll go away?"

But when another set of knocking comes a couple of seconds later, I realize those chances are slim to none. Which means telling whoever it is to go fuck off before coming back for another round is my best bet.

"I'm gonna make him leave."

There's a suspicious glint in Holden's eye—like he doesn't believe me—before he hums a low, "Mhmm."

"Don't be like that," I plead, grabbing my boxers from the ground and sliding them up to my hips.

"I'm not being like anything."

"Sure. And I didn't just fuck you halfway to Sunday," I say with a roll of my eyes. "I'll tell him to go away, and I'll be right back."

Not bothering to wait for a response, I head over to the door, ready to tell Theo to find Noah or Wyatt, or anyone else to room with tonight. It's his best option, seeing as Holden and I are nowhere near finished.

"Might wanna wipe the cum up first," Holden calls. "Unless you plan to save that as lube for round two."

I roll my eyes again despite his point and grab a towel from the bathroom—stepping over our clothes like they're landmines in the process.

"We can put a pin in that until I take care of this," I tell him before tossing the cum rag in his direction.

There's a hint of a genuine smile on his lips when I slip into a pair of sweats, and it makes my own lift in return. However, when another knock sounds, it falters, and I glare at the door some more while swiping my room key from where it lay discarded on the carpet.

"I'm coming!" I shout, annoyance evident in my tone as I go to give Theo a piece of my mind.

"I think you already did," Holden calls from deeper within the room, and the playfulness eases some of the tension coiled inside me as I flip over the privacy lock and nearly yank the door off its hinges.

"Theo, I told you I'd text you when it was—"

The rest of my sentence dies right there on my lips when the door opens fully, because it's not my teammate on the other side of the door.

It's Kason.

THIRTY-TWO

Phoenix

My heart drops to my stomach and clear out of my ass as I stare at my best friend, but I try to not let the panic show. Instead, I force a smile on my face as I step into the hall and calmly close the door behind me. Not an ideal situation while I'm only in a pair of sweatpants, but inviting him in where Holden is still naked and covered in my cum isn't exactly an option. And it's certainly not the way I'm looking to let him know about the two of us, whenever I'm ready for that moment to come.

"Kase. Hey," I say, my voice coming out a bit pitchy.

His green eyes crinkle at the corner while he looks at me, apprehension written all over his face. "Sorry, I didn't realize this would be a bad time."

Try a fucking horrific time.

"You just caught me off guard," I lie, trying not to wince at how hollow they've begun to sound. It seems to get worse with every one I tell him. "What're you doing here?"

"It's St. Seb's weekend."

The game. Right.

Had I not been so wrapped up in Holden lately, I'd have remembered him making these plans months ago when I first got my schedule for the season. He'd come down and watch the games with my parents before his obligatory drop-in to see his own family.

"Oh, shit. That's right." My hand rakes through my hair haphazardly. "I completely forgot."

"And here y'all say *I'm* the forgetful one," he says with an awkward laugh before his expression turns more pensive. "Are...we good, Phoe? I know you've been busy lately with school and ball and dating again, but it feels like something else is going on."

My lips part, ready to feed him yet another tasteless lie, when the door behind me opens from the inside.

"Round two is gonna have to start solo if Theo—"

My eyes sink closed, nausea slamming into me in waves at the sound of Holden's voice.

"Oh, shit," he curses under his breath, and I'm just praying to God he's at least put some clothes on. Anything besides just my jersey hanging open over his shoulders.

My gaze shifts, and even though I'm glad to see he dragged a pair of tight briefs up to his hips, the evidence is still pretty damning. A fact that's all-too apparent when my attention slides to Kason again.

His eyes are wide as they flick between the two of us in our states of half-undress, and I don't miss the way they lock on my jersey. But the shock in his gaze quickly wanes, and it's only a moment later that anger and betrayal take their place.

"Go back inside," I demand quietly to Holden, not daring to look away from Kason.

"Nix, let me—"

My gaze veers to him before I snap out a harsh, "You've done enough. Just go back in the room."

Hurt doesn't even begin to describe the emotion filling his golden irises, and while the rational part of me knows it's not fair for me to aim my anger at Holden, I can't seem to stop it. Yeah, he couldn't have known it was anyone other than Theo outside the room, let alone Kason...but fuck, if he would've just stayed inside the room, I could've—

Could've what? Kept blatantly deceiving my best friend? Continued disregarding Holden's wishes because I'm too afraid to own up to the mess I created?

Holden's Adam's apple bobs as he swallows, and with a quiet nod, he slips back into the hotel room and leaves me alone with Kason.

A seething, pissed-off Kason, if the way his eyes harden and nostrils flare are anything to go off of.

His lip curls back in a disgusted snarl, fury written all over his face. "Un-fuckin'-believable."

I stand silently, waiting anxiously for him to lay into me the way I know he wants to. The way we both know I deserve. Only to my shock—and even dismay—Kason opts to turn the other way and stomp toward the elevator.

I quickly snap out of the stupor the sight leaves me in and follow him. "Kason, just wait."

My hand wraps around his forearm, but he immediately yanks it free from my hold, whirling on me in anger. "Why? So you can lie to my face some more?"

The words hit their intended target, though it's not hard when I've been wearing my guilt so freely. Even with this newfound mantra of choosing myself first—one I've been doing my best to embody for weeks—old habits die hard. And when I have Kason staring me dead in the eye as all my deceit unravels before us, old habits have their way of creeping back in. Even taking over.

"I'm sorry," I whisper, knowing the words are hollow at best. Not because I don't mean them, but because I know they do nothing to fix the situation. "I didn't mean for this to happen."

"As if you couldn't be any more of a cliché right now." He scoffs and rakes a hand through his hair, the auburn strands sticking out a bit haphazardly when he's done. "The best friend and the boyfriend. It's fucking disgusting."

"The two of you weren't together," I murmur, though I probably shouldn't. "You technically never were and—"

A sharp, almost maniacal laugh leaves him. "That's not the point, Phoenix. I asked you point fucking blank at the Super Bowl party. I asked if you were seeing him, and you said no, gaslighting me into thinking I was seeing shit." His lips curl back in a sneer as he shakes his head. "But I did see it. That night. In Florida. Hell, I saw it that night at the Kappa Sig house in November. There was history between you two, and it was enough to get under your skin. But I asked you what the problem was time and time again, only for you to say it was nothing." His green eyes flare with fury as he looks me up and down. "I took you at your fucking word. Something I should be able to do with a friend, let alone the one person on this planet who has always been honest with me. Always had my back."

Agonized is only the tip of the iceberg for what I'm feeling right now. How can it not be when the twinge of pain in his voice he's doing his best to hide is still clear as day?

"But, you see, that right there is exactly why I didn't tell you. Because having your back and being honest with you was completely at odds with each other when it comes to Holden." I take a deep breath, steeling myself for what I say next. For what I *have* to say. "This is the first time since we've been friends that I've actually done something *for me*. Where I put my happiness above yours."

He shakes his head, a clear rejection of my statement. "Don't you dare put this on me, Phoe. I've never asked you to do that."

"But you did! You have!" I lift my hand and start ticking off examples on my fingers. "When you begged me to come to Leighton instead of going off to Foltyn for college. When you asked Holden to sit with us for lunch. Then again, inviting him down to Florida, along with your other teammates. You ask, and I fold. No matter what."

It feels like shit, keeping score this way, but to hell if I'll let him remain blind to everything I've done for him over the years—some of which without batting an eye.

I just can't do it anymore.

"You always put your wants and needs above mine," I murmur, my voice cracked and raw. "So why is it so wrong for me to finally do the same?"

"Because I never lied to you," he snaps, stepping toward me. The distance between us closes, becoming inches at best as he glares down at me so intensely…I'm actually a little afraid of him.

"I'm sorry—"

"Sorry doesn't cut it anymore, Phoe. Not when all I want is for you to tell the truth." If I didn't know him as well as I do, I'd miss the sorrow in his eyes as he glares down at me. All I'd see is the anger as he mutters the sentiment again. "Just tell the fucking truth."

So I finally do.

I step back and let all the lies and secrets, the deceit and betrayal, spill from me. I let the truth set me free as they land in a heaping pile at his feet where he can see each of them in all their ugly glory. Where he can sift through them, picking out the pieces and analyzing them under a microscope.

There's no reason to keep hiding anything now. No point in pretending this will hurt any less by keeping it from him. So I'm more than happy to tell him whatever answers he wants to know, especially if it means having any shot at earning his forgiveness.

Yet when I bring the sordid tale to a close and wait for him to say something, all he does is stare at me in silence.

And it's fucking deafening.

"Kase," I murmur, praying for him to speak. *Needing* him to say something.

Only, when he does, part of me wishes he'd let me drown in the silence instead.

"You sat there judging me for even thinking about sleeping with Holden, yet here you are, doing exactly that. For months without saying a damn thing about it." He wets his lips and shakes his head before continuing in a harsh whisper. "I don't even recognize you anymore."

His words are knives, and they cut deep. Mostly because I don't recognize myself anymore, either. The person I was would've never done this to him. He would've shoved down the feelings rising to the surface and fought against them. Pushed and kicked and beaten them away until they no longer existed.

But at what cost?

"Say what you want about me, but you played a part in this too," I whisper, the pain from his cuts causing me to lash out in return. "We might've done some shit, but the only reason we ever got this far was because we were forced together by you."

A scoff leaves him. "Then why am I only finding out about the first Kappa Sig party now? Because I'm pretty sure I have nothing to do with what happened between you two *that* night."

It's on the tip of my tongue to tell him it was a mistake. Hell, if I'd told him about sleeping with Holden immediately after it happened, I'm positive that's exactly what I would've said.

So much has changed since then, though, and saying that now is nothing more than another lie.

Nothing about being with Holden is a mistake. Nothing about him *feels* like one...apart from how it's destroying a decade-old friendship right before my eyes. Then again, maybe it wouldn't be if I'd just been honest from the beginning. This could've all been avoided.

But it's too late to turn back now and see if it'd play out differently.

"I'm sorry I didn't tell you what happened back in May. And I'm sorry I didn't tell you about Florida and—"

"But you're not sorry, Phoe! That's the whole fucking point. I can see it written all over your face." His eyes darken from an emerald to a deep forest as he stares at me, more angry than hurt now. "You're not sorry about what happened with Holden, you're just sorry you got caught stealing him in the first place."

This time, the words hit me like a bullet to the chest, knocking the wind out of me. Only no matter how much they hurt—how much guilt and regret courses through me for the pain I'm causing my best friend, I can't help the one thought circling through my head.

It's not stealing if he's meant to be mine.

But it does nothing to ease the guilt I've been working so hard to diminish.

"Except I really am sorry, Kase. I don't think you understand how much." My fingers link together behind my head as the aching, tormented feeling starts seeping back in through the chinks in my armor. "You're my best friend. I'm the one who's supposed to be protecting you, yet all I've been doing is protecting myself."

Kason grabs the back of his neck, eyes lifting to the ceiling in what looks to be a silent prayer. "When are you gonna stop acting like I constantly need you as some sort of guardian and savior? I told you months ago, we're not kids anymore. I can fight my own battles; I can win my own wars."

"If that's so true, why am I even here?" I toss my arms out to the sides, guilt again giving way to frustration. "If you don't need me, then why did you ask me to come to Leighton in the first place?"

"And we're back to this again?" he asks, tone snide and defensive as his focus snaps back to me.

"Of course we are, Kase! Because in one breath, you're sitting here saying you don't need me to protect you, but in the next, you're treating me like a security blanket or a fucking crutch to lean on."

His lips part slightly, and I'm prepared for whatever blow he wants to land next. But I watch as, right before my eyes, all his anger dissipates in the blink of an eye. In its place is nothing but anguish.

And it cuts me deeper than any words ever could.

"Clearly, this has nothing to do with Holden. He's just the catalyst. This is about you and me and all the shit that's so clearly broken between us."

His words sink in, and I hate the truth in them.

But this friendship is fractured, cracks and splinters forming just below the surface for longer than either of us has realized. Or maybe we did, and neither of us wanted to admit it. To ourselves, or each other.

"Maybe you're right." I shake my head and blow out a breath. "All I know is, you say you don't recognize me anymore, and I feel the same way. Things have been this way for so long—me giving into your every whim—that I don't even recognize myself. I have no idea who I am or what I want."

"It sure as hell seems like you know what you want," he mutters, and he doesn't need to elaborate on the thought. The way his gaze absently flicks toward my hotel room more than gives it away.

I gnaw at my lower lip, another wave of guilt dragging me under as I whisper the same sentiment I did earlier.

"I didn't mean for this to happen."

His eyes give nothing away as he stares at me, uttering a single word. "But..."

"But I can't change how I feel." I swallow down the emotion clogging my throat. "Just like I can't take back what I've done."

"No. You can't." Kason releases a long, slow sigh before walking toward the elevator and slapping his fist over the call button. "Choose him, Phoenix. It's clearly what you want to do. Just don't expect me to sit around and watch."

Two words spoken in Holden's voice swirl in my thoughts, and I try to grasp them. Hold onto the tiny threads that are barely keeping my existence together.

Choose yourself.

Standing here after a face-off with my best friend, I realize I'm on the precipice of just that. Choosing between my loyalty to him and the person who makes my entire world stop.

And for the life of me, I don't know how to choose. I don't even think I can.

Maybe because the reality of it is...I don't deserve either of them.

Which is why I'm left helplessly staring at the elevator long after Kason steps inside and the doors close behind him. I'm not sure how long I stay there either, only that the pressure on my chest is nearly too much to bear, and I'm ready to collapse under it.

Eventually, autopilot kicks in, and I head back toward my room. It's not until the door closes behind me and a fully-clothed Holden rushes toward me that I remember he was in here.

Though, I'm not sure how I forgot, all things considered.

"Oh, thank God." His relief is evident as his hands land on my arms. "What happened?"

The concern in his eyes as he maps my face rips my heart from my chest on the spot, and paired with his gentle touch, I'm in physical, aching pain that I fear will never end.

Because...this is what guilt demands I give up.

His fingers skim up and down my arms, as he continues watching me. Waiting for words to form on my lips, let alone fall from them.

"Nix. Baby, what's going on? What did he say?"

I'm useless to speak, and no matter how many times I clear my throat, hoping to alleviate the emotion clogged there, it doesn't get any easier.

I'm still choking on the regret. Suffocating beneath the weight of my lies.

"Just go, Holden," I say in barely a whisper. "I can't do this right now."

"Nix—"

I hold my hand up, stopping his words before they spill from his mouth. I've reached my limits, and there's nothing Holden can say or do to make this better right now.

Not when he's at the crux of the issue. The catalyst of the fall-out.

"Please." The word comes out choked. Anguished, even. "Go."

His gaze alone shows that leaving is the last thing he wants to do. If anything, he's looking at me like he wants to haul me to his chest and take every ounce of pain as his own.

But instead, he nods once, twice. A third time before releasing me, stepping back out of my personal space. The second his touch is gone, I simultaneously feel like I can breathe again, but I'm almost drowning from the surplus of oxygen surrounding me.

Like there's too much. Like I need someone else to take some of it.

Him to take it.

To steal it straight from my lungs like he's done countless times before.

Yet instead, he takes another step backward and reaches for his discarded bag before hauling it over his shoulder. That same soft gentleness in his eyes is still there when his attention moves back to me, and I swear I can see all the thoughts swirling in them.

But rather than speaking a single one, he presses his lips to my temple and silently walks out the door.

THIRTY-THREE

Holden

Thanks to the shit show last night, there's a feeling of dread swirling in my gut as we enter the stadium for Leighton's second game against St. Sebastian. There's tension in the air too. It might not be palpable to anyone else, but I feel it whirling overhead like a storm cloud ready to unleash a torrential downpour.

Yet I still climb toward my seat in the bleachers behind left field, despite my better judgment telling me to run the other way. My intuition has never led me wrong before, although I refuse to listen to it now. I can't, even if this could very well be the stupidest thing I've ever done. And I've done a lot of stupid shit, especially when it comes to Phoenix Mercer.

"You sure about this?" Harrison asks, observing me with a fair amount of doubt.

If I've ever been sure of anything, it's that Phoenix is it for me. Yet that doesn't erase the unsettled feeling low in my stomach as I stare out at the baseball diamond.

"Yeah, I'm sure."

I didn't see a point in keeping this thing with Phoenix a secret from the three of them anymore after the blow-up with Kason last night, and honestly, I'm glad to tell them. It's one less burden on my own chest. Three less people I'm keeping secrets from.

While I knew none of them would be shitty about it, I was surprised by just how supportive they were. Harrison especially, since he tends to keep more to himself. But last night, when I came back to our hotel room after Phoenix kicked me out, Harrison proved himself to be the kind of friend most people would kill for. Seeing me so numb and detached and just fucking hurt was a first for him, but he didn't try to fix anything. Just sat and talked me off the damn ledge after listening to me spew my guts.

Harrison gives me a tentative smile. "Then I think it's about time you get your man."

That's the idea, but unfortunately, *getting my man* seems to be easier said than done when I have no clue where the two of us stand now that Kason knows.

I texted him good luck well before he was due here before the game. I already left his favorite flavor of sunflower seeds in the dugout, thanks to Theo ensuring he kept Jerry tied around the package so he'd know exactly where it came from.

And seeing as the first pitch is about to be thrown, he should have gotten both those things by now. Should have had thirty seconds to type back a response or a thank you or send out a proof of life message.

But all I've received from Phoenix is radio silence.

Which makes me wonder if I'm really about to make a fool of myself for a guy who doesn't love me back. Who is too hung up on his best friend's approval to see that this thing between us…it's what people cross oceans for, what they write songs about.

It's the kind of love that only comes once in a lifetime.

The one worth breaking all the rules for.

"You got this," Noah says, placing a hand on my shoulder. "Just don't blow it like you almost did during our volleyball game in Florida."

"That was a seriously misplaced attempt at support," Luca tells him before glancing at me. "You'll be fine, all right? We got your back, no matter what happens."

It's good to know, because I honestly feel like I'm gonna be sick. Upchuck the breakfast I barely ate all over the seats in front of me. A feeling that only increases five minutes later when the Timberwolves take the field and Phoenix comes running out toward the outfield.

I can't even look at him without my heart racing. It'd be romantic if it didn't feel so fucking pathetic for him to have this much power over me.

But he does, which is precisely why I find myself walking down the stands to the same spot I met him yesterday, ready to say all the things I didn't when I had the chance.

His back is to me while he focuses on tossing the baseball with his right fielder, and thanks to the NCAA rule only allowing two minutes between innings, my time is already limited. A good thirty seconds have passed in no time, and I need every remaining one to get this out.

"Nix!" I shout, my fingers curled over the wall. But he doesn't look. In fact, it takes calling his name another two times before I finally feel those dark brown eyes on me.

"Holden?"

I nod, my fingers tightening on the padding. "Come here. Please."

There's a slight frown on his lips as he jogs over, and as the distance between us dwindles to nothing but a ten-foot vertical drop in no time, I hate it more and more. But it's the tired, dejected look in his eyes as they stare up at me that makes me wish I could grab him by the jersey, haul him up here, and wrap my arms around him. Take away some of the pain he's so clearly in.

"I didn't realize you guys were staying for both days."

My brows furrow, wondering why we wouldn't. "We want to support you. Support the team."

His ungloved hand adjusts the hat on his head before he glances over to his right fielder, who is openly waiting for him.

"What is it, Holden? I'm kinda in the middle of a game, and I shouldn't be over here at all."

God. The defeat in his voice is heartbreaking.

"I know," I whisper, the words coming out on shards of glass. "But I need to talk to you."

He lets out a sharp laugh. "It couldn't have waited another couple hours?"

Shaking my head, I tighten my grip on the barrier separating us and hope it's enough to keep me from vaulting over it to get to him.

His jaw ticks. "Well, I can't do this right now. I've got—"

"I'll be quick, but you need to hear this." I swallow past the baseball-sized knot in my throat, my fingers gripping the wall tighter. "You need to know that I don't care if your loyalty to Kason wins out, and all I'm doing here is making a fool of myself. It doesn't matter, and I don't care if you don't feel the same way, because I can't go another day keeping this shit to myself. Especially now that he knows."

There's pain and sorrow etched into his features that might as well run my heart through a blender as he goes to speak.

"Hold—"

"I'm sorry," I cut in, knowing my time is limited. "I have a lot of things to apologize for, and those can all wait 'til we have more time. Hell, I'm sorry for doing this now, during a game instead of waiting. But if there's one thing through this entire fucked-up situation I'm not sorry for, it's falling in love with you. And you need to know that."

His dark eyes give nothing away as they bore into mine. Neither does his body language, facial expression…absolutely nothing. And it sends my anxiety sky-rocketing into outer space.

"Say something," I plead, unable to stand his silence. "Please, say something."

The timer on the clock keeps ticking down, every second both flashing by instantly while also dragging on for eternity. Both of which are agonizing while I wait for the man I love to tell me he loves me too. Wait for some kind of answer from the guy who could…*fuck*.

The guy who could be my forever.

"Nix. Baby—"

"I have to go," he says, shaking his head. "I'll find you after the game, and we can talk, okay?"

On second thought, *now* it feels like my heart has been tossed in a blender.

"Okay," I manage to choke out. "Good luck."

All I get in return is a half-hearted smile before he turns and jogs back into position without a backward glance. Meanwhile, I'm left frozen where I stand, helplessly staring after him and wondering if this will be the last time I have to watch him walk away.

The game drags on forever, and because fate is a cruel bitch, it also goes into extra innings. Three of them, to be exact. And by the time some of Phoenix's teammates start filing out of the stadium toward the bus, I've just about lost my damn mind.

I wait, crouched against the brick exterior, as the sun begins setting off in the distance, illuminating the city in shades of orange and yellow. A beautiful sight, one I'd no doubt enjoy a lot more if I didn't feel like the sky was about to crash down on top of me.

At least I was smart enough to give Harrison and the others my keys to the Jeep. I don't want them around to watch this go down, especially if it ends badly. The last thing I want or need is an audience while having my heart ripped to shreds.

I sure didn't envy Quinton and Oakley when it happened with them a couple of weeks ago.

My fingers sink into my hair as more of Phoenix's teammates load their bags into the luggage hold of the bus before climbing the stairs to find a seat. Watching each one of them only causes my stomach to churn with even more anxiety.

Thankfully, Theo emerges from the stadium a few minutes later, spotting me the second he steps foot outside. And when he does, the look of sympathy crossing his face just about guts me. A feeling that only gets worse after he tosses his bat bag into the bus and approaches me.

He doesn't say anything when he squats down beside me; he just aims a gentle smile before squeezing my shoulder. It's meant to be reassurance, obviously, but it sure as hell doesn't feel that way.

It feels like the rest of my life is being ripped from my grasp.

"He's coming, right?" I find myself asking as my head sinks to my hands. "He's getting on that bus?"

There's another soft squeeze of my shoulder before Theo releases me and stands.

"Why don't you see for yourself?"

Once I register his words, my head snaps up to find a set of the darkest brown eyes I've ever seen already staring at me from only a few feet away.

Eyes I know so well, they might as well be my own.

"Nix," I whisper while scrambling to my feet. I'm caught between wanting to rush forward to haul him into my arms, while also realizing he might not want me to touch him. May need to keep some distance between us when all I'm craving is to erase it entirely.

I fucking hate this.

"Hey," he says softly before shoving his hands into the front pocket of his hoodie. "Sorry I had you waiting so long. When I said that, I didn't realize the game would go into extra innings."

"It's fine. It's not like you planned it," I tell him earnestly.

Yeah, maybe I was losing my damn mind thanks to the boatloads of anxiety I've been feeling since last night, but it's not like it was his fault the game went long.

Phoenix gives a solemn nod before he looks down at his feet and kicks at the pebbles resting on the asphalt.

Theo takes the hint and offers his hand out for Phoenix's bag currently draped over one shoulder. "I'll see you at home," he murmurs to me before heading back toward the bus.

I just nod and gnaw at my lower lip, thankful for my roommate leaving but also not knowing where to go from here now that we're alone. Not sure what to expect.

Phoenix has me all sorts of off-balance.

"Walk with me?" I finally ask.

"Yeah, but I can't go far," he says, nodding toward the bus. "Don't want them to leave without me."

It's on the tip of my tongue to say *let them,* and then I could drive him back to Chicago, but I keep the thought to myself and just utter a soft *okay* in response.

We fall into step beside each other and head away from the bus in silence. Unbearable, suffocating silence that drowns me with every step we take until his hand grabs my arm to stop me, and he finally breaks it.

"Listen, about what you said earlier…" he starts, trailing off before saying much of anything at all.

"I meant it," I whisper. "Every fucking word."

Unable to stand another second this far apart, I close the distance between us. One hand curls around the back of his neck, the other sliding down to entwine my fingers with his.

There's no way I'm saying these words for a second time without touching him. Only, he doesn't give me the chance when he pulls free from my grasp.

"Holden, just…" He pauses again and clears his throat. "Please, don't do this."

I can't help the scoff that slips free while I shake my head at him. "Don't, *what?* Don't love you? Because it's a little too fucking late for that, baby."

His eyes close, like my admission physically pains him.

And I don't know what to do other than forge on.

"Look, Nix. I'm sorry for the part I had in screwing up your friendship with Kason. I didn't expect to f—" I cut off and clear my throat, knowing I can't say those words again without hearing them in return. "Feel this way about you. I really didn't, and I think you know that. But it's still no excuse. There are a thousand ways I could have handled this whole situation differently, starting with ending things with Kason the moment I knew I was feeling something for you instead. Most of all, I'm sorry for not remembering that night last year. Because if I had…" I bite my lip when his lids lift, a somber imitation of a smile curling the edge of my mouth. "I dunno. I'd like to think if I had, none of this would've happened in the first place. Because you'd have been mine a long time ago."

"Except I'm not yours, Holden." His words come out in a whisper as his focus shifts to look past me, evidently unable to meet my gaze any longer. "I never was. Never will be."

That's a bunch of bullshit if I've ever heard it, and it ignites a blaze of fury inside me. Because how fucking *dare* he?

"Right. How could you be, when you're the one who acts like this thing between us is meaningless. Who treats me like some dirty secret you have to hide from your best friend." My jaw ticks, lined tight with anger. "You're the one who chased after Kason when he found out anyway, and now you're proving that you'll only choose him by ending this. Cutting us off at the knees before we even have a chance to be everything this could be."

His gaze shifts, dropping to the ground. "And what would that be?"

The words come out so characteristically detached, all I can do is gape at him. At this man who I've broken all my rules for, yet he can't seem to bend for me.

And all it does is piss me off.

"We could be fucking forever, Nix!" I swipe my hand over my hair, wondering how in the hell he can be so blind. "I look at you and see the rest of my life. All the shit I never knew I wanted. Or needed, for that matter. And you're standing here, ready to throw it all away…why? Because Kason doesn't approve? Because you feel guilty?"

He shakes his head, eyes still fixated on the ground. "Because it's one-sided, Holden."

Liar.

It's my immediate thought the second his words register, but damn if the words don't slice me to the bone anyway. But if that's how he wants to play this, I have no problem calling his bluff.

"So you feel nothing for me, then?" I snap, glaring daggers at him. At this man who is so dead set on breaking my heart the moment I give it to him.

The muscles in his jaw tick, and I see it again. The war in his eyes. The uncertainty waging the battle between his head and his heart. Between choosing himself and choosing...anyone else. And if my heart wasn't already a pile of minced meat in his hands, it would break even more watching the anguish in them.

Phoenix's tongue wets his lower lip before he glances away with a shake of his head.

"No, I don't."

Liar.

"I don't believe you!" I shout, stepping in closer to him. As close as I dare while he tries shoving what we have into some meaningless box to lock away and forget. "You can't even look at me when you say it, and until you do, I'm not going anywhere. So if you want me gone so badly, then look me in the eyes and tell me you don't love me." My eyes dart back and forth between his when he finally looks at me, searching for the truth that always lies within them. "That's when I'll leave. I'll drive to Chicago without a backward glance, but only if you can do that."

Phoenix steels himself right before my eyes, attempting to shutter his emotions from display while keeping his gaze locked with mine. As if he doesn't know I can see through him on his best days, let alone his worst.

Then again, maybe he thinks if he lies to himself enough, he'll actually believe the words falling from his lips.

"I don't love you," he says, his voice a rough whisper. "I never have."

Liar.

I wouldn't have to know him as well as I do to realize it. It's written all over his beautiful, lying face.

"Eyes and mouth, Nix. Eyes and fucking mouth."

"Not this time," he says, even as his voice breaks on the last word.

"Yes, this time. This time and every single fucking time, baby. Because I see your fear—hear it in your words—and I know it's what's controlling you. What's making you run away right now when we both know you love me too."

He opens his mouth, and I can see it right there on his tongue. The truth waiting to break free and end our misery. But instead, he says nothing and clenches his teeth to keep the words in.

I slowly reach up to take his face in my hands, terrified he'll pull away at my touch. He doesn't, but he's still strung tight; the hold on his emotions is a fragile one at best. A feeling I'm familiar with since I'm barely keeping it together myself.

My forehead drops to his, and the contact with his skin eases the tension within me while simultaneously creating more.

"I can wait for you. Or I can stay away," I murmur, brushing his nose with mine. "But I need you to tell me which. I need you to tell me what to do, because I can't read your mind. No more than I can change the way I feel about you."

He pulls back at the same time a strangled sound rips from his throat—some mixture of a gasp and a sob—and it splits me wide open. Severs whatever is left of my composure when his tormented eyes meet mine, and I watch helplessly while he drowns in a choice he never wanted to make.

And God, his pain is breaking me as much as it is him.

"Phoenix," I whisper, my hand shifting to cup the back of his neck.

"Baby, please. Tell me what to do."

All he does is shake his head. Over and over and over again while a war wages behind his eyes.

"I'm damned either way." He continues shaking his head. "No matter who I choose, I'll inevitably lose the other."

"Forget about me and forget about Kason." My thumb swipes over his cheekbone, and I don't miss the way he leans into my touch. "Forget us and choose *you*. Your happiness, your future."

Another tortured sound leaves him as he tries to look away, and then I feel a single tear collide with my thumb. It's silent, but it might as well make a sonic boom as it meets my skin.

Or maybe that's the sound of my heart shattering on impact. Because there is no worse pain on the planet than watching the person you love fall apart before your eyes, knowing you're helpless to stop it.

He's not going to survive this.

Not unless I take some of the pain or the fault or the choice for him.

Another tear collects on my thumb, and I'm quick to swipe it away. The knot in my throat aches as painfully as the heart in my chest at the sight of it, and I know what I have to do. Despite every cell in my body rejecting the idea, I'll do it anyway if it means saving him pain.

I'll choose to be selfless. Choose to live with regret.

Choose someone *else*.

Him.

The words catch on my vocal cords, but I push them out anyway— praying for my willpower and resolve to get me through breaking my own heart in order to save his.

"I'm yours, Nix. Always. You have to know that. So choose you, baby. 'Cause I'm choosing you too."

My thumb brushes his cheek, memorizing the feel of his skin beneath mine. Then, for the second time in as many days, I force myself to do something I don't want to.

I press my lips to his forehead and walk away.

Because I'll always choose him.

Even if he can't.

Even if it tears me apart in the process.

THIRTY-FOUR

Phoenix

April

I lean against the threshold of Kason's doorway and watch him tap away at his keyboard while sitting at his desk. Probably working on a paper, if I had to guess, even though his workload isn't knowledge I'm privy to anymore.

We've barely spoken in the past three weeks since the blow-up in Nashville, although not for my lack of effort. Even though I have no clue what I could say to make my deceit sting any less, especially since I'm still trying to do everything I can to make it right.

But he's made it perfectly clear he has little to no interest in talking to me right now.

His opting to stay home after the incident at the St. Seb's game for spring break—a decision not made lightly—should have been my first clue that the silence between us wouldn't just get better with time. It was a fool's wish to think a little time apart would do the trick, and I knew that. But damn if I didn't hope he'd return from Nashville with even an ounce of forgiveness.

But nope. Since the break, he's either not home when he knows I am or stays holed up in his room with the door locked on the off chance we'll be there at the same time.

I know, because I knock and wait to see if he'll talk to me. Every night, only to be ignored and walk away empty-handed.

That is, until tonight.

Tonight, I got home from practice to find his door wide open, and that could mean one of two things: he's ready to attempt a conversation… or he didn't realize the time and forgot to close it before I made it home.

I'm really hoping it's the first.

"You got a second?" I hedge, the words nearly getting caught in my throat.

His shoulders stiffen and fingers freeze over the keys, and my stomach drops at the sight. There's never been a time he's reacted to me this way before. Even in the worst of our fights over the years. But all hope must not be lost, because rather than telling me to get fucked or kick rocks or any other variation of that sentiment, he turns in his chair and faces me.

There's a hollowness to his expression, and it's one I know well. It's the one when you feel like you're missing a vital part of your happiness. It's the same one I've been wearing these past few weeks too.

"I guess, yeah." He clears his throat before nodding toward his bed. "You can sit if you want."

The tiniest bit of relief starts seeping through the anxiousness wreaking havoc on my nervous system. A minuscule amount, but it's still there as I cross the room and sit on the edge of his bed.

I roll my tongue along the inside of my cheek, searching for words to convey my thoughts and feelings. Anything to help him understand how and why we ended up here.

But it all falls flat, so I say the only thing I can at this moment.

"I honestly don't know where to start other than I'm sorry, Kase. I'm so fucking sorry."

He gives a slow, solemn nod while looking anywhere but at me. "So you've said before."

God, he's not planning to make this easy. Then again, he could put me through my paces only to tell me to go kick rocks, and it would still be merited.

"Me saying it now versus weeks ago doesn't make it any less true."

"Doesn't mean it makes what you did any less shitty," he replies dryly. Only from the way he cocks his head, he's more confused than anything. "I just don't get *why*. Why keep all the secrets? Why lie to me? And if you tell me it was because you didn't want to hurt me…" He trails off, shaking his head.

"That really was why," I whisper.

"And I've told you time and time again, Phoe, I don't need a fucking protector." A hand rakes through his hair as he tries to dial in his frustration. "And in the end, you hurt me worse with all the lies and secrets than by just being with Holden in the first place. You know that, right?"

My teeth scrape over my bottom lip before whispering, "Yeah, I do now."

"So then tell me why."

"You want a whole ass list of reasons?" I ask, giving him a wry smirk— anything to lighten the mood, even fractionally.

"I mean…" He trails off and gives me a shrug. "Might as well, at this point."

With a long exhale, I line out all the shame and embarrassment from the first time Holden and I got together. My state of mind when it happened, my out-of-character actions, and the fact that he's Kason's teammate. The fact that Holden acted like the whole thing never happened—even if it was because he didn't know it did.

I put it all on the table for Kason, and when I'm done, all he does is shake his head.

"None of those reasons are good enough for you to have kept it from me, Phoe. And even if you didn't want to tell me back when it happened, you still should have told me the night you stopped me from going home with him."

I nod, his point more than valid. "Yeah, maybe I should have. Except by the time the two of you started talking, it kinda felt too late. Months had passed, and it was like my window of opportunity to say, 'hey, I fucked your teammate after having a shit week' had closed."

"So naturally, becoming a human chastity belt was the better option?" he asks, and I don't miss the hint of a smile on his lips.

"Maybe not, but I honestly was coming at it from mostly pure intentions." I offer a gentle smile and shrug. "I didn't want you to feel like I did after sleeping with him the first time. So easily forgotten and discarded. Which, at the time, is exactly what I thought I was to Holden."

He nods before murmuring, "And that's exactly why you should have said something."

"But would you have listened? I mean, really, Kase? Would it have changed your mind?"

Because I don't think it would have. Kason can be one of the most bull-headed people I know, and from the look on his face at this moment, he knows it too.

He offers me a shrug. "I guess we'll never know for sure."

I give him a half-hearted smile as silent understanding passes between us. There's no way for us to know what could have happened, and we can't go back and rewrite history to figure it out. All we can do is take what's happened, learn from it, and move on.

Move forward. Hopefully in the same direction.

"I truly am sorry; I hope you know that." I rake my fingers through my hair before releasing a long exhale. "But you're right about one thing; this is bigger than Holden. This is about the toxic codependency we've fallen into over the years."

"I don't want to be." A solemn expression crosses Kason's face, and his head drops to his hands before continuing. "But you said it yourself; you're my comfort zone. My *security blanket*. And if this has taught me anything, it's that you can't be anymore."

The same bout of anxiety I've been feeling for weeks now starts infiltrating my thoughts all over again.

"I don't like the sound of that," I mutter. "Not one fucking bit."

"If we want to salvage this, I think it's the only way."

I hate knowing he's right, considering no part of this feels like the right thing.

"Why does it feel like we're breaking up right now?"

He lets out a choked laugh and shakes his head. "I mean, I wouldn't say breaking up. I don't want you to think I'm writing you out of my life for this, 'cause that's not the case. But we can't be like we were, and I do the work I need to do. Constantly looking to you and having you around isn't healthy for either of us. I…need to be on my own, you know? So do you, otherwise we don't stand a chance at getting past this."

"So we're just…" I pause, searching for the words I need, only to come up empty.

"We're on a break," Kason supplies, and I can't help how my lips curl up in a grin at his *Friends* reference. After all, it's one of the many things we bonded over through all the passing years.

"Just don't go finding a new best friend on this break, okay?"

A second round of soft laughter leaves him, and he shakes his head again. "Not in this lifetime, Phoe."

Another bout of silence falls between us, this one a lot more comfortable than the last. And though it might take a while for it to happen, I think this will work.

I think we're gonna be okay, but only if he can get past one crucial thing.

Kason's eyes study my face, and it's more than apparent he can still read me like a magazine when he asks, "Why do you look like there's something else you wanna say?"

Goddamnit.

I know saying what's on my mind right now is a significant step in the right direction for me. But retraining my brain to put my own priorities first has been a huge learning curve, and this is a perfect example of that.

My fingers trace over the stitching on his bedding, the bumps and ridges offering me a strange sort of comfort when I speak. "One of the things Holden kept telling me through this whole thing was that I needed to learn how to choose me. Choose who or what makes *me* happy, you know?" I wet my lips, and a wry laugh slips past them as I lift my gaze to him. "And though I know you don't want to hear this, Holden makes me happy, Kase."

"So you're choosing him, after all."

I'm silent for a moment before I say, "No, I'm choosing me."

From the way he frowns, he's not entirely following.

"You've always been my number one, but it's time I'm my own number one, Kase." I scrub the back of my neck awkwardly. "I fell in love with Holden. No matter how much sense it doesn't make, no matter if it all blows up in my face, I love him. He looks like the rest of my life, and I'll never forgive myself if I throw that away. Not for you, not for anyone."

There are plenty of reactions I'm expecting from Kason at my declaration, and most of them aren't pleasant. So when a single word comes from his lips, hinted with a smile, I don't know what to make of it.

"Good."

I blink at him, almost sure I heard wrong. "I'm sorry?"

"I said *good*."

"Are we in an alternate reality and I'm just now realizing it?" I say slowly. "I thought this would only piss you off even more."

The smile inching its way onto his lips is now a face-splitting grin. "You can fuck up and piss me off, but you're still important to me. And yeah, it might take some time for me to stop being angry and to rebuild the trust for all the lies and secrets you kept. But you're still my best friend, Phoe. I still care about you and will always want you to be happy. That's all I will *ever* want for you."

Deep down, this is something I knew. But his reaction in Nashville wholly contradicted that line of thinking.

"You made it sound like an ultimatum, though," I murmur, my gaze darting away before returning to him. "You, or Holden. Bros before hoes, and all that."

His lips roll inward and he nods, his expression immediately sobering. "And at the time, that's exactly what I meant. But then someone told me that rule doesn't apply if he's the rest of your life."

"Who told you that?"

"Holden did. Last week."

My eyebrows might as well shoot through the roof, and I can't help the way my heart stumbles in my chest at the sound of his name.

"You talked to him?"

He nods, smirking. "He cornered me outside the locker room and demanded ten minutes of my time. Wouldn't take no for an answer."

Yeah, definitely sounds like Holden.

I gnaw at the inside of my cheek, the question right there on the tip of my tongue before it finally breaks free. "What else did he want?"

Kason gives me a knowing look, a playfulness in his eye that I've missed more than I can describe. "I think that's between me and Holden, don't you, Phoe?"

"Jackass," I chide, but there's a smirk on my lips too.

"Consider it a taste of what it's like to be on the dark end of the secrets." Kason's expression sobers again as he gives me a stern, analytical look. "So, does it feel like that with him? Like he's the one?"

As much as it doesn't make sense, and as much as I wish it weren't the case, it does. He's the person I want to talk to every waking moment of the day. The person I want to punch people for at concerts or curl in bed with and study the steadiness of his heartbeat.

When I look at him, I see what my parents have. The kind of love that negates odds or logic.

I nod, but there's still a hint of guilt eating at me, and I can't help the words from sneaking out. "I'm sorry."

Compassion shines through Kason's gaze. "Don't be. You love him, and he loves you. That's fucking rare, man. You don't find it every day, and I'm jealous as hell you've managed to do this early in life. Not because I want Holden for myself or anything. More like I just wanna find it for myself." He leans forward in his chair, resting his elbows on his knees. "I'd be lying if I said I wasn't sick of being alone when so many of my friends and teammates are coupled up now. It was bearable when you were single, 'cause at least I had you…" He pauses to clear his throat before rerouting the topic away from me and Holden. "And I'm fuckin' tired of being a virgin. Of being the butt of the joke because I haven't had sex yet, even though no one out here feels worth giving it to."

"That person could be right around the corner, you know."

His head shakes, disbelief evident on his face. "At this point, he's either fictional, straight, or isn't alive."

My eyes roll instantly. "I think you're being a little over dramatic there."

"Well, dramatic antics aside, there's actually something I needed to talk to you about, too," he hedges before leaning back in his chair. "I'm moving out when the lease ends."

I'd have to be blind to not see this one coming, though it doesn't make the ache in my chest hurt any less.

"What are you planning to do?"

"I took a page out of Holden's playbook and answered an ad someone posted about an open room at another apartment down the road." His teeth scrape over his lip before he lets out a wry laugh. "Who knows, maybe I'll find a replacement best friend in the deal, too."

I wince, once again hating the tiny barb sticking out of the joke. But I do my best to flick it free from where it's latched onto me and give him a slight grin.

"C'mon now. We agreed we wouldn't be like Ross."

"I know, I know." Kason's penetrating gaze meets mine, and I can tell from the look on his face that my worries are clearly etched in my expression. "Me needing to take some time to get over this doesn't mean you still aren't my favorite person on this planet. It just means I need to put myself first, just like you are."

Yeah, this is starting to feel more and more like a breakup all over again.

Emotion clogs in my throat, and I do my best to swallow it down before nodding. Lord knows I don't trust myself to speak right now. Something Kason must realize, too, because he changes the subject.

"The real question is, if he makes you as happy as you're saying, then how are you planning to get your guy?" The look of confusion crossing my face makes him smile before he adds, "You forget, I know you better than just about anyone. So I know you've already got a plan in place."

He's right, I do have an idea. One that hinges on a lot of moving parts, but I also can't believe that's something he'd want to talk about right now. Not after all the emotional shit we just dumped at each other's feet.

"We really don't have to get into it," I start, shaking my head. "I know it's probably not—"

"It's fine. Seriously." He straightens in his chair like he's about to receive a briefing. "Now, tell me how Operation Get The Guy is gonna work."

THIRTY-FIVE

Holden

May

"Have you seen my keys?" I ask Theo while slipping my shoes on by the front door. He's standing over in the kitchen making some sort of strange smoothie concoction. The ones with kale and raw eggs in them and shit that never fail to make me gag on the spot. "I could've sworn I left them on the table by—"

"Island," he says, not even looking over his shoulder from where he's adding ingredients to the blender. And sure enough, they're sitting there on the kitchen island right behind him.

It's a strange place for me to leave them, but then again, I've been pretty out of sorts for weeks now.

"Thanks," I mutter, swiping them from the laminate and shoving them in the pocket of my hoodie before crossing back to the door.

My focus shifts to the window, locking on the rain pouring buckets from the sky on the other side of the glass. It's been like this all day, and it's befitting of the mood I've found myself in lately.

Maybe even more today, seeing as it's the sixth anniversary since my parents passed.

But it's knowing today is also one year since Phoenix and I started down this path that makes it feel all the more bittersweet.

I'm no stranger to loss, but this kind…it feels different than it does when I think about my parents. Maybe because I've still had to see Phoenix in class while he tries his best to keep his gaze from shifting to me. Hear his name when Theo or someone else mentions him in passing. And all this is happening while fighting the urge to go to him. Touch him, hug him, fucking love him with every inch of my being.

Everywhere I go, everything I do, he's there. And if he's not near me physically, then he's at the forefront of my mind like a beacon in the night. There's never been a time when another person has haunted my every waking thought, and trying to live without him while still being utterly consumed by him is driving me batshit crazy.

I can't escape him, and it's made this whole situation all the more unbearable.

"Holden?"

I glance up. "Yeah?"

His brows draw down, and he frowns. "I asked if you were on your way out for an exam. Did you not hear me?"

No, I hadn't. Not surprising, since I've been dissociating ever since Phoenix's rejection at his game down in Nashville at the end of March.

Though rejection might not be the right word for it, seeing as I was the one who walked away from him, not the other way around. But it sure feels like rejection, especially since I haven't heard anything from him in…

God, it's been over a month. The longest one of my life.

Suddenly, one of those little mandarin oranges flies across the room, hitting me square in the shoulder.

"Ow! What the hell, Theo?" I snap, glaring up at my roommate before picking it up and tossing it back at him. "I know you don't need the extra practice, so is there another reason you're chucking fruit at me?"

His brow arches at the snappiness in my tone. "Because you're so deaf right now, I'm ready to order you a hearing aid. Which begs the question, are your thoughts off on a different planet, or are you ignoring me because I won't give you any information on a certain teammate of mine?"

I pause, my answer initially being the former. But now that he's the one to mention it…

"Can it be both?"

A half-hearted smirk forms on his lips as I toss orange back at him. "I guess one probably relates directly to the other, right?"

Understatement of my life.

While I haven't been hearing a damn thing from Phoenix, Theo sure has.

He let it slip a couple weeks ago that Phoenix has been confiding in him a lot since the St. Seb's dual in Nashville. And like the addict I am, I've been shamelessly begging for whatever scraps of information he's willing to give me.

Of course, I couldn't pry any details out of him other than Phoenix is okay and working through things as best he can, all things considered. Which I'm glad to hear, but I'd much rather be hearing those things from *Phoenix's* mouth. Not Theo's.

As if reading my mind, Theo's lips lift in a sad sort of smile.

"He's doing fine, Hold. I'd tell you if he wasn't."

"Would you, though? 'Cause you've been tight-lipped anytime he comes up in conversation. He could be dead on the side of the road right now, and I doubt you'd say anything more than 'he's taking some *him time.*'"

Theo tries and fails to hide the smirk growing on his face, and the sight of it makes my irritation flare. But not as much as what he says next.

"Well, that's certainly not the case, seeing as he was just here half an hour ago, alive and well."

I press my tongue to the inside of my cheek, hating the knowledge that he was so close yet still not making any attempts to contact me directly. Because it hurts as much as it pisses me off.

Especially when it feels like Theo is using it for a gut punch.

"Now I really am just ignoring you," I snap before gripping the doorknob in my palm, ready to rip the thing off its hinges.

"Hold," Theo calls, and I don't know why, but some part of my intuition tells me to stop. Begs for me to turn around and hear what he has to say.

So I do.

Theo's pale green eyes soften. "He'll choose himself. You just need to give him time."

Those ten words—*three in particular*—breathe new life into me. Shoves air straight into my lungs, filling them with the oxygen I've been missing since the moment I walked away from him in Nashville.

Yet I still can't bring myself to believe it. Not until I hear the words from Phoenix himself. Not until he's back in my arms and this entire shitstorm is put behind us, and that's something I don't see happening anytime soon.

"You don't know that," I mutter, shaking my head. "You don't know."

Theo offers yet another half-smirk. "I know a lot more than you think."

I roll my eyes, once again irritated with him. Nevertheless, hope and relief rush through me, despite how dangerous it is.

"I'll keep that in mind," I say before shoving the door open and heading out into the pouring rain toward my Jeep.

Water soaks my head and the tops of my shoulders by the time I reach the driver's side door, and I silently curse Theo for distracting me from grabbing my jacket. The last thing I wanted to do was take this final, and now I get to do it while also dripping wet.

I'm about to slip into the driver's seat when my heart lurches in my chest, causing me to freeze on the spot. Because there, balanced precariously on the top of my steering wheel, is a little pink duck.

One that looks awfully like...a flamingo.

What the hell?

I pluck it from where it sits before climbing into the vehicle and letting the door fall closed behind me. My stomach somersaults as I turn it over in my palm, the note attached to its neck brushing against my knuckles as I do.

I don't even need to read it to know it's from Phoenix.

Theo mentioning he was here and my keys being mysteriously moved are enough to give it away. Besides him, who else would leave a tiny pink flamingo duck in my Jeep? It's too ironic, considering Francesco the Flamingo from our time in Florida.

Then there's the couple of times he's ducked me before this.

He might not admit to it, but I know the first one—the punk-rocker duck after the Icarus Ignites concert—was him. Then there was a second one a couple of weeks after the Super Bowl—when things were starting to get better between us—dressed as a little black sheep. His nickname for me plenty of times in the past.

It would only make sense for this to be him, too.

My heart twists and my stomach knots as I flip the paper over and read the message in the messy scrawl I'd recognize anywhere.

H—

Meet me at the Kappa Sig house tonight.
Seven o'clock, the bedroom at the top of the stairs.
I'll understand if you don't show, but I really hope you do.

—Nix

Taking a deep breath, I fold the note closed and beg the pulse in my throat to slow, except it's no use. Phoenix Mercer has my heart in a chokehold, and he's making no sign of ever letting it go.

Not that I want him to. It's just that moments like this…make me wish he'd loosen the grip a bit. Allow me to breathe a little easier.

Maybe luck will be on my side tonight, and he will.

Or maybe he'll rip it from my chest and crush it in his fist.

THIRTY-SIX

Holden

I walk up the steps to the Kappa Sig house thirty minutes late, a heavy feeling of nausea in my stomach. Or dread. Maybe both, because I have no idea what I'm about to walk into, even after playing out every possible scenario in my head all afternoon.

So much so, I almost didn't finish my final in time. Too busy thinking up different ways Phoenix can break my heart even more than he already has to focus on the test. And though I'm a pretty positive person, there's only one scenario where I get the guy in the end, so the odds aren't exactly in my favor here.

I push open the door, my gut still churning with anxiety as I internally chant one single sentence.

Here's to hoping I'm wrong.

Plenty of people greet me when I enter the house, including a few of my teammates. Luca and Noah are chatting with a couple of girls in the living room, and I even see Oakley milling around back in the kitchen. He spots me and heads my way the second his cup is topped off with beer.

"Hey, Hold. What's up?" he asks, eyeing me with concern.

My stomach rolls and twists into knots as I pull the little flamingo duck from my sweatshirt pocket and show it to him. He plucks it from my fingers, flips over the tag around its neck, and reads the note. His eyes widen slightly as he does, only for him to hand the whole thing back to me once he's finished.

"Looks like you're finally getting your answer after all," he muses, even as the apprehension is still evident in his gaze. "How are you feeling about it?"

I shake my head, trying to shove down all the emotions running rampant through me. "I'll let you know when my heart stops racing."

"Sounds about right." His answer comes out somewhat clipped, and I realize he knows this kind of love-induced anxiety well. It wasn't long ago that he put his own heart on the line—for Quinton de Haas, of all people.

It worked out in the end for him, though, and all I can do is hope it will for me too.

As if on cue, Quinton strolls up to us, and I watch with unmatched amounts of jealousy as Oakley slips his arm around his boyfriend's waist.

"What's going on?" Quinton asks, eyeing me through a pair of dark lenses.

Anticipation and fear war inside me as I glance at the stairs leading to the door where Phoenix said he'd be waiting for me—the battle between them causes my stomach to churn with more unease.

"I might actually be sick."

Oakley's hand squeezes my shoulder before giving Quinton a quick run-down, and I shift my focus back to them in time to see Quinton eyeing me quizzically.

"I know you have no reason to trust me on this, but speaking from personal experience…" Quinton trails off, shooting a quick glance at Oakley before his icy eyes return to me. "Phoenix taking the time he needs is a good thing. My temper didn't just go away overnight. It took a ton of hard work to get that shit under control, no matter how badly I wanted it to be instant. Change takes time. *He* needs time, but that doesn't mean he cares about you any less."

It's a concept I understand in theory. After all, breaking habits and forming new ones takes tons of work. But fuck, the part of me that craves instant gratification hates it anyway.

Oakley nods in agreement with de Haas before giving me a half-hearted smile. Compassion and empathy swirl in his eyes as he murmurs, "Go, Hold. It's only gonna get worse the longer you put it off, and it's better to know for sure. Otherwise, you'll just keep wondering about what could have been."

Oakley's wrong about one thing, though; the feeling only gets worse the *closer* I get to knowing. Builds as I climb the stairs and amplifies still when I reach the door, my fingers wrapping around the knob to turn it.

The second the door swings open, I spot Phoenix sitting on the bed. His head's resting in his hands and there's a slump to his shoulders that speaks of agony and regret.

It's a pose of defeat if I've ever seen one.

I take a step into the room and close the door behind me, the *snick* of the lock engaging finally grabbing his attention. It must take him a second to realize it's me, because a look of irritation I'd know anywhere is written all over his face—the same one he's aimed at me plenty of times in the past six months.

Only it disappears just as quickly, relief taking its place as he rises to stand.

"You came," he says, immediately stepping towards me. "I was starting to think you were so pissed at me, you wouldn't show."

It hurts a little that he didn't think I would. Even after telling him I love him. Words…I haven't said to anyone outside of my family. Words that somehow don't even do justice to what I feel for him; they just aren't big enough.

Then again, a small piece of me thought about not coming tonight. Debated whether or not I could show up, put my heart on the line for a second time, only for him to decide his best friend was more important than me. I've had enough loss in my life; I don't need the pain of losing him too.

Yet now that I'm here, standing in front of him, I realize maybe Oakley was right. Not knowing would be worse. It'd end up being the only thing through this whole fucking mess that I'd regret.

"Holden?" Phoenix whispers, and I realize I've yet to say anything.

God, I don't even know *what* to say.

"Yeah. I, uhh…" I try clearing the knot in my throat that grew three sizes the moment I saw him, but my voice still comes out raw and thick anyway. "I got your note."

Pulling the tiny flamingo duck from my pocket, I show it to him—as if he didn't know what I was talking about.

"I can see that," he says, a hint of a smile on his lips as he crosses the room to me. The swirling, bubbling feeling in my stomach intensifies once he stops right in front of me and takes the duck from my hands.

I hate how my skin lights on fire when his fingertips brush against my palm. Hate the way my body aches and yearns for this man—the way my soul reaches toward his constantly and without end.

Phoenix's eyes lift to mine as he slides the duck into the pocket of my hoodie, a little smirk on his lips. "Guess the cat's outta the bag though, right?"

I blink at him, wondering if he's lost his damn mind, because—

"It was never in the bag."

The smile is a complete grin now, and he whispers, "Yeah, you're right. Especially when you're so good at seeing right through me."

His gaze moves from mine down to my lips, and I don't have to be a mind reader to know what he's thinking. It's the same sentence running through my head.

Eyes and mouth.

The intimacy of the moment sends my pulse into overdrive, and I quickly look away. My focus skims over the room we're in, desperate for a distraction, but it doesn't work. Not when the part of my brain recognizes this as the room I woke up—naked, hungover, and alone—almost exactly a year ago.

My throat constricts as I look back at the man who continues shredding my heart into pieces while simultaneously being the reason it still beats.

"Who's room is this?" I find myself asking.

"Some guy named Grayson, who I paid to let me kick him out for a while," he says with a laugh.

The thought of him doing that has a smile quirking up the corner of my mouth. "You paid a guy off to use his bedroom? Seriously?"

He shrugs. "Call me sentimental, I just wanted to have this conversation with you where the whole thing began."

I shove my hands into the pocket of my sweatshirt in search of the duck he just placed there. My fingers wrap around the smooth rubber, squeezing it in my palm as if it's enough to ground me. Ease some of the tension coiled in my body like a snake ready to strike.

"So…" I start, going in the only direction I can think of, "You and

Kason are good, then?"

He opens his mouth to speak before his lips tilt into some semblance of a smile. But the most confusing part is the way it's still on his face when he shakes his head *no*.

"Not entirely. But I think we will be. Someday." His eyes hold a fair amount of sadness when he adds, "We need some time apart from each other."

"And you're okay with that?" I ask, slowly.

This time he nods. "He's choosing him...and I'm choosing me."

The last three words of his sentence cause my heart rate to spike immediately. How can it not, when that's all I wanted for him? For *us?*

But a lot of time has passed since we were in Nashville—where I saw the truth in his eyes as his mouth straight-up lied to my face. Six weeks' worth of time. And I don't know if, in that time, he's decided the words he let spill from his lips that day were the truth, after all.

Still, I have to ask. I have to know.

"What exactly does choosing yourself entail?"

He offers me a gentle smile. "Creating some healthy boundaries. Breaking some bad habits. I've spent a lot of time working on the guilt I've been harboring. Letting go of that shit so I can make way for all the good things. Accepting the past for what it is, even if I can't change it, and focusing on what I can." He pauses briefly, eyes locked with mine, before adding, "Learning to accept that sometimes it's okay to be selfish and put myself first."

My brows hike up. "Is this some sort of twelve-step program you found, or are you just kinda making it up as you go along?"

"Maybe a little of both?" he says as a soft laugh slips free, the decadent sound washing over me like whiskey and honey. He sobers quickly, though, and he rolls his teeth over his lip. "I'm sorry for hurting you, for shutting you out and not leaning on you when all you wanted was to take my pain away." His features show an endless amount of sorrow when he adds, "And I'm sorry for taking this long to reach out. The last thing I wanted was to do it before I felt ready, but that doesn't mean it hurt you any less."

"Six weeks is a long time to feel ready," I point out softly.

"Change doesn't happen overnight," he says, echoing a sentiment Quinton said not even ten minutes ago. "But I hope you know I would've done it faster if I could've."

His eyes reveal it's the truth, and some of the pressure in my chest eases because of it.

Phoenix is many things—loyal to a fault being one of them. But if I've learned anything about him over the past few months, it's that he has the biggest heart of anyone. He'd never do something to hurt me on purpose.

It actually…makes me glad to hear he's taken the time to do the work he needed. Truly put himself first. Just from looking at him, I can tell it's helping.

"Well, you look good," I murmur, my lips curling up at the corner. "Happier, you know?"

The smile on his lips—rare, bright, and genuine—steals my breath. Clenches the fist around my heart at the mere sight of it.

"I'm getting there. Still have a few changes I need to make to be there fully, though," he says, and though there's still a smile on his face, I hear the seriousness in his tone as well. "I have some wrongs to right. Mistakes to correct. And even alter some of the decisions I made that weren't entirely for me."

The last part causes the floor to drop out from under me, because I know one major decision he's made that wasn't his own. And for the fucking life of me, I don't think my heart can take this blow.

"Why do I have a feeling you're about to tell me part of that includes moving to Portland and playing your last college baseball season for Foltyn?" I ask, doing my best to keep my voice steady while clenching the duck on my fist.

His brows draw down. "Why in the hell would you think that?"

"You just said altering decisions, and the only reason you came here was for Kason and—"

"I'm not going anywhere," he cuts in, an amused smirk on his lips.

The relief flooding me would be comical to the guy I was six months ago. But now, I don't even care how sappy or pathetic it makes me. I want him here. I want to see him smile, hear his voice, and feel his skin against mine.

I want *him*.

He brings me a sense of peace I haven't known since my parents were alive, and I don't want to live without it anymore.

"You're staying," I repeat, wanting the words to be true yet barely believing them all the same.

Phoenix moves in closer, leaving only inches separating our bodies. Inches that feel like miles when both of his hands reach up and slowly cup either side of my face. The heat of his skin seeps into mine, and it instantly sends a warm fuzziness spreading through my extremities that's as grounding as it is addictive.

"I'm staying," he whispers, thumbs brushing along my cheekbones. "It might not have been my first choice in the beginning, but Leighton's grown on me. And I honestly don't think I'd enjoy attending a college halfway across the country from the guy I love."

I damn near choke on my spit before sputtering out, "What?"

A raspy chuckle I love so much spills from his lips. "Theo mentioned something about you going deaf recently. Guess he wasn't kidding."

Why in the ever-loving fuck are we talking about Theo when he just said—

"You love me," I parrot.

That little smirk is still on his lips as he shakes his head in obvious amusement. But rather than answering me, he draws my mouth to his in a long, slow kiss. One that sends my pulse into overdrive and has my heart skipping in my chest. Not due to lust or desire, but because it feels like coming home.

Like his lips molding over mine are all I need for the missing pieces to fall into place.

He pulls back far, far too soon, and those dark, midnight eyes dance back and forth between mine before he speaks.

"Out of all the lies I've told through this entire mess, telling you I didn't love you was the biggest one of all. There's nothing and no one I want more than you," he murmurs, fingers scraping against the back of my head. "I love you, baby. And I'm so fucking sorry for making you think otherwise."

I think my heart might burst right out my chest when I realize…they match his mouth.

Finally.

That's all it takes for me to haul him back in for another kiss, this one not nearly as slow and soothing as the last. This one is all the hurt and longing I've been feeling for weeks finally being released, since it's the last time I'll have to ever feel it.

Not another day will pass where he isn't mine.

I'm the first to break apart this time, resting my forehead against his while I beg the organ in my chest to slow and my head to stop spinning.

"I'm taking this as you accept my apology?" he murmurs, the warmth of his breath coasting over my lips. "Because I can pine and beg and plead and grovel for as many days as I've made you wait, if you want."

I laugh breathlessly. "You would, wouldn't you?"

He nods, his forehead rolling against mine. "Or we can put this whole mess behind us and start fresh. Say the word—whatever you want—and I'll do it. I don't care what it takes. I'm in this. Choosing me means choosing you, too."

Those words alone make my heart soar more than him telling me he loves me.

My gaze meets his while I pull back. "I'm just glad your eyes finally match your mouth."

"Because I meant it, Holden." His eyes dart between mine. "Until the day you decide you don't want me, I'm yours."

The sincerity in his voice causes my heart to ache, filling to the brim with the kind of love and happiness I never imagined. At least, not with him. Part of me is still a little disbelieving that this is my reality. That this man is mine, and mine alone.

Yet, by some miracle, he is.

"I doubt there will ever be a day that happens."

His smile sets my heart on fire. "Good, because I don't come with a return policy."

"Sounds like something I'd say," I point out.

The comment earns me another chuckle. "You're rubbing off on me, I guess."

"Mmm, I definitely could right now if you want," I murmur, bringing my lips to his again in a whisper of a kiss. "We've already got a bed and everything."

"Oh, shit. That reminds me." Phoenix pulls away, eyes wide.

The look on his face confuses the hell out of me, but not as much as when he steps back, links his fingers with mine, and drags me...toward the door?

I stare at him like he's lost his mind. "Wait, where are we going? The bed is right here."

Mischief and excitement line his features, and he cocks his head to the side before asking his own question in return. "Do you trust me?"

With my entire fucking being.

All I can do is nod, not following one fucking iota.

"Okay, good," he says, giving me a soft smile. "Then c'mon. I have a surprise for you."

With a final glance at me, Phoenix pulls the door open, revealing the chaos behind the wood. Nothing atypical under any circumstance, but especially with it being finals week. I'm not entirely sure how a surprise works into the equation here, yet something must be off when I spot Theo in the hallway as we step out of the bedroom.

Was he waiting for us?

A shit-eating grin plasters itself on his face when he sees me hand-in-hand with Phoenix. The kind that tells me he knew exactly what Phoenix was planning when he helped plant the flamingo duck in my Jeep earlier today.

I'm about to call him out for it too, when he crosses his arms over his chest and says, "I thought Oakley was taking you home ten minutes ago."

Oakley? Is he on crack—

Phoenix gently squeezes my hand, and my gaze flashes over to him. There's a reassuring smile resting on his lips as he nods his head toward Theo. "This is the part where you said something about Oakley being bossy like a dad, and if Theo is going to do the same thing, he should just walk away now."

I glance between him and Theo, still not understanding, when Theo smirks and says, "Someone's testy tonight."

"And then you said something about your roommates acting like babysitters all night," Phoenix murmurs in my ear. "Then you looked at me and asked Theo to introduce you to me."

I'm smacked square in the face with realization, and a knot forms instantly in my throat as I look at him. At this amazing, loyal, one-of-a-kind guy who loves me enough to do this.

To take a moment my mind erased and fill in the void.

"Nix," I whisper, his name coming out grated and drowned in emotion. But that's all I say. That's all I *can* say, or I'll be liable to break down on the spot.

He gives me a soft smile and another hand squeeze before glancing at Theo.

My roommate's smiling just as widely as he looks from Phoenix back to me. "Not a fucking chance, Hold." Then he steps forward and gives Phoenix one of those *atta boy* pats on his shoulder. "I'm heading out, but you played one helluva game, Merce. Don't think too hard on it."

"Thanks, man," Nix says, a small smile on his lips while his thumb traces over the back of my hand.

Theo's attention floats between us again before grabbing my shoulder and giving it a tight squeeze. An ear-splitting grin is still on his face when he says, "You're in the clear. Good luck."

And with that, he heads down the stairs, disappearing from sight.

Switching my focus to Phoenix, I find him already watching me with a mixture of apprehension and tenderness. The sight makes the organ pounding against my ribs beat a little faster.

"You with me so far, baby?"

All I can do is nod. I don't trust my voice not to crack and crumble if I dare attempt to speak.

"Good," he whispers. A little smirk tilts up his lips, and he steps away from me to lean his shoulder against the wall. "This is when I tell you that was one way to get a guy's attention."

Swallowing down the emotion as best I can, I croak out, "And what did I say?"

Another twitch of his lips, and then, "You said, *it worked, didn't it?*"

I choke out a laugh. "Yeah, that sounds about right."

"Absolutely, but I think this next part is probably my favorite." He gives me another winning grin, even as those dark eyes are teaming with just as much emotion as I'm feeling. "Because I stared into your eyes, then let my gaze fall to your lips. And before I could tell you my name, you told me you didn't care what it was, and—"

I close the distance between us and anchor my hand at the back of his neck, knowing myself well enough to see where this is going next. Knowing exactly what I'd do—drunk or not—at this moment.

Slanting my mouth over his, I kiss him like he's the only thing in existence. Like he is the air that fills my lungs, and the reason the sun rises, and is in every beat my heart takes.

Because he is.

"I love you, Nix," I whisper between each kiss I plant on his lips. "I love you so fucking much."

One of those addictive laughs leaves him as his nose brushes mine. "That definitely isn't part of the plot 'til much, *much* later. But I love you too."

The faint sound of metal rattling comes moments later, and then the door to Grayson's bedroom is pushed open. My gaze dances between Phoenix's eyes as he intertwines our fingers, pulling me through the threshold, only to be again enveloped in privacy.

His back collides with the wood behind him, and he reels me in until my hands land on either side of his head.

"Do you wanna know what happens next?" he whispers, sneaking his hands beneath my hoodie and linking them behind my back.

From the way he's looking at me, an intoxicating combination of love and desire in his dark irises, I know exactly what happens next. Even with the gap in my memory, it's obvious. And if I didn't already love him, his willingness to take us back to this very night a year ago would have made me fall on the spot.

But it's not until he offers up the moment I've begged for on a silver platter that I realize…I don't need it.

I don't *want* it.

I'm done with the drunken frat-house one-night stands. It might've been where we started, but that's not who we are.

Not anymore.

I shake my head, before pressing my forehead to his. "I want every moment we've ever had, no matter how messy. No matter how heartbreaking or fucked-up or stolen they might've been. I want all the pieces of our history, because those moments are what make us *us*."

Phoenix leans back, his gaze shifting between my eyes. "I feel a *but* coming."

I smile, wondering when he started reading me as well as I do him. "But we don't need to recreate the past. I just want to build our future."

"Are you sure?" he asks gently.

"I've never been more sure of anything."

He nods. "Well, I'll tell you anything you want to know, regardless. You just have to ask."

"Okay."

It's something to keep a pin in for later, though I doubt I'll change my mind on this. I got the guy in the end, and that's all I care about.

"And just so we're clear," he murmurs, his teeth scraping over his lip, "I paid Grayson to use his bedroom like a motel for nothing?"

A laugh bursts free. "Yeah, I guess you did."

"Unbelievable."

"So you've said once or twice," I tell him, cocking my head to the side. "I also vividly remember you saying it was bold of me to assume I could make you happy."

One of those sinful laughs leaves him. "How long are you planning to hold that over my head?"

I can't help my smile when I lean in and whisper against his lips.

"The rest of our lives, baby."

EPILOGUE

Phoenix

August—Three Months Later

The sunlight warming my skin is disrupted by a blanket of shadow, and I lift my lids to find a dripping wet and sinfully hot Holden leaning over me. He presses his mouth to mine in a feather-light kiss, and I taste tequila and salt on his lips.

"Hey, baby," I say, giving him a sleepy smile. "You finally left your perch?"

I swear, he hasn't left that damn flamingo float for a single waking moment since we arrived at the condo with my parents and sister two days ago. Much to Charlotte's dismay—even going as far as swimming under and dunking him off the thing. Twice.

So then he bought her an equally obnoxious unicorn float to make up for it, and all's right in the world now.

My boyfriend, ever the giver.

"Mhmm," he murmurs, nose brushing mine. "I only left it 'cause I found a better one."

Between my half-conscious state and the high his kiss gives me, I'm not entirely sure what he means by that. But when Holden straddles my lap, planting his feet on either side of the lounger, I understand perfectly.

His ass nestles into place on top of my dick, and a low groan escapes me.

"See? Perfect spot, right here." There's a sexy playfulness in his tone as he presses a kiss to the heated skin of my throat. "Wouldn't you agree?"

My hands grip his hips to hold him firmly in place, or else I'm at risk of popping a boner around my parents. "You're not playing fair."

His soft laugh makes my cock perk up even more than him sitting on it. "Let's be real. When have I ever?"

As if to drive his point home, he leans forward and captures my lips with his again, making my heart race and toes curl. His tongue tastes like the margarita he was drinking as it slides against mine, fucking into my mouth in a seductive dance I never want to end.

My hands grip his hips tighter, digging into his hard, smooth obliques in an effort to keep him still, but it's not enough to stop him from turning me on in other ways. Like with his fingers as they trail up my stomach and chest before sinking into my hair. Or the gentle suck he gives my lower lip before releasing it.

God, the things he does to me.

I'm convinced I'll never tire of kissing him. Touching him.

Loving him.

I'm the first to break for air, panting harshly against his lips as I catch my breath. He's just as starved for oxygen, but from the way his hips start rolling over mine despite my hold, there's something else he's craving more.

"Fuck me, Nix."

I let out a sharp bark of laughter that turns into more of a gasp of pleasure from the friction. "Not a chance in fucking hell."

His brows draw together into something of a pout. "Why not?"

I gape at him. While he might be extremely sexy and hard to resist, all the sun we've been getting must've made him lose his damn mind.

"I can think of plenty of reasons." I try stilling him again, but he's not having it. "One of the biggest ones being that my family is just inside."

"No, they're not."

"What?" Last I remember, they'd gone inside to clean up after lunch. I sit up as much as I can with him on top of me and peek under the carport, only to find it empty. "Where'd they go?"

"Charlotte wanted ice cream." A small grin lifts his lips. "You were sleeping, and I told them it was probably best not to wake you to ask if you wanted to go with."

"You didn't want to go?"

"And leave you here to roast like a lobster all alone?" His brow hikes up as he grins some more. "Plus, I might be new to this whole *boyfriend* thing, but I'm pretty sure ditching you for ice cream is not the right move."

My teeth sink into my lower lip, shamelessly enjoying the word *boyfriend* coming from his sinful mouth.

"You ditch me for the pit at concerts, so I don't think that's it," I remind him. "I think the real reason you chose to stay behind is for a little uninterrupted action instead."

Not that I can blame him, if I'm right.

We spent most of the last three months FaceTiming from different time zones rather than together, thanks to my baseball schedule running well into June. Worth it to win the College World Series—and to have him in the stands cheering me on—but it also took a serious chunk out of our summer together.

Besides my trip out to California to stay with him and his Gran for a long weekend, this week in Florida with my family is the most we've been able to spend together...and we've been looking to make up for lost time at every available moment because of it.

That mischievous look I love dances in his eyes, confirming my suspicions. "Wanting to get you naked also might have something to do with it, yeah."

As much as I'd love nothing more than to sink inside him here and now, I keep my libido reined in. I'm not looking to be arrested for public indecency heading into our final year of college.

"It's the middle of the day," I tell him, glancing around the pool area, "and they could come home at any time."

Or better yet, some random stranger in the neighboring condo could walk out onto their balcony and see everything. Or a random passerby on the beach.

"I'd say we have at least half an hour." Holden presses his ass down again, and my fingers dig into his hips harder on instinct. "That's plenty of time for an orgasm each."

I can't help the husky laugh from slipping out at his tenacity. "Did I not fuck you well enough in the shower this morning or something?"

The grin on his lips tells me that is most certainly not the case.

"You're telling me you're not wanting to spend every possible second of this week inside me?" he counters, brow arched. "Because the second I head back to Chicago for preseason training, you know our time is gonna go back down to basically zero."

I let out a low groan, hating the reminder.

Summer has flown by in what seems like the blink of an eye, and for once, I'm sad to see it go. All it means is we're back to being on opposite schedules.

But at least we'll be living together come the fall term, which is a major plus.

"You make a good point," I murmur, my resolve starting to wane.

"I know I do," he says, a teasing lilt in his tone. "Now, would you quit trying to change the subject and take off your trunks?"

Holden Sykes, relentless as ever. Though I must admit, it's become one of the many qualities I love most about him.

My cock twitches beneath him as the ache in my balls grows, and it's then, I cave. I don't have it in me to deny him a thing anymore. And I highly doubt any amount of time together will change that.

"That depends." My hands slide around to his ass, squeezing and kneading the fleshy muscle in my palm as my cock thickens some more. "Did you think to grab lube before trying to seduce me?"

A grin curls his mouth as he holds up a broken piece of a very familiar plant. I burst out laughing the second I recognize it, head falling back against the lounger.

"That's *not* what I meant," I say between laughter.

"It worked so well last time," he muses. "Figured we might as well go for a repeat."

"Then you're gonna have to get off me so we can get to the shower," I counter.

"We're not going anywhere." He grabs the waistband of my trunks and shifts off me to drag them down. "But these sure are."

I lift my hips, allowing him to pull them from my body and drop them to the ground. My teeth sink into my lower lip, watching shamelessly while he goes for his own waistband.

My brow kicks up as he shoves them to his ankles, and the ache in my balls rapidly intensifies. I'm ready to lick the bead of precum glistening on the tip and take him deep into my throat the second his cock comes into view, though God knows we don't have enough time for that.

"You want to right here?"

"Right here," he confirms, and I don't miss the hungry look in his eyes while his attention tracks down my naked body. "I wanna test out how sturdy these pool loungers really are."

This fucking guy.

"And what are we going to tell my family when we inevitably break it?"

"That I did something to piss you off and you threw it at my face." He smirks and shrugs. "Stranger things have happened."

"Then get over here," I growl, the lust turning into more of a feral need.

Holden wastes no time straddling me again and reaches for my cock, giving it a few long pulls that only build my desire. I do the same, reaching out and stroking him slowly, and making sure to play with that sensitive spot beneath the head.

"Playing dirty?" he murmurs while he breaks open the aloe and crushes it until gel covers his fingers and palm.

"With you? Always."

A smirk lifts his lips as he switches hands, and the cooling sensation of the aloe draws my balls up momentarily as he smothers my shaft in the lubricant. He coats me from root to tip, leaving no inch uncovered, and only when he finishes does he reach behind him to smear the excess up and down his crease.

"What if I wanted to do that?" I ask while giving his cock a firm squeeze.

His eyes lock with mine as he shifts, and the head of my cock presses against his rim.

"You snooze, you lose," is all he says before gently sinking down on my length.

My head drops back against the lounger, and my eyes sink closed as his body envelops me. It's these first moments I love the most—losing myself in the sensation of being joined with him like this.

It's only when I'm completely seated inside him that I lift my lids again to find him already watching me with a gaze so full of love, it leaves me breathless.

"Oh hell," I groan. "Keep looking at me like that, and this isn't gonna last long."

A grin forms on his lips, but it quickly disappears, taken over by a moan of pleasure as he rolls his hips after sinking down on my length again.

And I can't look away. Can't stop staring at his face while he uses my body to bring himself pleasure. Can't stop watching the way his lips part in soft pants as he takes us both closer to ecstasy.

It's an intoxicating sight I'll never be sick of.

"Fuck, baby," I murmur, my fist still stroking his dick. "That's it. Show me how well you ride my cock."

One palm uses my shoulder as leverage to lift off my cock before impaling himself on the length all over again. His other sinks into the hair at the base of my skull, taking hold and dragging me in for a kiss that I could live in forever.

Holden sets our rhythm, riding my cock as his tongue mates with mine with fevered passion. My hands travel his body, mapping the lines and planes of his shoulders and back before gripping a firm cheek in each palm. I massage the taut muscles, kneading and squeezing them before using one hand to give his ass a light smack as he bears down on my length.

He breaks the kiss, smiling into my mouth. "Are you unlocking a new kink right now?"

It's become a running joke between us, seeing as my experience in the bedroom falls severely short of his. But that's just an excuse for us to continue trying new things. Exploring what we both enjoy in the bedroom together.

Or, in this case…out on the pool loungers.

"Just trying to put you in your place," I murmur, my lips tracing the line of his jaw over to his neck while he drops down on my cock again. "Not that it'll ever work."

"Guess you just gotta keep trying," he taunts, a sexy arch to his brow.

I have every intention of it, because little does he know, some of my favorite moments are when he challenges me right back. When he doesn't just bend to my will at the drop of a hat.

Not that I'll ever tell him that.

I shift, sitting up so our chests brush, and meet him thrust for thrust. The new position doesn't allow me to slide in as deep, though it must apply the perfect friction against his prostate, because he lets out a low, sexy moan that goes straight to my balls.

"Oh, fuck," he pants as his ass clamps around me. "More, Nix."

Not one to deny my guy anything, both my hands fly to his hips to take over our rhythm. I'm relentless in my pace, dragging him down on my cock in thrust after untamed thrust while I explore the skin along his neck and collarbone with my lips.

The hand on my shoulder moves to his dick, and he starts stroking his length at a faster pace. They're wild and frenzied as he brings himself closer to release, ready to jump into freefall.

"Oh, my God," he mutters, the fist still anchored in my hair tightening as I peg his prostate again.

He continues jacking himself in time with my thrusts, the lounger creaking and scraping against the concrete beneath us with every frantic movement we make. And I don't care if we end up breaking the damn thing and falling to the ground. Nothing matters right now except him and me and how we're both driving each other mad with need.

Lust barrels down my spine when Holden's ass clenches around me, squeezing and pulsing in a way that lets me know he's close.

And I want it; his release. I want him to cover me in it.

For him to claim me as much as I am him.

"Come for me," I demand before nipping at his throat. "Come all over me, baby."

As if that's all he needed, Holden lets out a low groan and cum spills from his cock. It coats his fingers along with my abs and chest; all the while, his ass grips me to high fucking heaven. He nearly rips the hair straight from my skull as he works himself through his climax, and it's that bite of pain paired with the pulsing around my shaft that has my own orgasm slamming into me at break-neck speeds.

I continue driving my hips up with punishing thrusts, bottoming out so deep inside him, it's impossible to tell where I end and he begins. And he takes everything I have to give, his ass clamping around me like a vise and milking every last drop of cum from my body. Taking everything I have to give until we're both left a sated, panting mess of sunscreen, cum, and sweat.

His forehead collides with mine, and I'm quick to reach up and curl my hand around the back of his neck, looking to haul him back in for a kiss. It's slow, one that's meant to be savored while we take our time floating back to Earth. Gentle presses and sweeps of our lips that help calm my erratic heartbeat.

"I love you," I whisper before brushing my nose along his. "I love you so fucking much."

"Hearing that never gets old," he murmurs back in that sinfully addictive post-sex voice. All breathy and raspy.

"I know, so maybe you should say it back," I counter before nipping at his bottom lip.

He lets out a husky laugh that wraps a fist around my heart. "Someone's demanding."

"You're the one who just demanded sex, so why can't I demand an *I love you* in return?"

His lips part, and I'm sure he's about to give in. In fact, I can see the words sitting there on the tip of that naughty, wicked tongue.

"I…" he murmurs slowly, "think we should probably get cleaned up before your parents come back."

"You're fucking evil," I mutter before practically shoving him off me and rising off the lounger. Then I realize I'm still covered in his cum, so I grab my trunks off the ground and head toward the outdoor shower to rinse off.

Because, even if I'm annoyed with his little game, he's right. I don't think my parents would particularly enjoy finding the two of us like that when they came back with Charlotte.

"Where are you going?" Holden asks when I'm almost to the shower, and I hear the tell-tale sound of his feet padding on the concrete as he follows me.

"Cleaning up. Like you said."

I've just turned the water on when Holden appears at the opening of the enclosure. His head cants to the side as his eyes rake over my naked body.

"Can I join you?"

"I…don't think so."

He rolls his eyes before stepping into the shower anyway. Closing the distance between us, he backs me into the wall until our chests brush together and looks into my eyes like it's the only thing in the world he wants to be doing.

"Don't be like that, Nix. You know I love you more than anything."

I know in my heart he does. There's never been a moment where I've doubted it either. Even when we've been separated by time zones and hundreds of miles, he's always made it more than obvious that he loves me.

But I still want to hear it. The affirmation that I deserve it, despite all I put him through.

"You're still evil," I mutter, linking my arms around his waist.

He gives me an unamused look. "You say that like you don't enjoy it."

Yeah, he's got me there.

Most of the time, his little antics are just what I need to loosen up. To smile and laugh and remember that being with him is one of the best choices I've ever made for myself—the one I plan to continue making for as long as he'll have me.

"Fine, you win. But we seriously do need to get cleaned up before my parents come looking for us. Or worse, Charlotte."

A smirk lifts his lips, and he concedes, pulling away from me to rinse off his body beneath the spray.

"Hey, at least none of them were around to see anything. Or hear it, though you're really gonna have to get over that one come fall." He arches a brow playfully before adding, "Roomie."

A laugh burst from my chest. "You make it sound so dirty."

"I make everything sound dirty."

"That's very true," I say, my palms rubbing up and down his thighs. "But I thought you said Theo was moving upstairs and we'd have the basement to ourselves."

"He is. But the ceilings in that house are just as thin as the walls."

"Fantastic," I deadpan.

"Hey, I think two entire floors between us and the rest of the guys will be enough." He pauses before adding. "At least, I hope it is."

"Oh, Jesus," I mutter, shaking my head. "I might have to invest in a gag to go along with those handcuffs."

His brow arches. "Could be fun."

The look in his eyes tells me he's serious when I was just making a joke. "All right, now who's unlocking a new kink? Next, you're gonna be asking for nipple clamps or something."

I expect him to laugh or toss more banter right back at me, but I'm taken off guard when his gaze softens, and those imploring whiskey eyes stare straight into my soul. "You can do whatever you want to me."

"Baby," I whisper.

"I'm only ever gonna be yours," he adds, and my heart grows infinitely larger, taking up all the space in my chest while crashing against my ribs with every beat.

This guy. This fucking man who I'd have never dreamt to be mine... somehow is.

And it's the most incredible feeling in the world.

I crush my lips to his, stealing all the breath from his lungs as I kiss him. And it's not until I've owned every inch of his mouth that I break away to rest my forehead against his.

"You fuck me up, Nix," he murmurs, his lips brushing mine with every word.

I smile against his mouth. "I know, baby. You fuck me up, too."

THE END

Acknowledgments

This book is the bane of my existence, though that feels awfully on-brand considering the way these two felt about each other in the beginning. And though this story took on a life of its own—one I didn't even see coming—I hope you were able to enjoy meeting Holden and Phoenix.

To everyone who sat on FaceTime or Zoom with me while I wrote, outlined, or cried my way through this book or who constantly sent wellness checks: you're the real MVPs. The accountability, encouragement, and grace y'all gave are the only reason this thing was finished in the first place.

To Abby, for continuing on this journey with me.

To Emily, for this cover. I can't wait to see where we continue taking the series.

To my alphas/betas, Amy, Emily, Jackie, Holly, Nichol, and anyone else I'm missing: thank you for making sure this book wasn't a complete pile of garbage, and for arguing with me that it isn't no matter how many times I called you trash pandas after threatening to delete the whole thing.

To Marley, for helping me keep my sanity and for all the tough love.

To my editing team: Angie and Amanda. I don't have the words to describe how grateful I am for you turning this around so quickly. You two are angels and I'm so lucky to have you in my corner.

To my Enclave and my Legacies. Thank you for supporting me, promoting me, and being my core readership—some of you since the very beginning.

To anyone I missed in this list, and to my readers. Thank you for being here. Thank you for coming back for more. Thank you for changing my life.

I'll be forever grateful.

— CE Ricci

About the Author

CE Ricci is an international best-selling author who enjoys plenty of things in her free time, but writing about herself in the third person isn't one of them. She believes home isn't a place, but a feeling, and it's one she gets when she's chilling lakeside or on hiking trails with her dogs, camera in hand. She's addicted to all things photography, plants, peaks, puppies, and paperbacks, though not necessarily in that order. Music is her love language, and traveling the country (and world) is the way she chooses to find most of her inspiration for whatever epic love story she will tell next!

CE Ricci is represented by Two Daisy Media.
For all subsidiary rights, please contact:
Savannah Greenwell — info@twodaisy.com

Made in the USA
Middletown, DE
05 April 2024

52625688R00234